Chapter One

Wednesday 30th September – Justina Constantine

Bistro Mykonos, Tower Hamlets, London, England

Justina blinked as the sun flickered between the fast-moving clouds and shot bright, yellow beams through the Bistro's big windows, highlighting the dirt and the grime sprayed by passing traffic. Orestes, her darling Ore, had promised to clean the glass before the evening service, but, as usual, he would need another reminder. The forgetful man always needed one more reminder.

Her eyes stung, in part from chopping strong onions, and in part from worry over their financial troubles, but mainly from the loss of Papa Onassis. Three weeks after her father-in-law's untimely death aboard Flight BE1555, the tears still bubbled up when she least expected them. Such a dreadful waste of a wonderful human being.

Eventually, the pain would fade, as it had done when her own dear parents passed, but it would take time. The loss of Papa Onassis was still so terribly raw.

Justina sniffled and dried her tears with a tissue.

How long could they survive? How long would it be before the bank forced them to close their doors forever?

What had once been a thriving, family business, now struggled under the weight of falling sales and crippling debts. Where once the business generated a small, but steady profit, she and Ore now owed thousands of pounds to the bank and yet more to their suppliers. The darling man tried to hide the worst from her, but the business was in terrible trouble, that much could not have been more obvious. It could not be ignored.

Although he tried not to show it, she could tell Ore was scared. The official-looking letters—the ones he hid from her—made matters much worse. Every time she asked about them, he snapped at her, and Ore never did that. Not her calm, steady, loving husband. Not her Ore. And she could do nothing to help.

All she really knew was that their business would soon fail, and when it did, the family would lose their comfortable, little, upstairs apartment. They would be left homeless.

Sighing, she dabbed away another tear, scraped the finely diced onion into a plastic container, and placed it in the half-empty fridge ready for that night's service.

In the hope that dear Ore had added bookings without telling her, Justina checked the diary. Nothing. Not a single reservation for the evening, which was unusual, even for a Wednesday.

Preparing the rest of the vegetables and the meat could

The Fixer Novel series - book 5 - Kerry J Donovan

KERRY J DONOVAN
ON THE DEFENSIVE

ỼINCI
BOOKS

The Ryan Kaine series by Kerry J Donovan

To Sergeant Elaine Leishman, PTO, for her close-combat training and helping me keep the fight scenes as real as possible.

Vinci Books

vinci-books.com

Published by Vinci Books Ltd in 2025

1

A CIP catalogue record for this book is available from the British Library.
Paperback ISBN: 9781036701659

Printed and bound in Great Britain by Clays Ltd, Elcograf S.p.A.

wait. Why waste ingredients that might otherwise keep for one more day?

Justina had plenty of other tasks to keep her occupied while waiting for Ore to return after collecting the girls from school. Her little darlings would be hungry. They always were after school. Ravenous. She smiled in anticipation of hugging them tight. The quiet family time before evening service always was the very best part of Justina's working day.

She washed her hands, enjoying the warmth of the water and the aroma of lemon-scented soap—the only preparation that could take away the taint of garlic and onions.

Justina took a clean dishcloth from the drawer next to the sink and rolled the heavy canteen trolley into the dining room. It bumped over the slight lip between the hard kitchen floor and the dining room tiles, causing the cutlery to rattle and the glasses to clink. Happy sounds, she always thought—the sounds of friendship and hospitality. The sounds of joy.

As usual, she began at the four-setting table in the corner furthest from the entrance and worked her way towards the centre.

She smoothed the white, cotton tablecloths, set out the cutlery, folded the plum-red serviettes into attractive, serrated fans, and polished each glass to a shine before placing it in its correct position in the right hand of each setting. Finally, she added the centrepiece—a small, glass vase with its posy of fresh flowers. With only ten tables, Bistro Mykonos could never be described as large, and might not boast a fancy Michelin star, but no one would ever find fault with the food, or the front-of-house ambience. The *atmósfaira*.

In such things, Justina could still take great pride. She loved the precision of each table decoration.

The bell over the front door jingled.

Unexpected and harsh, the noise shocked Justina out of the familiar, mindless actions that had become her meditation. Her heart leaped. She placed a hand flat to her chest and turned. Two men, strangers, stood inside the open doorway.

She must have forgotten to flip the sign from "Open" to "Closed". But surely, she had locked the door? She never left it unlocked with the restaurant closed. Never. Perhaps Ore …?

The wall clock above the entrance showed half past three. Ore and the girls would not be home for at least twenty minutes. She stood alone against them.

"Excuse me, gentlemen," she said, surprised at how weak her voice sounded despite the relative quiet. "We are closed."

Being alone in the restaurant did not usually worry her, but something about the intensity of these men made her uneasy. The way they glowered at her. The way they carried themselves. It sent a shiver through her body. Ore, born and raised in London, would have called it a "bad vibe". In Greece, her homeland, it would have been given a different description. In her native Greek, it would be *"to simádi tou diavólou"*—the sign of the devil.

She stood behind the trolley, gripping the dishcloth tight. The trolley offered little security, but it acted as a barrier and hid her trembling knees.

"We do not open until seven o'clock," she called, forcing the words through a tight, scared throat.

The first man stood tall and straight. He had wavy, blond hair and the lean, athletic build of a soccer player.

With his smooth, angular face, strong jaw, and high cheek-bones, some women might have considered him handsome, but only if they ignored his hard, lifeless, blue eyes. He carried a shiny, metal briefcase in his left hand and moved quietly towards her, lips bared in a wide smile that exposed sharp, white teeth—the movements of a wolf closing on its prey. Circling. Hunting.

Again, Justina shuddered, and she gripped the dishcloth tighter.

Although the blond man was intimidating, his partner was worse. A dark-skinned giant, he had to turn sideways and duck to fit through the doorway. The expression on his tattooed face shouted anger. His eyes were as dark as his skin, the eyeballs yellow rather than white. Muscles bulged and rippled beneath a stretched T-shirt, and his grey, two-piece suit, although well-tailored and expensive-looking, seemed out of place on so square and large a body.

Justina's heart thumped faster, and she shuddered under the monster's fixed gaze. The dishcloth she had been wringing slipped through her sweaty hands.

The big man with the tattooed face shut the door and turned the lock. She *had* turned the sign to "Closed". He stood with his back to the door, feet apart, arms folded across his barrel chest. A man on guard. A rock. Immovable. Terrifying.

Dear Lord! What is this?

Beyond the windows, the world continued as normal. Cars still crawled past, but more slowly, and pedestrians still tramped the opposite pavement, but no heads turned towards her.

She stood alone. Helpless. Vulnerable.

The clouds chose that moment to break apart once again, and the sun burst through the windows. The monster cast a huge shadow into the room, but somehow, with his tattooed face darkened and hidden by the glare, his ominous presence became even more terrifying.

The blond man stopped in front of her, keeping a table and the trolley between them.

"Good afternoon, Mrs Constantine," he said quietly. "Or may I call you Justina?"

He knows my Christian name!

His voice carried a heavy, East-End-of-London accent and had the guttural rasp of a man who had smoked cigarettes for many years. The voice sounded older than his looks.

"My name is Alfred Lovejoy, but you can call me Alfie." Again, he smiled, but it was equally as chilling as the first. "It's always nice to call people by their first names, isn't it? Much more conducive to pleasant conversation. My rather large friend over there is known as Tugboat, for obvious reasons, but I call him Tuggy. It's much nicer, don't you think? Gentler. Friendlier."

The fact that Lovejoy stood over her, menacing and scary, was bad enough, but that he did not mind telling her his name seemed somehow worse. It showed he did not care that she knew.

"W-Who are you, and what do you want?"

Lovejoy's smile melted away and his cold, blue eyes drilled straight through her.

"Weren't you listening?" he said, his tone aggressive, harsh. "I just told you my name. Clear out your fucking ears, bitch."

Her mouth dropped open. She backed away until stopped by a table, but Lovejoy stayed where he was, his upper lip peeled back into an animal sneer.

"Yes," he said, nodding. "I thought that would get your

attention. I hate resorting to foul language. Swearing is the last resort of the ill-educated, don't you think? But sometimes, the shock value helps drive the message across. So, what do I want? Hmm. I'll tell you what I want." He hummed a familiar tune, jiggled his hips, and chuckled. "Ah, the Spice Girls. Lyrically brilliant, weren't they?"

He swung the metal briefcase, slammed it on the table, and pushed it towards the middle. Justina jumped. Glasses smashed and cutlery scattered. The centrepiece vase broke. Water spread over the tablecloth and dripped to the floor.

A long-stemmed wine glass, the final one, wobbled. Justina's arm twitched involuntarily. She wanted to rush forwards to catch it, but Lovejoy's presence locked her in place. Frozen in terror.

The glass toppled and fell slowly from the table. It hit the tiled floor and smashed into a dozen pieces. Only the stem and base remained intact.

Dear Lord, the mess.

Insurance would not cover such a small loss, but how could they afford to replace the broken glasses and the vase? A flash of anger pricked Justina's bubble of fear. How dare he do such a thing? She had only just finished setting the table!

She ground her teeth but kept quiet and lowered her gaze. The trolley's cutlery drawer was part-way open, showing her the wooden handle of a wickedly sharp steak knife. It lay within easy reach. She only had to stretch out a hand and take it.

Without removing his eyes from her, Lovejoy snapped the clasps of the briefcase, opened the lid, and removed a document bound in a clear, plastic cover. He dropped it on the table amongst the shards of glass, the flowers, and the crushed napkins.

"W-What is that?" she managed to say, lifting her gaze from the steak knife to stare at the document.

Lovejoy lowered the briefcase lid, secured the clasps, and placed his hands together as though in prayer.

"That there," he said, back to his smiling, quiet worst, "is a contract for the sale of this ... shithole."

For the first time since entering the Bistro, Lovejoy dragged his gaze from her and scanned the dining room through half-closed lids.

"Jesus H Christ, what a pitiful excuse for a restaurant. Not worth half the price we're offering, but the boss is a generous man. Too fucking generous if you ask me. He recognises the challenges involved in 'uprooting young families from their homes'. His words, not mine. I don't give a fuck."

He snorted and shook his head.

"If it was up to me, I'd torch the place one night with you, your hubby, and your sweet, little girls still inside." He jerked a thumb over his shoulder at the monster blocking the door. "Tuggy there's a dab hand with a Molotov cocktail. Aren't you, Tuggy?"

The giant did not move or make a sound.

Lovejoy continued. "Trouble is, that wouldn't give the boss what the lawyers like to call 'ownership with vacant possession'. Get me?"

Justina shook her head.

She had no idea what the horrible man was talking about.

"Stupid cow. It's all hubby's fault. He keeps refusing to sign the papers we send him. Damn it, the bastard didn't even acknowledge receipt of the fucking things. Didn't answer or return our phone calls neither. If he'd have responded, the boss might have been prepared to negotiate an even better price, but … Ah well, water under London Bridge. Too fucking late now. Much too late. Time's short and a new deal's out of the question. Orestes has caused too much irritation. Do you understand me now, Justina?"

Despite his supposed explanation, Justina did not comprehend any of it. Ore had kept so much from her, telling her things like they had to "soldier on" and "stay afloat until the good times returned". Sometimes, even after nearly nine years of marriage and ten years of living in London, Justina still had no idea what Ore was talking about. Although she spoke good English, and was proud of her ability to converse easily with the customers and the suppliers, some English expressions sailed way above her head like the wind over the Aegean.

What did money and papers have to do with one of the bridges over the river Thames? No sense. No sense at all.

"The rude bitch isn't listening, Tuggy. She isn't paying attention," Lovejoy said and sidestepped the table. As he rushed towards her, she stood transfixed, shaking, any hope of reaching for the steak knife gone.

He jerked the trolley aside and stopped within arm's reach, staring down at her. Even taller than she first thought, Justina had to tilt her head up to look at him, but she did not want to stare into the harsh, dead eyes. She wanted to scream for help. She wanted to run, but there was nowhere to go. Nowhere to hide. No one to save her.

She shuddered under his evil glare.

Lovejoy leaned closer. Justina's nose wrinkled in distaste at his overpowering, spicy aftershave.

"Let me make this perfectly clear, so even you can understand, you thick, Greek bitch."

The sweetness of his peppermint breath freshener made her gag.

"If your hubby doesn't sign the contract, Tuggy's gonna pay you a visit one night. You like playing house with sweet, little girls, don't you, Tuggy? Yeah. You love it."

My girls? My girls!

"Do not touch my babies!" she screamed. "I will kill you!"

Justina lunged forwards, clawing for his face. She wanted to scratch and tear, gouge the eyes from his head.

Laughing, Lovejoy dodged to the side. He caught her flailing arms and crushed them together, holding them by the wrists in one big, powerful hand. He slapped her so hard with the other, the blow rattled her teeth, and lights flashed behind her eyes. Her knees buckled, but he held her up by her arms and stopped her from falling.

Lovejoy grabbed her hair and tugged, snapping her head back. The skin stretched tight across her vulnerable neck. She was totally at his mercy.

Justina stopped struggling. Stopped fighting. He was too strong. His powerful grip hurt her wrists and her scalp stung where he pulled at her hair so hard. Her eyes watered again, more tears flowed. Her stomach churned. She fought the desperate need to throw up.

"Tut tut," Lovejoy said, his face millimetres from hers, his spittle wetting her chin. "Now, that's a rather aggressive way to react to a legitimate business proposition. And all because I mentioned Tuggy in the same breath as your offspring. That's likely to hurt his feelings. Don't let his size fool you. Tuggy has feelings, don't you, mate? I call that unjustified, Justina. Unjustified."

He laughed again. A horrible, cruel laugh, it turned her stomach. Loud sobs erupted, unbidden, from her mouth. She could not help herself, could not fight it. The thought of her babies in the clutches of these creatures tore her insides apart, but she could do nothing but struggle impotently against the powerful grip of the evil man.

Lovejoy turned towards the glowering monster and stepped to one side, lifting Justina's arms above her head, displaying her to the creature—a piece of meat for his approval.

"See what I did there, Tuggy? Justina—justified? That's what's called a pun. So, what d'you say, mate? Fancy paying a night-time visit to a couple of frightened kiddies?"

The monster tilted his head to one side as though appraising Justina. After a moment, he nodded and pointed a massive finger at her.

"You want this scrawny bitch, too? Yeah, you can have her if you like. Don't see why not."

Tugboat's lips peeled back. White teeth gleamed against the dark and brooding background.

Lovejoy pulled Justina's head close to his again and whispered in her ear. "Insatiable, he is, Justina."

Her cheek still throbbed from his slap, but her vision had cleared, and his dead eyes skewered her so badly, she could not look away.

"Tuggy's a dynamo, you know," Lovejoy continued. "Women have told me he can go all night. How would you fancy a man that huge on top of you hour after hour?" Lovejoy leaned away and shook his head. "Nah. He'd probably break a little thing like you. Wear you out from the inside."

The brute released her hair and her wrists, and pushed her away. Justina staggered to the side and stumbled against the trolley. She held on tight to the handle. She would not fall—they would not make her grovel in her own place of work, in her own home.

"On the other hand," the braying man continued, "I

could be wrong. A woman like you might enjoy Tuggy's attention. What do you reckon, Justina? I bet the thought turns you on, doesn't it! I bet you're wringing wet right now, hey? I wonder."

He stepped back and looked her up and down, undressing her in his mind.

"You know what? Despite everything, you aren't a bad looking bit of scratch. Quite tasty, in fact. Decent-sized tits and they still look firm despite having been used to feed your spawn. Flat stomach, too, and a nice, round arse. Wonder what you look like without that baggy apron and that daggy dress? Maybe I should find out. How about it? Fancy stripping for me and bending over that table? I can help you with the buttons if you like."

Justina's chin trembled, she gripped the trolley tighter, and prepared to strike for the steak knife. This time, she would grab it. No doubt. No hesitation. If he made another move towards her, she would stab him in the throat and run out the back way. She avoided looking directly at the part-open drawer and waited.

A car horn broke the near-silence. In the street outside, a man shouted something, and another, further away, laughed. Beyond the windows, traffic continued to rumble.

Clouds returned to block the sun, the shadow faded, and warmth bled from the room.

Lovejoy sighed and shook his head once again.

"Nah, don't worry, darling," he said. "Only kidding. I don't need to force myself on a bitch even if she is a bit of a MILF. Just making a point that there's no one to save you. And don't bother calling the cops. They'll do nothing. I can find fifteen friends and the barman who'll swear that Tuggy and I are in the pub, see? Right now, we're knocking back Belgian beers and telling bad jokes. The till receipts will show me using my credit card and everything. Got it all covered, see? In short, we're protected, and you aren't."

Lovejoy straightened his tie and smoothed back his blond hair before grabbing the handle of his briefcase and lifting it from the destroyed table. More pieces of glass fell to the tiled floor. He laughed again.

"You have 'til the end of next month to sign those papers. That's midday, October the thirty-first. Hallowe'en. Got it?"

He stopped talking, probably waiting for an answer, but she refused to give him one.

"Five weeks ought to be plenty of time for you to clear this place of your garbage and fuck off out of it."

Lovejoy pointed at the contract.

"Don't forget what I said. Sign and deliver those papers by midday, Hallowe'en, or we'll be back with a dirty, great 'trick' for you and a Tuggy-sized treat for your spawn."

The evil smile returned to his face.

"Now," he continued after a short pause, "we're going out the way we came in. And remember. If we hear you've gone blabbing to the filth—and we will hear it, believe me —all bets are off. You, your hubby, and your pretty, little daughters, are fair game. Right?"

He stared at Justina and held the look until she nodded. Only then, did they leave.

The moment they'd gone, Justina rushed to lock and bolt the front door, and collapsed into a chair. She buried her face in the crushed dishcloth and sobbed.

During the whole terrifying episode, the monster, Tugboat, had not uttered a single sound, which was perhaps the scariest part of the whole nightmarish incident. Not a sound.

Justina did not know how long she sat crying, but a

rattling on the door made her jump. She spun towards the sound, preparing to run, but found her beautiful, smiling girls tapping gently on the glass.

"Rena, Kora!" she cried again. "My darlings."

She jumped up, tore open the door, and swept the girls into her arms, squeezing tight. She absorbed their smell, their wriggling warmth, their love.

"Too tight, Mama," Kora said, squirming. "You're hurting me."

"Sorry, *moraki mou*," Justina said, easing the pressure but not letting go completely. "It is just that I missed you so, so much."

Rena ducked out of Justina's loosened grasp and darted inside. "Mama, did you have an accident?"

"I … tripped. Stay away from the table until I pick up the broken glass. It is dangerous. You will cut yourself."

Rena shuffled closer, her eyes narrowed, staring hard.

"Mama," she said, "your eyes are puffy. Have you been chopping onions?"

"Yes, my darling girl," Justina said, unable to stifle a laugh. The relief at seeing and hearing her babies was overwhelming. "That is exactly what I have been doing. And garlic. Do not forget the garlic."

Justina picked up Kora, locked the door, and carried her past the damage.

"Rena, come away from there. I told you it is dangerous!"

"Sorry, Mama."

"Now, upstairs and get changed while I clear the mess. I expect you are hungry?"

"Starving, Mama," Kora said.

Rena nodded and slid the satchel from her shoulder. "Yes please, Mama. School dinner was horrible."

Justina ruffled Rena's hair. "Help your sister change out of her uniform and, just this once, you can watch television before doing your homework, okay?"

She shooed them up the stairs to the apartment before rushing back to the kitchen in time to meet Ore, who had parked the car around the back as usual, off the busy street.

Before he had the chance to step fully into the kitchen, she flew into his arms and poured out her heart to him.

For the longest time, they clung to each other.

Ore listened, stroking her hair and whispering soothing words. Eventually, she recovered enough to let him clear the damage and make supper for the girls.

With Ore in charge, she ran upstairs and stood under the shower until it ran cold, scrubbing her skin raw to remove the stench and the feel of a man called Alfie Lovejoy.

She cried for a full hour.

———

LATER THAT NIGHT, after they closed the restaurant—six covers all evening, barely enough to cover the night's electricity bill—she and Ore sat in their living room. The girls were fast asleep and blissfully unaware.

They read the new contract together. She found the legal wording difficult to follow, but Ore snorted at the document's promised to pay them the full "independently assessed market value" for the leasehold of the building and the goodwill of the business. To Justina, the total purchase price—laid out in words and figures at the bottom of the final page—looked impressive.

"It ain't enough," Ore said, holding her close and gently kissing her bruised and swollen cheek. "After paying off the mortgage, we'd barely have enough to clear our other debts. There'd be nothing left over for a deposit on a new home. And worse than that, far worse, we'd both need to find new jobs straight away."

Despair wrapped around her, choking her, making it difficult to breathe.

"Ore, what are we going to do?"

He threw the contract on the coffee table and turned to face her, holding her hands, and kissing her wrists where the marks from Lovejoy's grip still showed red and sore.

"I don't know. I've been trying to find a way out, but …" Ore squirmed in his seat, creating a gap between them. "Before he died, Papa and I had a blazing row. He was planning to sell a share in the Bistro, but I hated the idea. The Bistro is the girls' inheritance, their future. Papa thought the money would tide us over until after the development company had finished renovating the block."

"Is that why Papa was on the flight to Amsterdam?"

Ore lowered his head. "Yes. He knew a man in The Hague, a rich man who owed him a favour. Darling, Papa died thinking I hated him."

Ore wept quietly and, even though she imagined herself all cried out for the day, tears also filled Justina's eyes. They held each other.

"Papa knew you loved him, Ore. He knew it."

They kissed and hugged, and for a moment, things were better.

Eventually, Ore leaned back on the sofa, his arm draped around her shoulders. Justina rested her head against his chest, listening to and feeling the slow, steady beat of his heart. The soft rise and fall of his chest lulled her, helping to calm her involuntary emotional and physical twitches.

"After Papa's funeral," he said at length, his soft words

vibrating through his ribcage, "I found the contact details of the man in The Hague, but … it's too late. He didn't want to help me. He said the debt he owed Papa died with him. Darling, I have no idea what to do."

She had no idea either and they sat in silence for hours and hours.

Chapter Two

Thursday 22nd October – Morning

The Villa, Gironde, Nouvelle-Aquitaine, France

The late-autumn sun flared off the water and sliced into Ryan Kaine's eyes, but the light breeze made the day pleasant. A cloudless, azure sky, miles of fine, silver sand, and the blue-grey Atlantic painted a picture-postcard beauty that would change by the day and with the seasons and never grow old. The villa and the Gironde Coast made a great base of operations. Comfortable, isolated, easy to defend, and with multiple means of ingress and egress.

In short, the place couldn't have been better.

The Bay of Biscay, calm in the autumnal stillness, stretched out to the gently curving horizon. The silence interrupted only by the breeze, the breakers wearing the sand into a finer powder, and the discordant cries of Audouin's gulls as they bickered over seaborne scraps. There were no ships or boats to spoil the sea's rolling majesty.

The view was stunning enough, but the smells wafting up from the sun-baked land, the salt-water ozone carried on the onshore breeze, completed it for him. The air held the tang of sun, sea salt, and marram grass. A fragrance no perfumer could capture in a bottle.

Kaine was in his element. For the first time in over twenty years, he could almost relax. The location made him as content as was ever going to be possible given the heavy load his conscience carried. The load he would carry for the rest of his life. However long that would last.

"Are you ready?" Lara called from the office.

He reached a hand to his left side and allowed his fingers to trace the raised, twenty-centimetre scar running along his rib cage. One of the most recent additions to his unwanted collection of body art. A legacy of the knife wound he'd suffered the morning after he'd shot down Flight BE1555. The gash had been serious enough for him to seek out the nearest medical treatment. Luckily for him but, as it happened, unluckily for Lara, his internet search had pointed him to her veterinary clinic.

She'd stitched together a rough and bloodied stranger without complaint and without a thought for herself. Saved his life. No doubt about it. He'd be in her debt forever but, in the weeks since their first traumatic meeting, things had changed. He'd started to feel more than gratitude—much more.

The growing emotions were wrong, inappropriate, forged in battle, and fostered by a sense of responsibility to her and his innate loneliness. He could never act on his feelings and worked hard to draw a professional but friendly line in the sand between them.

"Everything set up properly this time?" he asked, playing for enough time to roll himself out of his comfy chair and plaster on his game face.

"Yes, and it has been for the past five minutes."

"Is Sabrina online?"

"Yes, and has been——"

"Yeah, yeah. For the past five minutes?"

"No. She's been taking me through the system for the past hour. Get your backside in here, right now!"

And there it was, her patience threshold breached. Not saintly, but still beautiful. Angelic.

Kaine grunted as he rolled off the recliner and onto his feet. He hadn't been resting all that long, and the aches and pains from the early-morning workout had eased, but he'd have preferred more recovery time. His first training session of the day—a two-mile swim, keeping close to the shore, within sight and easy access of the villa, a thirty-minute run over the nearby dunes, followed by another thirty minutes spent throwing weights and punching bags—was the barest minimum, maintenance only. It took it out of him, and recuperation took longer than it used to—the cost of an aging body. Growing older could be a nightmare. On the other hand, it beat the alternative.

He snorted to himself.

Sabrina was doing them a huge favour and it would be wrong to keep her waiting any longer. Reluctantly, he turned his back to the sea and its gently rolling waves and padded barefoot across the hardwood deck into the cool shade of his whitewashed safe house.

He'd bought the single-storey, Mediterranean-style villa ten years earlier for cash—strike that—he'd picked it up for peanuts at the depth of a banker's recession. The original owner, a snot-nosed, London fund manager, needed a quick sale to help pay his legal fees and keep him out of prison, and he wasn't too keen to leave much of a paper trail. As a result, Kaine acquired the part-built property with its three bedrooms, open-plan kitchen-diner, and subterranean *cave* —wine cellar—set on acres and acres of dunes overlooking the sea as a retirement home. He'd since spent a fortune upgrading it into a self-contained, off-the-grid fortress, complete with its own triple-redundant renewable energy source—tidal, solar, and wind—and a bespoke satellite service.

For security, he'd used non-local artisans for separate parts of the project. As a result, no single firm, or single individual, had a comprehensive knowledge of the completed structure.

Although not averse to the odd glass or two of wine, Kaine didn't require a dedicated wine cellar, but did need a home for a secure communications hub and a state-of-the-art surveillance system. To that end, he'd called on the services of a couple of military engineer friends to help him convert the cellar into an office that could double as a panic room. They also spent a week deploying a security net of motion sensors and surveillance cameras—both standard and infrared—to protect the whole property.

Finally, before furnishing the place in a clean, minimalist style, Kaine added a hidden exit to the panic room. Only he, and now Lara, knew of the back door's existence. Kaine wasn't about to allow anyone to trap him or Lara inside a concrete cell, no matter how apparently secure it might appear.

What some might have described as paranoia, he'd seen as a healthy concern for his long-term personal safety. How right he'd been, and now he had Lara to protect, his extensive preparations had proven more than justified.

As an added security measure, since making the villa their temporary base of operations, Kaine, with Lara's help, had calibrated the surveillance system to react to any human-sized approach from land, sea, and air. They'd streamed the surveillance feeds through the comms hub in the office and each had access to the system via mobile phones and waterproof, military-grade, smart watches. As long as they had satellite access, mobile phones, and wore the watches, both he and Lara could monitor the villa and its surroundings at any time, and from just about anywhere on the planet.

Despite all the electronic wizardry, Kaine never forgot the human factor and regularly patrolled the area, often taking Lara with him as both cover—a loving couple out for a stroll—and to hone her surveillance skills. There were no real substitutes for human eyes and ears. Or for human intuition.

To complete the whole defensive arrangement, Kaine spent two hours each afternoon coaching Lara in what she had once jokingly referred to as "The Way of the Warrior". She did, however, take the training extremely seriously and, being bright and physically strong from her work with large farm animals, she made an ideal apprentice. In the few short weeks since their arrival at the villa, she'd developed a good grasp of military fieldcraft and had taken nine minutes off her fifteen-hundred-metre swim time. Kaine had rarely coached a more willing and able trainee and, he'd definitely never coached one as damned good looking.

He secretly loved the time he spent with her and looked forward to each session, but he knew it couldn't last. One day, they would clear his name and confirm that no one wanted to use her to get to him. On that day, Lara would be free to return to her quiet, normal life, and they'd never see each other again. Until then, he could never leave her alone and vulnerable. If ever he had to leave, there were people available at a moment's notice—men he trusted—to guard her in his absence.

He hoped neither day—his leaving on a new mission and her returning to her old life—would ever come, but knew, deep down, they must.

Chapter Three

Thursday 22nd October – Morning

The Villa, Gironde, Nouvelle-Aquitaine, France

After the warmth of the wooden deck, the textured, ceramic tiles of the lounge floor chilled Kaine's feet. He returned to the threshold and stepped into his trainers before descending the stairs and entering an office that wouldn't have looked out of place in the control room of a submarine.

The left side of the converted wine cellar was decked out as a compact living area with a small, galley kitchen, sofa-bed, and the necessary physical amenities. Half a dozen flat screens hung on the right-hand wall in front of a desk long enough to hold two full-sized computer stations.

Lara sat at the one further away and swivelled her chair to face him.

"About time, *mister*," she snapped, although her welcoming smile and twinkling, hazel eyes robbed the words of any hostility. "*I'd* quite like to lie in the sun all day and relax, too, you know."

He dipped his head and glowered at her over the rim of an imaginary pair of sunglasses.

"That's *Captain*, to you, *Doctor* Orchard. What do you have for me?"

She pointed him to the office chair beside her, and waved her hand at the larger of the two live screens, where Sabrina's youthful face smiled back at him. She'd changed her hair colour since he'd last seen her. The new, auburn highlights, a change from the pink she'd sported in London, suited her natural, olive complexion. She wore dangly earrings, a silver stud through her nose, and heavier makeup than usual. The ensemble gave her a neo-punk vibe.

Kaine suspected a darker motive for her new look, but wouldn't dream of asking for details upfront. She had her own life to lead, and he'd already stolen enough of her time.

He took his seat, intending to keep a professional distance, but Lara encroached on his personal space. Not that he minded in the slightest.

"Morning, Sabrina. Hate the new look."

"As do I, *Capitaine* Kaine," she said, frowning.

Her Parisian accent was as soft and appealing as ever, but her use of his rank and surname confirmed that his comment had irked her a little. As well as the time she'd spent on their joint IT project, he owed her a great, personal debt. He'd offered to pay for her expertise, but she'd taken it as an insult, and he hadn't broached the subject since.

"So," he said, "is everything working according to the design specs?"

"Oh dear Lord," Lara muttered, shooting him an exasperated look that suggested he'd clomped all over Sabrina's toes while wearing a pair of his size-nine, marching boots.

"What do you think I have been doing for the past month?" the French woman snapped, confirming Lara's interpretation.

"Sorry. My mistake. Can you give me the management summary? No big words, though. Imagine you're teaching the hard of understanding, or a primary school pupil."

"Ryan," Sabrina scolded, "you talk so much nonsense."

"You're quite correct," he said, relieved to be back on first-name terms.

"*Toujours.*" Sabrina nodded and her earrings flashed in the light streaming through the windows behind her. Clearly, Paris basked in the same, glorious sunshine as Gironde.

"Okay," she said. "I shall walk you through the system. On the main monitor you will see the primary folder."

A yellow folder icon appeared in the centre of the largest screen.

On a separate monitor—the one providing a panoramic view of the bay—their nearest neighbours to the south, Monsieur and Madame Dubois, strolled arm in arm along the beach.

Kaine pointed them out to Lara, who nodded that she'd noticed them, too. Hale and hearty, the septuagenarians were taking their regular, daytime constitutional. They posed no threat and often stopped for a chat if their stroll happened to coincide with a break in Kaine and Lara's beachside training sessions. According to Lara, whose grasp of conversational French far outshone Kaine's, the couple had been married fifty-two years and would drop the fact into the conversation whenever the opportunity arose.

Sabrina tapped a pen on her desk to regain their attention and continued. "As agreed, the system is secure and access has been restricted to the three of us, and to Sergeant Rollason and Corporal Pinkerton."

Lara raised a hand and Sabrina gave her the floor.

"Sorry to interrupt." Lara turned to Kaine. "Did you consider adding DCI Jones to the list?"

"Jones?" Kaine said, opening his eyes wide in horror. "The esteemed Detective Chief Inspector? Not a chance. I trust him with the evidence that proves I was set up, but he wouldn't want anything to do with this system or the tainted money. Can't say I blame him really. Even though he knows we're morally right and tacitly approves of our plans, we are stepping well over the bounds of legality here."

"*Oui*, that, I can understand," Sabrina admitted, nodding. "May I continue?"

"Sorry," Lara said, apologising for them both. "Please do."

"To open the main directory, you need to complete at least two of the four authentication options—retinal, facial, and thumbprint scans, and voice recognition. *Capitaine*, if you don't mind …" She waved her hand to encourage his action.

Using the mousepad on the networked laptop in front of him, Kaine rolled the cursor over the icon and clicked. He recited the opening few lines of the "To be or not to be …" soliloquy from Hamlet, and showed his thumb to the camera lens. After a short delay, the folder opened to reveal eighty-three sub-folders, each sporting the first name and surname of a victim.

The names brought flashes of light to his vision, and his

chest fought the imaginary sea for breath. His eyes snapped shut against the unwanted stimulus, but the horrific moment when he'd shot Flight BE1555 from the skies, killing the eighty-three innocent souls, played on a closed loop behind his eyelids. In quiet moments, the explosion—the massive fireball illuminating the darkening sky over the North Sea—kept returning to haunt him.

It would continue to haunt him for the rest of his life.

Kaine had been set up to take the blame and die in a booby trap, and the plot's real mastermind, Sir Malcolm Sampson, currently resided at Her Majesty's pleasure,

However, in its infinite wisdom, the UK government had decided that SAMS, with its tentacles in so many defence contracts, was too big to fail. They had covered up Sir Malcolm's part in the tragedy and buried the proof of Kaine's innocence. The proof Kaine had risked his life to obtain.

At the time, a significant positive to having Sabrina on his side, was the money she'd helped him "liberate" from Sir Malcolm—all three hundred and fifty-two million Euros of it.

One day soon, the real reason for Flight BE1555's destruction would reach the public domain, and clear Kaine's tarnished name. In the meantime, he had vowed to dedicate his life to helping the victims' families—*The 83*.

Three hundred and fifty-two million Euros sounded like a lot of money, and it was, but if split evenly eighty-three ways—as per Kaine's original plan—it would have led to imbalances and unfairness. Some families were smaller than others and the four and a quarter million Euros would stretch further. Others were wealthy and more able to cope financially. In addition, some of the victims had left no obvious beneficiaries.

No doubt, in some cases—most cases—money might help, but Kaine was under no delusions. Throwing cash at a problem wasn't always the answer. In certain situations, Kaine's other skills might prove handy. Either way, he vowed to help, even if the families didn't know exactly where the help came from.

It would be Kaine's way to seek redemption—as if that were ever possible.

Sabrina's words cut into his thoughts, and he opened his eyes to focus on her.

"...notice that a number of the folders are linked by two-way arrows. This indicates that the victims were directly related, either by marriage or as siblings. It reduces the number of individual families we need to monitor by twenty-nine and makes our task of dispersing the money slightly less complicated." She paused for a moment to let Kaine absorb the information.

"So," she continued, "I have produced dossiers on fifty-four individual families. You may click on any of the folders to access the data."

"You've identified the address and contact details of the heads of all the families?"

"Most of them, yes," she said, frowning. "Unfortunately, a number of the older people, the parents who lost children on the flight, have a smaller digital footprint than the younger ones. For these people, it will take longer to build a complete profile."

"How many letters have you posted so far?" Kaine asked.

While Sabrina was developing the program, Kaine and Lara had taken days to formulate a comprehensive letter of introduction to The 83 Trust. The letter included the link to the website, "www.the-83.com", where the family could apply for additional hardship funds as and when necessary.

The website sought to even out the income in terms of immediate need and was the only fair way Kaine could think to operate. Furthermore, the website provided a second vital function. Slap bang in the middle of the home page, Sabrina had stuck a big, red, "call to action" button:

*If you are in imminent financial or physical danger complete this form **now**!*

The button activated a questionnaire with multiple-choice answers and a text box for more detailed comments. Kaine was hoping most of the responses would be finance related. If, however, the challenges required his military skills, they would investigate and, should it prove necessary, he'd drop everything to rush to their defence.

"So far," Sabrina answered, "I have sent the letters to forty-two individuals, together with banker's drafts for nine thousand, nine hundred, and fifty pounds to ensure it doesn't trip any money-laundering alarms."

Kaine nodded. The amount and method of delivery was intended to make the initial payment frictionless and to show every recipient that The Trust was legitimate and meant business.

Lara leaned closer, giving him a hint of sandalwood body lotion, and nodded her understanding. "But that leaves twelve families totally unsupported?"

"So far, *oui*," Sabrina agreed. "I shall continue my research, but in the meantime ..."

"We have more than enough to be going on with," Kaine said. "Is the website live?"

"Ryan," Lara said, resting a hand on the arm of his

chair, "what do you think Sabrina and I have been doing for the past hour, comparing cake recipes?" She arched an eyebrow.

"Sorry," he said, staring into her soft, hazel eyes.

"As the website's already live, have there been any clicks or responses yet?" he asked Sabrina, forcing his mind back on the subject.

Sabrina shook her head, and once again, sunlight twinkled on the cut-glass jewellery. "Not yet, but I am expecting some activity by the weekend. What you call 'snail mail' takes a long time to deliver, no?"

"Shouldn't that be *escargot post* since we're *en France*?" Kaine asked, but continued quickly when Lara shot him another warning glance. "So ... you've had time to go through some of the dossiers. Anything I should be aware of?"

"Not really. Nothing that would require your specialist skills," Sabrina said, looking down at something on her screen. "At least nothing that stands out in my eye, but"— she raised her left arm and pointed at her watch—"I am sorry, time has flown. Feel free to access the system at your leisure. Familiarise yourselves with its configuration. There is no need to worry, you will not break it. Just make certain to shut it down properly between uses. It will automatically save the data to the cloud, and purge the search history."

"That's it?" Kaine asked.

"*Oui*, that is it. I have already shown Lara some of the more ... interesting elements, the ones that will help with your ongoing research."

"Really?" Kaine said. "You've added some toys?"

Sabrina pursed her lips before answering. "Nothing exciting. A few special applications to allow you direct access to some of the more useful national databases in the

UK. You know the sort of thing—police, military, DVLA, traffic cameras, and the like. If you ever need to interrogate databases in the EU or elsewhere, give me enough warning, and I will see what I can create."

"You are a genius," Kaine said.

"Correct," she agreed, and shot him the grin of a supremely confident IT specialist.

"And you're certain it's fully secure and can't be traced back to us here?"

"But of course," she said, her French accent deepening and confirming the perceived insult. "As is the location and origin of the money. The head of the Bank of England would sell his soul for the security I have built into this system. Nothing will filter back to you, or to me, and no one can access the funds without your authority."

"And in the event of my ... lack of availability?"

Lara flashed him a glance to tell him she knew he'd stopped himself saying, "In the event of my death?"

Sabrina clearly understood his meaning, too, but hid it better. Given the sometimes-clandestine nature of her work, she'd had more experience in hiding her emotions than Lara, but Lara would learn. She'd have to.

"I have built a number of redundancies into the system," Sabrina said. "You have no need to worry. In the case of your ... enforced absence, a trio of myself, Lara, Sergeant Rollason, or Corporal Pinkerton will be able to form a quorum to disperse the assets as we see fit and according to your expressed wishes. In the event of a disagreement, Lara will have the deciding vote, as per your instructions."

Kaine interlaced his fingers and cracked his knuckles. Not the quickest typist on the planet, he needed more time with a keyboard than many.

"Good," he said. "Anything else before I start my homework?"

Sabrina reached up to play with an earring. Kaine would never understand how women could wear the things. It was bad enough to have comms buds stuck in your ear during operations, but earpieces were taped in position and didn't move around much.

"There is one more thing before I go," she said, clearly not as eager to be on her way as Kaine imagined. "Earlier, we were talking about DCI Jones. When did you last speak to him? Is there any news of your status? How many people in authority know you were not to blame for shooting down Flight BE1555?"

Kaine and Lara shared a glance, her expression a curious mix of frustration and annoyance. He waved a hand for her to explain the situation to Sabrina.

"The delay is political and has nothing to do with justice," she said, anger bubbling closer to the surface. "It's so unfair. Ryan's being used again."

Lara made fists and pressed them into her lap.

Kaine took over. "When the PM sacked the last Home Secretary, her replacement wasn't inclined to stand by his predecessor's promises. DCI Jones was forced to hand over all our evidence to the Humberside Police Investigation Team and HOATU, the Home Office Anti-Terrorist Unit. Both are dragging their heels on the matter." He shrugged. "On the other hand, the police are no longer listing me as a 'person of interest' in the investigation, and, since my recent trip to Scotland, the media clamour related to me has died down a little. The news outlets have lost interest in hounding me and have returned to their fascination with celebrity marriages and divorces. Don't you just love today's investigative journalism?"

Kaine forced a smile.

A frown creased Lara's forehead. "Ryan, don't you dare be so flippant. The police and the government have had proof of your innocence for nearly two months, and they've done nothing about it. They didn't even charge Sir Malcolm with mass murder. All they did was lock him up for embezzlement and tax fraud!" She took a short breather before adding, "And what happened to that pardon you were promised? Where did that disappear to?"

Red spots darkened her cheeks and her voice rose in anger. God, she was beautiful when annoyed, and the fact she targeted her rage at the people she saw as doing the dirty on him did wonders to lift Kaine's mood.

"The wheels of justice—"

"Are rusted solid!" she finished for him. "It's just not fair, Ryan. Malcolm Sampson set you up and the world still thinks you're a terrorist madman."

He touched a hand to her shoulder, and she calmed a little.

On the screen, Sabrina rested an elbow on her desk and cupped her chin in her hand. As she stared at them, amusement brightened her eyes. "If you two are quite finished?"

Lara sniffed and dabbed her eyes with a tissue that had appeared in her hand as if palmed by a nightclub magician. Over her swimsuit, she wore a loose halter top with a plunging neckline, skin-tight, cutaway jean-shorts, and sandals. Where she'd stored the tissue was anybody's guess, but he'd love to find out.

"Sorry, Sabrina," Lara said. "The unfairness makes me so mad. Ryan's a good man and his reputation has been … shot to pieces."

"Oh dear," Kaine said, "I'll ignore that rather dark pun."

Had he allowed himself, Kaine might have blushed at her staunch support. Instead, he smiled and kept his embarrassment to himself.

Sabrina broke the short silence. "I fully understand, and on another positive note, none of my searches has indicated that Sir Malcolm's reward for your head on a platter is still active. Have you heard anything from your military contacts?"

Kaine scratched the beard he'd started growing on the day he became a fugitive. It itched to buggery and still had the irritating power to drive him nuts. "It's not likely to appear in *Soldier of Fortune*'s classified ads, but so far, everything's quiet on the contract killer front. My military mates haven't heard anything, but we can't afford to relax just yet. There are plenty of people in my former industry who'd just love to take a tilt at my crown of notoriety, even if there was no financial reward in the offing. Bragging rights alone would attract some of the sociopaths I've met and dealt with over the years."

"Ryan, stop it," Lara ordered, the frown deeper, her tone even more forceful. "This isn't a joke."

Tell me about it.

"Sorry, Lara."

"I should think so, too." Not readily placated, she continued. "The police could raise a warrant for your arrest any time they choose, and your photo would be on TV and in the papers all over again."

"I did apologise, Lara. And I do take it seriously. My gallows humour takes over sometimes. I'll try to keep it under control, okay?"

Still scowling, Lara returned her attention to the monitor and Sabrina.

"Do you have anything else to tell us?"

"You sound like an old, married couple, *mes amis*. Do I have your undivided attention?"

Lara blushed, and her frown softened.

"I object to that description," Kaine said, stretching out another amused grin. "Neither of us is that old ... but please continue."

Sabrina looked directly into the camera. "I have to leave Paris for an indeterminate period. Unfortunately, I will be inaccessible until my return."

Kaine raised his chin. "*Grand-père* Mo-Mo's in need of your talents?"

"*Oui*. Both he and *le Ministère de l'Intérieur*."

Lara frowned and opened her hands under the desk, out of shot of the camera.

Kaine whispered behind his hand, "Tell you later," before speaking up. "Thanks again for all your help, Sabrina. You have been completely and utterly superb. The 83 would thank you too, but they'll never have the chance to."

Sabrina arched one dark eyebrow. "Ryan Kaine, you are a charmer. It is no wonder Lara stays so close to you. I will leave you two alone to your marital bickering. *Au revoir, mes amis*."

Her screen snapped to black before either could comment or complain.

"Kids today, eh," Kaine muttered. "Absolutely no respect for their elders."

Lara pushed her chair away from the desk. "Okay, so who's this *Grand-père* Mo-Mo?"

He took a little time to think before answering. "What I'm about to tell you must not leave this office, promise?"

Lara returned his steady gaze. "Of course. You can trust me."

"I know, but the more information you have, the greater the risk to you. The abridged answer is, Faroukh probably isn't Sabrina's real surname."

Lara drew up her hands and placed them over her heart.

"Gosh, the shock," she gasped in mock surprise. "You really imagined I didn't know that? Honestly, Ryan, you must think I'm so naïve."

"Yes, okay. I know. I'm a complete bozo when it comes to women," he said, adding another shrug.

"So, are you going to answer me or not?"

"As you insist, my lady," he said, inclining his head in a slight bow, to which she sighed. "As I told you the day we met, Western Europe has two major and competing armaments companies. You already know about SAMS, formerly run by the top-of-the-pile arsehole, Malcolm Gareth Sampson. The other one is European Small Arms and Personal Protection, A/S." Again he scratched at the annoying beard.

"Headquartered in Paris, ESAPP is run by a chap with the name Maurice LeMaître. I met him once when doing some work for NATO. A charming individual and well-respected in the industry. The polar opposite of Malcolm Sampson."

"Thanks for the lesson in weapons manufacturers but what's that got to do with … wait a minute, *Maurice* LeMaître? Is he *Grand-père* Mo-Mo?"

Kaine raised an index finger. "Got it in one."

"So, her real name's Sabrina LeMaître?"

"Not necessarily. He's so well respected, everyone in the company calls him *Grand-père* Mo-Mo. It turns out that our young, IT expert carries out the occasional, undercover mission for ESAPP, as well as for the French government."

"Wow." Her eyebrows shot up. "She's a real-life spy?"

"Possibly. Let's just leave it at that and be grateful she's on our side, shall we?"

"Fair enough." She jumped to her feet. "Don't know about you, but I need some food before I can face wading through the system and the dossiers. Whose turn is it?"

"Yours. I cooked last night's dinner."

"Lobbing a couple of frozen pizzas in the oven isn't cooking, Ryan."

"It isn't?" he asked, wide-eyed.

Lara raised a hand and sighed. "Okay, okay. It's my turn. What do you fancy?"

"A cheese salad baguette would be nice, thanks. Give me twenty minutes to have a play with the system, and I'll follow you up."

Kaine watched her climb the stairs to the ground floor before turning his attention to his laptop. He started banging on the keys, trying to take his mind off the way she seemed to float over the treads, moving with smoothness and grace, and barely making a sound.

"Pack it in, Kaine," he muttered. "When did you turn into a lovesick teenager?"

Chapter Four

Thursday 22nd October – Early Afternoon

The Villa, Gironde, Nouvelle-Aquitaine, France

After a light lunch on the terrace, taking calories in with the view, Kaine and Lara returned to the office. For security and confidentiality reasons, they didn't print off hard copies of the documents. For the same reasons, the laptops needed to remain in the office. Reading from the screens was tiring on the eyes, but security took precedence over comfort and his being in close proximity to Lara could hardly be considered a chore.

While Kaine scanned through the dossiers, Lara familiarised herself with the intricacies of the new software system, and Kaine was happy to let her. He didn't have the greatest patience for non-military tech.

After close to three intensive hours, and with his eyes and brain tiring into fog, Kaine took his leave and carried out his regular, afternoon security sweep of the property. He masked it to any passing fishermen or casual beachcombers as yet another workout for an exercise freak.

He jogged the perimeter to check the function of the electronic defences—with Lara confirming the calibrations of the surveillance system—and finished with sprint-jog intervals along the beach. With Lara on her own in the villa, at no point did he venture more than five hundred metres away, but even such a distance, a maximum of two minutes flat out over the dunes, was too far for comfort. To do his job of keeping her safe, and maintain a half-decent level of fitness, physical conditioning was essential, so he encouraged her to spend the time locked in the panic room. When they first arrived, Lara baulked at the idea, but after telling her a little of his experiences in the world's flashpoints—keeping the details light and non-specific—she reluctantly agreed to his request.

As usual, he followed up the outdoor routine with thirty minutes of high-intensity exercise in the villa's makeshift gym—a corner of the spare bedroom. Still taking things easy with his left side, he punched light and heavy bags and lifted free weights, but his eyes maintained a constant vigil on the surveillance feed running into his smart watch and on the room's dedicated monitor.

While he worked away inside, Lara—a committed sun-worshiper—took to the deck and soaked in the late-afternoon rays.

Exercise completed, freshly showered, and feeling as relaxed as he could under the circumstances, Kaine lay, stretched out on a bentwood recliner, in his matching set of brilliant-white, Lacoste shorts and tennis shirt, ostensibly reading a paperback. But beneath the peak of his baseball cap, and behind his dark glasses, the words swam on the page. He couldn't concentrate to read. After twenty years in the military, many spent in the thick of major theatres of war, Kaine found it impossible to switch off his internal defences, even in so idyllic a place.

Despite the fortress-like setup, with the nearest neighbours more than a fifteen-minute beach walk away on either side, and a mesh of electronic tripwires blanketing the dunes, he couldn't relax, not fully. Lara, lying on her recliner at his side, was his responsibility, and he could never fully rest while there was even the remotest chance of her being at risk.

Besides, one of the reasons his eyes refused to concentrate on the pages was the way she filled out her sprayed-on, one-piece bathing suit. He found it impossible not to stare.

As though she could read his thoughts, she removed her sunglasses and looked at him.

"You haven't turned a page in five minutes. Something wrong?"

He hiked his shoulders and shook his head. "Not really. I'm always like this between operations. A 'quiet before the storm' kind of thing, you know? I never did learn to switch off fully."

In the fluid motion worthy of a dancer, she sat up, swung her long legs off the recliner, planted her bare feet on the deck, and leaned forwards.

"Living so much on the edge isn't good for you. Stress is a killer."

Still lying flat, he eased a crick in his neck. "I'm used to it. It's a way of life in my business."

"You can't even take a splash in the sea without turning

it into a training opportunity, and you've exercised twice a day every day since we arrived."

"I need to keep sharp. Stay in shape, you know?"

"Your shape's not too bad."

Blimey. She noticed?

"Thanks, Doc."

She tilted her head to the side, her eyes alighting on his chest and staying there.

"By the way, I've been studying your swim stroke," she said, as a throwaway line.

Kaine lowered his shades and stared at her over the top of the frame. To match her eye level, he dropped his feet onto the deck and sat up, only he likely did it with a damn sight less grace than Lara, and a load more grunting.

"You've been studying my swim stroke? Really?" He tried to avoid sounding incredulous, but failed miserably.

Frown wrinkles appeared around her mouth. Kaine half-expected her to growl.

"Yes, I know. I'm hardly the best swimmer in the world, but I've been online studying swim dynamics—"

"Swim dynamics?"

"Listen, buddy," she said, jabbing an index finger at his chest, "you don't have to be a great swimmer to be a decent swim coach."

She'd made a good point.

Smiling to diffuse the growing tension, he patted a hand in the air. "You've got me there. So, you've been looking at online swim coaching sites?"

"I couldn't think of a better way to spend my time than increasing my knowledge base. And don't worry, I used Sabrina's security interface. 'Safe surfing' as you keep insisting."

Smart woman.

"Good. And as a matter of interest, when did you do this internet searching?"

"Before Sabrina's monitoring system went live. While you were running along the beach. And don't worry, I kept the office door closed, too. Again, as you insisted."

Smarter woman.

"As I *recommended*. You're neither a prisoner nor one of my troops. I can't—won't—give you orders." He tried a smile but didn't think it worked particularly well.

"Okay. As you 'recommended'." Lara nodded, widening her hazel eyes and emphasising the words by wagging her head. "But I did lock the door."

"Thank you for listening."

"You're welcome."

She never stopped astonishing him. He'd been worried about her safety, and she'd been following his advice to the letter. The perfect client. The perfect partner. The perfect everything.

Pack it in, Kaine.

"Excellent. So, you have something to say about my swimming technique?"

Her expression became thoughtful and then morphed into one of serious, professional concern. In addition to her fitness and self-defence classes, he'd have to introduce a fieldcraft module on maintaining a poker face.

"You crab through the water a little. It took me a while to work out why, but it's because you pull a lot more efficiently with your right arm than your left. In fact, your left-arm reach is a great deal shorter than your right."

He forced a smile and said, "Good spot, but that's normal for me. A long-term stroke weakness. I've always been more efficient on my right side during the catch-and-pull phase. It's down to my being right-hand dominant and has nothing to do with the cut you stitched together so expertly—or anything else."

"Let me see your arm," she said, all business.

Without thinking, he offered her his right arm, but she batted it away.

"The left, idiot."

"Oh ... sorry." He smiled and thrust out the left as instructed.

With strong hands, she squeezed and prodded the forearm, and rotated the wrist.

"Any discomfort?" she asked.

"None."

"Really?" She sounded doubtful. "None?"

He shook his head. "Not a thing. Should have had those pins removed years ago, but I kept putting it off."

The surgically implanted screws and pins had helped stabilise a serious forearm break, but they'd done their job and more than outlived their usefulness. He'd had them removed at the same time as having the dental implant fitted. The small scars resulting from the keyhole procedure barely even showed anymore.

"Remarkable," Lara muttered.

"I've been taking things easy. Following doctor's orders."

"Not before time," she said, giving him his arm back. "How's that rib injury?"

"It's fine."

"Take off your shirt and let me see."

He hesitated for a second.

"Don't be shy, Ryan. I am a doctor."

"A horse doctor."

"You weren't so picky when you crashed into my clinic."

"Touché."

Reluctantly, he did as she instructed and, almost as a reflex, tightened his abs, hoping she wouldn't notice.

Lips thinned, Lara ran gentle fingers over his skin.

"See?" he said, trying to breathe normally despite the tensed abs. "Good as new."

"Not bad. The scar tissue is reasonably smooth and supple. Shouldn't cause any long-term discomfort. Make sure to keep it clean. To be honest, I've never seen a faster healing process, not even on horses."

"Great," he said, pulling away. "Now you're comparing me to Dobbin? Nice one."

The thread-like lines on her forehead deepened. "That's not what I meant, and you know it. I was making a point that with the number of stitches you kept popping when you were running around saving our lives, I'd have expected the scarring to be deeper and wider. Uglier."

The fact she saw his actions as life-saving, and had never once blamed him for dragging her into his screwed-up life in the first place, confirmed her status as a saint—or maybe an angel.

"Don't worry about it, Lara. What's one more scar to add to the collection?"

The marks of half a lifetime spent in battle hadn't worried him before, but he'd never really cared about what a woman might think of them before either. Under her keen gaze, the scars felt ugly, embarrassing.

As she continued her gentle examination, he stared out over the water and remembered all the missions he'd been involved in, the people he'd saved … the ones he hadn't.

Eventually, she leaned back and studied him full length. "Is that why you swim in a singlet and never take off your top in public? So many scars?"

He scratched the back of his neck. "More or less. Wouldn't want to scare the neighbours."

She stretched, shielded her eyes from the sun, and made a great show of scanning the empty dunes and the lonely expanse of beach.

"What neighbours?"

Kaine sighed and took a sip of lemonade. The ice cubes clinked—a happy sound that brought memories of simpler times. His mother used to make lemonade and they'd sit in the garden on long, hot summer days playing host to every kid in the village. Ma would relax in the sun while they played football, cricket, or endless games of chase and British Bulldog. He couldn't help smiling.

"You have a decent body, for an older guy," she said. "Pity it doesn't see much sun."

He tried to pull down the tennis shirt, but for some reason, it stuck to his skin. Eventually, he untangled it enough to free his arms and grab his glass again. He took a large gulp of the lemonade and crunched on an ice cube.

"The sun and I aren't best mates," he said at last. "I've spent too much time in too many deserts."

He didn't mention that someone walking around a quiet, coastal town in France looking as though he'd been standing next to Daniel during his stroll through the lions' den, didn't exactly merge into the background. Military fieldcraft basics—in the field, blending in was an essential part of staying alive.

"And anyway, who are you calling an 'older guy'? We're not that far apart, age-wise. Born within eight years of each other. I even know how old you'll be on your next birthday."

Her smile fell. "I never told you my age. Or my birthday."

Kaine tapped the side of his nose. "That sort of information doesn't stay hidden for long, not with the contacts I have at my disposal."

"Don't you dare ask Sabrina to hack my personal details. Some things are best left unknown."

Oops, too late.

As soon as he'd had a spare minute after their initial life-changing meeting, he'd found out everything he could about the beautiful veterinarian.

For operational purposes, of course.

She took a breath as though to say something else, but shook her head and stretched out on her recliner once again, lips together, skin glowing in the light reflecting off the water.

The longer she remained silent, the more uncomfortable he became.

The time would come when they would have to make a decision—soon, but not right away. Lara needed time to consider her options. After all, she was a young woman, a professional. How long could he expect her to spend lying in the sun on an extended holiday from her real life?

He'd love nothing more than for her to be part of his life forever, but she deserved better, much better.

Because of his oath to The 83, the course of his life would be forever dictated by their needs, not his own. When he'd run off to Scotland to search for the missing lad, Lara had been worried and upset, and for good reason. He might never have returned as a free man. It wouldn't be fair to keep putting her through the same thing time after time.

He should have sent her away weeks ago, but having her beside him seemed the most natural thing in the world.

Why couldn't he have burst into the life of a bow-legged, wizened, old bloke with a hook nose, brown teeth, and halitosis? Things would have been so much easier. He'd have set the old boy up with a new life somewhere safe and out of the way. Somewhere like New Zealand.

Kaine should have done the same for Lara. He should have had Sabrina build her a new identity, in a safe place, and ensured her safety, but no, he'd been selfish. So bloody selfish.

Some days, he wanted to scream at the world for its cruelty. Other days, he wanted to dance for the colour she'd brought into his life.

"It's … getting late," he said, jumping to his feet.

"Yes, it is."

She pointed her toes, rolled her shoulders, and sighed.

He stood tall over her and cleared his throat. "What do you fancy for supper? Eat out, or stay in?"

"Do you mind if we eat in, please? I don't really like the idea of getting dressed for the restaurant."

"Good decision. Barbeque?"

Lara nodded.

"Okay, barbeque it is."

She stretched into a comfortable, back-arching yawn—which made Kaine yawn in sympathy—and settled back on the recliner once again.

"There's no rush, though," she said languidly. "I can wait an hour or so. This is so peaceful. Let's enjoy the last of the sun."

"Keeping a hungry man from his grub? Fair enough, abstinence makes the stomach grow fonder."

She covered her eyes with a hand. "Oh dear."

"Sorry. Not one of my better jokes."

"You make jokes?"

"Clearly not." He winced. "Guess I deserved that."

Kaine drained the last of his lemonade. The ice had

melted and diluted it down to mostly water. He lifted her empty glass from the table.

"Another?"

"No, thanks. I'll have some wine with dinner," she said, and stared at him for a few seconds before letting out another gentle sigh. "Think I'll carry on with my book for a while."

She hitched a smooth shoulder, took her e-reader from the table, and turned her back to him.

The cold shoulder? Kaine couldn't really blame her. He needed a better joke book. Maybe he'd order one for Christmas. *1001 Jokes for the Modern Fugitive*. It would be a hoot.

Kaine hovered over her, unsure of what to do next.

"What're you reading?"

She touched the e-reader's screen, and it lit up.

"Women's fiction. A light romance. Nothing you'd be interested in."

He leaned against the back of her chair and glanced at the screen—*Chapter 14, Alison's Dilemma.*

"You'd be surprised," he said with forced enthusiasm. "I love a good, soppy romance, me. Especially the ones where the recently widowed heroine has to take over her Great Aunt's antique shop in the Yorkshire Dales. Towards the end, she has to choose between the nice but solid and boring doctor, and the devastatingly handsome but dangerous rogue."

"Philistine! It's not at all like that. Not anymore," she said, looking up and shooting metaphysical daggers at him. "The genre can be much more realistic and gritty these days."

"Really? Do tell. Care to give me the synopsis? What exactly is Alison's dilemma?"

He drummed his fingers on the back of her recliner, waiting.

"Alison is a high-powered, New York lawyer defending a banker accused of tax fraud. They've just had an argument and she's stormed out of a late-night meeting. Now she's about to hook up with a guy in a bar."

"A guy in a bar? A ruggedly handsome biker who sweeps her off her feet and rides them off into the sunset, perhaps?"

Lara lowered the e-reader and placed it face down on her flat stomach. "No, this guy's a professional hit man who kidnaps her and holds her captive in a house near the sea."

"Ouch. Art mirroring life?"

"Now *I'm* joking," she said, lifting the e-reader again. "This one's really about a woman trying to rebuild her life after the only man she's ever loved dies in her arms."

"Ha! Told you. Art mirroring life."

"Yes, you did. Now, go fetch your drink and leave me in peace."

"Yes, ma'am."

She dismissed him with a curt wave of her hand. He wandered into the kitchen to replenish his glass, adding the merest hint of vodka for the kick and, after a quick scan of the surveillance monitors, he returned to the deck, drink in hand.

In his brief absence, the temperature had dropped enough for Lara to have tied a silk sarong as a beach wrap over her bathing suit. She'd discarded the e-reader and sat, looking out over the ocean. The cooling breeze pressed the silk against her body, folding it into her curves. Kaine couldn't resist staring and was grateful she was concentrating on the glorious view of the bay.

He stood, watching her enjoy the lowering sun. Both views—her and the bay—were stunning.

Reluctantly, he broke the spell and stepped forwards.

"May I ask a question?" she said without turning or looking up.

Damn it, she'd sensed his presence, and there he was, so proud of his ninja skills and the silent approach. Either he was slipping, or she'd picked up more from their fieldcraft sessions than he'd realised. He couldn't work out whether to be disappointed in his failing abilities, or pleased with her improvement.

He sank into his recliner and raised the back to match the level of hers.

"Ask away. Though I can't promise to answer if it's operationally sensitive."

He winked as she turned her head and frowned at him.

"Try to be serious for a minute, will you?"

Kaine snapped her a short-arm salute. "Will do, Doc."

She grumbled and shook her head, then took the drink from his hand and sipped.

"Vodka?"

He shrugged. "Just a dribble. The sun's well over the yardarm."

She frowned. "The yardarm? What does that mean, exactly?"

"No idea, but it sounds vaguely naval."

"Oh dear Lord," she said, shaking her head in exasperation. "I'm going to slap you in a minute."

He straightened his face. "Sorry, Lara. I'll be serious. You have my word."

"I'll hold you to that, but coincidentally, the navy is one of the things I wanted to ask you about." She waved an arm towards the ocean. "We're living right by the sea. Why have you never taken me sailing?"

Kaine paused and took in the vast expanse of water little more than a good grenade's throw from the edge of the deck. He took a second to decide. Taking her away from the secure confines of the villa and the local village always carried a slight risk, but, given enough time to scope out the nearest boat hire shop, he might be able to work something out.

"You fancy hiring a speedboat to explore the coast?"

"No, I mean proper sailing. You know, yachting. With canvas and ropes and winches and stuff. Wind in the hair. That sort of thing."

"Sailing?" He coughed, slapped a hand to his chest, and signalled for her to hand him his glass. "Oh dear, oh dear. The very idea." He knocked back a mouthful. "Damn it. Should have added more vodka. Or maybe a tot of rum."

He coughed again, this time into his hand.

"Lara, I have to be honest with you. I don't know the first thing about sailing. Couldn't tell you the difference between a jib and a jibe."

"You can't sail? But you were in the Royal Navy, for goodness' sake."

He lowered the glass to the table and twisted at the waist to face her square on.

"Not at all. I was a Royal Marine before I transferred into the Special Boat Service. Marines are waterborne soldiers. Think of us as highly skilled infantrymen, but based on ships and working from boats. Give me a RIB with a Mercury outboard, a canoe, or a kayak, and I'm your man. Underwater? No probs given the right bit of SCUBA gear. At one stage, I used to be able to cite the dive tables from memory. Strap a compressed air cylinder on my back, or an oxygen rebreather, and I'll show you a good time in the water, but sailing? No way. Not a chance."

"That's disappointing. I'd love to try. Looks so … exciting. Romantic even."

"Sailing, romantic? Try it in a Force 10 gale with twelve metre waves crashing over the bow. Nothing romantic about it, I can assure you."

"You said you didn't know anything about sailing."

"I don't, but that doesn't mean I haven't been stuck in a small boat in heavy seas, swallowing mouthfuls of salt water and throwing up over the side. Happy days. No, love. I want my boats powered by a big, strong, marine engine, not a bedsheet."

Bloody hell.

Did he really just say "love"?

He stopped ranting long enough to take another drink and hand her the glass. She accepted it and sipped delicately. Perhaps she hadn't notice his gaffe. He cleared his throat once more.

"Seriously though, if you're that keen to sail, perhaps we could learn together. There's a marina along the coast in St Marcel. We could take a drive over there one day and try enrolling in a course."

A smile lit her eyes. "That sounds like a lovely idea."

"I'll have to vet the place thoroughly first, though," he said, sharing her excitement internally. "I could maybe send Rollo on a fact-finding tour. We have to make sure it's safe."

"Of course. We don't want to risk exposure."

"No, we don't," he said, happy she fully understood the challenges. "And, I've just found out that there's an equestrian centre a few miles inland from here. You must miss your horses."

"Oh Ryan. You have no idea." She sat up and turned

towards him, her face alive. "I grew up around horses. My father taught me to ride almost as soon as I could sit up on my own. Magnificent creatures ..."

Kaine watched her eyes light up, amazed at how animated she became when talking about the powerful, hooved beasties. Her infectious excitement swept him along and, at one stage, he convinced himself it might be fun to learn to ride. They spent the better part of an hour making plans like carefree and excitable youngsters.

For those few brief moments, Kaine allowed himself to dream of a future that, deep down, he knew could never happen.

Chapter Five

Thursday 22nd October – Early Evening

The Villa, Gironde, Nouvelle-Aquitaine, France

After barbequed steaks, jacket potatoes, corn on the cob, tossed salad, and a fiery sauce—eaten during a glorious, orange sunset—Kaine and Lara settled back to watch the sea extinguish the last of the sun's flames.

Lace ribbons of stratus cloud, backlit in red, orange, and purple, hovered above the pale horizon. The sea was as flat calm as it would ever be.

"Breathtaking," Kaine said, offering Lara the last of a full-bodied Bordeaux.

She refused, and he set the bottle aside. Two small glasses was his limit when on duty and, with Lara under his care, he'd never be truly off duty.

"The seascape's pretty special, too," he added softly.

She winced. "Oh dear."

"Too cheesy?"

"Like a camembert left too long in the sun, but I'll accept the compliment. What girl wouldn't?"

"Thank you."

"You are welcome, and I'll have my coffee now, since you were about to offer."

"You're a mind-reader now? But your wish is my delight."

Her musical laugh lifted his spirits and, coffee brewed and poured, they chatted like comfortable friends for ages, relaxing to the sound of the waves lapping the sand and the gentle wind sighing through the dunes.

By ten thirty, they'd emptied a full carafe of coffee, and covered Lara's life history from growing up on a Hampshire farm, through her early childhood, and all the way up to her first proper date. Kaine felt an unreasonable pang of jealousy when Lara described her first serious kiss.

"Okay, Ryan Liam Kaine," she said, lifting a blanket to cover her bare shoulders. "That's more than enough from me for one night."

"Oh, you're turning in? Are you too cold? Would you like another blanket?"

"No, no. It's not that. I'm having a lovely time and you're being very attentive. Charming, even."

Charming? Moi?

"Uh-oh, I sense a 'but' here."

Her smile hit home. Would he ever grow tired of seeing it aimed at him?

"But …" she said, raising a finger and dragging out the delay, "I've been talking more or less non-stop for hours. You know so much about me, but I know next to nothing about you or your past life. And, before you fall back on that terrible, old cliché that if you told me you'd have to kill me, I don't want to know any military secrets. I want to know about you. The real you."

"The real me?" he asked, puffing out his cheeks.

"Yes please."

He shrugged. "You're right, of course. I can't talk about my military activities, not that I'd ever do anything to harm you. It's the one thing I would never joke about. As for the rest of my life, there's nothing much to say other than it's too boring for words."

"Let me be the judge of that."

She scrunched up and tucked her legs under the blanket.

"You are cold, aren't you?"

She nodded. "A little, but don't think you're getting out of it that easily, *mister*. I need answers to some questions."

"Okay, hold that thought."

He jumped up, rushed into the villa, and emerged with a sweater for him and another blanket, which he draped over her shoulders and tucked under her legs.

"Thank you."

"You are more than welcome."

Kaine dragged the sweater over his head, but pulled the sleeves up to his elbows, keeping the smart watch exposed. He didn't want to ruin the vibe and make it obvious when he kept checking its readout.

"So?" she asked. "Ready to come clean?"

"Okay," he said, with a degree of apprehension. "I'll give you three questions and promise to answer them to the best of my ability. But choose wisely, you only get three."

"I'm honoured."

"And so you should be. Few people are afforded the opportunity."

"Ready?" she asked.

"Yes, and that's one. Only two left. Fire away."

"Hang on, that's not fair."

A hand shot out from under the blankets and slapped his bare thigh. He said, "Ouch," and made a show of rubbing away the non-existent sting.

"I demand a recount."

"Okay," he said, smiling at her angry frown. "Just this once."

Christ, she was stunning. He couldn't remember the last time he felt so relaxed.

"First question, where did you grow up?"

"Seriously? You have three questions and that's your first? I'm a little disappointed."

"Why? And"—her hand pushed out from under the blankets again—"don't you dare count that as another of my questions."

"Wouldn't dream of it. I've learned my lesson well." He rubbed his thigh again. "No, what I meant was, I'd have asked a more open-ended question and maybe added a rider or two. Something like, 'Would you please tell me all about your childhood and your family in particular?' Technically two questions, but I'd have given you a pass for ingenuity."

"Getting information out of you is like pulling impacted teeth from a Shire horse."

"No idea what you're talking about there, but I'll take your word for it being difficult. So, you want to know about my childhood?"

"Of course."

"Fancy another coffee first?"

"Yes, please, but stop hedging. I can hear you from the kitchen if you talk up."

He sighed and dragged himself off the recliner once again. "At your command, my lady." He opened his arms and bowed expansively while backing towards the villa. "I was born at a very early age——"

"Ryan, I'm warning you! You promised."

Amid a rumble of the boiling kettle and a rattle of cups and saucers, Kaine started his story. "I was born in Pompey, Portsmouth, and brought up in a small village north of the port. My mother ran a grocery shop, and my father was an officer in the Royal Navy."

"So, you're a military brat following in his father's footsteps. And before you start, that's a statement, not a question. Your father must have been very proud when you joined the marines."

Kaine emerged with a tray full of the makings and a plate of dark chocolate biscotti, her favourites. He deposited it on the table separating their seats and poured. They both took it white with no sugar. Still snuggled deep inside the blanket, Lara cupped her hands around the mug, blowing across the top.

"Your father? Was he proud?"

Kaine shrugged. "I guess he would have been, but Dad died on active service when I was still a kid."

"Oh I'm sorry, Ryan."

He allowed himself a wistful smile and shook his head. "Why? You had nothing to do with it. You would have been in nappies at the time."

"There you go again trying to be funny. I meant, I'm sorry to have made you talk about it. Forgive me?"

"Nothing to forgive. Dad was a hero who died fighting for what he believed in. I'm okay with it now. Tore me apart at the time, though. Of course it did. I went off the rails for a while, but Ma was a rock. Strong, you know? Irish stock." He paused to sip his coffee and threw his mind back so many years. "She was a feisty, auburn-haired Colleen. Real name Myra, by the way. I lost count of the number of times she'd take me by the ear and drag me to Father Angelo for confession. I hated it and soon pulled myself together."

He smiled at the memory of the overly aggressive pre-teen, wailing and scrambling as his mother dragged him to the church. If he'd been any stronger or more resistant he'd have lost an ear.

"Would you believe I did a couple of years as an altar boy? They tried to make me join the church choir, but apparently, I'm tone deaf. A long time ago, someone told me my singing reminded them of a plumber cutting a pipe with a hacksaw. If you ever see me opening my mouth in preparation to sing at a Karaoke bar, you have my permission to shoot me. Okay?"

"Okay, it's a deal," Lara said, lighting the deck with a wonderful smile. "By the way, your mother sounds wonderful. I'd love to meet her."

Again, he shook his head sadly. "Mum passed away over fifteen years ago. Her big, Irish heart finally gave up. I'm glad neither is around to read what they're saying about me now. I wouldn't be able to contact them to explain—"

"And bad people might use them to get to you? The same way they might try to use me?" she asked.

That question, he refused to answer. He'd never opened up to anyone before, and although he enjoyed talking to her, he couldn't make a habit of the process. It turned out to be a little too painful for an old military man, and anyway, she'd be gone soon. The way she'd come alive when talking about her old life made it clear. At the first opportunity, she'd want to leave the villa and head for home and her horses. She'd leave him. In fact, he was surprised she'd been so patient. Every morning, he expected her to demand he do something to make it right. It could only be a matter of time.

"Hang on a minute," she demanded. "If it concerns me, I have the right to know."

Kaine shook his head. "Nope, sorry, that's it. You've used up your final question."

"No I haven't!"

He studied her for a moment before responding. "Now, let me see," he said, counting off the memorised points on his fingers. "'Your father?' Question mark. 'Was he proud?' Question mark. 'Forgive me?' Question mark. Yep, that's three questions all right. Sorry, you're out."

She shook her head and huffed. "Insufferable man. Okay, you win, for now. But I reserve the right to resume this interrogation at another time," she said and finally broke out a wry, but overwhelming, smile.

Crisis avoided, he returned the smile, but dropped it when her hand appeared from under the blanket to hide a yawn.

"Tired?"

"Nope. Not really. I could stay out here all night, just chatting. Getting to know my guardian angel. This is lovely."

Yes, it is.

"Cold?"

"Really, Ryan. I'm fine."

"Look," he said, pointing up high over the bay.

A cloudbank shifted and the waxing, gibbous moon, ninety percent visible, threw a bright, wide line on the sea. The gentle glow from the kitchen LEDs provided plenty of illumination, and he'd developed enough natural night vision to pick out the silvery detail of the coastline.

Lara's skin glowed under the soft, silver light. Christ, the clichés were true. There was something wondrous about moonlight. The lyrics of an ancient song ran through his head.

Good job she'd reminded him about his singing voice, or he might have made a complete tit of himself.

Lara took his hand.

Kaine jumped, surprised by the contact. He jerked his hand away and instantly regretted his reaction when he saw the hurt in her eyes.

"Sorry," she said, "I didn't mean to upset you."

"No, no, it's my fault, I was miles away. Thinking about … well, things, you know. Please"—he opened his hand and laid it palm-up on the table—"forgive me. Can we start over?"

She smiled and put her hand in his once again. He squeezed gently and she responded in kind.

"Gorgeous," she said, nodding at the moonlight dancing over the water.

"Can't argue with that. The moon on the water's nice, too."

"Ryan, you really are so very corny. Nice, though."

"I do try."

"Agreed. Sometimes, you are very trying, but, as I said, nice."

Her hand felt small in his, but strong from working with animals. She was tough, as well. The way she'd reacted to danger, to their escape from the gunmen in the helicopter, and a dozen times since, showed a determination and an inner strength few civilians would have been able to muster.

It would be great to have Lara as more than a friend,

but that was out of the question. She deserved better, and he didn't deserve a comfortable life after what he'd done to the plane. He had so many victims on his docket and felt responsible for their families, The 83. Protecting them would be a lifelong mission.

No, forget it, Kaine.

A romantic relationship between him and Lara couldn't work. His job was to protect her and, if possible, return her to her old life if he could do it safely. It was what she wanted, what she deserved. It was what he'd do.

But why had she reached for his hand?

She squeezed again and turned to face him, her expression serious.

"Ryan, I need to tell you something."

Yep. This is it. She's had enough. She wants to leave.

He waited, not really wanting to hear the words he'd been expecting ever since he'd brought her to the villa.

"This is really difficult. I've been trying to find the right words, but ..."

"It's alright, Lara. You don't need to say—"

"No, Ryan, hear me out. I've been putting this off for days and can't bear it any longer. I know you're only staying here out of a sense of obligation. I know you don't like me the way I like you."

A dagger sliced through his heart.

"What?"

"Don't make this harder, please. You're only staying here because you dragged me into danger, and you want to keep me safe. You want to protect me, but you've also dedicated your life to protecting the families."

The words tumbled out in a breathless torrent.

"Don't get me wrong, I-I'm so proud of your decision to help The 83, but my being here ... is holding you back, dragging you down. I know I should go away somewhere safe … but I don't want that. Ryan, I'm … I think I might be … falling for you."

Moonlight picked out her glistening tears. The weight on Kaine's chest increased.

"Lara, I—"

"Ryan, could your feelings for me ever change?"

He should have lied, should have told her theirs could only ever be a working relationship. He was her protector, her bodyguard. A friend only. That's what he should have said, but he could never tell her a direct lie.

"No. Lara. Not a chance."

She covered her mouth with a hand before he realised what he'd actually said.

"No, no, I didn't mean it like that. My feelings for you can't ever change because …"

"Yes?"

Go on man, bloody say it!

"I—"

A mobile phone vibrated on the table.

Lara jumped, the blood drained from her face.

"Which one?" she asked.

"The burner."

"Oh God!"

Kaine snatched up the burner and read the screen. No caller ID.

"Code Yellow!" he barked.

Kaine ripped the SIG from its position taped under the side table, racked a bullet into the breech, and pointed Lara to the back door. Without hesitation, she ran.

Chapter Six

The Villa, Gironde, Nouvelle-Aquitaine, France

Kaine waited and watched as Lara reacted precisely the way they'd practised. No reluctance. No question.

She raced into the living area, pulled open the panic room door, and slammed it shut behind her. Inside, she'd have full access to the surveillance equipment. Her job, to monitor the tripwire net. His job, to sweep the grounds.

The mobile buzzed again. He picked it up, checked the screen.

One text. Unknown number.

Shit.

Not part of the agreed protocol.

His smart watch showed "all clear". None of the field

sensors had tripped or the internal alarms would be howling.

So far, they were safe, but it couldn't stop there. He couldn't rely on the technology. A wrong number? What were the odds? No time to delay.

He slipped the burner phone into his pocket. Heart racing, breathing rate up, villa lights off, night vision at its optimal for the conditions, he completed a fast sweep of the immediate perimeter, bent low at knees and waist to minimise his target profile.

No intruders.

No obvious disturbance to the close grounds. No unusual smells or sounds.

He ran a second boundary check with the same results before spiralling outwards slowly, edging towards the beach, but keeping in close contact with the villa.

The smart watch vibrated, and he took a knee in a hollow behind a thick tussock of marram grass. He read the message.

Villa clear. Grounds clear. Only you.
Two people on beach, heading south.
The Dubois?

Kaine jumped up, sprinted for the edge of the dunes, and dropped to one knee again. He waited for his breathing to recover.

In the distance to the south, two dark figures stood out clear in the moonlight, standing out sharp against the white sand. One was tall and slim, stooped over, the other short and squat. The Dubois for certain. She loved the beach at night, and he, ever the gentleman, refused to allow her out on her own.

Kaine scanned the beach to the north—nothing. The sea—empty. He held his breath for one more listen—silence, except for nature at night.

He stood, dusted the sand off his knee, and returned for a final search of the house.

None of the circuit breakers had been tripped. None of their high-tech traps had been sprung. The bungalow stood secure.

Lara was safe.

He exhaled deeply.

She's safe.

The only thing that mattered.

Kaine leaned against a wall and buried his face in his hands, taking a moment to recover before returning to the living area. He looked up into the lens of the camera hidden above the panic room door and tapped two fingers against the site of his most recent injury—his tooth implant—a signal only he and Lara knew. The door clicked open, and he breathed more easily. Without Kaine's signal, had anything larger than a rabbit activated more than three of the infrared sensors, Lara would have stayed inside, called for Rollo, and waited for his arrival.

Kaine made the SIG safe and tucked it in the holster sewn into the back of his shorts. Lara popped her head around the blast-resistant door.

"That was fun," she said, smiling, although her pale face and trembling hands gave lie to her bluster. "Who was it?"

"No idea. Text message."

"We did all that for a text message?" She stepped further into the main room. "Why didn't you just read the bloody thing?"

"There was no caller ID."

Close to tears, Lara's lower lip trembled.

"Oh God."

Kaine rushed forwards, wrapped her in his arms, and guided her towards the couch.

"You know the protocols, Lara. An unexpected contact without a caller ID and the security code is unacceptable. Any break from the norm and we protect ourselves first and ask questions second. If we'd been compromised, stopping to read the text might have been all the distraction an attacker needed. I couldn't take that risk. Safety first, remember?"

She nodded. He tried to release her, but she held onto his arm and pulled him down to the chair with her. Even with his internal defences still on high alert, her touch and proximity were distracting.

"Okay," he said quietly, "let's see who's sending us text messages."

He retrieved the mobile from his pocket and opened the message.

> Constantine Family.
> Bistro Mykonos, Tower Hamlets, London.
> Help them!

"What does it say?" Lara asked.

Kaine handed her the phone and tried to work out the implications. Apart from him, Lara, Sabrina, and Rollo, only two other people knew the burner's number, and he trusted them both with not only his life, but Lara's as well. And her life happened to be worth considerably more than his.

Lara returned the phone. "Rollo?"

He shook his head. "He'd have used the code, which is?"

As was his way, he tested her. Driving in the safety protocols the only way he knew how—through repetition. Being a civilian, everything in the field was new to Lara, and she needed the safety protocols ingrained, a second skin. Reaction, action, and only then, thought. If the processes came naturally to her, she might stand a chance if he was no longer around to protect her.

She nodded. "The text starts with a day of the week. Yesterday—that's Thursday as it's way past midnight—if things are okay, but tomorrow—Saturday—if there's a threat."

"Rollo would never break the code. Neither would Sabrina or Danny."

"DCI Jones, then. Does he know it?"

Kaine read the message again. "Yes, but he's not the type to ignore an agreed protocol."

"Who then? Have we been discovered? For this to happen the same day Sabrina rolled out the new program is suspicious, isn't it?"

Kaine had been thinking along similar lines. Despite Sabrina's assurances, he doubted there'd ever been such a thing as a totally secure computer program. Lara's guess was as valid as his, but he didn't want to show her any weakness. She looked too close to losing control.

"Do you recognise the name, Constantine?" he asked, giving her something practical to focus on.

Lara closed her eyes, frowning. "It does seem familiar somehow. Shall I check Sabrina's folders?"

"Yes, please," he said, smiling his encouragement. "Good idea."

She peeled herself away from him and stood. He watched her all the way back to the office staircase. With the door open and the situation normalised, it no longer held the designation "panic room".

"I'll call Jones." He checked the time. 01:37 local time, which meant 00:37 in the UK. He dialled Jones' number. "He'll probably still be up."

Lara said something he didn't catch, and the veteran police officer answered with his usual, terse, "Jones here."

"Sorry, wrong number. I was looking for Mr Mariner."

Jones grunted and disconnected the call. Kaine started counting. He usually didn't reach ten elephants, but the phone vibrated in his hand on the fifteenth pachyderm.

"What took you so long, Mr J?"

"Never you mind."

A voice in the background Kaine didn't recognise called Jones by name and rank.

"Are you still working?"

"Always."

"Nothing serious, I hope?"

"Do you have a problem, Mr Gabriel?"

Kaine winced at the name Jones had assigned him. Gabriel, the Guardian Angel. It made him sound like something out of an Old Testament movie.

"Possibly. A short while ago, I received a text. Wasn't from you by any chance?"

"A text? From me?" Jones scoffed. "I doubt that'll ever happen."

Shit.

If not Jones or his friends, then who?

"I thought not, but had to check, you understand?"

"Have you been compromised?" The policeman's lowered voice took on a note of urgency.

"That's what my ... companion and I were wondering. I'll let you go. Sorry for calling so late."

"Not a problem. I'm at work anyway." Jones hesitated a beat before adding, "Be safe, Mr Gabriel, and please give my fond regards to your companion."

Kaine cut the call and followed Lara down the stairs into the office. He took his usual spot at the desk, sitting as a guard between her and the exit. Four of the six monitors showed wide-angle, monochrome images of the perimeter, each set to the cardinal compass points. The remaining two displayed the front and rear entrances. The barbeque still glowed hot, its temperature indicated by a white flare on the infrared picture.

"Any luck?" he asked, leaning closer to look at her laptop screen.

She leaned back unexpectedly, and her hair brushed his cheek. It smelled of the sun, the sea, and something subtle he didn't recognise.

"I was right. Orestes and Justina Constantine are members of The 83," she said quietly. "They own Bistro Mykonos, a Greek restaurant in Tower Hamlets, London. They have two daughters. Kora, aged five, and Rena, aged seven."

Kaine didn't want to open the wounds, but he had to know.

"Who did they lose?"

If he weren't such a miserable coward, he'd have asked, "Which of their family members did I murder?" but Lara knew what he meant and wouldn't torture him with it.

"Onassis Constantine," she said. "Orestes' father and Justina's father-in-law. He opened the restaurant in the early '70s. Orestes' mother, Renata, died about ten years ago. Breast cancer."

Kaine kept monitoring the other screens. After the

apparently false alarm, his defence mechanisms wouldn't settle down for hours.

"The message told us to help them. Anything on the system to suggest why they'd need my type of help?"

"The Constantine dossier is huge. It'll take ages to read it all, but I haven't found anything obvious so far. So, what do we do?"

Although he loved her use of "we", as though they were a proper team, the decisions had to be his. His world—his responsibility.

"I need to think."

"The message might be a trap. Someone could be trying to lure you to London."

He scratched at his new beard. Would he ever get used to the annoying, bloody thing?

"That's a distinct possibility."

She dipped her head and her shoulders slumped in resignation. "You're going to London, aren't you?"

When he didn't answer right away, she repeated the question more forcefully.

"Not sure I have any alternative. If the Constantines *are* in trouble, I need to be there for them."

"In that case, I'm coming, too."

Kaine expected her to say exactly that and was ready. "Oh no. No way. Safety first. You're staying right here in the villa."

"But I'll be safer with you, and I can help. You know I can."

He tried to ignore the eyes that could slice through his defences in seconds and hardened himself to her pleas.

"I'll call Rollo and ask him if he can babysit." Kaine winced as a spark of anger coloured her cheeks, and added, "Sorry, I meant, I'll ask him to come and protect you."

Nice one, Kaine. You bloody moron.

"Hopefully, Rollo can be here before I have to leave. If not, I'll drop you off at his place. He can drive you back here and stay with you until I'm done. Okay?"

She looked away. He put a hand to her cheek and turned her head gently to face him.

"Please, Lara. Don't fight me on this. You can help from here. You can use the system to provide intel I can't find on the ground."

He released her cheek and allowed her to work through the arguments in her head. She was intelligent, one of the brightest people he'd met in a long time, and a fast learner. It wouldn't take her long to see the sense in it.

Eventually, she nodded. Tears shone in her eyes.

"You go pack." She spoke quietly, her voice resigned, shoulders held stiff and back. "I'll call Rollo and work out the quickest way to get you to London. What identity will you be using?"

He took a moment to consider the ramifications. "I thought Vincent Abernathy would make a good cover in London," he said, relieved by her agreement if not her reaction. "What do you think? Do you reckon I'll be able to sell accident insurance to small businesses?"

He broke out a cheesy grin and opened his eyes wide.

Lara turned away and picked up the secure desk phone. Clearly, she didn't appreciate his levity.

Where was the bloody joke book when he needed it?

Chapter Seven

Friday 23rd October – Pre-Dawn

The Villa, Gironde, Nouvelle-Aquitaine, France

Packing only took a few minutes. Kaine rolled all the clothes he needed for a short stay into his Bergen. His grab-bag containing cash, keys, and a few other essentials, was always prepped and close to hand. To it, he added his identification of choice. Years of living a life on the move, never knowing when he'd need to travel at a moment's notice, had instilled a familiarity in the process. And this time, it wasn't as though he was heading into the Afghan Kush or the Scottish Highlands. If he forgot anything other than his fake passport and driving licence, and his wallet, he could pop into the shops and buy it.

Having London as a destination held another advantage. He kept a few things he couldn't buy over the counter —illicit military hardware, for example—securely stored in his London property. Protected by surveillance equipment similar to the French villa, his long-term safe house had remained undisturbed since his most recent visit some six weeks earlier.

By the time he returned to the office, Lara had the printer fired up and spitting out sheets of paper.

"Ready to leave? Or is Rollo on his way?" he asked, from the bottom step.

"There's no rush," she answered, swivelling her chair to face him and pointing him into his usual one. "Your flight doesn't board until a half past six this morning." She handed him the paper from the printer. "Here's your boarding pass. Air France, Flight AF254."

"A flight? That's more than a five-hour delay. I expected to leave as soon as Rollo arrives, and then drive north to Calais."

She shook her head. "No point. It'll be much quicker to fly than to use the ferry. Driving through the night would be a killer. You'd be exhausted when you arrive. Unless I shared the driving."

"I told you. That's not happening. You're staying here."

"Yes, okay," she snapped. "I've got the message. The flight will get you to Heathrow inside five hours, including the transfer at Charles De Gaulle airport."

Kaine nodded and gave himself time to work the journey through. From the villa to Calais, the drive would take at least nine hours, including refuelling and rest stops. Then he'd have to wait for a Eurotunnel train. And after that, there'd be at least a two-hour drive from Dover to London. Even if he missed any traffic snarl-ups and had minimal delays getting through the Chunnel, the trip would take the best part of fifteen hours. A cross-channel ferry from St Malo would take even longer, eighteen hours or more.

Lara was right. Few surprises there. Flying was the much better option.

"Okay, agreed," he said, taking the boarding pass. "The plane it is."

Lara seemed relieved, but she didn't manage even a grudging smile. He folded the document and stuffed it inside his passport in the grab-bag.

"You can take a train from Gatwick station and reach Central London well before midday. All things being equal, that'll be less than ten hours from now. What's more, you'll be fresher and better prepared for action—assuming there is any."

He couldn't see a flaw and didn't really fancy driving through the night especially when he had no idea what he'd face at the other end of the journey.

"And there's one more thing," she added. "While we wait for Rollo, I can finish reading the Constantines' dossier. Better than going off into the night on some sort of fool's errand, isn't it? There's no telling what you'll be walking into."

Her eyes were still clouded with anger and worry. He dropped the Bergen and the grab-bag on the sofa-bed and took his seat beside her. She edged away, but not too far—just enough to make her point.

"You've made your case, Dr Orchard," he said, pointing to his laptop. "Mind if I use this?"

"Help yourself."

"Thanks."

He wanted to say more, to apologise again for his monumental "babysitter" gaffe, but they'd both shifted into operational mode, and it was hardly the time.

"I'll pull up Google Earth and zoom in on the Constantines' address," he said. "I need to check out the lay of the land. Let me know if you find anything in their files."

"Yes, *sir*," she said, attacking her keyboard with enough force to beat it into submission. "Already doing so, *sir*."

"Lara, please?"

She sniffed. "Please what, *sir*?"

"Please don't be mad. I don't want to leave with you angry at me."

Especially if I might not be able to return.

Lara stopped bashing the keys, kept her eyes on the monitor, and sighed. "I'm not really mad at you, Ryan. I'm angry at the situation. Frustrated, but I'll get over it. You have to do what you have to do. I can see that, but I'll ..." She growled and started typing again, this time with less aggression, less force. The keys must have been so grateful.

"If it's any consolation, I'll miss you, too, Lara."

Having found what she wanted, she stopped typing and, still looking at the monitor, shook her head. "That's not it at all. I'm not going to miss you one little, tiny bit. I was just going to say, that I'm looking forward to some peace and quiet ... and to seeing Rollo again. That's all. Now, you carry on with your research and let me get on with mine."

Her brief smile, when it finally arrived, came as a huge relief. Kaine hit the spacebar on his keyboard and the system kicked into life, with the internet browser open and ready to go. Lara had anticipated his first move. She was turning into such an asset.

He entered the Constantines' address and the map of London opened up.

"Speaking of Rollo," Kaine said. "Did he kick up much of a fuss?"

"You're kidding," she said, shoulders relaxed, voice softer. "He was delighted to have an excuse to leave. He'll be here within the next two hours."

"Really? Last time we spoke he reckoned he'd found a permanent billet with Marie-Odile. A restaurant near the coast with a voluptuous, French widow who clearly likes her men on the beefy side. He was loving it. What's wrong? No trouble in paradise, I hope?"

Lara laughed. "I'll let him tell you himself when he arrives."

She'd finally forgiven him. Maybe.

"Sounds ominous. Let's get to work."

"I already am, *sir*."

He fell silent. It felt good to let her have the last word.

———

ROLLO ARRIVED a full twenty minutes ahead of schedule. He blew into the drive in his understated, spotlight-festooned, midnight-blue, Mitsubishi Shogun and parked it in the triple garage. He burst through the interior door—almost unrecognisable without his bushy, salt-and-pepper beard—carrying a well-stuffed Bergen and a huge rectangular case with metal corner protectors.

From the way the case clunked on the living room tiles when he lowered it from his shoulder, the big, former-SBS sergeant had arrived packing some serious hardware. Kaine had no idea how Rollo sourced his matériel, but the former quartermaster had retained most of his military contacts, and he kept their identities top secret. Even if someone tried removing his fingernails with rusty pliers, Rollo would never give up his sources.

It wasn't as though the villa lacked for weaponry. The hidden armoury behind the sofa-bed in the office contained enough equipment to win a military coup in a small, developing country. On the other hand, Rollo's lifelong motto, "You can never carry too many guns," was rarely up for debate.

Lara rushed to him and planted a kiss on the older man's smooth cheek.

"Hi, Rollo," she said. "Thanks for coming at short notice. I wouldn't have asked, but His Nibs over there"— she scowled light-heartedly at Kaine—"insisted I needed a 'babysitter'."

Rollo beamed at her welcome. "No problem at all, Doc. And he's right. We need to keep you safe until we're certain no one's looking for you. Sorry, but you'll have to put up with my ugly mug until the captain's done his thing."

"If I can take his sourpuss over my croissants every morning," Lara said, flashing another gentle glance at Kaine, "I can certainly cope with yours. What happened with the beard?"

Rollo rubbed his chin with the back of a hand. "Marie-Odile said the fuzz made me look like an old man." He shrugged. "I feel naked without it. It was a dear, old friend. Had the thing for years, but ... you know. I have to keep my better half sweet."

"She's right. I love the new look. Takes years off you."

Kaine relaxed. With Rollo's arrival, Lara couldn't be in more capable hands.

"Evening, Sergeant," he said, grabbing Rollo's Bergen and leading him to the guest bedroom. "Trouble in paradise, I hear?"

"Excuse me, boss?" Rollo said, grunting under the weight of the weapons case.

"Lara said you were pleased to escape Bordeaux. How are things with you and the delightful Marie-Odile?"

"Bloody marvellous," Rollo said, his voice tinged with irony. "There's talk of wedding bells."

Kaine stopped and spun to face him. "You? Getting married?" He made ready to clap a congratulatory hand on his friend's shoulder but stopped when he caught the sergeant's wry expression.

"No, I meant Marie-Odile was making noises about it. I always considered myself a confirmed bachelor."

Rollo lowered his head, his naked face flushing red with embarrassment.

"How long have you known her now?" Kaine asked, resuming the walk to the spare room.

"Five years, but this is the first time we've spent more than a few weeks together at any one time."

"Been getting along all right?"

"Well enough. Living in a restaurant with a bar is an old marine's dream"—Rollo patted his washboard stomach— "but, her mother's on an extended visit and ... let's just say I needed a break from all the talk of family, churches, and preachers. So, on the subject of cohabitation"—he glanced over his shoulder and lowered his voice to a near-whisper— "what about you and the doc? Anything I need to know?"

Kaine sidestepped the question. "Just keep her safe, okay?"

Rollo showed a toothy, boyish smile. "Will do, Captain. You can rely on me."

"I know, Sergeant. I know." Kaine set Rollo's Bergen on a chair in the corner of the bedroom and Rollo heaved the metal case onto the bed. The mattress sagged under the weight. "You can store that in the armoury later. Lara knows the combination."

Rollo arched an eyebrow. "She does?"

"And she knows her way around a handgun, too. Both revolver and semi-automatic. Won't be long before she'll be outshooting you."

"Really?"

"Yes, really. You never were much of a shot." A sense of pride flooded through Kaine as he spoke of Lara's improving skills. "I've been taking her through some basic fitness and fieldcraft drills, but she's a long way off the finished article." He looked past Rollo. "While I'm away, you might put your mind to developing a basic training programme for her. She needs a better understanding of fieldcraft and defence optimisation. I've made a start on her physical conditioning … wipe that smirk from your face, Sergeant. I mean she's a better swimmer now and can handle a ten-kilometre yomp over dunes wearing a twenty-kilo backpack."

"You're kidding. That little slip of a girl?" Rollo said, clearly impressed.

"Anyone working with sick horses and large farm animals has already developed core strength. Now all she needs is specialised training from an expert drill sergeant. Trouble is, I don't have access to one of those, so I'll have to rely on you."

Rollo arched his right eyebrow. "Highly amusing. Highly original, too. Nice one."

"Thought you'd appreciate that."

"All joking aside, it's a good idea. I'll pull something together. The doc's one sharp cookie. It won't take her long to pick up the basics."

"Very good, Rollo. Be gentle though. Treat her as a raw recruit, not someone drafted in from the marines."

"You know me and training, boss. After all, didn't they used to call me Uncle Cuddles during the Beasting?"

"No, Rollo. They didn't."

Not in your hearing.

"Must have called me something else then. Don't worry. I'll look after her, boss. She's a special lass."

Yes, she is.

"Excellent. You might want to join her in the training. It looks as though you could use a little exercise yourself. I've never seen you looking so—how can I put this kindly—so well-padded." Kaine arched an eyebrow. "Are you fit for active duty after swanning around in a French restaurant for the past six weeks?"

Rollo's baleful glare ended the discussion before it started.

"Right," Kaine said, clearing his throat, "let's see what the good doctor's discovered. And, by the way, we're not in the service anymore. There's no need to call me 'boss'. Ryan will do."

"Not a chance. I'm here on duty, you're paying me, and you're calling the shots ... boss."

Kaine sighed. He thought better of arguing and let the matter slide.

———

LARA DREW AWAY from the keyboard.

"Sabrina is absolutely brilliant. The files are incredibly comprehensive. Take a look at this." She nodded to the big monitor. "Bistro Mykonos has an online point-of-sale system and Sabrina tapped directly into it. Doesn't make good reading, I'm afraid. The till receipts have plummeted since the start of the last year, and their bills for consumables have fallen by two thirds," she said, reading from her screen. "They've been receiving calls from the bank and their suppliers. I've no idea what was said, but I can't imagine the bank was calling to wish them a good morning."

Sitting on the sofa-bed to give Kaine and Lara plenty of elbow room, a mystified Rollo sighed. "Such easy access to all that information. Makes me glad I'm pretty much a fossil and keep well away from the net."

Lara grinned and hovered a hand over her mouse. "You'd be surprised what she found on you. Want to see?"

Rollo shuddered. "Absolutely not. I'm happy in my ignorance. She really investigated me?"

"No," Lara said. "I'm kidding."

"So," Kaine said, "to summarise for the sergeant's benefit and for mine, the Constantines run a small, family restaurant on Hardwicke Row, Tower Hamlets. Its fortunes have been in freefall since way *before* Flight BE1555 ... went down."

Rollo nodded. "That seems clear enough."

Lara asked, "What does that tell us?"

Kaine took a moment to think before answering. "It tells me their problems, whatever they are, have nothing to do with the death of Onassis Constantine. And that, in turn, suggests our anonymous texter might be genuine. He— assuming it *is* a man—definitely hasn't caused the Constantines' problems to draw me into the open."

Rollo spoke. "I don't follow your logic, sir."

"If this was an elaborate plan to drag me out of hiding, the Constantines' problems would be more recent. And, it seems to me, our mystery man, the texter, would have set up something more spectacular. Maybe a kidnapping, or a physical attack on a member of the family."

"Or maybe you're overthinking this and the texter is using an existing business situation to set the trap," Lara, the realist, suggested.

"Either way, it won't stop me going."

She crossed her arms and compressed her lips.

"So, you're planning to walk up to the restaurant, knock on the door, and offer to help with a situation no one is supposed to know about?" Lara asked, not hiding her growing exasperation with his attitude.

"Not at all," Kaine answered. He worked the mouse and scrolled the cursor over the street view on his laptop screen. "How can I put this up on the big screen?"

"Hold down the control key and hit F6," she said, rolling her eyes towards the ceiling as though he should have known how to do it already.

Kaine followed her instructions and a corresponding image appeared on the largest wall monitor.

"I plan to set up an observation post in one of those boarding houses across the street and monitor the Bistro for a day or so." Kaine used his cursor to indicate the area on the screen. "I might even take a meal or two in the place. Haven't tasted Greek food for a while. It'll make a nice change from French cuisine and barbeques, even if the view and the company is far less impressive."

Lara failed to acknowledge his olive branch of a compliment and all but scowled at him.

Kaine paused for a beat and carried on, but softened his tone. "Charging in without gathering intel first does not form part of my standard operating procedure."

He wasn't used to having his decisions questioned. With Lara around, gone were the days when he could simply issue an order and be confident it would be carried out. Sometimes, the good old days were exactly that—good.

Kaine manipulated his mouse and the street view pulled back into a wide-angle shot.

Bow Road ran in front of Hardwicke Row and appeared to have good foot traffic, leading as it did from the local underground station towards the city centre.

"See all the pedestrians walking by? And look at the businesses on either side of the Bistro." They included a pub, a toy shop, a betting shop, a sandwich bar, a bijou jeweller and watchmaker, and a house and business letting agency. On the corner with Old Road, a butcher and green-grocer completed the run. "Don't know about you, but they look to be thriving to me. Agreed?"

"Agreed," Lara and Rollo said together.

"So, why would the Bistro suddenly be rushing headlong towards bankruptcy?"

Rollo spoke. "I don't know that area of London too well, boss. Can you do a three-sixty?"

Kaine tweaked the mouse and slowly rotated the image through a complete circle.

"Looks like a mixed business and residential area," Rollo said after the picture centred on the Bistro once more. "Close to the city. Plenty of tower blocks, and the parked cars are all high value. I can't see much in the way of graf-fiti, either. Small businesses in that area should be raking it in."

"That's what I thought. Now look at the date on the image capture. January of last year. I'd like to know what's changed for Bistro Mykonos in the last twenty months."

"Can't you just call the Constantines and ask them what's wrong?" Lara asked, but her expression said she already knew it wasn't a good question.

"Oh yes, I can imagine that conversation right now," Kaine said, putting a thumb to his ear and sticking out his little finger. "Hello, Mr Constantine? May I call you Orestes? I understand your business has been going down the toilet this past year. I've just sent you some money, is it enough? No, no. I can assure you, this is not a joke. ... Me? Oh, my name's Ryan Kaine, and ... Hello? Hello? Mr Constantine, are you there? ... No, don't call the police, Mr Constantine. They won't do anything to help you."

"Ryan!" Lara snapped, flicking a hand at him. "There's no need to be so sarcastic. I'm only trying to look at things from all angles."

Waves of regret showered over him. He'd upset her again. She didn't deserve it, but he needed to play the tough guy, for her sake.

"I'm sorry, Lara, but I have to go and see for myself. Their situation might just be a question of financial mismanagement or illness. In which case, extra money will help. I'll just go and take a look. Don't worry, I'll be careful. Promise."

"What do you think, Rollo?" Lara asked, her tone pleading.

Rollo held up his hands. "The captain knows what he's doing, Doc."

Kaine didn't like the idea of Rollo acting as mediator between him and Lara, but he really did hope the big sergeant was right.

———

THE JOURNEY, although extremely short notice, passed without incident or delay. After a power nap, an early-morning breakfast of coffee and croissants on the villa's deck, Rollo—with Lara in the back—drove Kaine to Bordeaux International Airport. Rollo stayed in the car and a teary Lara waved him on his way.

"I'll be back before you know it," he said and hurried off before her tears did any further damage.

Thanks to the one-hour time difference, the flight landed at 10:35 UK time. The journey had been too short for the airline to provide a cooked meal, and he wouldn't have offered the prepacked, curled-at-the-edges, cheese-and-pickle sandwich triangles to a prisoner on death row. He'd made do with a lukewarm coffee and a packet of dry-roasted peanuts—taking care not to crunch too hard and risk damaging his new tooth. A young lad in the seat beside him slept through the flight, clutching a threadbare teddy while his mother read a fashion magazine.

Oh for a normal life.

In a damp and dreary England, he took the shuttle from Gatwick Station to London Bridge Underground Station, and continued to his Camden safe house to pick up his nondescript, age-old Vauxhall Astra. He also collected some provisions that wouldn't have been allowed on any passenger plane anywhere on the planet, at least not since 9-11. It took a further two hours to find a room with a good enough view and see the changes to Hardwicke Row that appeared to go some way to confirming the texter's positive intentions.

After a ninety-minute, dry-eyed vigil, Kaine's stomach started grumbling.

Chapter Eight

Friday 23rd October – Early Afternoon

Bow Road, Tower Hamlets, London, England

Kaine lowered the binoculars and rolled his eyes behind closed lids.

Basic rules of covert observation—dry eyes, equals tired eyes, equals compromised vision. The coloured contact lenses he wore to match his fake identity only aggravated the situation, and eye drops didn't do much to alleviate the problem.

He yawned. Obbos didn't used to be so tiring, but at least he had plenty of activity to study from his second-floor window. It was certainly an improvement from the long-range, desert patrols where he'd be staring at nothing but sand and windblown dust clouds day after day.

The tip of his tongue found the still-unfamiliar implant in his upper jaw. His long-term dentist had made a good job of it and the ceramic implant fitted well and looked good, but it still felt unnatural and would do for a little while yet.

He grabbed the Costa mug from the windowsill and took a swig.

Cold and bitter. Was there a drink in the world that tasted nastier than cold coffee?

Stupid question, simple answer.

Cold tea, not one shadow of a doubt.

Without losing sight of his target, Kaine stood and stepped away from the window. He backed into the centre of the room and performed twenty-five squats followed by heel lifts, breathing in on the ascent and out on the descent. Next, he took up an orthodox boxing stance, bobbed and weaved, stepped forwards and danced back, and threw rapid, five-punch combinations—left double-jab, right uppercut, left cross, right cross—coughing and turning the wrist at each imagined impact point.

He repeated the routine until he'd loosened out all the kinks from his journey, driven up his heart rate, and blown away some of the mental fug. Solo stakeouts weren't exactly optimal, but Daniel Pinkerton—"Danny" to his friends, "unreasonable bastard" to anyone who tried calling him "Pinkie"—wouldn't arrive for hours. Kaine needed to stay awake at least until the foot and road traffic had died down for the night.

He'd managed to grab a little sleep on the plane and would be good until Danny arrived to pick up his share of the load.

Breathing heavily, but recovering quickly, Kaine dropped into the hard-backed dining chair and worked through a well-practised, seated stretching routine. He worked from the top down: neck, shoulders, arms, abs, waist, and finished with knee and ankle flexes. He'd designed the stretches specifically to maintain his swimmer's flexibility, but they worked well enough for all aspects of his working life.

Outside, the dank, grey afternoon stretched out towards a grey, early evening as the clouds grew heavy and dropped their load in a steady drizzle that did little to wash away London's grime.

After spending more than a month on France's isolated and pristine Gironde coast, the shock of returning to his adopted home city both surprised and depressed Kaine more than he could have expected. Missing the company he'd been keeping during his enforced holiday only added to his low mood.

Hardwicke Row, a complete city block situated on the eastern side of Bow Road's wide thoroughfare, was bordered by Old Road to the south and Grafton Lane to the north.

The row had been given a new set of clothes since Google Earth had taken its pictures. Construction workers had framed the four-storey block with scaffolding and covered the three storeys above street level with debris netting in an eye-watering shade of dayglow orange. A huge waste chute snaked down the Old Road side of the building. It ran from the top floor and spat its load into a skip so large it blocked the whole of the pavement and one of the lanes.

In the two hours since Kaine's arrival, the monstrous skip had been emptied twice. Builders working flat out? Extraordinary. It must have been part of a fixed-cost contract.

Bistro Mykonos sat in the middle of the row.

Most of the shops on either side of the Bistro stood

empty, either having been sold or wearing signs that boasted variations on the theme of, "Under New Management" or "Closed for Refurbishment". Clearly, the whole block had been earmarked for a major, cosmetic makeover. A significant and expensive makeover, judging by the amount of ongoing building work.

The silent pub on the corner of Bow Road and Grafton Lane, The Red Lion, should have been jumping on a Friday afternoon, but the windows had been boarded up and the punters forced to find another venue for their afterwork revelry.

Although Kaine had yet to see the place at night, he had no doubt the lights of the Shard and the London Eye would be visible over the Hardwicke Row rooftops.

Being so close to the city, the block couldn't have been better placed for "gentrification", and the only hold-outs still running live businesses, or trying to, were the Constantines in the Bistro and the grandly named Findlay & Sons Turf Accountants to Royalty. The glorified betting shop window also sported one of the "Closing Down Soon" posters.

Other things that caught Kaine's attention included broken street furniture and graffiti, although he hadn't seen any teens hanging around on the street corners. There were no schools nearby or sinkhole tower blocks, and nowhere local for kids to hang out, like parks or underpasses. So, where did the graffiti come from? None of it suggested any skill or artistry. It wasn't as though Banksy had made a welcome appearance to add his artistic talent to the scene.

Nor had Kaine seen a single police officer pass by, either on foot or by car, despite the presence of a major police station less than two miles distant. Hardwicke Row appeared to have been abandoned by the local authority, too. The litter fluttering in the light breeze and gathering in the doorways spoke volumes.

The light drizzle increased to heavy rain and visibility reduced. Kaine cracked open his sash window and kept having to wipe the condensation from the glass or risk losing sight of the Bistro.

He stretched out his arms and, still seated, ran through a few more stretching exercises. He waited. For what, he hadn't a clue.

At 16:14, a dark blue Ford Focus pulled up outside the Bistro and double parked the car long enough to disgorge two young girls, both smiling happily. They wore wide-brimmed hats, green blazers, white blouses, grey skirts, white, knee-high socks, and carried brown, leather satchels. Pretty little things, they had dark colouring and long, bubbly hair, and skipped through the front door to be greeted by their mother with hugs and kisses.

Kaine grinned in remembrance of a time when he'd return from school to the same reward. Although decades ago, the memory still had the power to make him smile. His old family home didn't serve hot food to paying customers, but the days were always sunny, the kitchen was always open, and it always smelled of fresh-baked bread. At least it did in his mind. Nostalgia was hardly the most reliable aide memoire.

Justina Constantine—he recognised her from the photograph in Sabrina's comprehensive dossier—took the satchels from her daughters and ushered them to a table near the window overlooking the street while Orestes filtered the car back into the near-stationary traffic. After a five-minute crawl to complete an eighty-metre drive, he turned the car left into Old Road, squeezed it past the skip, turned left again, and disappeared into the alleyway behind the block.

Kaine turned the binoculars back to the Bistro. The girls had books open on the table and drinks in hand. The older one, Rena, wrote in an exercise book, while the tiny Kora made busy with colouring crayons. Again, Kaine smiled at the familiar memory. He was surprised to see youngsters doing what looked like old-school homework. He'd expected modern kids to be buried nose-deep in tablets or laptops.

Justina ruffled Kora's hair, moved behind the kitchen counter, and started stirring things in pots, all the time talking to her girls. To Kaine, Justina's smile appeared forced, but he couldn't be certain. Maybe the reason for his presence was colouring his interpretation.

The chalk board inside the Bistro window announced the dish of the day as beef and onion *stifado*. Kaine's stomach growled at the imagined deep bowls of steaming, dark stew, green salad side dishes, and baskets of home-made pitta for the mopping-up exercise.

Hours had passed since his early-morning croissants and coffee with Lara and Rollo. Hunger wouldn't help if he had to spend most of the night alone and awake. Kaine patted his grumbling stomach.

Easy, buddy. I haven't forgotten you.

He could have popped around the corner for a pizza but *stifado* sounded far more appetising. He'd have to wait a couple of hours until the Bistro opened, but he'd survived without food longer than that in his life. One time, behind the lines in Iraq, he'd gone without rations or clean water for five days. A short delay wouldn't do any damage.

Besides, eating at the Bistro would give him the chance to interact with Orestes and Justina Constantine and study the family close-up. He'd be safe. It was highly unlikely anybody would recognise him with his darkened hair, new beard, and green contact lenses.

Yep, *stifado* would make a nice, warming dinner. Worth the wait. His mouth watered at the thought. Pavlov's dogs had nothing on Ryan Kaine.

He settled down with the field glasses pressed to his eyes. His stomach complained again but, this time, he ignored it.

In the Bistro, a door at the back of the kitchen opened, and Orestes entered. After shaking off his rain-soaked coat and hanging it on the back of the door, he kissed Justina. They chatted for a short while with heads close together, apparently whispering, before she waved him towards the girls. He strolled to their table and sat with his back to Kaine, facing his daughters.

A few minutes later, Justina emerged from the kitchen, carrying a large tray heavily laden with bowls and a large tureen. Orestes jumped up to help her dish out the meal from the tureen, and the girls put away their books. Justina stood for a moment, beaming down at her family, full of maternal joy, before returning to the kitchen.

Everything appeared normal and nothing out of place.

Faced with such a pleasant, domestic scene, Kaine lowered the binoculars and took in the wider picture. The scaffolding, the building work, the lack of pedestrian traffic, all fused together in a single, extended view, partially obscured by the incessant and driving rain.

The building work!

Of course.

It was there, laid out in front of him, but he hadn't put it together until that moment. He'd been such a bloody idiot.

No wonder the Bistro's trade had foundered. The building work discouraged the lunchtime foot traffic and drove away the evening trade. The Constantines were racing towards bankruptcy, and it was all down to the building work.

Simple.

All they needed was an injection of funds and Kaine could help them out immediately with that. Not a problem. Except …

The momentary relief brought with it a nagging question.

If it was a mere financial issue, why the warning text message? The question ate away at the lining of his empty stomach. Why had the texter pointed him at the Constantines if they only needed money and not his specialist skills?

The answer, when it came, struck him with the force of a stun gun.

Oh shit!

A diversion. The texter wanted him in London—away from Lara!

Chapter Nine

Friday 23rd October – Afternoon

Bow Road, Tower Hamlets, London, England

Heart racing, Kaine jumped to his feet, grabbed the mobile from the windowsill, and punched the number from memory.

Answer. Oh God, please answer.

The call connected immediately.

"Doc?" he gasped.

"Vince?" Lara asked, calm-as-you-please, and using his current alias as agreed. "Is everything okay?"

Thank God.

He took a breath. No point in scaring her.

"Yes, it's all good here, love."

Crap.

He'd called her "love" again.

"Can I speak to Alphonse?" he added quickly, using the alias they'd given Rollo.

"Not at the moment."

"Why not?" Kaine snapped. "Damn it, he's supposed to be keeping watch—"

"Vince, he's outside running a circuit of the grounds. I'm in the office with the door closed. Everything's perfectly okay here, but ..."

"But?"

"Well ... you sound stressed."

"I do?"

He coughed quietly.

"You don't sound like yourself. Are you sure you're okay?"

"Yes, yes, I'm ... fine. Really. Why?"

"You're not due to report in for another hour, and what's with the 'love' thing? You've, ahem, never called me that before."

He had, but only the once, and she'd clearly missed it.

"Sorry, Doc. Slip of the tongue. How long's Alphonse going to be? I need to talk to you both. It's urgent."

"Hang on a sec, I'll text him ... Oh, not necessary, he's just coming."

Kaine paced the worn carpet. Eons passed, which couldn't have been more than a minute, before Lara spoke again.

"Vince, you're on speaker. What's the problem."

He explained the situation and gave them his interpretation of what he'd been staring at for the previous few hours. "I'm worried Texter just wanted me out of the way. Take that on board."

"No problem, Vince," Rollo said, slightly out of breath.

"I'm all over it. There's been no unusual activity here, but I'll take extra precautions."

"Full lockdown, until I say otherwise," Kaine said. "Or until I miss a comms report."

"Yes, boss."

"What does that mean?" Lara asked.

"It means you stay inside the villa and sleep in the safe room until Vince says otherwise," Rollo answered, his words quiet but firm.

"What? You're putting me under house arrest? For how long?"

Kaine sighed. "Until I return or give you the 'all clear'."

"That's ridiculous. You're overreacting."

"Perhaps, but that's what's going to happen. Understand?"

Silence.

"Doc, do you understand?"

"Yes, *sir*," she said, the anger evident in her low voice, "I understand. And what are you going to do in the meantime? Are you on your way back?"

On his way to the door, Kaine grabbed his rain jacket.

"Yes, I'm coming back, but first I want to check in with the … clients. I need to make sure I haven't misinterpreted the situation. If they're okay, I'll take the next available flight back to you. Oh, and Alphonse?" Kaine said, slamming the door behind him.

"Yes, boss?"

"Don't take any arguments from the doc. Keep her safe."

Kaine ended the call and took the stairs two at a time and, at the ground floor, narrowly avoided bumping into the well-upholstered landlady, Mrs O'Halloran.

"Mr Abernathy," she said, giving him the benefit of the full twenty-watt smile, "is everything okay in your room?"

He tried to brush past the woman, but she defended the dark hallway with the ferocity of a Rottweiler.

"Excuse me, Mrs O'Halloran, I'm—"

"I told you before," she said, holding her ground and offering a coquettish smile that exposed a set of teeth that were stained brown by nicotine, "you must call me Maureen. All my guests call me Maureen."

The hallway reeked of stale smoke and the "No Smoking in the Rooms" sign on the reception desk was stained as yellow as the woman's skin. Under normal circumstances, Kaine wouldn't have set one foot inside a place so grubby, but the room on the second floor offered the only uninterrupted view of the Bistro available, and beggars weren't able to do much choosing.

She held an unlit cigarillo between the enlarged, arthritic knuckles of her right hand and clasped a gold cigarette lighter in the other.

"Maureen, I really must go. I have an urgent appointment with a client," he said, giving his best "travelling sales-man" delivery. "But the room is excellent. It's comfortable and clean, and I couldn't ask for more. Now, if you'll excuse me?"

Behind her, car headlights shone through the frosted glass of the front door, picked out bright in the gloom of an early, cloud-driven dusk. As usual for London's rush hour, which seemed to last most of the day, the cars barely moved. In this particular instance, the snarl-up resulted from drivers waiting for the traffic lights at the junction between Bow Road and Grafton Lane to turn green. A car horn blared long and hard. A second answered. The wild call of the angry driver in its natural habitat.

Mrs O'Halloran raised the cigarillo to her thin and wrinkled lips, but gave no indication of stepping aside any time soon.

Somewhere outside, beyond the grimy window, a heavy glass panel shattered. A woman cried out. Young girls screamed.

A big motorcycle revved hard. Tyres squealed and faded quickly, but the screaming continued.

Oh God!

Senses aflame, Kaine barged past the landlady, bunting her into the wall, and sprinted to the door.

Chapter Ten

Friday 23rd October – Justina Constantine

Bistro Mykonos, Tower Hamlets, London, England

With eight days remaining until the deadline, Justina still had no idea what they were going to do. Each day that passed was more worrying than the last, and she found it increasingly hard to concentrate on everyday chores. All she could think of was the idea that Hallowe'en would mark their last day in the Bistro, the last day in their home. Worse still, they had yet to find another place to live.

How could they cope? Where would they go?

It was true Arana did have a spare room. Her sister would be able to take them in for a short while, but it could never be permanent. They had little income, no savings, no future.

Justina had made a start on packing the clothes, but had barely put a scratch into the surface. They had no money for packing crates, or to pay a removals company, and nowhere to send their belongings anyway. Storage facilities in London were far too expensive to even consider, and Arana's garage was already full. They had no one else to turn to. In Greece, it would have been different. In Greece, the community would have helped, but in Kos, the same situation would never have arisen. It would not have been possible.

Oh dear Lord, what are we going to do?

Orestes kept telling her it would be all right, he'd think of something, but the deadline drew ever closer and with the unstoppable relentlessness of the Mediterranean tides.

Pressure built upon pressure, making life evermore intolerable. She felt most upset for the girls, her innocent babies. None of this was their fault. They deserved so much better than a sad, terrified mother and a worried, guilt-ridden father.

Some days, Justina thought it would be better to close the Bistro and find work. With their culinary skills and reputation, both she and Orestes would be able to find positions in other restaurants, but ... where would that leave the girls? They would have to relocate to a different school. What would such upheaval do to the overly sensitive Kora?

Justina put aside the knife—leaving the boning of the lamb ribs incomplete—then washed her hands and wiped them on a clean cloth. She turned, leaned her back against the kitchen surface, and took in the view for what would be one of the last times. Although not the most luxurious and up-market restaurant in London—the dining room wallpaper was tired, the tables were scratched beneath the tablecloths, and the customer-facing area had not been redecorated in years—it was still homely and welcoming. It was still a place of which they could be so proud.

The Bistro had been in the Constantine family since 1971, more than five decades. Orestes had known no other home, and Justina had lived there ever since they married, shortly after she had arrived from Kos. Eight years earlier, she and Orestes had held their wedding reception within those very walls. And the girls loved their home, their school, and their friends.

So many memories. Happy memories.

Through the years, the Bistro had hosted celebrations and parties, and delivered countless meals to smiling, satisfied customers but, within days, it would close forever.

Why? For what reason?

The greed of bullies.

She wiped away a tear before it could run down her cheek and sniffled into a tissue.

Why did life have to be so horrible? Why did the Blessed Saviour not intercede to help them?

Justina scrunched her shoulders up to her ears and let them fall, but the action did nothing to ease the tension in her neck and the crushing headache it caused. They needed a miracle, but if the Good Lord heard her prayers, He was not acting on them.

She forced a smile onto a reluctant face and pinched some colour into her cheeks. The girls would soon be home from school, and they mustn't see their mother upset. Instead of crying, she would smile and, what was it the English said? "Put up a brave face." Yes, that was it. She would put up a brave face for her girls.

Justina would hide the darkness from them for as long as possible. She would try to make their lives happy even though it was all she could do not to scream and throw her fists in the air at the injustices of life. Papa Onassis was dead, and bad men had moved against them, circling like vultures over a rotting carcase.

As Hallowe'en approached, she replayed the visit of the two evil men in her head over and over. It remained as fresh and as clear as though it were happening all over again, and the recollection still had the power to make the breath catch in her throat. It still sickened her.

For the first time in her life, she felt cold hatred. For the first time in her life, she wanted to kill. Not just the man who had grabbed her and threatened her babies, but the huge and silent monster at his back, and their boss, the person who pointed the evil men in her family's direction. She wanted to attack them with the ferocity of a mountain lioness protecting her cubs.

She wanted to kill Alfred Lovejoy. Lovejoy! What a ridiculous name for such a vicious and evil creature.

Justina imagined him lying in a gutter, with blood pouring from a gash in his throat. She imagined plunging a knife deep into the blond man's neck, slicing open an artery. Each night for three weeks, as Hallowe'en grew ever closer, the day they would be chased from their home, she had fantasised about Lovejoy's death and the death of the hulking, silent brute.

She would often wake with the soaking sheets bunched around her legs, afraid she would scare the girls with her yells and her tears. Ore, too, lost sleep over the matter. The situation was making them both ill, but they could do nothing to prevent it.

She could do nothing but dream of murdering their tormentors. It was wrong to feel that way. It went against all the teachings of her faith, but the Lord had put so many obstacles in their path, how could she continue to remain strong?

At confession, Father Michael told her that God never gave his followers more than they could endure, but Father Michael was wrong. The weight of their suffering was more than she could bear, and it had nearly killed poor Orestes. Were it not for her and the girls, he would surely have done something stupid by now. Instead, he slowly disintegrated before her eyes. Her darling man. Her handsome, honest, brave husband had been bent low by forces beyond his control.

Justina made the sign of the cross and prayed to the Blessed Mother for deliverance and forgiveness. She massaged her aching shoulders. The pain in her neck had become a permanent feature of her waking life, the cross she had to bear, like the one Jesus carried on the Road to Calvary, but He had prepared all His life for the suffering. He had endured the pain so humanity would gain access to Paradise. She was just a weak woman with no one to turn to for help.

Again, Justina wiped her eyes. She turned her back to the dining room and stirred the big pot. Her beautiful girls loved *stifado*. On such a cold and wet day, it would bring them warmth and comfort.

FOR WEEKS, the building work had increased in intensity, the booming, crashing noises above and around their heads became less and less bearable. The dust it created in their first-floor apartment and the Bistro made it impossible to keep the kitchen and dining areas properly clean.

Some nights they served no covers at all and had to

discard all the prepared food. Such a waste. So expensive. Whenever she broached the subject of what they were going to do, Orestes would clamp shut his mouth and turn his back. To see him so beaten down and defenceless was almost the worst of it, almost more than she could withstand. She cried every day, but only on the inside. On the outside, she tried to be the same, smiling mother as always.

And still it worsened.

Another official-looking letter had arrived that morning, but Orestes had taken it with him to the office upstairs, unopened. Knowing him the way she did, he'd probably fed it through the shredder, still sealed. Her husband was always a man to bury his head in the sand.

Dear Lord, what will become of us?

Justina read the time from the clock above the front door. Ore was late with the girls. The bad weather had brought more cars onto the road and made his return journey from school even slower.

A car horn tooted three times.

Beaming, she hurried into the dining room and pulled open the front door.

As usual, Ore stopped the car outside, having to double park. Kora and Rena jumped from the back and rushed into her waiting arms. Despite everything, they were still full of life, still the main reason for Justina's existence.

Justina absorbed the latest news from school while herding them to their usual table. She closed the door against the driving rain, which glistened on their school hats and blazers, despite the distance between the car and the front door being so short. Justina helped Kora remove her outer clothes and took Rena's to tidy away.

"Mama," Rena said, looking up through Ore's dark

brown eyes, "Miss Gupta said I could be Mary in the Nativity play."

"Oh that is wonderful, *moraki mou*. And what role is there for you, Kora?"

Kora popped out her lower lip and tucked in her chin. "I'm a shepherd, Mama. They're gonna make me wear a beard and Billy Philippoussis says they stick it on with glue and it's scratchy and tickly at the same time. Will I have to use Poppy's razor? 'Cause Billy says I will."

Justina pulled her baby into another hug. "Don't listen to that Billy Philippoussis. He is a foolish, little boy. Everybody knows they use a magic potion to grow beards on beautiful, little girls for just such occasions. The whiskers grow like that"—she clicked her fingers on one side of Kora's head—"and they disappear just as quickly." She clicked her fingers again on the other side.

Kora giggled.

Rena shook her head. "Oh Mama. Nobody believes in magic anymore. Not even baby Kora."

"I'm not a baby. I'm nearly six!"

"You must be a baby if you believe what Billy Philippoussis says. Everyone knows he's a big fibber. Duh!"

"What about Harry Potter? He uses magic."

"Baby Kora. Kora's such a baby!"

"Mama, Rena stuck her tongue out at me. She did!"

"Tattletale."

"Rena, that is enough," Justina said, trying to be firm, but not having the heart. "Now, sit while I finish making your supper."

"*Stifado?*" they cried in unison.

Justina nodded. "I did promise. Your job as the Bistro's chief tasters is to tell me if it is good enough to serve the customers tonight or if I should start again."

"Oh Mama," Kora said, "you and Daddy never have to make over. Not ever."

"Thank you, *moraki mou*," she said, nudging Kora's chair closer to the table. "Now, you behave yourselves while I finish cooking and serve you two *tiny* bowls."

"The big ones, Mama. The big bowls," Kora cried.

Justina helped Kora unpack her satchel. "Start on your homework, I shall be right back."

Kora sorted through her pack of colouring pencils, no doubt looking for the pink ones, Rena started her spelling exercises, and Justina returned to the kitchen. She hung the blazers on the rail beside the back door, smiling sadly as she listened to the girls chattering away as though the world was all butterflies and sweetness. As though men such as Lovejoy and the silent Tugboat did not exist.

The back door burst open, allowing a blast of chilly, rain-heavy air into the kitchen. Ore dived inside and leaned against the door to help it close more quickly. He peeled off his coat, hung it up, and stood still, breathing warm air over his hands, and rubbing them together hard.

Although he smiled, his red, puffy eyes, and the dark lines beneath, showed the effect of weeks without proper sleep. Normally impeccable, he had not shaved that morning, and the stubble on his chin scratched as he bent to kiss her cheek. He was tired, but putting on a brave show for the girls.

"Winter's arrived early. Chuffing freezing out there."

She nodded. "It never was like this on Kos. Sometimes I wonder why I ever left the island."

Ore pulled her close and wrapped his arms around her. His clothes were cold and damp.

"In that case, my darling, we would never have met, and our beautiful girls would never be."

She shook her head into his shoulder. "The Good Lord would have led us to each other."

"Perhaps."

He relaxed his grip and held her at arm's length. "How's it looking tonight? Any more bookings?"

"A table for four, and the Spanos will be here at eight o'clock as usual."

Ore frowned and allowed his shoulders to fall.

"Seven covers on a Friday night. That's all?"

"It is not what we would expect, but …" She eyed the girls at the table and lowered her voice. "What are we going to do, Ore? We have such little time."

He drew her close once more. "I'll think of something. I'll protect my family."

Typical of Ore. He could never face the truth, never make a decision. In the past, he had left everything to Papa Onassis, but now the problem fell on his shoulders, and he could not manage.

She patted his chest. "Go sit with the girls, I will bring supper. Tomorrow, we can talk to my sister and to Christos. They may be able to help."

"That'll only be a stopgap. I'm working on something for the … longer term." He ran his hands through his thick curls and pulled so hard his eyes opened wide.

"What, Ore? Where were you this afternoon? I called many times, but you did not answer your phone."

There it was again, the same pained expression she saw every time he looked at her since the attack. It was as though he blamed himself and felt guilty for not being there to protect her. Poor Ore, his manhood had been challenged, and it had been found wanting. For a Greek man to be unable to protect his family was the worst thing imaginable.

Emasculation. Many Greek men would prefer death to such dishonour.

He frowned. "Sorry, the battery's dead. Forgot to charge it last night. But don't worry, I might have found a way to get us out of this mess. You keep the restaurant ticking over, and I'll handle the … other matter. Okay?"

Justina's heart lurched.

"Ore, you are scaring me. What are you planning?"

"I've been talking to Ivan."

The breath caught in her chest. "What? No, you promised. No more gambling! That will not help us."

"No, you don't understand. I promised you I'd never play poker again, and I always keep my promises. Always."

"So, why did you talk to Ivan?"

He stepped closer, took both her hands in his, and clasped them to his chest. "It's my job to keep you and the girls safe, and I can't do that without a weapon." He cast a glance at Rena and Kora before whispering, "I've asked Ivan to find me a gun."

Justina gasped. She tore her hands free of his and covered her mouth in case she screamed and frightened the little ones.

The *stifado* simmered in the pot, the traffic crawled past the window, and the girls chatted happily at the table.

One part of her mind rebelled against the thought of having a gun in the house. It was wrong. Worrying. Illegal. Another part—the mountain lioness part of her—roared with defiance and hate. Yes, she would happily point a gun at Alfie Lovejoy and the dark monster, and pull the trigger. She would do that to protect her family.

But what of the Good Lord's teachings? What of her faith?

The argument raged within her breast, but one look at

her girls, sitting at the table, playing so nicely together, made the decision for her. Yes, a gun might well be the answer.

"Do you know how to shoot?" she asked.

Ore's mouth dropped open. He had clearly been expecting a heated argument. That she could still shock him into silence after all these years came as no surprise.

"No, no. I've never even held a gun. On the TV it looks easy. Just point and pull the trigger. But I thought if Lovejoy knew I had one, it would be enough."

Pah! Silly man. So naïve.

She had married a fool and had known it since the first time they had met. A soft, lovable, wonderful fool, and one she adored with all her heart and soul.

"You have not thought this through, have you, Orestes."

"What do you mean?"

"So, you are going to wave a gun under the nose of Lovejoy, and hope he soils himself and runs away crying to his boss? Or are you going to put a sign in the window that says, 'I have a gun and am not afraid to use it'. Is that it?"

Ore took her by the arm and led her deeper into the kitchen, further away from the girls.

"No, I was going to spread the word around the neighbourhood. The message would work its way back to Lovejoy that we aren't going to let him force us from our home."

Justina caressed his cheek and softened her stance.

"You silly, silly man. This is not Greece, Orestes. It is illegal to have a gun in England. This, I saw on the television. If Lovejoy found out you have a gun, he would simply call his friends in the police, and they would come quickly to take you away."

Ore's lower lip trembled, and heavy tears filled his beautiful, brown eyes.

"I can't think of another way, Justina. When you told me what he did to you ..."

Justina leaned against him, burying her face in his chest. "I know, my love. But telling people we have a gun here is not the way. We need to keep it a secret."

Ore jerked her away.

"What? What did you say?"

Justina wiped her eyes with the tissue once again. "I said, we will keep the gun a secret, and we will use it when Lovejoy next comes to call."

"I-I ... are you sure?"

"When will you collect it from Ivan?"

"Tomorrow afternoon. It's all arranged." He blinked twice as though unable to believe what he was hearing. "Are you sure? I haven't paid him yet and can always cancel. Ivan owes me big time, and he wouldn't be upset."

She stiffened her back. "I am certain. You will collect the gun, and I will keep it safe from the girls."

"You will? You don't mind holding a gun?"

"Of course not. I am familiar with weapons of all types. On Kos, my Uncle Stefanos had many guns and was a good teacher. When I was still a small girl, he showed me how to use them. Semi-automatic pistols, revolvers, rifles. It has been many years, and I was never what the American cowboys might call a 'crack shot', but in a confined space such as this one I would hit the object at which I was aiming. Of that you can be certain."

Ore's shocked and relieved smile filled Justina's heart. She could tell this one was genuine. She could always read the language of Ore's body.

"Now that this decision is made," she said, returning to the stove, "go sit with your daughters and get ready to eat. I hope you are hungry."

The weight of the world seemed to slip from her husband's shoulders. He stood taller.

"I'm starving, and that smells delish, my angel."

Pausing only long enough to wash and dry his hands, he rushed into the dining area and sat with his back to the window, facing the table. The girls showed him their homework. He studied each book in turn, made encouraging noises, and told them their favourite jokes. It was like the old times. The good times.

She filled a large bowl with salad, a pottery tureen with the stew, added a plate of pitta, and carried it all out to them on a large tray. Orestes rose to help her serve.

"Enjoy, my darlings."

"Thank you, Mama," all three said together, giggling in unison and picking up their spoons.

"Napkins, girls. Remember your table manners."

Justina returned to the kitchen, happier than she had been in weeks. Although not the best solution for their problems, a gun gave her power and strength. She would point it at Lovejoy and would even pull the trigger to defend her family. Anyone who threatened her, or her babies, would not live to brag about it to their friends. As for the police and the legal situation, she would face all that when it arose.

Maybe the Good Lord would find a way to help them before she was forced to use the gun. He had certainly failed to do anything so far. She made a hurried sign of the cross and begged His forgiveness for the doubts she had shown. Perhaps the gun *was* the sign she had been looking for. Perhaps the Sweet Saviour had answered her prayers after all.

Justina washed her hands with antiseptic gel, dried them on a cloth, and bent low to take a large saucepan from the floor cabinet.

An explosion shattered the quiet.

A shower of what sounded like pebbles cascaded to the floor. The traffic noise increased. A loud engine roared.

Justina jumped up, the saucepan heavy in her hand.

Rena. Kora. My babies!

She turned.

A pile of glass fragments covered the tiles near the front table, twinkling under the lights. One of the large windows was smashed and opaque, a large hole in its centre through which beat in the rain.

Justina dropped the saucepan. It crashed to the floor, the lid clanged like a cymbal and rolled towards the back door. She screamed and rushed into the dining room.

The girls, mouths open in silence, eyes wide, stared straight ahead.

In front of them, Ore lay slumped forwards over the table. A pool of red spread across the white tablecloth. It mixed with spilled stew, granules of glass, and broken crockery.

"Ore!" she yelled.

As one, the girls screamed.

Chapter Eleven

Friday 23rd October – Afternoon

Bistro Mykonos, Tower Hamlets, London, England

Kaine crashed through the boarding house door and entered the late-afternoon gloom, immediately swamped by the deluge and battered by the cold. Stationary cars filled all four lanes. Rain bounced off roofs and bonnets, adding to the racket. He darted across the road, dancing between the cars, climbing over bumpers, heading directly for the centre of attention, Bistro Mykonos.

One of the Bistro's large windows had disintegrated and showered the inside with bullet-sized pellets. The frosted remains of the pane clung to the corners of the frame, ready to cascade.

The screaming and crying continued.

Drivers sat safe and dry inside their cars, staring at the damage, but doing nothing to help.

Justina kneeled in the debris hugging her distraught daughters tight, keeping their faces tucked into her chest, turned away from the table. She stared in horror at her husband, who had slumped forwards in his chair. His head, right arm, and upper body lay across the table, unmoving. Blood flowed from a gash on the side of his head and ran onto the snow-white tablecloth, mixing with the remains of the unfinished meal.

Orestes' left arm hug loose, dangling towards the floor.

Kaine charged through a small crowd of onlookers filling the pavement outside the Bistro. A woman had a phone to her ear. She spoke urgently. He heard the words, "Ambulance and Police," and put away his own mobile.

A young man, his expensive coat protected by a black umbrella, pointed his phone at the damage. Filming. The bastard was standing there filming the destruction, not making a move to help.

What the hell's wrong with people?

On his way into the restaurant, he barged the film director hard enough to send him crashing to the pavement. The mobile spilled from his hand. Continuing the movement, Kaine kicked the phone ahead and stomped on it as he passed. The man yelled something, but Kaine silenced him with a single glare that yelled, "Don't tempt me, son!"

He stared into the brightness of the Bistro. All but one of the tables stood empty—tablecloths white and starched, silver cutlery shining, candles unlit, standing ready for the evening's service. The table nearest the smashed window had taken the brunt of the attack. It was a mess of broken dishes, spilled stew, and red.

Blood.

Orestes groaned.

Alive. Thank God.

His left arm moved. The fingers twitched and he groaned again. Orestes raised the hand to his head and struggled to sit up, still groaning. Blood oozed from between his fingers and dripped down his arm.

Half a concrete breezeblock lay on the floor between the table and the window, part-buried in a mound of granulated glass. Blood on one corner of the block showed where it had connected with Orestes' head. Mercifully, the window had been fitted with tempered glass and had disintegrated on impact. Float glass would have formed razor-sharp, flying splinters, and the damage could have been a hell of a lot worse. The girls would have been in the firing line, too.

Kaine studied the half-breezeblock's flight trajectory. If Orestes hadn't been in the way, the block would most likely have hit the younger one, Kora.

He stared down at the weeping girls wrapped in their mother's arms and quietly seethed. The bastards responsible for such an act of cowardice would pay.

By God would they pay.

Kaine crunched through the granules and squatted in front of the injured man.

"Best you keep still, mate. An ambulance is on the way."

Orestes groaned once more. "No, I-I'm … okay. Really." He lifted his head.

"No neck pain?"

"No … just a headache."

Good, probably no spinal damage.

"The … the girls?"

"Don't worry, they aren't hurt."

Orestes placed his elbows on the table and rested his

head in his hands. Blood ran down his left arm and stained his white shirtsleeve bright red.

Justina climbed to her feet and stood in front of the damage, hugging her daughters tight against her legs. They still wept, but she had fallen silent. She turned to Kaine, eyes wide, pleading. He'd seen the same desperate, confused look on survivors in the aftermath of a hundred different battles.

"Help him," she said. "Please, help him."

"The ambulance will be here soon. Are the girls okay? No cuts?"

She tilted their faces up, inspecting each in turn for damage—wild eyes, tears, pale skin, shaking. Clearly in shock.

Justina looked down at Kaine, chin trembling. She shook her head. "N-No cuts. No blood."

"Excellent. Are they your daughters?" he asked, playing the ignorant stranger.

Justina frowned as though unable to process the question.

"Do you live upstairs?" he asked, more forcefully.

She blinked and nodded. "Y-Yes. I …"

"Good. Take them away. I'll look after your husband until the ambulance arrives."

Justina hesitated, clearly not wanting to leave, but Orestes flapped a hand. When he spoke, his words were mumbled, he sounded groggy. "Yes, love. Take them … upstairs. I'm … good. S-Shocked is all."

She shot a suspicious glance at Kaine. "Are you sure?"

"Yes, certain. Look after your little ones."

Reluctantly, and keeping Orestes in sight, she shepherded her daughters into the kitchen and took them through a door at the back marked "Private".

Kaine took a napkin from a nearby table and approached the injured man. "Mind if I take a look?"

"Are … are you a doctor?"

"No, but I've seen one or two injuries in my time."

Orestes peeled his hand away from his head, sucking air between his teeth as clumps of hair stuck to his fingers and pulled on the wound.

Without touching it, Kaine inspected the damage. A five-centimetre, L-shaped flap of skin peeled back to reveal livid, red-and-purple muscle and a flash of white skull. The concrete block had made a good start at a scalping, but at least the bone appeared intact. Orestes yelped as Kaine used the napkin to fold the flap back into place and push the edges together. He pressed the napkin to the injury.

"Looks worse than it probably is. Head wounds always bleed to buggery. Here," he said, taking Orestes' bloody left hand, "hold it against the wound. It'll help stem the bleeding. The wound's going to need a good clean and quite a few stitches. The medics will probably keep you in overnight to monitor for concussion. You were lucky."

Orestes winced and pointed at the half-breezeblock with his free hand. "Call that … call that lucky?"

"Well, yes," Kaine said, frowning. "If the bastard lobbed a full block, it would have had more impetus after crashing through the window."

"Oh my God. The girls …"

"As I said, you were lucky."

Kaine stood and took in the damage once again. "What's up, mate? You annoy one of the local hooligans?"

The man squeezed his eyes shut. "No idea. Probably just a random act … of v-vandalism."

Yeah, right. Maybe Texter wasn't playing silly buggers after all. What are you mixed up in, Orestes?

"Kids these days, eh?" Kaine said. "Too many drugs and no sense of right and wrong. I don't like moving you, but do you think you can stand? We need to get you clear of the window."

He also wanted to move away from the rubberneckers and their phone cameras. Even though he'd kept his back to them, and his face hidden, he couldn't risk being recognised.

"I think so."

Kaine helped him to his feet, eased him clear of the destruction and the driving rain, and lowered him into a chair deeper in the room.

"Well done. By the way, I'm Vince Abernathy. If you don't mind, we can shake hands later."

Kaine smiled, but his attempt at levity missed the mark. He needed more practise to perfect his bedside manner. That, and the imagined joke book.

"Orestes Constantine ... Orestes. Thank you for your help, Mr Aberna—"

"My friends call me Vince. Only my boss calls me Mr Abernathy. My boss and the taxman. How are you feeling now?"

"Weak, and a little ... unwell."

Orestes' colour changed from grey to green, and he swayed in his chair. He placed his elbows on the table and cradled his head in his hands once again, keeping the napkin pressed hard against the wound.

"Breathe deep and slow, it'll help with the nausea. With a head injury it's best you don't have anything to drink until the doctors give you the okay. Meantime, try to stay awake."

"Don't feel well. Dizzy. I think I'm going to throw up."

Kaine jumped to his feet. Concussion was a distinct

probability. "Okay, let's get you off that chair. I don't want you falling over and damaging the tiles."

He lowered his patient to the floor and placed him in the recovery position, injury side up. He used a rolled-up tablecloth as a pillow to keep Orestes' spine in alignment, and two knotted napkins held a third in place to keep pressure on the wound. A battlefield dressing in the middle of a London restaurant, how his military skills kept coming in handy. Although, maybe the Constantines wouldn't have needed his help if those same military skills hadn't killed the family patriarch in the first place.

For pity's sake, Kaine. Concentrate.

He sat cross-legged on the floor and tried to keep Orestes awake and lucid.

"So, I'm new to the area. How far is the nearest emergency hospital?"

"I don't ... Um, not far. St Catherine's on the Green. ... About twenty minutes, I guess."

"Okay, that's good. The ambulance shouldn't be too much longer even in rush-hour traffic. Try to keep your eyes open."

"The lights ... so bright."

Kaine shifted around to his left, throwing his shadow across Orestes, making sure to keep his face turned away from the crowd outside.

"Better?"

"Thank ... thank you."

"No problem. Did you see who threw the block?"

"No, I ... had my ... back to the window. Why are you asking ... all these questions?"

"You need to stay awake. Just thought we could chat to pass the time. Your colour's improved, by the way. How are you feeling?"

"Better. Much better now I'm lying down. Thank you."

"No worries. Headache?"

"No, thanks, I … I've already got one."

Kaine laughed. For the man to crack jokes was a good sign.

"After the window exploded, I heard a motorcycle roar away. Have you upset any Hell's Angels recently?"

"No, how many times—"

Ore tried lifting his head, but grimaced in obvious pain and lay back down again, resting his right cheek on the back of his left hand.

"Who are you, Vince? And what … do you want?"

"I've rented a room across the street. I'm hungry and saw your restaurant. Looks like I'll have to order a pizza instead."

"I apologise for the inconvenience," Orestes said, his voice stronger and taking on an ironic edge.

The man showed spirit. Another good sign.

Kaine warmed to him. He preferred to like the people he decided to help and, just as importantly, it was good to be appreciated in return. It wasn't always the case. A few years ago, in the Sudan, his patrol had stumbled upon a village under militia attack. After eliminating the threat, the villagers turned around and threw stones at him and his men. Without hanging around for an explanation, Kaine ordered an immediate and strategic withdrawal, assuming the colour of his skin and his uniform had something to do with the villagers' angry reaction.

Strange times in a stranger world.

Head lowered, he shot a quick glance towards the damage. The crowd had increased in number and stood on the pavement outside in the wind and the rain, gawping through the near-empty frame. Some talked through the sides of their mouths, others had phones held high, jostling for a better view and a better photo opportunity. Kaine moved further around Orestes to hide from prying lenses.

Ambulance sirens wailed in the distance, growing louder.

Ideally, he'd have scarpered before the ambulance arrived along with the police, but to run off would likely draw even more attention to himself than he'd already done by rushing in to play the hero.

Way to keep a low profile, Kaine.

"I'll wait with you until the medics arrive, but then I'll have to go. I have an important business meeting tomorrow and need to prepare my notes." He offered an apologetic smile. "I also need to find somewhere to eat. Don't mean to sound callous, but I doubt you're going to be open for a day or two."

The door in the kitchen opened. Justina hustled through and rushed to her husband's side. Kaine scrambled to his feet and gave them space.

Orestes raised his head again, this time holding it up for longer. "Rena and Kora?"

"Neither is hurt. Only shocked at the loud noise and worried about you and all the blood. I left them talking to Arana on the computer. She will keep them calm and will telephone if they need me." Justina showed him her mobile and looked enquiringly at Kaine. "Mr ...?"

"Abernathy. Call me Vince."

"Mr Abernathy, I must thank you for all your help."

Kaine raised his hand to halt further appreciation. "I did nothing. I'm glad your daughters are okay. I think your husband is going to be fine, but he felt a little queasy." He shot another glance at the empty window frame. "You'll need to call someone to board this up at some stage, but don't touch anything until the police arrive. They'll want to see the damage as it is."

At his mention of the police, the couple shared a worried look that spiked Kaine's internal alarm system. Neither wanted police involvement.

"Did I say something wrong?"

Justina started to speak, but Orestes frowned and tried to hide it from Kaine.

"It is not you, Mr Abernathy. My husband does not want me to speak out, but I must. The police here do nothing. They will come and make a report, and they will give us a crime number for the insurance claim. But that is all. They will do nothing to protect us from—"

"Enough, Justina," Orestes said, his voice even stronger. "Mr ... Abernathy doesn't need to hear any of this. I'll be fine, angel. You go back to the girls. They'll be terrified."

"No, they are good with Arana. You need me and ... I ..."

Orestes held out his hand to her. "Okay, okay. Stay until the ambulance gets here, but don't leave the girls for too long. I tell you, I'm ... okay. Bloody ... headache is all."

The sirens grew louder and cut off as the ambulance arrived and parked outside, its emergency lights washing the darkening streets with a pale blue strobe. The paramedics, a man and woman in green fleeces and coveralls, exited the bus and slalomed through the gawpers. The man carried a stretcher, and the woman led the way into the restaurant with a big, medical holdall. With the minimum of fuss, they set to work on Orestes. She introduced herself as Bridget. The man didn't speak.

A few moments later, another set of blue lights arrived, but without the accompanying siren. The police patrol car parked behind the ambulance. Two uniformed officers climbed out. The taller, younger one started dispersing the crowd, and the other, an inspector, pushed open the door. He paused in the doorway to appraise the scene.

Kaine slipped into the background, trying to make himself inconspicuous. Ordinarily, he'd offer the medics a case history, but decided it would be better to keep quiet.

The inspector, a sour-faced man of similar height and vintage to Kaine, but at least twenty kilos heavier—mostly around his midriff—took a cursory look at the damage. He wrinkled his nose at the breezeblock before rolling towards Orestes and the paramedics. Thankfully, he paid almost no attention to Kaine.

The cop introduced himself, to no one in particular, as Inspector Blackstone from the local station, and pulled an old-fashioned notepad from his breast pocket. Kaine half-expected him to lick the tip of his pencil before he started writing. So much for the much-vaunted, twenty-first-century, hi-tech policing.

Kaine stood against the kitchen counter and studied both the paramedics and the local law enforcement at work. He was impressed by the former, but not so much by the latter. The inspector did nothing, and his junior colleague did little more.

The paramedics were effective and efficient. Working together and keeping Orestes' head and shoulders in line, they rolled him onto his back, fitted a collar, and attached him to a backboard.

Finally, Blackstone acted. He strode forwards, leaned over the kneeling paramedics, and pointed to the smashed window. "See who did it, sir?"

His bored delivery didn't instil a whole lot of confidence in Kaine.

Bridget scowled up at Blackstone. "Hang about there,

Officer. This man isn't well enough to answer any questions."

After checking his vitals, Bridget took a penlight from her breast pocket and shone it in Orestes' eyes. He groaned and tried to pull his head away.

"Sorry 'bout that, sir," she said, speaking with calm, quiet authority. "I think we'd better put you on that stretcher and get you out of here."

"This is ridiculous," Orestes said, lifting a hand to the spinal collar. "I can walk ... walk to the ... ambulance. Not that I need one."

Kaine smiled.

Bridget took Orestes' arm and firmly placed it at his side. "I'll be the judge of that, Mr Constantine."

"Jackson," she said to her colleague, "what's that head laceration look like?"

Jackson answered. "Deep and ugly. Needs stitches, and I really can't completely rule out a skull fracture."

Bridget nodded. "Agreed. His pupillary reactions are a little sluggish, and his pulse is racing. Let's get him on the stretcher and into the bus. Sir?" she said, looking at Kaine and ignoring the inspector. "Fancy giving us a hand? I'll talk you through the process."

"Happy to help," Kaine said, stepping forwards. "I used to be a lifeguard and have taken a few first-aider courses, but you lead, I'll follow."

She smiled. "Good. Take the feet, roll, and lift when I tell you."

Bridget scooted around and took a firm hold on Ore's head. Jackson took control of the shoulders.

"This is ... is embarrassing," Orestes grumbled.

"Won't be long, sir," Bridget said, smiled down at Orestes, and started her countdown.

They had Orestes strapped onto the stretcher in a couple of minutes.

"Thank you, sir," Bridget said. "That went really well."

From his position off to the side and well away from the blood, Blackstone coughed.

"Where you taking him?"

"St Catherine's on the Green. He'll need a scan and overnight obs at the very least."

Justina gasped and threw a hand to her mouth.

Orestes grimaced. Tears squeezed out behind his closed lids. "I-I'll be okay, angel. You need ... need to look after the girls."

"I'll ask Arana to take care of them and will follow you."

"No, they'll need you now. Stay here. I'm in ... in good hands." His eyelids fluttered and then closed.

Bridget nodded her thanks to Kaine, but arched an eyebrow at Blackstone. "Thanks for all your help, Officer. Couldn't have managed without you."

"You only had to ask," Blackstone said and opened the door for them after they hoisted the stretcher—his first constructive action since arriving. "Constable," he said, crooking a finger at his subordinate, "carry that medical bag to the ambulance, would you?"

Justina burst into tears and followed them outside, holding tight to Orestes' hand until they'd loaded him into the big, white bus.

Kaine eased towards the door, wondering whether he could use the emotional scene as a distraction to slip away, but decided against it. An overhasty disappearance would definitely raise some interest.

Justina stood on the pavement until the ambulance left, before returning to the Bistro. As she reached Kaine, she paused, tears spilling down her cheeks. "Thank you, Mr Abernathy. Thank you so much for helping."

"That's okay, I was just passing. And … you know. Well, I'm so sorry it happened."

She wiped her eyes with a tissue and blew her nose. Blackstone stepped in front of her before she could move away. Justina gasped and threw her hands up to her face as though expecting a blow.

Kaine tensed. The woman was terrified, and it seemed more longstanding than the recent crisis. Orestes didn't strike him as the type to hit a woman, so what was she afraid of?

"Mrs Constantine," Blackstone said, softening his tone a fraction, "I understand how upsetting this must be for you, but I have a few questions before you go."

She turned pleading eyes towards Kaine and shook her head. "I need to be with my children."

"Mrs Constantine, you aren't being at all helpful here. What did you see?"

"Nothing. I saw nothing. I was in the kitchen and heard the window smash and my babies screaming. Then … then I turned and saw the smashed window and the blood. That is all I know."

"Do you have any security cameras on the premises?"

Again, she shook her head. "No. Why would we need such things? We are a small business only. There is no spare money for security cameras."

Blackstone scratched the side of his nose with the blunt end of his pencil. "That's a pity. You're not giving us much to work with here, madam. Are you sure you don't know who could have done this?"

"Why don't you listen? I am telling you, no!" Justina shouted, her voice cracking. "Let me go to my babies."

Blackstone hesitated, but before Kaine could intervene, he stood aside and allowed Justina to rush into the kitchen.

"I'll have one of my colleagues call back in the morning," Blackstone shouted after her. "When you've had a chance to recover a little."

Kaine forced his jaw muscles to relax before his new tooth cracked under the strain. He'd just witnessed the single most insensitive interview since the "resistance to interrogation" module of the SBS boot camp. All Blackstone needed was a pair of thumbscrews and he'd be up there on top of the list with the worst of the instructors.

Blackstone sneered and ran his appraising eyes over Kaine, head to toe and back again.

"Now, sir. And who might you be, then?"

For the first time since his arrival, the inspector's pencil touched his notepad.

Crap. Here we go.

Chapter Twelve

Friday 23rd October – Early Evening

Bistro Mykonos, Tower Hamlets, London, England

"Vincent Abernathy," Kaine answered. "I'm very pleased to meet you, Inspector Blackstone."

"Just passing through are you, sir?"

Kaine stared at the policeman. "Something like that, Inspector. I was hungry and looking for some decent grub. Haven't had Greek food for a while."

"Do you have any identification? A driving licence perhaps?"

"I do indeed," Kaine answered, but made no move to show it.

He wanted to slap the supercilious expression from the police officer's chubby face, but that would, no doubt, be counterproductive. It certainly wouldn't do anything to help the Constantines.

"Well?" Blackstone asked, an angrier edge to his voice.

"Sorry?" Kaine frowned.

"Where is it?"

"Where's what?"

"Your driving licence. Are you being deliberately obtuse?"

"Ah, yes," Kaine said, lifting his chin as though finally understanding Blackstone's intention. "Sorry, it might appear that way."

"What?"

"It might appear that I'm being deliberately obtuse."

It's a pastime of mine when I meet officious, bullying clots.

Kaine shrugged and added another apologetic smile. "Sorry, I'm a little hard of hearing. Was yours a rhetorical question? I'm not sure. You'll have to speak up a little."

"Huh?"

"I said," Kaine shouted, touching a finger to his ear, "I'm a little—"

"Yes, yes, okay. I did hear you."

For the first time since leaving France, Kaine was having fun, albeit at the expense of a dullard.

"If I heard you correctly, Inspector," he said, "you asked whether I had a driving licence, and I said I did. You didn't actually say you wanted to see it."

Blackstone glared at Kaine and shook his head. He wasn't expecting a discussion on semantics.

"Where is it?"

"What, my driving licence?"

"Yes, your bloody licence!"

"Inspector Blackstone. There really is no need for that sort of language. You're scaring me. I get flustered when

I'm scared and my hearing … sorry. The licence is in my wallet," Kaine answered quietly, keeping his eyes open wide and his expression innocent.

"Well, get it out, man. Show me!"

Blackstone's face and neck turned a deep shade of puce and darkened with each beat of his heart. A vein distended on his temple, threatening to pop.

Without rushing, and patting each pocket in turn before he found it, Kaine took out his wallet and removed the realistic-looking driving licence. It should be realistic, the darned thing cost enough to pass the most serious scrutiny.

"And while I'm at it," Kaine added, "please … take this."

He dug a business card out of the wallet and handed it to Blackstone. It contained details of an office with a Derby address and a phone number that would redirect the calls to Lara via at least one military satellite. Lara would, of course, take a message and immediately ignore it.

"In your line of work," Kaine added, "you can't have too much personal insurance. If you don't mind my saying, the company I represent is currently offering a very special Whole Life Insurance package targeted specifically at members of the uniformed services. If you like, I could arrange a visit to your station so I can speak to you and your colleagues?" He leaned closer, lowering his volume to a conspiratorial level. "I am in a position to offer a significant discount to people who introduce me to new clients."

Kaine didn't mention renting the room across the road. Some things, the buffoon didn't need to know.

"Not a chance," Blackstone said, his colour restored to its original shade of sun-ripened tomato, "police officers are all fully covered."

He took the card and put it, unread, into the same

pocket the notebook came from. Somewhere between Kaine showing the licence and Blackstone tucking away the business card, he'd resumed the air of a bored official at the tail end of a long, long shift. He didn't actually yawn, but he did keep scribbling notes onto his pad and barely spared the time to look up, which suited Kaine well enough.

Kaine still kept his back to the street, but monitored the actions of Blackstone's partner through the reflection in the mirror on the far wall of the dining room. The constable, a twenty-something man with a pale complexion and narrow shoulders, asked a few questions of the remaining crowd, but didn't spend long with any one individual. It seemed that no one had anything interesting to say.

"Did you see what happened, Mr Abernally?"

"Abernathy, Vincent Abernathy," Kaine corrected and, ever so helpfully, spelled it out for him. "You'll find it on my business card."

Blackstone made great play of correcting his notes.

"Thank you, sir. So, did you see what happened?"

Kaine shook his head and showed his apologetic face. "I'm afraid not, Sergeant—"

"Inspector."

"Oh, Inspector, right, sorry. I actually saw nothing," Kaine answered truthfully. "I was on the opposite side of the road, coming up from the tube."

He jerked his thumb over his shoulder in the general direction of Bow Road Underground Station. "I'd just passed the Co-op when I heard this tremendous crash. Then I saw the damage and rushed in to see if I could help."

"Very public-spirited of you, Mr Abernathy."

"Thank you, Inspector. Wherever possible, I do aim to be of value to the community," Kaine said, smiling sadly.

"When I heard Mrs Constantine and those poor, little girls screaming, it tore my heart out." More truth. "Wasn't able to do much, but I always try to be helpful. I took a first-aider course a few years ago. … Actually, this is the first time I've ever had to use it outside of the St John Ambulance classroom." And again, he was back to the lies. How easy it was to slip between fact and fantasy.

Enough, Kaine. Don't volunteer too much information.

He coughed in embarrassment, covering his mouth with his hand while doing so.

Blackstone grunted. "What did you see when you arrived? What did you do?"

Kaine reprised his actions from the time he entered the Bistro, until the paramedics' arrival. He left nothing out. Blackstone took precious few notes.

"I expect you'll find plenty of CCTV images of the attack," Kaine said after wrapping up his story. "This is London after all, second only to Beijing as the surveillance capital of the world—according to last week's Sunday Times."

Blackstone shook his head a little too quickly. "Doubt it. Not with all this building work going on. Most of these businesses have shut down. I reckon whoever did this will have gotten clean away by now."

Kaine failed to mention the motorbike he heard roar away immediately after the window exploded. He had his own resources and the last thing he wanted was for the police to reach the biker first. Although, given the inspector's lacklustre approach to criminal investigation, that didn't look likely.

Blackstone flipped his notepad shut, apparently satisfied with Kaine's version of events.

"Well, thank you, Mr Abernathy. That will be all for the time being. We'll be in touch if we need anything else."

"I suppose the forensics team are on their way?"

The inspector snorted.

"Have I said something amusing, Inspector?"

"Forensics? For vandalism?" he scoffed. "You've been watching too much American TV, sir."

Kaine's face warmed and he took a moment to control his breathing before pointing to the bloodstained table. "Two young girls were sitting right there. If their father hadn't been in the way they could have been seriously hurt. Why don't you check the breezeblock for prints, DNA, any—"

Blackstone sighed. "From part-time first aider to crime scene analyst?" he asked. "God save us from amateurs. Thank you for your concern, Mr Abernathy, but we know how to investigate a crime. Leave it with us, sir. There's a good fellow."

Blackstone took Kaine by the upper arm and edged him towards the door. If he didn't already want to leave, Kaine might have ripped the man's arm from its socket and beaten him over the head with the bloody stump.

"When can I expect your call, Inspector?" Kaine asked on his way through the door. "I'm only in town for a couple of days, but would happily extend my stay if you'd like to make that appointment."

He added a wink and tapped the side of his nose.

"Please move along now, Mr Abernathy. You'll find a burger bar and a chippy further down the road."

Blackstone called to his subordinate. "Constable Callow!"

Kaine avoided reacting to the youngster's unfortunate, if somewhat apt, surname.

"Please direct this gentleman to the nearest restaurant. Apparently he's hungry. And Mr Abernathy." Blackstone leaned closer, allowing Kaine a full blast of his tobacco breath. "Mind how you go, sir. There's a good chap."

Kaine touched his forehead at Blackstone, smiled at the callow youth, and made a hurried but circuitous return route back to his digs.

By the time he'd reached his rooming house, after a fifteen-minute contemplation, he still couldn't figure out Blackstone's game. The cop had given off a strange vibe. Either the man genuinely didn't care about the attack on the Bistro, or he was doing a damn good job of hiding the fact that he did.

No doubt about it, Inspector Blackstone deserved some of Lara's investigative time.

Chapter Thirteen

Friday 23rd October – Early Evening

Bow Road, Tower Hamlets, London, England

Kaine opened the front door quietly and closed it even more so. He didn't want another encounter with the malodorous Mrs O'Halloran. Fortunately, he made it past her door and up the stairs to his room unmolested.

The room looked undisturbed, and the camcorder he'd propped, apparently carelessly, on the windowsill with its lens pointing through the part-open window hadn't moved. The red light showed it still recorded the scene across the road.

Before leaving for his meal, he'd gambled that Mrs O'Halloran wouldn't enter his room and discover his surveillance rig. A risk worth taking given what had transpired at the Bistro. Ideally, he'd have attached the camera to its tripod stand for a better image, but if the landlady had entered the room in his absence, his cover would have been shot. In its current state, he could have explained it away as an accidental recording. On a tripod stand, not so much.

Kaine hung his dripping coat on the hook behind the door and crossed the room. He hit "stop record", "reset", and "play", but didn't bother with "fast forward". The attack had taken place within minutes of his vacating the room and he didn't want to miss anything first time around.

The tiny image on the view screen was canted at a forty-five-degree angle from the horizontal. It looked like something they'd show in a '60s arthouse retrospective, or at a modern-day Cannes Film Festival. He couldn't make out anything until the Bistro window caved in and the headlights of a motorcycle lit the scene and left the shot in the correct direction—heading away from the camera.

Excellent. Precisely what he was hoping for.

A rear view of the bike speeding away would give him a shot of the number plate. If the vandal was an amateur and hadn't swapped the plates, it would make Kaine's job easier.

Throughout his time in the SBS, Kaine always preferred the active approach. Attack rather than defence. Or in the words of a former commanding officer, "Go on the offensive before the opposition even knows you're in his stadium."

Despite his fall from grace, Graham Valence had possessed a fine military mind. Shame it turned out to be a greedy one, too.

Kaine paused the image at what he thought would be the optimal place to show the motorbike's arse end. He retrieved the cable from the camera bag and plugged the recorder into the back of the room's TV using the yellow RCA connection.

The TV took a few moments to warm up, and the results were disappointing. The still frame showed the bike well enough—an old, black Kawasaki Z750, if he wasn't mistaken—but the picture was too small to make out the number plate. Zooming in with the camera resulted in a pixilated image, impossible to read. Poor light, bad weather conditions, and filming through a rain-spotted window had conspired to render the picture useless in its present state.

Bugger it to hell.

Kaine tried manipulating the colour contrast and the brightness, but nothing cleared the image enough to make the plate legible. He paused long enough to scratch at his annoying beard. Nothing for it but to call in the big guns.

He unplugged the camera from the TV and connected it to his laptop. After cutting thirty seconds from either side of the window shattering, he converted it to an MP4 file and uploaded it to the storage area Sabrina had allocated them in the cloud. Kaine trusted her with stuff he knew little about. If Sabrina told him their cloud storage was as secure and unbreakable as anything on the planet, he wasn't about to start arguing with her.

Now for the difficult part.

He grabbed his mobile and dialled. Disappointingly, a newly clean-shaven, former Royal Marine answered instead of a beautiful veterinarian.

"Hi, Alphonse," Kaine said. "How's it going?"

"It's about time you called. Since you missed your report deadline, the doc's been having kittens. We thought you'd been taken. Been watching the TV and online news expecting to hear about the capture of the notorious terrorist …"

Kaine let his old mate rattle on for a few more seconds. Having someone else worry about him warmed his tired heart.

Eventually, Rollo ran out of steam and the line fell silent.

"If you've quite finished verbally attacking your employer, Alphonse, perhaps you'd allow me to get a word in?"

Rollo coughed. "Sorry, boss. But you had us worried."

"Yes, I gathered that, but as you can hear, things are good. I'm free and clear, and in need of some technical assistance. Where's the doc?"

"In the shower. Just a sec, I'll give her a shout."

"No, don't disturb—"

The muffled scratching of a hand covering a mouthpiece followed by an even more muffled shout of, "Doc, it's the boss. He's okay," told him he was too late.

The hand swiped free of the mouthpiece and Rollo said, "One moment, boss. She's on her way," the sound much clearer.

"You didn't have to disturb her. You could have passed along a message."

"Kidding aren't you? She'd have killed me … Hang on, here she is."

"Ry—Vincent?" Lara said, slightly breathless.

He smiled at the sound of her voice.

"Yep, it's me."

"Why didn't you call earlier? I've been worried sick."

"Something came up. Can you put me on speaker? Alphonse needs to hear this, too."

A change in the background tone confirmed she'd hit the speaker button.

"Okay, we can both hear you," she said. "What happened? Did you contact the clients?"

"Yes," he said. "Sort of."

"What d'you mean, 'sort of'?"

Kaine told them about the attack.

"Oh God, that's terrible," Lara gasped. "How is he?"

"No idea. The paramedics took him to hospital while I hung around and made a statement to the police."

"You did what?" Rollo barked.

"Couldn't avoid it. If I'd sloped off, it would have been suspicious."

Kaine ran through what happened with Inspector Blackstone and reviewed the film he'd captured on the video recording and ended with, "I've sent a short, MP4 file to the server. I need the bike's licence plate enhanced and the owner identified. Can you do anything with it, or do you need to ping our friendly IT guru and ask for her help?"

Rollo answered. "We tried contacting her this afternoon, but she's not answering."

Kaine nodded to himself.

"She's gone abroad on a mission for her grandfather," Kaine said, not needing to elaborate. He'd briefed Rollo earlier and he knew as much about Sabrina as Kaine and Lara did.

"Okay, understood. It's a shame she's not accessible. I'd love to know more about our mysterious texter."

I hear you, buddy.

"Me too."

Lara cut across his words. "But from what you say, he seems legitimate, yes?"

"So far," Kaine agreed, "but I don't like the idea of someone leading me by the nose. I'll be happier when we can put a name to his text."

"Boss? Might I make a suggestion?" Rollo asked.

"Be my guest."

"Why not try calling him back? Perhaps he's waiting for your response."

Kaine winced. "Sorry, mate. I should have told you. I did that last night before you reached the villa. No reply so far."

"When was the last time you checked your other phone?" Lara asked.

"Before I left my room this evening. Good point, though. Hang on." He pulled the second burner from his pocket and checked the screen. "No, nothing new from our man."

"What the hell's he up to?" Lara said.

"Who knows? Doc, can you download the MP4 file and see if you can read the number plate? You'll stand a better chance with your monitors than I do with the ancient TV I've been using."

"I'm on that now. Our … technical director left me an idiot's guide to her picture enhancement app. I'll try working on the image myself. Get some sleep and I'll have the information to you by morning."

"Sleep? Yeah, sure." He laughed. "Like that's going to happen."

"You need your rest."

"Thank you, Mother."

Plenty enough time to rest when I'm dead.

"I have another suggestion, boss," Rollo said, this time with less enthusiasm.

"Go ahead, Alphonse."

"Why not send a copy of the film to the police and let them do their job?"

"Yes," Lara said, reinforcing Rollo's suggestion. "That

way you can come back here where it's safe."

"And leave the clients unprotected?" Kaine snapped. "Not a chance."

"Alphonse is right, though," Lara called, sounding more distant. "Who knows the texter's real agenda? You should come home."

Although she'd probably turned away from the phone to upload and work on the images, Lara still had the spare capacity to question his decision making. Not good for his leadership position.

"Listen you two, this isn't a bloody democracy." Kaine paused, took a breath, dialled back the aggression in his voice, and continued more quietly. "Sorry to play the old soldier, but I'm the one on the ground. I'll be making the operational decisions."

"Vincent Abernathy, behave yourself," Lara interrupted, using her best schoolmarm delivery. "We're only trying to look out for you."

And I'm trying to look out for The 83.

"I understand that and, believe it or not, I did consider your suggestion, Alphonse."

For all of a microsecond.

"But?" Rollo asked.

"I rejected it for three reasons. First, the police might get to the biker first, and I wouldn't like that. Not one little bit. Second, the police would be able to use the film to work out where it was taken from, and I'd have to relocate. Not a good idea since this is the best obbo point I could find. And third, the cop, Blackstone, gave me a bad vibe. Either the Metropolitan Police aren't all that fussed about what they see as a simple act of vandalism, or someone is encouraging them to look the other way."

"Bent cops?" Rollo asked, his tone incredulous. "For

pity's sake, boss. You can't think every second cop in the UK is bent! Paranoia's setting in."

"After what happened in Scotland, I reckon I'm justified."

After a momentary silence, Rollo said, "Yes ... well, I suppose you have a point." He laboured the statement. Kaine could imagine him scratching at his missing beard.

"So, what happens when we identify the biker?" Lara asked.

"You're going to have a little chat with him," Rollo suggested.

"Exactly. Someone paid the bastard to lob that breeze-block through the window, and I intend to find out who."

"And then?"

"And then, I'll visit the paymaster. He isn't getting away with it. End of!"

"Okay ... okay," Lara said, resignation in her voice. "I understand. Will you promise me one thing? Please?"

"If I can."

"Be careful. Don't take any unnecessary risks."

"Me?" Kaine scoffed. "Take unnecessary risks? As if."

In the background, Rollo let out a false laugh.

"Please?"

The plaintive tone in Lara's plea did it to him every time.

"Okay, Doc, I promise. Until I hear back from you, all I plan to do is sit in my room until the traffic dies down, and then I'll sit in my car and watch the restaurant. If the client leaves, I'll follow her. Such a simple task shouldn't be beyond me."

"Thank you," she said, flatly. "I'll see what I can do with this file. I'll message you if I find something. Keep your mobile powered up. Oh, and one more thing ..."

"Yes?"

"Can I assume that I'm no longer under house arrest?"

"Excuse me?"

"You heard, *boss*," she snapped.

He couldn't tell whether she was joking, but assumed not.

"Yes, Doc," he said. "You can assume that very thing."

"Good."

She ended the call without allowing him to apologise again or to thank her. The unexpected silence left Kaine with an unfamiliar sense of loss.

Chapter Fourteen

Friday 23rd October – Evening

Bow Road, Tower Hamlets, London, England

After a quick change into dark clothing, Kaine retrieved his Astra from the multi-storey car park around the corner. He confirmed its London Congestion Charge account was topped up, and found an empty parking spot with a decent view diagonally across the road from the Bistro. He kept the engine off and all four windows cracked open a couple of centimetres in an effort to combat the build-up of condensation. He also scooted low in his seat. Most casual observers would see an empty car. Anyone passing close enough might see a guy asleep behind the wheel. Either way, Kaine needed fast access to transport. Judging by what

Justina had told Orestes, she was unlikely to stay at the restaurant for long.

After powering up his tablet—with the brightness turned down low—and committing an online street map of the area to memory, Kaine kept his mind occupied by dictating anonymised notes into his digital recorder. He had no idea what he'd use the recording for—maybe posterity—but it helped pass the time. Perhaps he'd ask Lara to print them out using their system's voice recognition app. If she learned how boring stakeouts actually were, she'd maybe think twice about demanding to join him on every mission.

He took a moment to consider what it would be like to have Lara at his side during such moments, but shook the thoughts from his head. Such distractions, he did not need.

Back to work, Kaine.

He peeled open his eyes, rubbed the circulation back into his face, and yawned. His stomach grumbled yet another loud complaint, reminding him the attack on the Bistro had derailed his dinner plans. He could have murdered a coffee and a bite to eat, but leaving the car to head for the nearest burger bar would be out of the question. The lack of amenities highlighted another challenge with solo stakeouts. If Lara was with him, she could not only keep him company, but allow him to pop out for refreshments and a natural break now and again.

Bloody hell, Kaine. Pack it in!

During his evening stakeout, three events made the recorder.

Within minutes of Kaine relocating the car and settling in for the long haul, Inspector Blackstone and the callow youth at his side had departed the scene, leaving the Bistro unsecured and Justina and her daughters alone and vulnerable.

For pity's sake!

Their dereliction of duty had Kaine spitting nails. He wanted to race across the street, knock their lazy, useless heads together, and force them to do their bloody job.

Considering the injury sustained by Orestes and the damage caused to their business, Kaine would have expected far more from the local cops. They should have initiated a proper investigation, which would have included protecting the Bistro and its occupants. In the existing political climate of heightened racial tensions and anti-immigration rhetoric, an attack on a Greek family might even warrant treating the case as a hate crime.

The police were supposed to protect the public, and if the Constantine family didn't need protection, who the hell did?

Blackstone and his lackey had shown themselves, at best, as useless and, at worst, complicit. Either way, Kaine would find out. And in any event, the Constantines had Kaine's protection, even if they ended up knowing nothing about it.

At 20:57, with the rain as heavy as it had been all evening, a dark blue Ford Transit with a glass transport frame bolted to the side panel approached from the east. It pulled up in front of the Bistro and two men wearing smart boiler suits jumped out. They removed two weatherboard sheets from the window frame and revealed a decal on the side of the van that made Kaine smile.

T&J Patel, General Building Repairs.
"Fed Up with Cowboy Builders? Try the Indians!"

Kaine watched the men work, impressed by their speed and efficiency. They chatted and joked, while each knew his task and carried it out with precision. He'd seen army engineering units less well-disciplined and less well-organised.

It took the men a little under an hour to clear the glass pellets from the pavement and fit the weatherboard panels to secure the premises. The lashing rain bouncing high off the pavement didn't seem to hamper their progress or dampen their enthusiasm. If anything, the weather acted to spur them along.

After they'd finished, Justina Constantine signed the older man's worksheet, shook his hand, and they were on their way home after a job completed in impressive time. Quick and efficient emergency repairs—one of the benefits of living in the nation's capital. Although if the Constantines lived in the sticks, Kaine wondered whether anyone would have smashed the window in the first place.

Soon after the builders left, a small, Fiat hatchback arrived and stopped in the spot vacated by the builders. A dark-haired woman, no doubt the sister, Arana, slipped out and knocked on the restaurant door. Justina arrived within seconds and the two fell into each other's arms. Kaine was too far away to hear their words, but their body language spoke of distress mixed with worry and relief. Justina led her sister inside and through to the back of the dining room. At least she finally had company. Being alone in the building with her traumatised daughters while waiting for news of her husband couldn't have been easy.

Kaine's phone vibrated. He snatched it up from the passenger seat, hit "accept", and spoke without checking the caller ID.

"Doc?"

"Sorry to disappoint, boss. It's me," announced a happy Danny.

"Ah, right. Evening, Corporal."

"Didn't mean to ruin your day, boss. I mean, I know you'd rather be speaking with the doc, but——"

"Less of the backchat, son," Kaine snapped, but couldn't keep the smile from his voice. "Where are you?"

"In the entrance to Bow Road Underground Station. It's pissing down. How do I find you?"

Kaine gave him the directions. "Should only take you five minutes if you hurry."

The "call waiting" signal interrupted Danny's response and Kaine cut him off to accept it.

"Vincent?" Lara asked.

"Doc. Hi. You have something already?"

"Yes," she said, "I thought you might like to know I managed to clean up that image and identify the owner of the motorbike."

She spoke quickly, excitement and pride clear in each word.

"That's brilliant. Thanks."

"The detailed handover notes made it easy."

"Sorry to be so brusque, Doc, but I was talking to our visitor from Canada."

"He's reached London already?"

"Yes. He made good time. Should be with me in a couple of minutes."

"That's wonderful. You having support, I mean."

"Exactly. So, the biker?"

"I've emailed you his details."

"No trouble with the DVLA?"

"None," she said. "The app was simplicity itself. It allowed me right into the heart of their database. All I had to do was plug in the licence number and it popped back with the owner's name and last known address." She paused as though waiting for a response from him. "Although we can't be sure he was the one riding the bike this afternoon."

Kaine smiled. "True enough, but he's a good place to start. I don't suppose you managed to check whether the bike's been reported stolen?"

"Funny you should ask that—"

"You're kidding. You had time to check the local police logs, too?"

A large delivery van roared past, throwing a sheet of muddy spray across the Astra's windscreen and part-open side window, wetting Kaine's face in the process. He raised the glass and wiped the dampness away with his sleeve.

"I had Alphonse do that while I was accessing the DVLA database," she explained.

Kaine considered turning on the ignition and working the wipers, but decided against. The driving rain did a good enough job of clearing the screen on its own.

"I really don't know what I'd do without you. Can you run a background check on the biker?"

"Already completed. I attached a dossier to the email. Alphonse and I plan to spend more time on the research over the next few hours. I'll send what we find when we have something useful."

"That's ... really great work. Thanks again. Both of you."

"What are you planning?"

"I don't know yet."

"Really?"

"Really."

"Why are you being so evasive?"

"Listen, Doc. Things are pretty fluid here, and I'm in

operational mode. There's so much to think about. I have to keep things tight. Professional. When I get back, we'll talk about how this will work in future, okay?" He winced, hating how stiff he sounded.

"Okay, if you insist."

"Yes, I do. Is ... Is Alphonse there?"

"I'll put him on," she said, sounding curt, flat.

The scuffling of a phone changing hands preceded Rollo's, "Yes, boss?"

Kaine waited a beat before asking, "Are we secure?"

"Yes, sir. Problem?"

He relaxed a little. Rollo had not only confirmed that Lara couldn't hear their conversation, but he'd make sure it stayed that way.

"No real problem, but you need to talk to our new recruit about operational expedience. Can you tell her ... well, you know what I'm saying?"

Rollo's chuckle grated down the line.

"I understand, boss. You really like the doc, and you don't want her upset with you. No problem. Leave it with me. Guess I'll have to change my name from Uncle Cuddles to Cupid."

Frustration boiled up from Kaine's gut. Uncontrolled emotional entanglements could ruin the best military units. He could envision his tight, military discipline collapsing in a heap at his feet.

"This is serious, Alphonse. Lives are at stake. While I'm here, you are responsible for the doc's safety. Do you understand my meaning?"

Rollo coughed. "Yes, boss. Sorry."

The frustration subsided, leaving behind a bitter aftertaste. He hated losing control, much less snapping at people he considered his friends. Yet another way his emotions could lead everything and everyone he cared about into the mire.

A double-tap on the front passenger window nearly gave him a coronary. He twisted, braced for action, but Danny's smiling and rain-soaked face appeared through the flooded glass. Kaine cursed his inattention. He'd completely missed Danny's approach.

Kaine popped the locks and Danny slid inside after slinging his Bergen on the back seat.

"Alphonse," Kaine said into the mobile, "a half-drowned rat has just arrived from Canada. Looks like he's swum across the Atlantic. I'll contact you in the morning for a sitrep. Meanwhile, carry on with the deep dive into the biker."

He ended the call, fished in his Bergen for a swimmer's micro-towel, and handed it to Danny.

"Hello, Corporal. Still raining, I see," he said, as though the heavy drumming on the car's roof and the water washing down the windscreen and windows hadn't given the game away.

"It's great to be back in dear, old Blighty," Danny muttered, rubbing his face and hair with the towel. "I missed this place so much."

He struggled out of his raincoat and threw it into the back, spraying Kaine with castoff water.

"Thanks," Kaine said, wiping a hand over his face.

"You're welcome, boss. Think nothing of it."

Danny flashed a smile that couldn't have been less apologetic.

"And thanks for dropping everything. It must have been hard to drag yourself away from the delights of a Canadian autumn. The colours of all those falling maple leaves."

"Not really. There's only so much field training the

Mounties will accept from a Brit. Besides, your email was interesting. What's my role?"

"Long term, I need you as backup. Short term, depends on what happens in the next few minutes."

Kaine gave Danny a full briefing on the day's events, and anticipated his demand for the biker's address and for permission to remove the bastard's testicles with a rusty hatchet.

"Permission denied, Danny. I'll be taking on that particular responsibility."

"You sure, boss? If you don't mind me saying, you can be a little on the gentle side when it comes to interrogating a prisoner."

Kaine snorted. "Yes, Corporal Pinkerton, I do mind. And anyone who can do that"—he pointed to the weatherboard sheets—"with children in the firing line, doesn't deserve gentle treatment."

"Fair enough, boss." Danny rubbed some warmth into his hands. "So, what now? We wait to see what happens here?"

"That's right. My guess is Mrs Constantine goes to the hospital and leaves the girls here with her sister. If that's the case, you stay here and watch over the girls, and I'll make sure Justina reaches the hospital in one piece. After that, I'll go pay our biker friend a middle-of-the-night social call."

"And if the sister takes the kiddies to her place, should I follow them or stay here and guard the premises?"

Kaine gave Danny what his dad would have called an "old-fashioned" look.

"Do I really need to answer that? The girls take priority. As far as I'm concerned, whoever's putting the pressure on the Constantines can do what they like to the restaurant. The building can fall into rubble so long as the family's safe.

We can always pay for a rebuild—or, better still, 'encourage' the bad guys to do it."

Kaine grinned at the throwaway idea which, on reflection, merited much more thought.

"Okay, just making certain of the operational parameters, boss. I take it the rules of engagement are unchanged?"

"That's correct," Kaine said. "We're here to discourage the bad guys and protect the good guys. Luckily, in this case, the good guys are easy to spot. Check out the area."

He handed Danny his tablet—still open to Google Maps—and they fell silent while Danny studied satellite images to generate a feel for an area that might one day become a field of operations. Kaine wanted Danny to know every alleyway, every takedown spot, every piece of high ground that might be used as a sniper's nest. Urban warfare presented its own specific difficulties and required its own particular methods, and Danny Pinkerton happened to be one of the best exponents Kaine ever had the pleasure to work with—hence his contract with the Mounties. Short-sighted defence cuts had deemed Danny as superfluous to the nation's military requirements. The same myopic, political bollocks had thrown Kaine on the scrapheap along with him.

In the case of Danny Pinkerton, the nation's loss would turn out to be The 83's gain.

"You happy with what you've seen?"

"Yes, boss," Danny said. "Piece of cake."

He powered down the tablet, zipped up its case, and placed it in the back beside their Bergens. After settling back into his seat, Danny shot Kaine a sideways look and opened his mouth to speak, before closing it again and turning his head to face front. But he kept shuffling in his seat.

"Come on, Danny. Something's bothering you. Out with it."

Danny paused for a moment before speaking. "Sorry to bring filthy lucre into the proceedings, boss, but ... your email said something about full expenses."

"That's right. Why?"

"Well ..." He paused again. A pained expression crossed his boyish face. "I've just flown in from Toronto, and Air Canada only had business class tickets left on the last flight of the day. Cost a small fortune. Six thousand Canadian dollars."

"Ouch. That's what? A little under four grand?"

Danny shrugged. "Sounds about right. Nice, full-length, reclining seats though, and the flight attendants weren't exactly hard on the eye. The email did say you wanted me here *tout-de-suite*. I'm happy to donate to the cause, but I still need to make a living, you know? Besides, it's not as though you're short of a few quid. How much did you take from Sir Malcolm Sampson? Three hundred million, wasn't it?"

"That money's for The 83, Danny. Not me. Untouch-able. I'm funding this operation out of my own pocket and anything we might, shall we say, 'liberate' from the bad guys along the way."

"Fund liberation?" Danny cocked an eyebrow. "Sounds rewarding."

"And," Kaine said, pausing to add impact. "Since this is a voluntary and cooperative venture, we're going to split everything we earn equally. No sliding scale governed by former military rank. Is that agreeable?"

Danny double-hiked his eyebrows. "You won't find me arguing against such a division of equity, boss."

Kaine put an end to the discussion by staring through the rain-streaked windscreen. With two people in the car—

one wringing wet—and the windows now closed against the driving rain, the condensation built, and it was becoming more difficult to see across to the other side of the road.

Danny loosened the laces on his boots and pushed the seat back as far as it would go. "Couldn't you find a bigger car, Captain?"

"This one is inconspicuous."

"Really?"

Danny stared pointedly at the pearl-white Aston Martin ahead of them and the dark blue Lexus beyond that.

"Okay, Danny. Point taken. I'll pick up something larger and more comfortable next time."

Danny reclined the back of his seat and groaned as he stretched out. "Mind if I have some shuteye, Captain? Jet lag's a killer."

"Business class seats, you said."

"Still a long flight, though. Wake me when something happens."

Minutes later, with Danny's deep, open-mouthed snores rattling the windows, the Bistro's lights flickered on, and the women reappeared. Justina carried a sleeping Kora and a large suitcase, and Arana held Rena's hand and protected them all with a large golf umbrella. They piled into the Fiat.

Kaine fired up the Astra. Danny woke with a snort and looked around him as though trying to figure out which continent he'd landed on.

"Wipe the spittle from your mouth, Corporal. We're off for a little drive."

Danny opened his eyes wide, raised the back of the seat, and clipped his seatbelt into place. He pulled in a great, big, loud yawn and rubbed his eyes. "How long was I asleep?"

"Ages and ages. I'm amazed you're still tired."

Danny read the dashboard clock. "Nine minutes. Bloody marvellous."

"That's nine more than me, Corporal."

Kaine smirked as Danny lowered his head. One thing in the lad's favour—he knew when to keep his mouth shut.

They followed the Fiat at a discreet distance, keeping at least three cars between them. After a short drive, the little car turned into St Catherine's on the Green's car park, and pulled to a halt in a dropping-off bay.

Justina climbed out of the passenger side, ran to the covered entrance, and turned to wave at her family.

"Okay," Kaine said. "Here's where we part company. Take the Astra and follow the girls. Stay with them until I tell you otherwise. Okay?"

"You're stopping here?"

Kaine nodded. "Until I'm certain Mrs Constantine is settled in for the night."

"After that, the biker, right?"

Kaine grabbed the door handle. "That's right, Danny. After that, the biker."

"Say hello from me."

"Oh, I will do."

"Just a thought, boss. I'll have the car. How will you get there?"

Kaine ducked out into the rain and grabbed his Bergen from the back.

"Look around you, Danny," he said, waving to the high-priced vehicles lining the consultants' car park. "There's a veritable smorgasbord of cars to choose from if I can't find a taxi. By the way, you'll find a weapons safe in the boot. To unlock it, key in our old troop's designation, but add twelve. You'll find a nice, friendly SIG P226 in there with your name on it. Plenty of ammo, too."

Danny smiled, said, "Thanks, Captain. You know I feel naked without a SIG on my hip," and scooted into the driver's seat as the Fiat drove away.

Kaine hung the Bergen over one shoulder, pulled down the peak of his baseball cap, and headed towards the brightly lit hospital entrance.

Chapter Fifteen

Friday 23rd October – Alfred Lovejoy

Halcyon Tower, Kensington and Chelsea, London, England

Alfred "Alfie" Lovejoy stretched out his long legs and wriggled his toes. Coming up to winter and he was walking around on ceramic tiles barefoot. Jesus, nothing invented could beat underfloor heating. Since gaining access to the flat, he'd spent a load of his time walking around barefoot, luxuriating in the toasty glow.

Yep, he belonged in a place like this and one day, he'd own one just like it, only bigger and with an even better view. Although the one through the balcony window wasn't too bad, he couldn't really see the Houses of Parliament unless he stood on a chair outside on the balcony and leaned far out to the right. Not ideal. Not the safest thing he'd ever done, either.

He'd lived the first seventeen years of his life on the twenty-third floor of a tower block in Southwark. Once he'd left, young Alfie swore he'd never go back to high-rise living. But that was before setting foot in the penthouse.

Those Southwark tower blocks were a different animal altogether, though. Built after the slum clearances of the '50s to house the post-war baby boomers, they were still slums, only built vertical, and had been roundly condemned as "unfit for human habitation" within ten years of the first people moving in. Useless fucking planners. Useless fucking builders.

Alfie stretched out again.

Yes, this was the life. This, he could get used to. Penthouse comfort with a view of London people spent a fortune to glimpse, and here he was, living the highlife, literally. He chuckled into his beer.

Sitting on his comfy chair in the corner by the lift, Tuggy raised an eyebrow in question. Although the big guy could actually speak when he wanted to, he rarely bothered, preferring an intimidating growl or a moody frown to more regular methods of human communication.

Hey, whatever works for you.

And it usually worked a treat. One reason to keep the big bastard around. There were others. Alfie had few real friends, but he considered Tuggy as one of the best.

"Don't worry, Tuggy," he said after taking another sip of his Dutch beer. "Just reminiscing. Can't get over this here underfloor heating. Why don't you kick off your size-sixteen trainers and feel the warmth?"

Tuggy grunted, shook his head, and opened his left hand three times. After that, he crossed his arms over his huge chest, and his pecs bunched under the form-fitting exercise vest. All natural, too. No "Arnie" implants for Tuggy. The man may have been a monster, but he was Alfie's monster.

"Okay, my mistake. Size fifteens. I've seen smaller bloody canoes. Still"—Alfie made a big show of sniffing—"given that I've been downwind of you in the gym changing rooms before now, best you keep the fucking things on."

He laughed and Tuggy did that thing with his mouth that could have been either a smile or a sneer, Alfie never could tell. Didn't matter, though. They'd been mates for so long, Tuggy never took offence at Alfie's jokes, and Alfie paid no heed to Tuggy's guttural responses.

As the Yanks might say, "Everything was copacetic between him and Tuggy," whatever the fuck that meant.

He drained his beer and jumped to his feet. "Ready for another?"

Tuggy checked the time on his gold Rolex. He liked shiny things, and no one could find anything with much more bling than a Rolex Submariner with an old-gold wrist band. Pathetic really, but if it kept Tuggy happy it was okay by Alfie.

"Don't worry, it's late enough for a second, and we've got plenty of time. I'm having another even if you don't want one."

He sauntered to the kitchen, dropped the empty into the bottle bank—it made a satisfying clink against all the others —and pulled a fresh one from the cooler. He loved the old-school, flip-top stopper.

The desk phone burbled. Bloody stupid noise. First time he'd heard it, Alfie thought Tuggy had backed up the toilet again.

"The boss is early. Fucking arsehole."

Alfie set the unopened bottle on the draining board, jogged to the desk in the designated office area, and snatched up the handset before the fourth ring. The boss got real pissed off if he ever had to wait much longer than that.

Deep breath, Alfie. Play it cool, son. Keep the old fucker on side.

"Good evening, Sir Brandon."

"Alfred, dear boy, what do you have for me?"

A shiv in the kidney if you keep talking down to me like that, you fucking tosser.

"It's done, Sir Brandon. It went down before five o'clock just like I promised."

"Casualties?"

Background laughter on the phone line told him the boss was entertaining again and, once more, Alfie hadn't been invited. Not that it mattered. Alfie had a two-pronged plan in place to slide his feet under the high table permanently. One prong included recording every phone conversation and backing up every email between him and the boss, and storing it on the laptop and in the cloud. Boring, but a necessary defence and attack strategy. The second prong, the seduction of Sir Brandon's airhead daughter, Lady F, was proving a much less onerous task than he'd imagined. Women born to money liked to party. They also loved a bit of rough, and Alfie could be as rough as anyone. Although he did know where to draw the line. Leave no marks that showed. Usually.

He snorted. A mantra to live by.

"One casualty. The owner's in hospital. Apparently, the poor man had his head cracked open. Such a shame."

The old man's laugh rattled down the line. "Restaurants can be such hazardous places. What happened? Did he slip on a greasy kitchen floor?"

"No, according to my source, it was much more spectacular, but still anonymous. Apparently, some hairy-arsed lout on a motorbike lobbed a brick through his window."

On the other end of the phone, a deep-voiced woman started belting out a tune. Jazz. Atonal. Scat singing they called it. Fucking hard on the ears and on the pocket, especially when played live. The boss had to be shelling out the big bucks. Probably schmoozing some more foreign investors. Towelheads and Russians seemed to be the flavour of the year. No shortage of money in those quarters.

"Oh dear," Sir Brandon said in mock distress. "Is nowhere safe in London these days?"

"Must have upset someone important."

The old man snorted.

"Perhaps his misfortune will act as a warning to others who might think about dragging their feet."

The jazz singer was well into her thing and fighting to make herself heard over the backing band. The geezer thumping the piano keys was winning against all comers.

"Anything specific you want me to do next, Sir Brandon? If you want my advice, it might be best to hold off for a couple of days. We need to make sure nothing blows back on you or the firm."

"How many times do I have to tell you? We're protected. The Boys in Blue won't lift a finger to help the family concerned. Just make sure they sign the papers by the end of the month. Hear me?"

Alfie shot a glance at Tuggy, who was listening on the extension. Sure, Sir Brandon Banner-Hardy might be paying off the filth, but that protection wouldn't extend to him or Tuggy if the doggy doo-doo hit the spinning blades.

Not a chance.

Alfie had been protecting himself from the day he ran

away from Cecil Rhodes Tower, and he wasn't about to stop any time soon.

"I hear you, Sir Brandon. They'll sign the contract after tonight's little persuader. There's no doubt about it."

"Don't wait too long. I have everything in place for a fast turnaround. Architects, surveyors, contractors, the lot. I want that contract signed by Friday of next week at the latest. Any delay will cost me millions, and you know what that means, dear boy?"

"Yes, Sir Brandon. You'll take it out of my cut."

"I'll take it out of your hide, more like," the oily bugger said, his voice edged sharp as a razor. "And don't think that musclebound freak Tugboat's gonna save you. With one phone call, I can have five men twice his size at my back. Do you hear me?"

Alfie squeezed the phone so hard the case creaked. "I hear you, Sir Brandon. You can rely on me, sir."

"I know that, dear boy," he said reverting to his condescending worst. "Is there anything else?"

"Just confirmation on the price."

"What price?"

"The price we're now offering the Constantines for the signature."

Sir Brandon scoffed. "A big, fat zero. The bastards rejected a very fair market offer. Now all they get is whatever remains of their health. Stupid, Greek bastards think they can say no to me and get off with nothing more than a broken window?" The man paused for a moment before adding. "Fuck it. I've just changed my mind. Make an example of her for the rest of the block. Go in hard and fast, and do it tonight."

Alfie mouthed an obscenity down the phone. The next part was going to be dicey. How could he spin it without stepping into danger or coming across like a weak-kneed wally? He could hardly tell Sir Brandon a date with his daughter took precedence over business. A little lie wrapped in the truth might do.

What the old bastard didn't know wouldn't hurt him— or Alfie. And nothing would ever hurt Tuggy.

"Sorry, boss. I'm afraid that ain't gonna be possible."

"Why the fuck not?"

Sir Brandon's speech rose to a high-pitched squeak. He really could be a little girl when he didn't get his own way. Spoilt arsehole.

"Mr Constantine is in hospital. The quacks are operating right now, and the geezer's missus is with him. The kids are being minded by his sister. There's no one in the Bistro or the upstairs flat."

"Which hospital?"

Fuck.

The fat bastard wasn't making it easy.

"St Catherine's on the Green."

"Well? What are you waiting for? Get to the hospital and lean on the fucking bitch!"

Arrogant fucker would have them all nicked.

"I can't exactly turn up at St Catherine's with a load of muscle. They'll have CCTV all over the place.

Give the tosser an alternative, Alfie. Take his mind off of things.

"Of course, I could always torch the Bistro, but that'll increase the price of the refurb. Make things a little messy, too. The insurance company will stick their oars in the water. Whatcha reckon?"

"No. No. I don't need that kind of scrutiny. How do you know all this? Your hired thug only smashed the window a couple of hours ago."

"I've got eyes on the ground over there. I called my watcher before reporting in."

The arsehole growled. "Okay. I hear you. Give it a couple of days. Wait until the bitch and the kids are back home. It'll be easier to put the pressure on when she sees what'll happen to her kids if she keeps playing silly buggers."

"You want me to hurt the girls?"

Of course he does, so long as his hands stay clean.

"I don't care what the fuck you do to the little bitches so long as it gets me the signature on the bottom of that contract. Have I made myself clear enough?"

"Yes, Sir Brandon. I understand you perfectly. I'll pop around to the Bistro over the weekend and pay my respects to the wife. She'll be all alone and in need of a strong man to offer some comfort."

"Planning to go yourself, or send your pet gorilla?" he said, barking out a mirthless laugh.

Tuggy made a fist with his free hand. His knuckles cracked. Alfie shook his head and patted his hand in the air.

Cool head, Tuggy. You'll have your moment.

"No, Sir Brandon," Alfie said, pretending to laugh along. "Tugboat and I are a team. We share everything."

"The gorilla's okay with your sloppy seconds? Never could understand why you keep that dummy around. He gives me the creeps. Pay your social visit on Sunday. The builders won't be around to hear her scream."

"And the kiddies, you're sure?"

The fucker hesitated for a moment before answering. "Second thoughts, leave them alone. No point bringing too much attention on the place. My influence over the authorities isn't infinite. At least, not yet."

"Yes, Sir Brandon. Leave it with—"

The phone line clicked into silence. Alfie grunted.

Tuggy drew back his hand and threatened to throw his phone at the wall.

"Ignore him for now, Tuggy," Alfie said. "One day, I'll let you loose on the ignorant prick. Won't be long, but I need one or two more things in place first. Then we'll see who's laughing. Right, mate? Have yourself a beer and think about Sunday. That Greek bitch ain't gonna put up much of a fight, but she'll bleed red enough for you to get your rocks off."

Tuggy smiled. Yep, definitely a smile this time. No mistaking that one.

Got to love a man who took pride in his work.

Alfie dropped the phone back into its cradle, retrieved his beer, and settled back into the reclining chair to stare out over the stunning, London skyline. Would he ever get used to the view? One day, he wouldn't be just minding the penthouse for the boss. One day, he'd own it, or something like it, and Lady F, Daddy's little Baby Girl would buy it for him.

In his corner by the entrance, Tuggy rolled his shaved head, rotated his shoulders, and cricked his neck. Pretty soon, after the visit, he'd go downstairs to the gym and punch seven bells of shit out of the leather bags for an hour before they picked up Lady F and hit the town. But he'd only do it after Alfie gave him permission.

Hierarchy worked like that, mostly.

Yeah, most of the time, people kept to their dedicated places in life and rarely climbed to the next rung up the totem. Not Alfie Lovejoy, though. Nah, Alfie was riding to the top of the greasy pole, and Lady F was going to provide the ticket to first class.

First things first, though. A family was standing in his way, and they had to be shifted.

Chapter Sixteen

Friday 23rd October – Barnard Mortensen

Halcyon Tower, Kensington and Chelsea, London, England

Barnard "Barney" Mortensen slid into a bike bay, out of the pissing rain. He dropped the kick stand, killed the burbling engine, and the heap of shit's hacking cough died. Bloody thing needed a new exhaust at the very least, but that crap were expensive. Not worth stumping up any more money on the rusty bag of bolts. If the meeting went good, he'd be able to buy a new bike. Maybe a shiny, red Ducati 999. Always did fancy one of them babies. Shit hot, they were. Power to spare and rode as smooth as silk.

If there were a better way of shooting 'round London in rush hour than on a motorbike, Barney hadn't found it yet.

He patted the Kawasaki's dented, black fuel tank and smiled. Although he were desperate to get shot of her, the old bitch had done him proud once again. She'd been with him years. Man and boy. When Barney finally hit the big time, when he were flush, he'd keep the Kwaka for the rough jobs and save the Ducati for impressing the boys.

Barney tugged off his skid lid, stuffed the leather gloves inside, and hung it on the handlebar by its strap. Despite parking in full view of the road, there weren't no lowlifes about. Not in this hood. No, this hood were too upmarket for that kind of bullshit. The bike were gonna be safe outside a gaff like this one. Probably even had security. Maybe one of them uniformed doormen were gonna salute him on the way in and out.

Wouldn't that be cool.

He ran his fingers through his long hair and wiped the grease on the arse of his jeans. Yeah, the hair deffo needed a wash. Should have scrubbed up before coming. Too late now, though. Maybe next time.

Now he'd pulled off the job with the brick, he'd worked his way in. He'd pick up the rest of the wedge and say, "Yes, please," to the next job. Any job. As part of Alfie Lovejoy's growing team, he'd be one bit closer to "made man" status. Untouchable. For once, Barney's life were looking on the up.

He sniffed the air. It didn't smell no fresher than nowhere else so close to the river, but it did look a damn sight smarter. No graffiti or nothing. Weren't no homeless bums holding out the begging bowls. No peeling paint on the doors and windows, no litter-filled doorways, and no overflowing dumpsters. He'd be willing to bet the big ones he saw in the car park were emptied regular, too. Weekly even. The owners probably had to pay some private firm to keep the place this spotless.

How the rich fuckers lived.

One day, Barney. One day, mate.

Smiling at his good fortune, he bounded up the steps to the entrance of Alfie's block. He paused at the top to take another gander at the area.

Nice. So, so nice.

He punched the "Penthouse" button on the security panel like what they told him to do, lifted his face, and stared, straight into the security camera. He smiled.

Steady, Barney. Make this count.

This were like the second part of a job interview, the one after the practical test. Fuck's sake. He should have washed his fucking hair. He tucked a stray lock behind his left ear and waited.

After holding his pose for an age, the system clicked and a message on the security screen read, "*Take lift to Penthouse. Wipe feet.*"

The latch popped. Barney pushed on the door and stepped inside, making sure that any fucker watching the CCTVs could see him wipe his boots on the *Welcome* mat.

The foyer were a bit of a disappointment. There weren't no uniformed concierge, just a rubbish bin in the corner, a fire-evacuation plan on the wall, and two potted plants either side of the lifts—great, big, ugly, green things they was, too. Took up space and gave back fuck-all in return. Far as Barney could tell, they might even be plastic. Not that he'd risk pissing anyone off by touching the ugly fuckers.

The quiet inside the lobby made the ringing in his ears seem louder. The Kwaka's knackered exhaust was fucking up his hearing. Owning a Ducati couldn't come soon enough. Barney didn't think he could cope with going deaf. No music in his life would drive him round the bend.

Note to self. Until you can afford the Ducati, buy a skid lid what cuts out the sound a bit better.

The lift doors stood open and ready to take him to the dosh—another example of the way his luck were running.

Barney stepped into the box and punched the top button. He closed his eyes. One day, he'd have his own place with air-con what sprayed perfume into the air. Wouldn't take long, not if he passed the rest of the entrance exam. Dosh from a few more drive-by attacks would put him right up on top with the rest of the fuckers in their expensive suits. The pay were plenty good enough, and he didn't mind sticking it to the filthy immigrants and their snivelling brats. Not one little bit. If an ordinary bloke like Alfie Lovejoy could afford to live in a place like this, why not the likes of Barnard Harold Mortensen?

It were stifling inside the tiny, metal box. Made him sweat like a pig in heat. Barney yanked down the zip to his leather jacket and pumped the front of his T-shirt, but it didn't do no good.

Why keep the place so pigging hot?

Probably needed the warmth for the fucking potted plants. Rubber bastards. He wouldn't have plants in his new place, no way. Them poncy fuckers could take their clutter and their fucking potted plants and stuff them up their arseholes.

The lift rose the twenty-two floors in next to no time and the doors slid open right into Alfie's front room. Tugboat's huge frame blocked his access. Probably named after his huge, fuck-off face, the square-built, Kiwi body-guard pointed for Barney to leave the lift and waved a wand over him—arms, legs, crotch, front, and back.

Security conscious or what?

Once satisfied Barney didn't have an assault rifle hidden up his jacksie, the big fucker pointed to Barney's boots and jerked his thumb. It took a moment to work out what he meant.

"You want me to take me boots off?"

Tugboat dipped his head and pointed to a mat just inside the room. Showing respect for other people's homes? Yeah, Barney could do that. No probs.

He unzipped his boots, kicked them off, and placed them carefully beside the other outdoor shoes on the mat.

Only then did Tugboat move aside and stand back by the side of the lift.

Barney took a moment to gawk.

Jesus H Christ!

How much would a place like this set someone back? Million and a half? Two? Three?

Barney's heart rate climbed. More sweat flowed, but this wave didn't have nothing to do with the heat.

"Mr Lovejoy?" he called.

"Out here on the balcony. Grab a beer from the fridge and come join me."

"Thanks ... Mr Lovejoy. Be right there."

Booze and a private audience with the main man. How cool were that?

Barney stepped into a pair of guest slippers before padding across the cream-and-white floor tiles. A double-doored, American refrigerator filled one corner of the kitchen. He helped himself to a bottle, flipped the lid, and sucked the froth before it had the chance to dribble over his hand and spill to the floor.

"Come on, Mortensen. I don't have all evening. I'm off out to the Midnight Club, and I hate being late."

The Midnight Club? Where the fuck's that?

Barney sniffed. What were the point of dropping the name of a place nobody'd ever heard of?

"Sorry, Mr Lovejoy."

Barney looked lively and pushed through the door to the balcony before pissing off the main man. The minute he stepped out of the super-heated room, the freezing, London air burned his lungs. He coughed, only just remembering to cover his mouth with his hand.

The balcony wrapped around the building and the only thing stopping anyone from going arse over tit into the black were a weak-looking, glass safety screen. Barney stuck as close to the inner wall as a limpet to a rock, and he waited.

Alfie Lovejoy lay back on an upholstered recliner. Protected from the icy wind by a heavy coat and knee-length suede boots, he sucked on a cigar the size of a baby's arm. A cloud of blue-grey smoke hung around his head, mixing with the steam from his breath.

Chuffing cold, it were. Barney tried not to shiver. Didn't want to make it look like he were a weakling.

"Freezing out here, isn't it?" Lovejoy said.

Barney set his bottle down on the glass-topped table and pulled the jacket zip up to his throat. Thank fuck he'd put on the slippers. Otherwise, his feet would have stuck to the floor tiles.

"It is a touch parky, Mr Lovejoy."

"So why aren't I sitting inside, you might ask?" Alfie asked, taking another deep draw on the fat cigar.

Barney grabbed his beer, not that he needed a drink, but he thought it best not to refuse the hospitality of his new boss. Wouldn't want to cause no offence, like. There weren't no telling how a guy like Alfie Lovejoy would react. And that safety screen didn't look all that pigging safe.

He took a sip and tilted his head towards the view. "That there is worth a bit of a chill."

Alfie sat up and placed both feet on the tiles. "That's nothing special. You get used to it after a while. Give me the East End any day but"—he stubbed the cigar out on a silver plate and must have left thirty quid's worth of stub smouldering, unused—"Lady F doesn't like the smell of stale cigars."

"Lady F?"

Alfie nodded and showed Barney his teeth in a wide smile. Fuck, he were a good-looking bugger. Barney's heartbeat jacked up to high speed, and he heaved in a deep, chilly breath.

"Yeah, she's the squeeze I'm taking to the club tonight. Loves to see the flashing lights. So, enough about my love life. I understand you did a good job at the Greek place."

Barney's mouth dropped open. He couldn't help it. He snapped his jaws together and swallowed before recovering enough to speak again. "You know 'bout that already?"

"Of course," Alfie said, smiling. "I have my sources. I know everything that goes on in my manor."

His manor. Right.

Barney nodded and powered right into it.

"It went down exactly the way you wanted it, Mr Lovejoy. Exactly the way you told me to do it. I lobbed a brick through the window and scarpered."

Alfie nodded. "So I hear. You did really well."

"Thank you, Mr Lovejoy. Thank you."

Barney sniffled and waited a sec before taking another sip of beer. He wanted to ask about the rest of his money but couldn't appear too needy. Locking in a place on the team had to be more important than the folding stuff right now, and most bosses preferred their employees to speak only when they was asked a direct question. Barney's dad told him that. About the only thing the miserable, old git ever learned his son before drinking himself into an early grave.

Alfie's smile broadened. Looked like he'd had his teeth whitened since Barney'd last seen him. They shone bright against the fake tan. It looked good on him, though. Strong face, square jaw, baby blue eyes, fuck-off gorgeous. No wonder he were knocking around with a proper Lady.

Lucky bloody cow.

Barney swallowed hard, trying to ignore the stirring in his jeans. It wouldn't be good to let Alfie, or Tugboat, know Barney's dirty, little secret. There weren't no queers in the underworld, not at Barney's level. He'd have to stay in the closet for a good bit longer.

"Excellent," Alfie said, "that'll teach the Greeks to say no to us."

"Sorry, Mr Lovejoy?"

"Doesn't matter. And you can call me Alfie, now you're on the team."

"I am? Fantastic. Thanks … Alfie. Do you 'ave anything else for me?"

"As a matter of fact, I do. Get back here by noon Sunday. You can run interference and play lookout while Tuggy and I pay a call on an uppity, Greek bitch and her filthy spawn." Alfie stood and waved him towards the door. "Now bugger off and let me get ready. Can't keep a Lady waiting. Tuggy has the rest of your cash. We owe you another monkey, yes?"

"That's right, Alfie. A monkey. Ta."

Barney tried not to drool. A thousand quid for something he'd have done for free just to get his foot in the door? What weren't to like? Whoever said Barney Mortensen weren't going to amount to nothing wanted shooting. He managed to play it cool. Didn't smile too much. Didn't hold his hand out too eager.

It had been a great day.

Best ever.

Time to celebrate.

Chapter Seventeen

Saturday 24th October – Barnard Mortensen

Charles Street, Camden, London, England

Barney belched loudly and lined the empty beer bottle up next to all the others on the coffee table. Frankie stared at him through bloodshot, half-closed eyes. Jo-Jo snored heavily beside him, cramping Frankie for space, but Frankie didn't seem to mind much.

"Tell me again, man," Frankie pleaded.

He slurred so much Barney had trouble understanding what the dozy fucker said. Still, he didn't mind repeating his story. It weren't every day he made a mark with the big boys. If he were being honest with himself, Barney loved the attention. When he'd waved the five hundred quid in crisp, clean twenties under their noses, he nearly creamed his jeans at their reaction.

Hero worship. Barney loved it. Couldn't get enough of it.

Fucking aces!

"Go on, man. I want all the details."

Barney raised the bottle to his lips and tilted.

Fuck.

Being pissed screwed with his timing, and he dribbled some of it down the front of his T-shirt. Shit, it were his last clean one, too. Best make a trip to the laundrette before the meeting tomorrow. Couldn't turn up for his next job looking like a fucking dosser. Wouldn't be professional.

"Wish I'd been there, man," Frankie said. "I'd have filmed it for prosperity."

Barney snorted. "Posterity, Frankie-boy. You mean posterity, not prosperity."

Frankie winked and pointed at the notes spread out on the table.

"Nah, man. I mean prosperity. We is loaded, good buddy," he said and started giggling. "Loaded."

The giggle turned into a hysterical cackle and then became a hacking, choking rasp until Frankie doubled up, arms wrapped around his chest, struggling to breathe.

"Jesus, mate. You ought to see the quack about that cough. Sounds like you puked up half a lung. Fucking 'orrible. It ain't right."

Frankie came up, gasping for air and stared at him, white-faced and sweaty. "Nah. I'm alright. Doctor's only gonna tell me to jack in the booze and the fags. What's the joy in that? What else do I got to live for?"

He wiped phlegm and lager from his chin and took another deep swig.

"So, go on, Barney. Blow-by-blow, full-colour description. You was on the bike and pulled up outside the restaurant, and then you …"

Frankie made a rolling-forward movement with the hand holding the bottle. More lager spilled onto the stained and threadbare carpet. Maybe they'd get a new rug, someday.

Barney scratched at his chin. As well as the trip to the laundrette, he'd shave before meeting Alfie. Wash his hair, too. Had to smarten up if he wanted people to take him serious.

"Yeah. There I were, nose-to-tail traffic outside the place. It were all lit up like on display, you know? Calling in the diners for their grub, only there weren't nobody eating but the owner and his brats. Frizzy-haired, little mongrels. They was at the table right by one of the windows."

Frankie lurched himself forwards, forearms resting on knees, both hands gripping the bottle, roll-up sticking out the corner of his mouth. He blinked away the smoke drifting into his eyes.

"Go on. Describe the place."

Barney's heart started racing. Just talking about it gave him a hard-on.

"Here it is. You got these two fuck-off, big windows either side of the door, right? I could've chosen the one on the left, but there weren't nobody sitting by that one, and I had my orders to scare the crap out of the Greeks, right?"

"Right," Frankie echoed, his eyes shining bright.

"So, I thought to myself, 'fuck the empty window, do the other one'. That's when I slung the brick. Lobbed it overarm straight through the glass. Crash, bang, fucking wallop. Shattered into these little pieces that sparkled like Christmas lights, y'know? The old man were like, out of it.

Lying across the table with 'is head pumping blood. And the snivelling little brats was screaming. Then I burned rubber. You should have seen me, man. I rode the Kwaka like Steve McQueen in that old war movie. Only I didn't get tangled up in no barbed wire at the end."

Frankie snorted. Beer and snot blew out of his nose. He wiped it clean with the back of his hand.

"You having that?" he asked, eyeing the last unopened bottle.

Barney looked at it for a moment before shaking his head. "Nah, better not. Got things to do later on. Places to go. People to meet. Alfie's setting up another job for tomorrow, and I need to be ready."

"In that case."

Frankie drained his bottle and snatched up the spare.

"Yeah, knock yourself out. I'm for my pit. Laters, man."

Frankie waved the bottle at him. "Yeah, man. Laters."

Barney stood, staggered, threw a hand against the wall to right himself, and groped towards the stairs. "And keep the fucking noise down. I need my kip."

When Frankie didn't respond by the time he reached the staircase, Barney grabbed the banisters for support, and looked back. The Rasta tosser lay sprawled against Jo-Jo, eyes shut, mouth open. The contents of the open bottle flowed into his lap.

"Stupid fucks."

As his dad kept on telling him, "In this world, you snooze, you lose."

Yeah, Dad. You kept saying that all the way from the dole queue to the pub. Fucking arsehole.

Barney climbed up the four flights to his converted attic bedroom, tugging on the wobbly handrail to help him all the way.

He made it to the top in a bath of sweat. The minute he'd firmed up his place on Alfie's crew, he'd be out of the squat and into his own flat. Maybe it wouldn't be as flash as Alfie's penthouse right away, but his bedroom wouldn't be in no cramped, fucking attic.

His crappy, unmade bed squeaked in complaint when he dropped into it from a great height. He kicked off his boots, but didn't bother removing his clothes. A shower could wait until morning.

BARNEY COULDN'T BREATHE.

No air.

Couldn't breathe!

Cold. Wet. He were in the river, drowning. Weeds filled his mouth. He gagged. Sank deeper. He fought, struggled, tried to kick for the surface, but his arms and legs wouldn't move. They was paralysed. Fish nibbled at him, bit into his wrists and ankles.

Oh God.

He couldn't breathe!

He opened his eyes. Light streamed in through an open doorway.

A familiar, dark stain on a sloping ceiling and a skylight confirmed his bedroom.

Thank fuck, but ... he still couldn't move his hands or legs.

A nightmare? Heart attack? Stroke?

Movement flashed in the corner of his eye. A man. A man in his room? How?

Barney turned his head. Looked at his hands.

Fuck. No! No!

Cable ties bound his wrists to the bedposts.

He lifted his head and looked down. His ankles were bound, too. With jeans at half mast, around his calves, only his briefs covered his dick. Exposed. No fucking protection.

Jesus Christ. Jesus Christ Almighty!

Barney strained against the bonds. He pulled and twisted and tore, but nothing gave. He tried screaming, but a gag muffled the sound. A gag? His heart pounded. Sweat poured off him and soaked his sheets.

The man moved from Barney's peripheral vision and his face came into view, unmasked. Unknown, but memorable, and somehow familiar. The man didn't care if Barney could see his face.

Oh Jesus fuck. I'm gonna die! The fucker's gonna kill me.

He tried not to look, but he couldn't close his eyes or turn away. He didn't want to see but couldn't help himself.

An outline stood over him. Framed in the hall light.

Dark hair, dark beard, pale green eyes. Old, maybe forty, but hard and good-looking. Rugged. So fucking handsome, but tough. Expressionless. A face of stone.

A hired killer?

Why me? What have I ever done?

One of Alfie's opponents come to take revenge? The unblinking man leaned close; too close. His breath warmed Barney's face.

"You, son, are a rank amateur," he said, speaking normally, not bothering to whisper.

Barney tried to say, "What?" but it came out as a strangled, spit-slobbered garble.

The man seemed to understand.

"Using your own motorbike during the attack was crass stupidity. I expected you to claim it had been stolen, but there it is, parked outside in your front garden plain as day.

Couldn't believe it. That rookie mistake's going to cost you, son. It really is."

English and softly-spoken, the fucker might as well have been discussing the weather. The man patted Barney's cheek and stood up. His scarily good-looking face moved away.

Barney tried to swallow, but the gag made it impossible. Spittle pooled in the back of his throat, and he struggled to breathe. He turned his head to the side, trying to take in air. Didn't help. He still couldn't breathe.

Oh God. Oh God.

He were drowning in his own spit!

The bedside lamp snapped on. The light hurt his eyes and glinted on shiny metal. A knife in the man's right hand, its blade sharp and smooth on both edges, tapering to a wicked point.

A dagger!

Something else in the man's left hand. Small. It looked like a gas canister with a nozzle sticking out the top. Scary shit. Terrifying.

Fuck! What's that?

Barney lost control of his bladder. Warm piss ran between his legs, pooled around his butt cheeks, and slowly cooled.

The scary fucker twizzled the knife. Steel flashed again. He smiled. Not pleasant.

"Recognise me?"

Barney squealed behind the gag and shook his head.

"You should do, son. I'm Ryan Kaine."

Who? Ryan who?

Why were that name so familiar? The memory flared, punched Barney in the gut.

The crazy bastard what killed all them people on that plane. Oh fuck! I'm a dead man.

That's how come he recognised the face.

"Ah, I see by your reaction you do recognise the name. Good. It means you know my capabilities. Although I'm happy to demonstrate if you like."

More piss joined the first flush. Warm then cold. Barney started crying. Whimpering, like a fucking baby. He hated himself.

"Listen carefully, Mortensen. We need to chat. I'm going to remove the gag, but if you try to scream I'll sever your vocal cords. Then I'll slice off the tips of your fingers, and you'll have to write your answers in your own blood—assuming you can write. Your records say you didn't finish school so I'm not sure."

He knows I were excluded from school?

How the fuck?

"What do you say, Mortensen. Can you write?"

Barney nodded.

"Okay, well done. But forcing you to write your answers in your own blood would be such a waste of time, don't you think?"

Barney jagged his head up and down. He couldn't say yes quickly enough.

"I'm glad you agree. Keep doing that and we'll get along fine."

What about Frankie and Jo-Jo? If he could keep the mad bastard occupied, make some noise, maybe they'd come help him. Barney tried not to look at the doorway. He tried to concentrate on Kaine, but the fucker smiled and shook his head.

"No point waiting for a saviour, son. Don't think your two buddies downstairs are going to come flying up here to the rescue. They're in no condition to help anyone. Not ever again." He hitched his eyebrows. "Do I make myself clear?"

Barney blinked through the tears. The blade swished and the mad-eyed fucker ripped the tape from his mouth. He spat out the cloth gag—one of his own dirty socks—and gulped in huge mouthfuls of air.

Oh God. Thank you, Jesus!

"Who put you up to it?"

"Huh?" Barney said, still panting.

"The Bistro. Who put you up to it? Don't make me ask again."

"W-What you … t-talking about?"

"Tut tut, Mortensen. You haven't grasped the basic concept here. I ask questions, you answer them truthfully. No compromises. Mess that up once more and you'll begin to understand pain. Okay, one last time."

He twizzled the blade again.

"Who put you up to it?"

"M-Mr Kaine, I-I can't tell you that. They'll kill me."

Kaine shook his head slowly, almost apologetically. Barney felt his chin dimple and twitch.

"Wrong response, Mortensen. So now comes the pain."

He moved the point of the blade closer to Barney's left eye.

Oh God.

Despite the warning, Barney screamed.

Chapter Eighteen

Saturday 24th October – Pre-Dawn

Charles Street, Camden, London, England

Kaine waved the blade in front of Mortensen's left eye. The coward squealed and tried to pull his head away, but Kaine held it in place, leaning close and braving the man's foul sleep-breath.

"D-Don't 'urt me, please. I'll tell you everything … all I know, but please don't 'urt me."

It hadn't taken much to find his weakness. One flash of the dagger's pointed tip and the cowardly bastard had wet himself. Pitiful.

"Didn't mind hurting two little girls, though. Did you!"

"I-I …"

Kaine lowered the knife and dragged the edge carefully

across Mortensen's throat. Mortensen's Adam's apple quivered. From his position on the bed looking up, the biker wouldn't have been able to tell what Kaine was doing. To Mortensen, it would have felt as though his throat was being cut. The power of the mind worked in Kaine's favour.

He twisted both the metaphorical and the real blade. An honest lie or two would reinforce Kaine's menace.

"One of those little girls caught a piece of glass in her eye. Might be blinded. What was it you called them? 'Frizzy-haired, little mongrels', wasn't it? And the broken glass 'sparkled like Christmas lights', did it?"

The terror in Mortensen's eyes multiplied and his whole body shook. Kaine could feel it through the mattress.

"You … you heard me talking?"

Kaine jerked his head towards the bedside table where he'd rested his digital recorder. It stood upright, the LED recording indicator shining bright in the darkened room.

"Your confession is all on there, clear as day. It's amazing what a laser microphone can pick up. I didn't even have to leave the comfort of my car. All I had to do was roll down the window, point, and click, like one of those garage door openers. Wonderful. Now, where was I?"

Kaine rested the flat of the blade on Mortensen's right cheek, immediately below the eye, making sure he could see the needle-sharp point. The biker trembled like a man in the middle of a two-day fever.

"Oh yes. The poor lass will likely never see properly again. Five years old and you threw a breezeblock through her window. And her father's lying in a coma. What do you think I'm going to do to you?"

"Please don't 'urt me. It weren't my fault. I were only acting under orders."

"Orders? You're not a soldier, and this isn't the Nuremburg War Trials."

"Huh?"

Mortensen's face creased. He clearly didn't have a clue what Kaine was talking about. Kaine let it slide. He had no time or inclination to deliver a history lesson.

"How much were you paid?"

Mortensen tried to look away, but Kaine added a little more pressure to the blade and the breezeblock thrower's head locked into place. "Answer me, damn it! How much?"

"A monkey before. ... Same again after."

"One thousand pounds for a little girl's eyesight?"

He fanned out the notes he'd found on the coffee table downstairs, and waved them under Mortensen's nose.

"This it?"

Mortensen closed his eyes.

"Y-Yes."

"There's only eight hundred here. Where's the rest?"

Hesitation.

Kaine added more pressure to the knife blade, it bit into the skin. Blood trickled down Mortensen's cheek and into his ear.

"We needed ... shopping," he said, whimpering.

Kaine scoffed. "You mean the six-packs, the bottles of whisky, and the weed downstairs in the lounge?"

Mortensen blinked, struggling to keep his eyes open. Tears and sweat mixed with the blood in his ear. The stench wafting up from the bed wasn't at all pleasant.

"S'right. Shopping."

Kaine folded the money and stuffed it in his back pocket.

"Don't mind, do you? No? Good. It'll help pay for the replacement window."

Kaine pulled the knife away from the biker's cheek. It left an open cut that would probably scar. He stood and stared down at the pitiful sight for a moment before dragging a dining chair next to the bed. He straddled it and leaned forwards against its curved back, making himself comfortable. The vertebrae in his neck cracked as he rotated his head from side to side to loosen his shoulder muscles.

He lifted the knife in one hand and the black canister in the other and studied them, raising and lowering one at a time as though weighing them on a set of balances. Slowly, he lowered the canister. Its time would come a little later.

Mortensen's gaze flicked from the dagger to the canister, then locked on the dagger as Kaine kept it in sight.

"Now, are you going to keep answering my questions, or do I need to get nasty?"

Mortensen nodded, eyes pleading, eager, desperate to please.

"Y-Yes. Yes."

"Sorry? You want me to get nasty?"

Mortensen nodded and then shook his head.

"Yes … I mean no."

"What's it to be. I need precision."

"I'll answer your questions. Honest, just please don't 'urt me no more."

"Good. Now, I'm going to ask each question once. Lie to me or hesitate, and I'm going to start slicing bits off you."

He took a wrinkled carrot he'd found in the kitchen after he'd secured the two drunken idiots downstairs, and held it up by the fat end for Mortensen to see it easily.

"Imagine this is part of your meat and two veg. Get me?"

Mortensen's eyes latched onto the drooping root vegetable.

Slowly, Kane drew the blade across and down. The carrot fell apart. The severed tip dropped onto Mortensen's belly and rolled slowly onto the sheet. His scrawny stomach rippled as the carrot fell.

"Think of that as your one and only demonstration," Kaine said, adding a manic chuckle. "Do I have your full attention?"

More tears rolled down Mortensen's face, and snot ran from his nose. The snivelling coward had been prepped and was ready to start squealing.

"Question one. Who ordered you to attack the restaurant?"

"Alfie. A-Alfred Lovejoy."

Mortensen threw out the answer without hesitation or reticence. The truth. No doubt about it.

"Next question. Where do I find this Alfie Lovejoy?"

Mortensen gave the address as an upmarket tower block near the Thames. Expensive. It seemed as though the biker moved in rarefied circles. Kaine didn't bother trying to take notes, the digital recorder would capture it in perfect clarity.

"Ever been inside the apartment?"

"Yes, I w-were there earlier tonight to … to make my report."

"And collect the money?"

"Y-Yeah," he answered and took another shuddering breath.

"Describe it to me in detail. Leave nothing out."

Kaine listened intently as Mortensen struggled to explain the penthouse suite's layout. Kaine asked question after question, but the miserable thug's powers of observation were not far away from being useless. The only thing he learned of any value was how the entry system and the lifts worked, and how the bodyguard operated the security wand. Either by direct or indirect means, he'd have to augment Mortensen's sketchy information. Time would tell.

"How long have you been working for him?"

"This were my first official job. A sort of trial."

"How did you meet him?"

Mortensen's face creased in pain. Kaine checked the colour of the creep's hands—red, darkening to blue at the fingertips. The cable ties binding his wrists were tight, but not too tight. The thug was suffering, but he'd have to tough it out.

"Keep talking," Kaine said, using the knife as a razor and shaving a tuft of long and greasy hair from Mortensen's scalp.

The clump fell across the biker's face and stuck to the sweat. Kaine leaned away and Mortensen sneezed. The lock of hair slipped southwards.

"So … Alfie and 'is … m-minder come into my local the other day asking who owns the Kwaka, parked outside. That's my ride, a Kawasaki. Motorbike, y'know?"

Kaine flicked his wrist, and the knife nicked Mortensen's earlobe. He screeched and jerked his head away. Blood dripped onto the filthy pillow.

"Don't insult my intelligence, Mortensen. I know what a Kwaka is."

Kaine wiped the blade on the pillowcase, probably making it dirtier.

"Oh God. I'm sorry," Mortensen cried, panting. "D-Didn't mean nothing by it."

"Keep going with the story."

Mortensen's trembling increased in tempo and depth, but he gathered himself enough to continue.

"So, Alfie turns up asking who owns the bike and ... I tells him it's mine. Then we goes outside, and he gives me the restaurant job."

"A complete stranger walks into a bar and picks you at random?"

"Nah, it's like, a well-known place for people to hang out looking for ... for work. N-No questions asked, y'know? And everyone in the hood knows Alfie, and nobody would never grass him up 'cause he's protected, and I don't just mean by Tugboat. He's connected, right? Works for people with money and power. Names, y'know?"

"Tugboat?"

"Yeah, that's what they call Alfie's minder. He was the one with the magic wand thing. Ain't nobody's never seen Alfie without Tugboat at his side." Mortensen swallowed and tore his eyes away from the dagger's blade long enough to look at Kaine almost for the first time. "Listen, I'm being straight with you, man. Really. Don't go near Tugboat. He's a total monster. A nut job. Word is he don't just hurt people to protect Alfie, but 'cause he enjoys it. I once saw him put a guy in 'ospital for dissing his face tats. Horrible it were. Broke both the poor bugger's arms and smashed his kneecaps with a pool cue. Nearly killed him and smiled while he did it. Horrible, scary smile it were, too. Like one of them heads on top of churches. A fucking ghoul." Mortensen swallowed before carrying on. "Alfie's tough enough on his own, but don't go up against Tugboat without no army."

Kaine sneered. "Really. Is that your considered advice?"

"Yeah, it is, and I-I ain't kidding, man. And no one's never heard Tugboat speak, neither. Might be a ... a dummy, but ain't nobody's had the stones to ask him. He's too fucking scary."

"I can be scary, too."

Mortensen's chin quivered, and he squeezed his eyes closed. Kaine patted him on the uninjured cheek and his eyes snapped open. Fear wafted up from the bed on waves of stale sweat.

"Please don't 'urt me no more."

"I've hardly touched you, yet." Kaine released a wicked smile. "Only a few more questions left then you can do something for me, if you don't mind."

"Anything. I'll do anything. You only gotta name it."

The fear in his eyes turned to hope.

"Out of professional interest, why did you use your own bike for the job? Why didn't you steal one?"

He nodded vigorously.

"Yeah, that's what I said to Alfie, but he told me it didn't matter 'cause the bizzies wouldn't be arsed to investigate properly. Alfie said he 'ad the place sewn up, and I 'ad a free 'and to do whatever I wanted."

"Well, Alfie Lovejoy was wrong. The Constantine family is under my protection."

"Who?"

Deep anger flared again. The little shit didn't know or care about who he hurt for his money.

"The Constantines own the restaurant. From now on, they are untouchable. Like I said, they're under my protection. In fact every business left operating on Hardwicke Row is untouchable. Have I made myself clear?"

"Yeah, yeah. I understand. Want me to spread the word?" he asked, keen as the dagger's blade. "I'll let everyone know they're off limits."

Mortensen thought he could see a way out when none existed. Desperate hope gave flight to words that tumbled out on a puff of lager-soaked halitosis.

If Kaine hadn't seen the results of the attack, he might almost have felt sorry for the biker.

Kaine shook his head again. "No, I'll take care of the warning, you won't be in a position to warn anyone."

"Oh God. Please don't—"

"You see, I can't stop thinking about that five-year-old girl and her comatose father."

He lowered the knife and rested the tip at a point between Mortensen's navel and the top of his briefs.

The fear returned. Sweat shone on Mortensen's face and his body shook from head to toe.

"P-Please don't."

His face crumpled and he whimpered, waiting for death.

Kaine felt nothing.

"You see, Mortensen, I can't trust you not to go blabbing to Lovejoy and his boss the moment I let you go. I'm thinking of gutting you like a fish right here and now ..."

He paused to let option one sink in. Mortensen opened his eyes and strained to see the knife. Kaine slid the blade lower, adding more pressure.

"...but that would be too quick. You deserve to suffer, and that's why I brought along my little present."

Kaine placed the knife next to the recorder and brought up the canister again.

The brief flash of hope in Mortensen's expression died.

"Wh-Wha—"

"What's this?" Kaine asked, finishing Mortensen's question. "This is a CO2 injector. A chemical delivery system. A bit like the hypospray the doctor uses on Star Trek. You've seen them? Started off as science fiction, but it's science fact now. Thing is ... this nifty, little device doesn't only deliver medicine. Ah yes, I can see in your eyes you get where I'm going with this."

Kaine pointed to the nozzle on the top of the canister.

"This here gizmo is a spring-release valve. All I need to do is press it against the skin, like this …"

Kaine lowered the device to Mortensen's shoulder and pushed. The injector emitted a loud hiss and a puff of condensation. Mortensen would have been able to hear the hiss, but not see the puff of harmless carbon dioxide.

Screaming, the biker struggled against his bindings.

Kaine slapped him hard across the face rather than wait for him to pipe down.

"…and there you are. Dose delivered. No fuss. No bother. No needles. No blood loss. No need for an alcohol swab. It'll probably feel cold around the entry site for a while, but don't worry, you'll feel nothing soon. Nothing at all."

"Oh God," Mortensen cried. "What … w-what did you give me?"

"Fifty grains of Gypsophila 980-delta."

Mortensen started shaking and didn't stop.

"Oh God. No!"

"Gypsophila 980-delta. If you can remember that name, it might just save your life. The 'delta' part is the most important. Repeat that name for me."

The terrified biker recited the name aloud, squealing and desperate.

"Good," Kaine said, "you've got it. Well done."

Kaine had no difficulty keeping a straight face despite having just told the biker he'd been dosed with a flower more commonly known as "Baby's Breath". He only had to remember Orestes Constantine's head injury and the blood on the restaurant tablecloth for the last grain of humour to leech from his system.

"Oh fuck. What … w-what is it?"

"It's a slow-acting, systemic poison. Remember that Russian spy who drank the tea laced with Polonium 84? He took weeks to die. You have three days. Four at the most."

Mortensen stopped moving. Stopped breathing.

"That's good, Mortensen. Very good indeed. Keep your heart rate down and your movements slow, and you might just get out of this alive."

"What?" he whispered.

Kaine pocketed the pressurised tyre inflator—available at any good quality automotive and bicycle retailer—and stood.

"I'm not a vindictive person," Kaine said. "I believe in giving a person a second chance. Even an evil, little scrote like you, Mortensen. Are you still listening?"

The terrified biker nodded fast and hard.

"Good. You have one opportunity here. Just one."

"Please. Please, I-I'll do anything."

Kaine nodded and pulled in a deep breath. "Ever heard of a place called Porton Down?"

"N-No. Not never."

Typical. Ignorant fool.

"It's the government's military science park, near Salisbury. Amongst other things, they run a unit specialising in chemical warfare. The unit conducts human trials and has an experimental therapy for the poison that's currently coursing through your bloodstream. It's long and painful, and involves some invasive therapies." Kaine smiled and paused to let the message sink in.

"When I cut you free," he continued, "you need to find

your way to Porton Down and ask for Colonel Andrew Chavasse. He's the scientist in charge of the research. Give him the name of the poison, which is?" Again, Kaine paused.

"Er … Gypsophila 980-delta?"

"Good. That's right. Remember to move slowly, though. If you rush or raise your heart rate in any way it'll increase the potency of the drug. Take your bike and ride slowly and carefully. If you have even a minor shunt along the way, the increased flow of adrenaline will probably prove fatal."

Kaine hoped he'd primed the pump well enough. It wouldn't take long to find out. He sliced through all four cable ties and stood back.

Rather than jumping up and rushing around the room in a mad panic, Mortensen sat up in slow motion, his breathing ragged but controlled. Ignoring the urine drying on his legs, the filthy biker pulled on his jeans and stood even more slowly.

"Salisbury you say?" he whispered.

"That's right," Kaine said, nodding. "Head west and don't forget to ask for Colonel—"

"Ch-Chavasse," Morton said, still shaking.

"And don't say anything to your mates downstairs. Or they'll get a dose, too."

"Huh? You didn't hurt them?"

Kaine frowned. "No need. Luckily for them, they were both out of it when I let myself in. Booze and drugs will do that to you."

Mortensen lowered his eyes. He tiptoed towards the exit, unhooked his leather jacket from the back of a chair, and moonwalked along the short landing to the head of the stairs.

Kaine listened to every creak on every tread and waited for the Kawasaki's engine to grumble into life before crossing to the window. He tugged back the thin curtain in time to see the motorbike pull away. If Mortensen had ridden any slower, he would have toppled off the ancient machine.

Again, Kaine smiled.

"Oh dear. Some things are just too easy."

He grabbed the recorder and chuckled as he hit the stop button. Lara and the guys would probably get a kick out of the playback.

In his car outside, Kaine pressed redial on his mobile. He didn't have to wait long for the slightly sleepy answer.

"Chavasse here. Is that you, Captain?"

"Hi, Andy. Our nasty, little friend's on his way."

"You're kidding. He fell for it?"

"He's not the brightest spark in the bonfire. Frighten an idiot into thinking they're going to die, and they become ever so receptive to an alternative scenario."

"A natural, human response to fear," Andy said through a loud yawn that Kaine couldn't avoid copying.

"Can you treat him as one of your guinea pigs? I need him kept on ice for a week or so. You'll find him amenable to the most intrusive of tests. Don't suppose you have anything requiring daily rectal probes?"

Andy laughed. "I'll think of something. When can I expect him?"

"Five or six hours. You have plenty of time to go back to sleep."

"Christ, I thought you were in London? That's only a couple of hours away at this time of the morning."

"Yes," Kaine agreed, "but I thought it best to slow him down a little. Didn't want him panicking and causing a pile up on the M3."

"How on earth did you manage that? No, on second

thought, don't tell me. I'll let Mr Mortensen fill in the details when he arrives."

"It's a good story, I promise you'll enjoy it," Kaine said, still smiling. "Might go well with an audience and a bucket of popcorn. Thanks for this, Andy. I owe you one."

"No, you don't. My family and I will never be able to pay you back for what you did in Falluja."

"I did very little. Right place, right time."

"Less of the bullshit, Captain. I know what you and your team did for my little brother. He sends his regards, by the way. Or would do if he knew we were talking right now."

"How is he?"

"Doing really well. Rachel popped out another sprog last March. Their first boy after two girls. Never guess what they named him."

Kaine couldn't help rising to the bait. "Don't tell me. Andrew, right?"

The medic laughed. "That's right. Ryan Andrew Chavasse. A handsome, little chap with a really powerful pair of lungs. So, what's next for you?"

"Me?" Kaine asked, already planning his next move. "I've another house call to make, but I doubt it'll be as easy as the last one."

Or as bloodless.

Chapter Nineteen

Saturday 24th October – Early Morning

Halcyon Tower, Kensington and Chelsea, London, England

The rain had eased during the short drive from Mortensen's grotty, little squat in Camden to Alfie Lovejoy's lofty domain in Chelsea. It was almost as though the rarefied atmosphere of the palatial residences close to the river were exempt from the worst that the British weather could throw at them.

Kaine found an empty parking bay on a side street with a good view of Halcyon Tower and stretched out in the driver's seat. The Mercedes he'd liberated from the hospital car park—after pilfering the keys from a jacket in the doctor's lounge—allowed plenty of legroom. Danny would have been pleased with Kaine's selection and, even better, the "Doctor on Call" certificate displayed on the windscreen ensured nobody would question its presence in the area.

Halcyon Tower, Lovejoy's block—one of seven within easy walking distance—stretched up and disappeared into the low clouds. Twenty-two storeys, according to Mortensen, but the top few were lost to the murk. Many of the visible floors were dark, but some shot beams of light out into the darkness. No doubt, if its lights were on, Lovejoy's penthouse apartment would illuminate the sky like the beacon of a lighthouse.

He took out his mobile, dialled a number, and waited.

"Morning, boss," Danny said. He sounded tired.

"Where are you?" Kaine asked.

"Golders Green. Parked outside the sister's house. Nice gaff, too. She's doing quite well for herself. The girls are inside, tucked up in bed for the night. You want me to keep babysitting?"

"That's an affirmative. Anyone else follow them?"

"No."

"Anyone follow you?" Kaine asked, waiting for the explosion.

"Boss!" Danny snapped, clearly pissed at the implied insult to his countersurveillance skills.

"Well, you do keep banging on about how jetlagged you are."

"I'm not *that* jetlagged, boss. I'll never be *that* jetlagged." *Oh the confidence of youth.*

"That remains to be seen," Kaine said, dryly. "Hopefully, after my next meeting, we'll be one step closer to ending this and we can all get some decent shuteye."

"Your chat with the hairy biker netted good intel?"

"It did indeed."

"Where are you now?"

"In the city."

"Certain you don't need me to come hold your coat again?"

Despite the seriousness of the situation, Kaine laughed.

He'd first met Danny in a Munich dive a decade earlier. A trio of local neo-Nazis had been picking on a non-white barman and Kaine took offence. Danny and another mate, Will Stacy, offered to help, but Kaine told them he had it covered. While he made short work of the skinheads, Danny looked after Kaine's new and very expensive leather jacket. Danny and Will also made sure no one else joined in the quarrel. No one would ever consider three neo-Nazis against one SBS captain as anything other than a fair fight.

Off and on, Danny had been "holding Kaine's jacket" ever since.

"You keep watch over the girls. I'm not certain who we're facing or how big the organisation is. I'm just about to run a gentle recce. My coat's safe enough for the moment."

"Hmm," Danny muttered. "I've been involved in enough of your so-called gentle reconnaissance operations to know what's involved, boss. Why don't you hold off until we call in some of the guys from the old troop. We could get Fat Larry and Slim here by tomorrow evening and a couple of others by Monday afternoon. There isn't a man among them who'd turn you down. You know that."

"No can do. I'm still a wanted man. Anyone found working with me might end up in serious trouble."

"People like me and Uncle Cuddles, you mean?"

"True enough, but he's too smart to get caught," Kaine said and waited a beat before adding, "and you're not worth anything."

"Nice one, boss. Way to make a man feel good about himself."

Headlights raked the Merc's rear-view mirror. "Hold on a second. A car's pulling up. BMW M Series. Could be my targets."

The Beemer slowed as it drew alongside Kaine. He took a good look at the occupants. Big driver, whose head scraped the roof and right shoulder brushed the side window, and a normal-sized couple in the back. The woman, a blonde in a skimpy top, fawned over the man. He, also blond, almost seemed bored by her attention. The car turned into the underground parking beneath the tower block, and the steel shutters rolled down behind it.

"Sorry about that," Kaine said into the phone. "The targets have arrived. I'll let them settle in for a while. Where were we?"

"You were saying how expendable I was, boss."

"Was I? Oh dear, awfully bad form of me, I'm sure. But to address your point, we are spread a little thin, and I would like some added backup. Unfortunately these jokers have something planned for tomorrow and I can't wait. They might already know about the sister's place in Golders Green. I need to chat with them right away, to find out what they have in mind. Maybe I can discover who's pulling their strings and for what reason. I've contacted Uncle Cuddles and the doc. They know everything. If I suddenly drop out of contact, your kindly uncle will take over command. Understood?"

"Right you are, boss," Danny said sombrely, under-standing what Kaine meant by "drop out of contact". "Stay safe."

"Always."

Kaine powered down the mobile and tucked it into a side pocket on his Bergen—he didn't need it ringing at an inopportune moment, and he didn't want it falling into the wrong hands in the event of a disaster. He climbed out of the car, hid the Bergen in the boot, and took a moment to soak in the atmosphere.

Slow-moving traffic on the nearby Cheyne Walk drove away any possibility of silence, and the not-so-sweet fragrance of the river after heavy rainfall snaked across the distance easily enough. Rain-slicked pavements, still surprisingly well-populated with weekend revellers, showed a city that rivalled New York's famed insomnia. It suited Kaine to have plenty of noise and movement covering his tracks.

He completed two slow circuits of the tower, scouting the ground floor for alternative points of entry. He found none.

Security appeared pretty solid. The western face of the building with its service clutter of pipes and venting ducts was protected by anti-climb paint, which matched the rest of the building for colour, but acted like the dye packs attached to clothes to deter shoplifters. No way up on that side. Flush walls and smooth-facing windows offered no easy means of scaling the other elevations, at least from the lower levels. The balconies didn't start until the tenth floor, and every means of ground-floor access—main entrance, emergency exits, and lower windows—were alarmed and fitted with expensive locks that would prove difficult to pick.

Given time and the right equipment, Kaine could have broken in easily enough, but he had neither available. A parachute drop onto the roof and an abseil onto the penthouse balcony would be another option, but he didn't have easy or fast access to a helicopter. And obtaining a permit for an aerial approach in a no-fly zone might prove a tad challenging for a suspected terrorist.

Mortensen's information presented him with a fast and direct entry method, but one he'd hoped to avoid. A frontal approach exposed Kaine to risk, but he could find no viable alternative.

Kaine decided to rely on his target's complacency.

As a well-known, local hard man, Alfie Lovejoy was assured of his position in the hierarchy of the area's gangs. He'd probably consider himself one of the "untouchables". On top of that, he had a big bodyguard for protection. The man would likely be confident. Hopefully, overconfident.

Kaine would use that and was going to bet his life on it.

He returned to the Mercedes, deposited his Fairbairn-Sykes fighting knife in the hold-everything Bergen, and left his SIG, too. Each would tip Kaine's hand, and neither would make it past Tugboat's magic wand.

Modern metal detectors could identify more than just ferrous metals. They could be configured to pick up radio transmissions and other electronic bugs. Inquisitive little buggers.

Kaine had something to fall back on besides his hand-to-hand combat training. He had stealth, surprise, and hard-baked clay.

Hopefully, he had luck, too. And he'd need plenty of luck if Tugboat's abilities came even close to matching his reputation.

KAINE ALLOWED a full hour to pass, watching and waiting, before pulling on a pair of thin, leather gloves. He locked the car door—too many thieves in London to leave it unlocked and vulnerable—and headed for the building's well-lit main entrance, dropping into the character of a significantly older man. With rounded shoulders and a pigeon-toed shuffle, the camera would capture a short, thin, stooped man carrying a slight limp. A man who posed no physical threat to a local "made man" and a monster the likes of Tugboat.

He trudged up the three steps, one at a time, and rested at the spotlit porch, which was part-protected from the spitting rain by a wide, concrete awning.

The CCTV camera above the front door swivelled on its servos. Kaine assumed that someone sat at a desk on the receiving end of the circuit. He could almost feel Tugboat's eyes upon him as the camera rotated, centralising his face in the lens.

Kaine pressed the intercom button and waited. Time dragged. He pressed the button again and held it down for a count of five.

The electronics clicked. A computerised voice asked, "State your business," with all the lifelike warmth of a robot.

"Alfred Lovejoy?" Kaine asked. "I-I'm looking for Mr Lovejoy."

The pre-programmed message repeated itself.

"I'm sorry about the time, but I need to speak to Alfred Lovejoy on a … mutually beneficial matter."

The intercom clicked, fell silent, clicked again, and an angry human shouted, "Who the fuck are you? Haven't you got a watch?"

"Mr Lovejoy?"

"What of it?"

"You … you don't know me, but Barnard Mortensen told me you have a problem with one of my neighbours … the owners of the Bistro Mykonos. I … I might be able to help."

"I don't need any help. Now, fuck off."

"Please hear me out, Mr Lovejoy. My information is time sensitive."

Kaine lifted his face to the camera, his expression pleading, hopeful.

"What information?"

Kaine looked over his shoulder as though checking the area for eavesdroppers.

"Not here, it's too exposed. There are too many people about. Can I come in? What I have to say won't take long."

"Come back later. I'm busy."

"It'll be too late by then. Time sensitive, you see? I'm no threat to you, I promise." He held out his hands, showing them as empty.

The intercom clicked again. Seconds seemed to stretch into minutes.

Come on, Alfie. You have to be a little curious.

"If you're yanking my chain, you're a dead man. Take the second lift and hit the button marked PH, for the 'Penthouse Suite'."

Lovejoy's words were harsh, but coloured with smug pride.

"Thank you, Mr Lovejoy."

The door latch fizzed, and Kaine stepped into the foyer.

First line of defence breached, he entered the open lift and pressed the "PH" button.

An alarm dinged, the lift stopped, and the doors slid silently apart. The monster filled the opening. A bloody, great, big creature of Polynesian descent, his neck so thick, his shoulders seemed to run straight up to form a rounded point at the top of his boulder for a head.

Two metres tall, at least one-forty kilos—and all of it muscle, bone, and gristle—Tugboat stood with feet shoulder-width apart, glowering. Less a tugboat and more a frigate protecting the entrance to its home port.

What the bloody hell are you doing here alone, Kaine?

He'd fought big men before, but Tugboat wasn't named by accident or with irony. Kaine swallowed hard and cowered into the corner of the lift, gloved hands open and raised to his chest. Making himself a pitiful sight.

Tugboat beckoned him with curled fingers the size of courgettes. In his huge fist, the electronic wand looked like an electric toothbrush.

Kaine hesitated and looked from side to side, lower lip quivering, before stepping into the den.

Tugboat grabbed him by the shoulder, spun him around, and slammed him face first against a cream-coloured wall. Kaine whimpered and let the air explode from his lungs. The wand squealed as it passed over Kaine's body, up and down the arms, torso, legs, crotch, but found nothing. Not that there was much for a metal detector to find—not since he'd had the pins and screws removed from his forearm.

The vice-grip on Kaine's shoulder loosened. Tugboat spun him again and repeated the performance on Kaine's front.

As he'd hoped, the big goon relied on the technology and ignored the personal touch. If he'd augmented the wand with a standard pat-down, Tugboat might not have come up quite so empty-handed.

The wand spoke to Kaine, too. It told him Tugboat wasn't carrying a concealed weapon, either. The big guy shouldn't have stood so close to Kaine while waving it around so randomly. The user's manual recommended full arm's length, or it would react to a gun worn by the operator—a gun or a knife. In the trade, such a result was called "registering a false positive".

At times, untrained amateurs with flashy toys could be their own worst enemies.

Perhaps Tugboat thought he didn't need a gun to protect his boss. Or maybe his fingers were too big to work a standard trigger. Either way, it gave Kaine a slight advantage, assuming Lovejoy wasn't carrying either. Then again, why would he carry a weapon at home when he had a minder the likes of Tugboat?

During the sweep, Kaine kept his head lowered and scanned the penthouse through hooded eyes.

A large, open-plan room decorated in cool chic—white, cream, and chrome. A solid wall to Kaine's left held four, flush-fit, white doors, which probably led to the bedrooms and the amenities. The right-hand wall housed a kitchen with black granite surfaces, white cabinets, no clutter, and no signs it had ever been used to prepare food. The full-width, landscape windows above the kitchen units framed a stunning view of the river and the south bank.

In front of Kaine and directly opposite the lifts, a floor-to-ceiling glass wall faced east and boasted a view to put the penthouse firmly in the multi-million-pound bracket. It held an almost-uninterrupted panorama of London's most famous landmarks—the garishly illuminated London Eye, The Shard, and St Paul's. On a sunny day, the view might have allowed him to see into the gardens of Buckingham Palace—not that he'd want to. The royal family deserved all the privacy they could muster.

Lovejoy sat in a leather armchair side-on to the magnificent panorama. Barefoot, he wore skin-tight jeans and a snug-fitting, silk shirt. Judging from the absence of holster-shaped bulges, Kaine doubted the man was carrying.

Although there were plenty of places to hide a handgun in a room the size of a basketball court.

The young, scantily clad, blonde woman he'd seen in the back of the BMW, lay sprawled on one of two sofas, apparently asleep, possibly comatose. A glass-topped coffee table, dusted with lines of white powder, formed a centre console to the leather, three-piece suite.

Finally, a small area in the far corner contained a brushed-steel office desk, a leather swivel chair, and all the electronic trimmings necessary to run a small multi-national corporation. A huge laptop occupied the centre of the desk. Its lid stood open, and the screen backlit the office area in a pale orange glow. An impressive piece of equipment—expensive, too. Kaine guessed Lovejoy did all the typing. He doubted Tugboat's fingers could operate a standard-sized keyboard and, according to Barney Mortensen, the monster certainly wouldn't be able to use voice-activated software.

Tugboat shoved him forwards.

"Well? What are you trying to sell?" Lovejoy shouted.

Tugboat returned to his station next to the lift but maintained easy access to the room. Kaine took three halting paces forwards, giving himself plenty of space to operate when he chose to.

Second line of defence breached.

One more to go.

"Stop there. Don't come any closer with those shoes on, and you aren't invited to take them off. Well?" Lovejoy barked. "I don't have all day and neither do you."

He looked behind Kaine to the man-monster, who snorted.

Kaine took another step into the middle of the open part of the room.

Lovejoy raised a hand.

"I said, that's close enough. What you got to say for yourself?"

"This is sensitive information." Kaine pointed to the woman. "What about her?"

"Don't worry about Lady F. She's in dreamland." He wiped his nose with his fingertips and sniffed. "Loves a bit of rough and tumble, but still not totally used to the blow. Not yet anyway, but give her time."

A red mark on Lady F's cheek suggested Lovejoy's idea of a "bit of rough and tumble" might not have matched hers. Kaine bunched his gloved hands into fists. The bruise had sealed Lovejoy's fate. Kaine made a slight sideways turn to keep both men in view.

"I heard you were ... er, how can I put this? Er, *leaning* on the Constantine family. If you want, I can give them to you."

"Oh can you now?"

Lovejoy leaned back, stretched out, and put his feet on the coffee table, crossing one leg over the other at the ankle. The height of relaxation.

"I know where Mr and Mrs Constantine are right now."

Lovejoy's smile didn't falter. "So do I, you stupid, old fuckwit. They're at St Catherine's Surgical Unit. Poor, little Justina's in a real state, but Orestes is on the operating table and doesn't know what day it is."

Kaine hadn't expected that, and he allowed it to show on his face.

Lovejoy's feet slapped to the floor, and he sat up straight, hands resting on his thighs. "Think I don't know a setup when I see one? There's no way Barney Mortensen gave up my name to a stranger unless they forced it out of him. I only let you up here to find out who you were and what you wanted. We could tell you were alone from the moment you stepped into the lights at the entrance."

He looked at Tugboat, and the smile morphed into a sneer. "Get to work, Tuggy. Don't make too much of a mess, and make sure he can still talk when you're finished."

Tuggy? How affectionate.

Kaine shook the tension from his hands. He'd seen it coming, but not quite so quickly.

The sneering Māori danced forwards, light on his feet for such a massive lump of inhumanity.

Lovejoy laughed and rubbed his hands together.

"Looking forward to this. Better than watching cage fighting on the TV. Much more realistic."

Lovejoy had just called Kaine a fuckwit. Maybe the smiling, blond gangster's assessment hadn't been too far off.

How much would Kaine give for Danny's coat-holding right about now?

Chapter Twenty

Saturday 24th October —Early Morning

Halcyon Tower, Kensington and Chelsea, London, England

Kaine backpedalled until he bumped into the wall with all the doors.

So much for plenty of room to manoeuvre.

Tugboat stopped three metres in front of him. He threw a few air shots to loosen his shoulders, bending and twisting at the waist to increase his reach. The big man's fists whistled through the air in a blur and snapped with a final twist at the end of the punch. Kaine felt the pressure of the air moving in front of his face. Tugboat knew how to throw a punch, that much was clear.

If one of the blows ever connected ... game over.

Kaine raised his hands, fingers open and relaxed. Huge men could be powerful, but slow. He watched Tugboat's movements. Studied their timing and direction, looking for the giant's pivot point and range of balance. His rear heel stayed anchored to the floor. A minor weakness, but a weakness, nonetheless.

No doubt, Kaine had speed and experience over Tugboat, but the old boxing adage cut through his thoughts, "a good big man always beats a good small man".

Being good wasn't enough. Kaine had to be better, faster, more decisive.

With powerful shoulder muscles bunched, Tugboat danced forwards and popped out a lightning left jab. Kaine ducked. The massive fist brushed the top of his head and smashed through the plasterboard wall behind, trapping the fist.

Bent at the waist, Kaine drove a right uppercut into the giant's groin and ducked left in time to avoid a knee to the face. Kaine's punch hit its target flush on, crushing the soft tissue. Most normal men with normal testicles would have gone down under such a blow, but Tugboat barely grunted. He shook his head, yanked his forearm from the hole in the wall, and swivelled to face Kaine.

Behind them, still lounging in his chair, Alfie cackled.

"Low blow! Low blow. I ought to disqualify you for ungentlemanly conduct. It won't do you any good, though. Tugboat doesn't have any bollocks on account of a boyhood accident. He's what you might call a eunuch. He doesn't like me talking about it, but you're not going to be around to tell anyone. Boy, are you in big trouble now. He's likely to tear your head off. Aren't you, Tuggy?"

The giant Māori's mouth snapped shut. He grunted again and kept moving forwards.

Kaine danced backwards and circled to the left.

Move, keep clear, wait for the opening.

If he didn't stay out of range of the forceful left jab, or the piledriver right, the fight wouldn't last long.

Kaine dipped inside another clubbing blow and threw a flurry of punches—a double left jab followed by a right cross—but the Māori took them well, barely pausing in his forwards momentum.

Tugboat sneered and shook his head as if to say, "That all you got, little man?"

It wasn't, but Kaine had to put on a bit of a show. He needed to close the gap between himself and Lovejoy. He had to lull the blond man into not going for a hidden weapon, keeping him as a spectator not a participant.

Panting hard for effect and maintaining his distance from the giant, Kaine lowered his arms, relaxed his hands, and shook them out. He raised his fists again and bent into a boxer's crouch, keeping one eye on Tugboat, the other on Lovejoy.

Tugboat stood still and beckoned Kaine with his courgette fingers. An invite he had no intention of accepting.

"Doesn't say much does he," Kaine said, jinking to the right and faking a left jab, before sliding right again and stepping further back.

Nearly close enough. One more shimmy.

Tugboat matched Kaine's movement, teeth bared in a smile.

"Ha," Alfie said, "Tuggy's what's called a 'selective mute'. He can speak, but chooses not to most of the time. Weird, eh? Works for him, though. Helps him concentrate

216

because he doesn't have any distractions. He spends most of his spare time in the gym throwing weights around."

"I can see that," Kaine said, panting and ducking inside a swinging, roundhouse left.

Without thinking, Kaine snapped out a left uppercut. The blow landed hard, mashing Tugboat's ulnar nerve into his elbow.

The big man grunted, shook his head, and took his first backwards step.

No. Too early. Too bloody early.

Lovejoy was still too far away. Well beyond Kaine's reach.

Tugboat stared at his elbow. A questioning frown formed on his tattooed face. He clenched and unclenched his fist, trying to regain some sensation.

Kaine's elbow strike would have paralysed a normal arm, but Tugboat shook off the blow in seconds.

Fast recovery. Very fast.

It would only take one slip for things to deteriorate, and Kaine would be in real trouble.

Stop toying with him, Kaine.

Tugboat shook his arm and howled. He lurched into an attack, arms outstretched, attempting to lock Kaine into a bear hug. Kaine ducked underneath the encircling arms and threw a rabbit punch to the kidney. His fist landed on granite.

Tugboat screamed again and stumbled before righting himself. He turned slowly, his eyes narrowed, his expression pained. The kidney punch had ignited the monster's pain receptors. Rage blazed behind the big man's dark eyes.

Kaine sucked in more air, panting for real this time. Sweat dripped down his hairline and stung his eyes. He blinked rapidly to clear the blurring vision.

Lovejoy continued his taunting, seemingly unaware of the damage suffered by his pet.

"He used to box all the time, but we can't find any sparring partners. They're all terrified. No one will step in the ring with him. Everyone reckons he's too dangerous, but he's a pussycat, really. Aren't you, Tuggy. What do you think, old man?"

Tugboat dipped his right hip, lunged, threw another left jab, and followed it with a right cross. Kaine twisted at the waist, parried the jab, but let the second shot strike him a glancing blow to the top of the head. He grunted, buckled at the knees, and waved his hands in front of his eyes as though suffering with blurred vision.

"Ha!" Lovejoy cackled. "Has Big Ben started ringing early, you old bastard?"

Okay, finish this, Kaine. Finish it now.

Kaine dropped his guard and staggered backwards, moving ever closer to Lovejoy. His right heel struck the leg of the coffee table. He fell backwards and landed on the tiled floor in a crumpled heap, keeping his hands close to his ankles.

Tugboat raised both arms and bayed in victory.

Alfie cheered.

"Kill him, Tuggy. Snap his fucking neck. I've seen enough. Can't be arsed to question him after all. Kill the bastard for me, Tuggy."

The monster took one pace forwards but stopped mid-stride, his howl of triumph cut short, eyes and mouth opened wide in shock. He looked down. The handle of Kaine's ceramic throwing knife stuck out of his chest, between sternum and left nipple. No blood. No signs of injury. Just the jutting handle of the knife.

Tugboat staggered forwards, fingers scrambling for the knife.

From the floor, Kaine kicked out. The heel of his boot hit the giant's standing leg, crushing the kneecap. Blood gurgled in Tugboat's throat. He toppled headlong and face-planted onto the tile floor, driving the knife deeper into his chest. He lay still. Blood flowed, slowly spreading across the nice, warm tiles.

Lovejoy's cackle stopped as quickly as Tugboat's howl. Shock registered on his tanned face, and he watched the pumping blood reach out to him across the white tiles.

For a brief moment, time stopped. Nothing moved but the flowing pool of red on white. It reminded Kaine of Orestes Constantine's blood spreading out over the starched, cotton tablecloth.

Lovejoy's scream broke the short spell. He jerked out of his chair and scrambled towards the office area.

Kaine shot out a foot and kicked the glass-topped coffee table. It tripped Lovejoy, who tumbled to the floor. He tried to stand, but his hands slipped on the blood. He fell again, sprawling face down on the floor.

Kaine planted his hands on the tiles on either side of his head, "kipped up" onto his feet, and used the forwards momentum to carry him into a flat-out dive. As he landed, he drove the point of his elbow into the small of Lovejoy's back.

Lumbar vertebrae crunched.

Lovejoy screamed. Stopped moving.

Kaine scrambled away from the bodies, alive for any signs of danger. There were none.

He climbed to his feet and leaned against the balcony door, breathing hard, waiting for his body to recover and the shaking to stop.

Kaine wiped the sweat from his face with a jacket sleeve and tried to still his trembling hands, but adrenaline still surged through his system, speeding his heartrate, driving blood to muscles hungry for oxygen.

Adrenaline, part of the human "fight or flight" response, had saved him again. Most people didn't know how to use it, but, to a trained fighter, controlling the adrenaline response made the difference between success and failure—the difference between life and death.

Close, Kaine. Too damn close.

As a rule of thumb, Kaine didn't care much for the "flight" part of the equation, but perhaps he needed to rethink his rule. This time, he'd cut it fine. He'd come close to losing—much closer than he expected. Maybe he should learn caution. Maybe he should learn to accept the help offered by his cobbled-together team of specialists. He owed Danny an apology. Next time, he'd listen. He was getting too old to take on youngsters in unarmed combat.

Far too bloody old, Kaine. Idiot.

Lovejoy groaned.

Kaine straightened, pulled back his shoulders, and closed the gap between him and the human-shaped rubbish dump on the floor.

"Still alive, young fella? Good. You and I'll need to talk in a moment. Just let me get my breath back. Your dead mate was almost as tough as he looked."

Lovejoy groaned again, this time louder. His fingers scratched at the tiles, but nothing else moved except his mouth and eyes.

Kaine wasn't worried. Judging by the bruise developing on his elbow from when he crippled the pathetic lump, Lovejoy wasn't going anywhere, not of his own volition. He doubted the man would ever walk again. The bastard wouldn't be commissioning attacks on families, or hitting defenceless women, either.

Three deep breaths, in through the nose, out through the mouth, lowered Kaine's heartrate and paid back some of the oxygen debt he'd generated during the fight. His stomach calmed and the shakes melted away.

Thinking of defenceless women, the young blonde on the couch hadn't moved since his arrival. Keeping his eyes on Lovejoy in case he'd misdiagnosed the severity of the spinal injury, he pushed away from the wall. Steering a wide path to avoid the spreading pool of claret, he stepped around the bodies and crossed towards the north-facing wall and the leather suite.

The young woman, Lady F, lay still. Unnaturally still.

Crap.

Kaine placed two fingers on the side of her neck and found a steady beat, slow but strong. He made sure her airway was open and relaxed a little.

"Now then, Alfie," he called out. "Why were you in such a hurry to reach your office?"

Before searching the desk, he removed the leather gloves and replaced them with a more practical, latex pair—no point making it easy for the crime scene investigators.

In a bottom drawer, he found a loaded Ruger 9mm and two spare, seven-round magazines.

"That's interesting, Alfie, what else am I going to find?"

He carried out a quick-and-dirty search of the apartment and found two other weapons in interesting places. Once he'd finished, he rolled Tugboat onto his back—no easy task considering the man's bulk and while trying to avoid treading in the small lake of blood. He dug his knife out of the big guy's chest and washed it with bleach in the kitchen sink before returning it to its ankle sheath.

From a block in the kitchen, Kaine took a carving knife and wrapped Alfie's fingers around the handle before planting it into Tugboat's wound. Its blade was wider and longer than Kaine's throwing knife. The ploy probably wouldn't fool a half-decent pathologist, but if the police used an overworked or inferior one, it just might pass muster. It would certainly add confusion to the issue.

To screw with the immediate crime scene a little more, and to sell the idea that Lovejoy stabbed Tugboat, he pushed an unresisting but still groaning Lovejoy further into the puddle and squirmed him around a little.

"Pity about your nice, silk shirt, Alfie, but needs must, old chap. Send me the cleaning bill—I'll leave my address with the doorman."

He stood back and examined the scene with as much of a forensic eye as he could manage.

Jagged hole in the wall. Disturbed coffee table. Two men, possibly a couple. One dead, the other close to it. Lovejoy's prints on the handle of the apparent murder weapon. Bruising to his face where he'd hit the floor. Broken back where Tugboat landed a final blow before succumbing to the work of the blade.

It might pass as a lover's tiff taken to extremes. Alternatively, the white powder on the glass coffee table offered an alternative "drug deal gone wrong" scenario.

Of course, Lovejoy would tell a different story, but would the tale of a scrawny, old man getting the better of poor, defenceless Tugboat sound any more realistic?

With the scene set, he searched the room more thoroughly, starting with the office.

The laptop on the table proved interesting, and its two-factor security—password and thumbprint—didn't provide any sort of a challenge. He found the password written in long-hand on a card taped to the underside of a desk drawer—a pathetic breach of security and one that Sabrina would have justifiably screamed at Kaine for employing. The thumbprint he obtained from Lovejoy, not that he was in any condition to refuse permission. The laptop, being more portable than Love-joy, made the job easy, although Kaine did have to wipe the suffering man's thumb clean of blood to make the reader work.

Stealing the laptop would have been one way of doing things, but he didn't want to give the police any more reasons to suspect outside involvement. Fortunately, he found an empty external hard drive in the same drawer as he located the password. He plugged it into a USB port and set the system to copy the entire hard drive.

"Lovejoy," he called again, "thanks ever so much, old chap. You've made my job a hell of a lot easier. If you don't mind, I'll look through the files later. No doubt you'll have all your bank details on file, and here's little, old me, maxing out on expenses. You don't mind if I borrow some of your money, do you?" He waited for a negative response. "No? Excellent. Thanks millions, old chap. I've been digging deep into my savings recently and your generosity will help me take care of business."

Kaine stretched his arms over his head and yawned.

"There's an awful lot of data on your hard drive, though. It means I'll have to hang around for a while. Don't mind a little company, do you?"

Still no response.

"Excellent. You're being extremely hospitable. Thanks ever so much."

Kaine stood and looked down at the sorry pair, but felt no regret, no pity.

Given the chance, Lovejoy would have killed Kaine, the Constantine family, and anyone else who stood in his way.

No, Kaine had no room for regret. That particular cupboard was already full to overflowing.

Next, he turned his attention to searching the rest of the apartment. The hub for the surveillance system featured high on his wish list.

Chapter Twenty-One

Saturday 24th October – Early Morning

Halcyon Tower, Kensington and Chelsea, London, England

Kaine prodded the young woman's shoulder with his gloved index finger. She stirred and swatted his hand away. He poked again.

"Leave me alone," she moaned, her words slurred.

As she rolled onto her side, her left breast popped out of the strapless top. Kaine averted his eyes.

"Cover yourself, young lady."

"Huh?"

She woke more fully, looked down through bleary eyes, chuckled, and pushed herself into a seated position, slumped forwards, elbows resting on her thighs.

"Like them?" she asked, dropped the other side of the bodice, and jiggled both breasts at him. "Big aren't they? Firm, too. Wanna check them out?"

Seriously?

He stifled a yawn—boredom mixed with long-term fatigue and the after-effects of the fight.

"They'll be down around your knees in twenty years."

She jiggled her assets once more.

"Oh no, not these girls. Daddy bought them for me ahead of my coming-of-age party. Guaranteed not to sag or Daddy's going to pay someone to kneecap the surgeon." She chuckled again, arched her back, and squeezed the "girls" together with her upper arms. "Nice, aren't they?"

"Put them away, child. I'm not impressed by a couple of silicone sacks."

The girl pouted and stuffed the overlarge implants back inside the heavily stressed top.

"Duh. They don't use silicone anymore. Too dangerous. These girls are filled with saline. Don't you know anything?"

Lord above, save me from airheads.

"Name?"

"Excuse me?"

"What is your name, dear?" he asked slowly, enunciating each word clearly.

She scrubbed her face with both hands, winced when she found the bruise, and looked at him through heavy lids and false eyelashes.

"If you must know, I'm Lady Fenella Penelope Jessica Banner-Hardy. Some people call me Lady F, or Fen, if you prefer."

He hiked an eyebrow. "Fen it is. I'm not much into titles unless they've been earned."

"What's in a title?" she shrugged and nearly unloaded the implants again.

"Precisely."

She rocked forwards, trying to stand, but fell back into the leather sofa. A deep frown creased her high forehead, and her vacant, blue eyes finally found focus on the mess behind Kaine.

"Why are Alfie and Tugboat on the floor? Too much powder?" She sneered. "And he calls *me* a lightweight."

"They annoyed me. Keep asking stupid questions and you'll join them."

She waggled her fingers at him. "Oooh, listen to Mr Tough Guy."

The girl tried standing again. This time she made it to her feet, but staggered sideways. She threw out her hands and leaned on the arm of Alfie's chair. The sky-high youngster stared past Kaine once again and discovered a better view of the mess on the floor. Her eyes widened and her face turned pale. One hand pressed against her belly, the other flew up to cover her mouth, and she dashed to the kitchen. She made it just in time to vomit into the sink.

"Good catch," Kaine said, impressed by the turn of speed in a woman previously so unsteady on her feet. And in six-inch heels, no less.

She ran the cold tap, testing the temperature with a finger. When it was to her liking, she held back her hair and took a mouthful of London's finest, oily sludge. She swilled it around her mouth and spat it out. After another mouthful —this one swallowed—she turned to face him, leaning her backside heavily against the surface and gripping the marble edge with both hands. The livid bruise on her cheek stood out clear against her pale skin.

"How's you cheek?" he asked.

She frowned. "Huh?"

"Someone hit you."

Kaine indicated the location of her bruise by pointing to the relevant spot on his face.

She turned and studied her reflection in the window above the sink, but dismissed his concern with a wave of her hand.

"It's nothing," she said, facing him again. "Not that much swelling. We went a little heavy on the foreplay tonight. A liberal dab of foundation will hide it from Daddy. Alfie and I sometimes get carried away, but I give as good as I take." She raised her hands and mimed scratching the air with red-and-glitter-painted nails standing in as claws. "If you remove Alfie's shirt, you'll see the damage these babies can do to a man's back."

Yet another giggle grated on Kaine's nerves. He was starting to think the girl's fondness for recreational drugs might have done some permanent damage. Beautiful, without a doubt, but seriously flawed unless she was putting on a bloody good act.

He sighed. "You paint a charming picture, Fen."

"Are they ... dead?" she asked, her voice growing firmer and more steady with each passing moment.

"Tugboat won't see another sunrise, but Alfie's still breathing."

"You did that?"

"Who ... little, old me?" he said, pulling in his chin and adding an expression he hoped passed for astonishment. "Do I look as though I'm capable of causing damage to so huge a man? Oh no. Dear me, no. I mean, look at the size of him."

"Of course not, but you said ..." She scrunched up her

face, a question taking its time to form in her coke-addled brain. "What was it you said?"

"When? I've said a lot of things in my life."

She sniffed and shook her head in annoyance. "Can't remember. It'll come to me. By the way, who are you and what are you doing here?"

Kaine gave her a stiff bow and clicked his heels together. "Major Alan Bingham Carstairs, OBE, formerly of Her Majesty's Coldstream Guards. At your service, ma'am. Happen to be house-sitting downstairs for a … friend who's away on business with the Foreign Office. I heard a commotion up here. Sounded like an old, married couple arguing." He smiled vacantly. "Anyhow, I rushed up the stairs. Found the door wide open, and there they were, on the floor, like that. You were over on the couch, and … exposed."

She stared at him, slack-mouthed through the whole fabrication, nodding occasionally.

"They did it to themselves?"

"It rather looks that way, don't you think?"

She frowned. "Why?"

"Who knows? A lover's tiff perhaps?"

Kaine made a point to keep up the forced, "old soldier" vibe, and she seemed to be falling for it.

"Okay, but why's Alfie making that horrid moaning sound?"

"I rather expect it's because he's in a certain amount of discomfort."

Hardly surprising with at least one crushed lumbar vertebra, and it couldn't have happened to a more deserving arsehole.

Kaine glanced at his watch. Time was a-flying, but the file transfer was still running and, short of tying her up and locking her in one of the bedrooms, he had no idea what to do with the idiot woman-child.

"Should I call an ambulance? My phone's in my handbag."

Finally, a decent, human reaction from the empty-headed one.

"Don't worry about that. I'll call them after I've helped put you into a taxi.

Fen frowned. "Hang on a minute, that's a bit harsh, isn't it? I hate seeing anyone suffer. Even if he is only Alfie."

Kaine nodded—she did have a point.

"Before calling, I need some information. I'm going to ask Lovejoy a few questions."

"What are you going to ask him?"

"A number of things. The name of the man he's working for will do for a start."

She frowned and tilted her head to one side. Kaine suspected that confusion would be her default expression.

"That's silly. Why do you need to know that to call for an ambulance?"

Kaine leaned forwards at the waist and put a finger to his lips. "Between you and me, his boss will want to know what's happened to a valued employee. Don't you think?"

"Alfie valued?" she scoffed. "What makes you think he's valued?"

"Well, isn't that obvious? This apartment is worth a fortune. Lovejoy has to be making big money. That would make him someone's valued employee, wouldn't it?"

She peeled a hand from the granite worktop and fluttered it in the air. "But this is Daddy's flat."

"Daddy's, is it? I thought it belonged to Lovejoy."

Fen snorted, pinched her nose, and ripped a square of kitchen towel from a holder on the wall.

"Don't be silly," she said and blew hard. She stared at

Kaine while crushing the towel, opening a door, and dropping it into the exposed bin. "Alfie couldn't afford anything like this. Daddy owns this whole building. Alfie was just looking after the place for him. He's live-in security, y'know. And anyway"—she pointed at Kaine, and her fancy nail varnish sparkled under the lights—"who *are* you again?"

"I told you, dear. I'm Carstairs. So, Lovejoy works for your father?"

"Yes. He's something to do with ... oh dear, I've forgotten for the moment." Her frown deepened as the brain cells tried to coalesce, and her mouth twisted before the answer popped out as, "Security? ... Protection? No, that's a different one of Daddy's staff. Darn." She hit the side of her head with the meat of her hand. "So frustrating. My mind's a bloody sieve these days, I need some more ... some more medicine." She glanced longingly at the coffee table. "Oh, I have it. Alfie deals with property clearance and contract issues. Yes, that's right. Property clearance."

Pleased with herself, the idiot girl smiled and eased away from the kitchen surface.

Kaine threw a look at the creature writhing on the floor. With Fen apparently happy to divulge the information he wanted, perhaps an extended and unpleasant interrogation —unpleasant for Alfie Lovejoy—would be unnecessary.

"Let me get this straight, Lovejoy works for your father."

"Yes. Has done for the past four or five years."

"And your father is?"

"You don't know?" she asked in a stunned manner that suggested everyone in the country would know who her father would be.

"If I knew that, I wouldn't be asking."

"Daddy is Sir Brandon Banner-Hardy, of course."

"Ah, I see," Kaine said, shrugging.

"The millionaire construction magnate."

"Yes. I have heard of him. Vaguely."

"Of course you have. Everyone's heard of Daddy. Most people have heard of me, too."

"I haven't."

I don't follow the gossip columns.

Fen tottered back to the sofa, where she picked up her clutch bag and rummaged through it for a moment. Kaine looked on with interest when her hand came out empty.

"Looking for this?"

He held up the Ruger Mark IV 22/45 Lite he'd removed from the bag while she was still away with the fairies.

Fen lowered her head. "No. Thought I still had some ciggies left, but can't find the packet. Must have finished them after we left the club. As I already said, my memory's pretty scatty these days."

He stuffed the small pistol back into his pocket.

"Hardly an essential piece of costume jewellery for the modern girl-about-town. You know there's a minimum five-year prison sentence just for carrying one of these without a permit?"

She snorted again, but this time, she didn't need to reach for a kitchen towel. "Of course I have a permit. Daddy knows a man who knows a number of men high up in the police force. And as for costume jewellery, that's a little sexist, isn't it?"

"I suppose it must be." Kaine gave her a little half-bow. "You have my abject apologies."

"Accepted. And don't worry, I know how to use it. Attended my first hunting party at the age of eleven. 'Blooded' on my first day out with the adults. Bagged a twelve-point stag, I did. Daddy was most impressed. Proud of me, y'know."

She sighed.

"Daddy never leaves home without his gun, and he absolutely insists I carry one for protection. Says he deals with lots of nasty people in his line of work, and if I want to live without a permanent bodyguard, I have to take one with me at all times. Hate the wanking thing, but I've had special lessons on the shooting range. Like I said, I know how to use it."

"Do you, indeed?"

She dropped the bag on the coffee table and folded her arms. "So, can we go now please? This place is starting to smell bad."

Movement in Kaine's peripheral vision made him snap-turn and reach for Lovejoy's Ruger 9mm. He relaxed when his eyes found Lovejoy. The pitiful creature had managed to lift his chin from the floor. He stretched an arm out towards Fen and whispered, "Help ... please, help me."

His head dropped back onto the tiles, and he sobbed quietly.

She looked from Lovejoy to Kaine, her flippant attitude replaced by one of genuine concern and real tears.

"Call an ambulance. Please. Look at him, he's in terrible pain."

Kaine sighed. "I've seen injuries like that before. I'm afraid he'll have to get used to pain, and to wheelchairs, and to peeing into a plastic bag."

Fen's chin trembled. "Why are you being so horrid? Does he owe you money?"

"No, *not me*," Kaine said. He paused for a moment, shook his head, and continued with, "It serves him right for upsetting the wrong people."

"What?" she asked. "What did you say?"

"Never mind, lass. Come, let me help you find a taxi."

Kaine held out his hand and, despite a sideways glance at Lovejoy, she took a tight hold. He helped her to her feet and walked her past the human detritus.

Lovejoy—lying on his front, cheek pressed into the tiles, legs splayed, feet pigeon-toed—had lost control of both his bladder and his bowels. The stench of urine and faeces mixed with Tugboat's rapidly drying blood was already beginning to ripen thanks to the modern wonder of under-floor heating. Kaine could almost imagine a dark miasma wafting up from the bodies.

"But Mr Carstairs, aren't you going to call him an ambulance?"

Kaine frowned and tilted his head.

"Okay, if you insist." He pointed at the squirming man on the floor, said, "Alfie Lovejoy, you are an ambulance," and dragged her away. "Come on. We're off."

Her jaw dropped. "That's horrible. Are you serious? We can't leave him like that!"

"No, just kidding," Kaine said. "Always did like that joke, but the nearest hospital is only a few minutes away. It shouldn't take an ambulance long to get here this time of the morning. Your father wouldn't be pleased to see you on the news being led away as a witness to murder. Worse still, a suspect. You need to leave here and forget you ever saw me—for your own good, of course, not mine. No, we'll get you to safety first. As I said earlier, I'll call 9-9-9 the moment you're in a taxi. Then I'll wait for the police. Make a state-ment, y'know. Do you have a coat?"

"Of course."

Kaine waited, but she wasn't getting the message. He pushed his head towards her. "Go find it then!"

She blinked and shook some of the less sticky cobwebs from her head. "Yes, yes. Right. Of course."

While she headed to a door beside the lift which opened into a walk-in cupboard, Kaine returned to the desk. The transfer had completed. He stuffed the external hard drive into his jacket pocket and turned to find Fen carrying a heavy, full-length, woollen overcoat.

Kaine helped her into it, and she held out her hand.

"Can I have my little gun back, please?"

Not a chance in the world.

He almost laughed at her audacity.

"I'll send it to you next time I pass a post office."

"You don't know where I live."

"Don't worry about that. I'll find you."

She took Kaine's hand and he half-led, half-dragged her to the lift. A button-press later, the doors closed on the carnage, and on Alfie Lovejoy's pitiful whimpering.

Chapter Twenty-Two

Saturday 24th October – Brandon Banner-Hardy

Banner-Hardy House, Hampstead Heath, London, England

Sir Brandon "BB" Banner-Hardy jumped to his feet.

"You stupid, little bitch!" he screamed.

He raised his hand, preparing to strike.

Fenella cowered away, covered her face with her hands.

"Daddy! No! Please."

BB breathed deep. Relented. He controlled his urge to launch a backhanded slap to his idiot daughter—but only just.

"How many times do I have to tell you to stay away from Lovejoy and stay off the drugs?" he bawled. Breathing hard, he lowered his arm and stepped away from the trembling child.

"I-I'm sorry, Daddy. I-I'm so sorry," she said, lower lip trembling and tears brimming.

She'd used the same tactics since she'd been old enough to work out how to manipulate him, but this time, it wouldn't work. By God, it wouldn't. She'd involved herself in a killing, for fuck's sake. Indirectly involved BB, too.

Stupid, stupid, stupid.

"What happened?" he demanded, lowering his voice and turning it into a growl.

"I-I don't know."

"What d'you mean, you don't know? You were there, child. You were right bloody there!"

Again the lower lip trembled. The tears finally fell.

"I-I fell asleep. Wh-When I woke, Alfie and Tugboat were lying on the floor in a pool of blood, and this man was standing over me."

BB frowned. Brutus hadn't said anything about a man being in the penthouse. Neither had the police.

"A man? What man?"

She shrugged and shook her head.

"I-I don't know, Daddy. A scary man. I'd never seen him before."

"What was this 'scary man' doing?"

"Nothing. He was just standing there, looking down at me." She lowered her head, blinked the tears away, and sniffled.

BB took a moment. Breathed deep and slow. In this situation, bullying wouldn't work. Ranting and raving never worked on Fenella. She'd just clam up. BB changed tactic. He smiled. Edged forwards. Took her gently by the arm and led her to the sofa. He eased her down and sat beside her, leaving a slight gap between them.

BB allowed the silence to stretch out until the crying had subsided.

"Would you like a drink?" he asked. "Tea? Coffee?"

If Fenella didn't, BB certainly did.

"C-Coffee please."

"Okay. Good idea."

He reached across to the occasional table, picked up the remote, and pressed the button for the maid.

She had two minutes to arrive or face his wrath. After what he'd been through so far that day, he needed to vent on someone, and Fenella wouldn't do.

Fenella took a tissue from somewhere and blew her newly sculpted nose.

"Daddy?" she said, looking up at him through plucked and hooded brows. Fear showed in her blue eyes. Her mother's eyes. The dead bitch.

"Yes, love?"

"H-How did you know I'd been at the ... the penthouse?"

BB hesitated, trying to decide the value of owning up.

Shit.

Telling her the truth wouldn't matter. This latest escapade had already sealed her immediate fate.

"There's a tracker app on you mobile."

BB waited for fireworks, but they never erupted. Perhaps she knew what he had in store for her and was prepping herself for the imminent banishment.

"Oh," she said, simply.

"I had it installed a couple of weeks ago, after your last balls-up," he confessed. "It was for your own good. I wanted to protect you from yourself."

She nodded and they lapsed into silence again. He'd wait for the coffee before resuming a more gentle interrogation.

After a light rap on the door, it opened, and the maid stepped into the room in her French maid's outfit Penelope had designed on BB's instructions. This was the good-looking one who hadn't been on the staff long. The one who'd piqued BB's interest, and would be the next target of his advances. Lucky for her, she'd made it with seventeen seconds to spare. He'd timed her by the clock on the mantlepiece. The clock that had been in the family for centuries.

The maid, whose name BB had yet to commit to memory, curtsied and said, "You rang, Sir Brandon?" Her Scouse accent was the only flaw he could make out on an otherwise-decent package. Still, it was an improvement on the last one, whose piercing, Welsh voice could have shattered glass crystal. Whoever said the Welsh were all musical hadn't heard that one speak.

"Two coffees," he ordered.

"Yes, sir."

She curtsied again, crossed to the breakfast table, and poured two coffees from the electrically heated carafe. She added cream to each, two spoons of sugar to Fenella's, and carried them on a tray to the occasional table at BB's side.

It would have been much quicker to serve himself, but why keep dogs only to bark yourself? Besides, the delay had given him time to recover his poise after the shock of the news. It had been years since he'd been so close to hitting Fenella, and he needed to regain some sort of composure.

"Will that be all, Sir Brandon?" the Scouse maid asked.

"For the moment. Tell Brutus he can come in again."

An emotion flickered in the maid's eyes. Fear? Disgust?

Both? It didn't matter what. BB didn't give a stuff for the house staff's reaction to the Georgian. Brutus Novikov was BB's minder. His personal rottweiler. The house staff either put up with him, or they buggered off. Without another word, the maid turned and left, closing the door behind her.

"Brutus?" Fenella asked. "Why Brutus." Fear cracked her voice.

"You know why."

"H-He scares me."

Good.

That was the way BB liked it.

Fenella reached out for her coffee. The cup rattled in its saucer. She lifted the cup by its handle, sipped.

No longer thirsty, BB left his drink on the table, untouched.

Seconds later, the door opened again. Brutus, who'd been stationed outside in the hallway, entered and stood, hands clasped in front. He kept back from the table to avoid intimidating Fenella too much. Silent. Brooding. The dark man exuded menace. A magnificent beast.

Her cup and saucer still rattling, Fenella lowered them back to the table.

"Yes, sir?" Brutus said, his voice deep, rasping.

BB turned to face his trembling daughter.

"Now, let's get back to the man you woke up to at the penthouse," he said gently. "Can you describe him to Brutus for me?"

Fenella shuddered. Closed her eyes, refusing to look at the shaven-headed, dark-eyed minder.

"I-I can't really remember. He wasn't anything special."

"Age?" Brutus asked.

"Really old. At least forty-five. Maybe even fifty. Slicked back hair and a beard."

"Tall? Short? Muscular?" Brutus asked, a man of few words.

"A little taller than me. Slim. Stoop shouldered. H-He walked with a slight limp."

"How dressed?"

"Dark jacket and jeans, I think," she answered, shaking her head, which she kept lowered, refusing to raise her eyes to meet Brutus' scowl. "I'm not sure. It's a bit fuzzy. I-I was a little ... wasted."

Of course you were, fool.

"What sort of accent did he have?" BB asked, taking his turn.

"Posh," Fenella answered, crushing the tissue in her hands. "Like one of us. An army man, I think. An officer."

"How do you know that?" BB snapped, sensing a break-through.

She glanced up at Brutus and turned towards BB. Her eyes widened in surprise.

"I-I remember. I remember. He told me his name." She frowned and tapped the side of her head, as if trying to unlock the elusive memory. "It was ... Major ... something."

BB edged closer.

"Go on, Fenella."

He reached for her hand. Squeezed gently.

"Major Carruthers ... No, Carstairs. Major Alan Carstairs." She smiled in delight and relief. "He ... He said he was staying in the downstairs apartment. Housesitting for a friend."

"Is that all?"

"He had a funny sense of humour."

"Funny?"

She nodded.

"In what way?"

"I don't know. Weird. He said Alfie was an ambulance and then … and when I asked him why he was being so horrible to Alfie … he said … Oh dear, what did he say?"

"Try, Fenella. Try to remember."

She closed her eyes for a second then opened them again. "It was something like, Alfie shouldn't have upset the wrong people."

BB turned to Brutus, who nodded. They'd both heard enough.

"Thank you, darling," BB said. "That's all we need."

Fenella swallowed.

"Did I do well?" she asked, giving him an eager smile, desperate to please.

"Yes, Fenella," BB soothed, stroking her hand. "You did very well."

"Good. I'm glad." She sighed and finally caught BB's eye. "I suppose you're sending me to the clinic again?"

"Yes, darling. The ambulance is on the way."

Her smile dimmed and her chin dimpled.

"It's for the best, darling. You need to stay out of sight for a little while. You know that, right?"

"I know," she said, resigned to her fate. "How long for this time?"

"Long enough for you to dry out and for all this to blow over. A few weeks. Maybe a couple of months. The media fuss will have died down by then. You understand? I'm doing this to protect you. Because I love you."

Fenella gave him a sad, vacant smile and dipped her head. "I know, Daddy. I know."

"I'll visit you often."

"Promise?"

"Yes," he lied. "I promise."

BB had no intention of setting foot in the bloody clinic. After Penelope and now Fenella, the Maidstone Clinic had swallowed up more than enough of his time. Bloody place gave him the willies.

"Should I go and pack now?" Fenella asked.

BB nodded and added an encouraging smile.

"That's a good idea, darling. Go and make sure Margaret hasn't forgotten anything."

"Yes, Daddy. I will."

Head still bowed, she rose, skirted around Brutus, and hurried from the room, meek as a kitten.

BB sighed. That was so much easier than he'd expected. No screaming. No wailing. No gnashing of teeth. Nothing but acquiescence. Waking up to a dead Tugboat lying in a puddle of his own blood and a crippled Lovejoy—BB had almost gagged at the crime scene photos—had scorched all the fight out of her.

BB waited for Fenella to close the door before speaking.

"Any idea how Carstairs could have gained access to the penthouse?" BB asked.

"No," Brutus answered, his voice deep and low. "Surveillance cameras not working."

Bugger!

"Did the doctors tell you when we could talk to Lovejoy?"

"No. They keep him isolated. Waiting for swelling to go down before they operate."

BB closed his eyes to fight the migraine that had been growing since he'd received the call from the police. He pressed the heels of his fists into his eyeballs, but it didn't do any good. He groaned, opened his eyes, and stared up at his personal bodyguard.

"Well?" he said. "What d'you think?"

Brutus did the thing with his head that BB took as a nod, but it could have been a shrug. He didn't seem able to bend his tree trunk of a neck all that easily.

"Lovejoy upset wrong people," Brutus suggested.

"Drug dealers?"

Another nod-shrug.

"He bought coke from somewhere. Mixed with lowlifes."

"Yeah. The moron probably short-changed them or tried to muscle in on their business. Always did have his eye open for a business opportunity. Trying to climb the ladder. Stupid bastard. What about Carstairs?"

"Prob'ly not real name. But he might be enforcer."

Again, on the balance of probabilities, BB had to agree.

"Why did he let Fenella live?"

Hesitation. Brutus raised his left eyebrow.

BB repeated the question.

"If he know Lady F your daughter …" Brutus opened his hands and allowed the rest of the thought to hang in the air between them.

"He didn't want to start a war, you mean?"

The Georgian's head dipped in an actual nod. "It my guess. If he is professional, he will know about me and my men. And he will know what we do if you threatened."

Brutus smiled. Not a pretty sight.

BB considered the idea for a moment. It seemed to make sense. Once again, he had cause to be grateful for employing the pitiless Georgian and making his presence known in all the right circles.

"So," BB said, "this has nothing to do with Hardwicke Row or the Constantines?"

Brutus's scowl deepened. "I think not."

BB relaxed a little. Nodded.

"Just to make sure, talk to Blackstone in person, not over the phone. Give him Carstairs' description. If Carstairs *is* an enforcer, Blackstone can find out for certain."

Yet another nod-shrug.

"And the Constantines?" the Georgian asked.

BB made a snap decision.

"Leave them alone for the time being."

"Yes?"

"Yes. Leave them alone."

"How long?"

"A week or two. Time for the fuss to die down, and I need to find someone to replace Lovejoy. Someone a damn sight more reliable."

"Yes, sir. Is that all?"

"Make sure we have eyes on Hardwicke Row. Someone other than the builders."

"Yes, sir. Anything else?"

BB leaned forwards and reached for his coffee, giving himself time to think. He took a sip, grimaced. It had already grown too cool for his sensitive tastebuds. He lowered the cup to the table.

"Not for the moment."

Brutus turned and left the room.

BB sighed again, reached for the remote, and summoned the maid. He couldn't abide cold coffee.

Chapter Twenty-Three

Sunday 25th October – Morning

Safe House, Camden, London, England

After a full six hours' sack time, Kaine woke refreshed to a dull, grey morning. Two mugs of coffee and three slices of toast, butter, and thick-cut marmalade set him up for the rest of the day. One of the reasons for Kaine's relatively early *réveille* was his upcoming video call with a certain veterinary surgeon. Overnight, he'd send an SMS tasking her and Rollo with finding out all they could on Sir Brandon Banner-Hardy and his various business enterprises.

Kaine was expecting their call at midday, UK time, and no matter how hard he tried to hide it from himself, he was looking forward to seeing Lara again—not that he'd ever let on.

By 10:30, Danny still hadn't surfaced and, judging from the deep rumbles reverberating through the upstairs hallway, he had little intention of doing so in the foreseeable future.

It suited Kaine to let Danny rest. He wasn't used to houseguests cluttering up the place and preferred the solitary life. At least he had done before spending time in the villa with Lara.

On a more practical level, Danny had been watching the junior female contingent of the Constantine family since his return from Canada. The willing corporal needed rest and recovery, or his performance would be compromised for the ongoing mission.

As for Kaine, he'd spent most of the previous day cobbling together a unit he could count on. Fortunately, his second call met with success. Two members of his old SBS unit, Laurence "Fat Larry" Kovaks and Anthony "Slim" Simms, had been available at a moment's notice—as Danny had predicted.

Slim had reached London first. Kaine briefed him on the situation and sent him straight to Golders Green to relieve a jaded Danny. Finessing Orestes Constantine's around-the-clock protection took slightly longer and required a thirty-minute internet search, followed by a little bribery and a certain amount of corruption.

The first part turned out easy enough. A recent press release posted on St Catherine's on the Green's website proudly announced that the Hospital Trust had saved thousands of pounds of taxpayers money by outsourcing their security to Secure-Brack Ltd. With Orestes still in his intensive care bed, but scheduled to be moved into a recovery room shortly, Kaine buttonholed Secure-Brack's owner in a pub after locating him through the company's emergency contact number. Kaine had explained the Orestes Constantine situation and the reason he needed around-the-clock protection. He kept as close to the truth as possible and, after a cursory study of their résumés, the owner was happy to accept Danny, Slim, and Larry as temporary—and unpaid—employees. He also accepted the résumés of two other, as yet unnamed, officers into his company. The owner, a former army colonel, was even happier to accept ten thousand pounds in folding money to forego his company's usual security screening protocols, no questions asked. As Colonel Brackley's actions demonstrated, in the security industry, not only did firms find it difficult to source reputable staff, but also, money screamed loud and opened many doors. Not that Kaine was complaining about the lapse too much.

As a result of Kaine's generosity, by 19:30 on Saturday evening, Larry Kovaks took the first watch on the hospital's private recovery ward, protecting a very special patient. Only Kaine and his team knew Larry was armed, Kaine having decided there were some things the colonel didn't need to know.

The four of them—Kaine, Danny, Slim, and Larry—would take twelve-hour, rotating shifts to guard the Constantines until Kaine could boost the team's numbers. It would be tiring, but unavoidable. He had a few trustworthy individuals in mind, but their whereabouts were proving somewhat difficult to identify—globetrotters all. By the time Kaine turned in, exhausted, he'd left enough feelers out to give him hope.

After a solitary breakfast, Kaine called Slim and Larry individually but, as he hoped, neither had anything significant to report. He then resumed his search for the elusive backup to augment his thinly spread team. He struck gold early and completed the arrangements in time for his mid-morning coffee break.

11:55 found him prowling the ground floor, wondering why the clocks were running so bloody slowly.

When the call finally came, he raced to the dining room that stood in as an office, pulled on his serious, "officer on duty" face, and touched the green "accept video call" button on the laptop's touchscreen.

France's bright sunshine picked out the amber highlights in Lara's windblown hair. She smiled a greeting, and, despite himself, Kaine returned it.

"Morning, Vincent," she opened, warmth and promise weaved through the innocuous greeting.

"Hi there, Doc. Are you out on the deck?"

"Well spotted."

"I should have been a detective."

She turned her smartphone and panned the picture slowly, from right to left. After showing the empty dunes, beach, and sea, the image came to rest on the beefy Rollo, lolling in the recliner—Kaine's recliner.

"Morning, boss."

"Morning, Alphonse. Hard at work, I see."

Rollo yawned and pushed his arms out in front of his chest, stretching the thin cotton of his workout vest. "On watch, boss. Always on guard. Everything okay in dear, old Blighty? How are the troops?"

Kaine ran through the team's disposition and ended with his morning's success. "I finally got hold of Peewee and Pat. They'll be here tomorrow afternoon at the latest, which will give us enough men to run the minimum protection roster. Eight-hour shifts."

Lara manipulated the phone and the picture returned to her, a much better choice than "Uncle Cuddles".

"Are you going to let the client know what's happening? She'll surely spot your men at the hospital and outside her sister's house."

"Apart from at the hospital, where the guys will be in security uniform, standing outside the recovery room, she'll see nothing we don't want her to see. But"—he dropped his shoulders and started breathing normally— "you're right. To ease her worries, I'll talk to her tomorrow when the rest of the team arrives. She needs to know how she's being protected and by whom. By the way, has there been any activity on the Constantines' bank account?"

The sun picked out more of Lara's warm highlights as another gust of wind ruffled her hair. She shook her head. "They haven't deposited the banker's draft, if that's what you mean."

"It is. I wonder if she knows about the money? Might be a good way for me to break the ice. I'll tell her about The Trust's hardship fund when I introduce her to Peewee tomorrow."

"Boss," Rollo called from out of shot, "if you don't mind a little advice. Be best to wait for Pat. He's a little easier on the ear than Peewee."

Rollo referred to Pat's soft, Irish brogue as opposed to Peewee's harsh, and sometimes indecipherable, Geordie twang.

"Yep, fair point. I'll wait for Pat. Right, time's passing. What do you have on Sir Brandon Hyphenated?"

After a brief sideways glance in Rollo's direction, Lara frowned. "All business with you, isn't it?"

"It's what I'm here for, Doc," he said, but softened the

impact of his words by tilting his head and adding a smile. "So, what do you have?"

A soaring gull stood out white and clear against the otherwise-unbroken blue of the sky behind Lara's shoulder as she paused, no doubt to gather her thoughts. "Okay, I've just sent you an email with the full dossier attached, but in brief, Sir Brandon's is a riches-to-rags-to-riches tale."

She ran through the bullet points of their target's public and private life.

Sir Brandon Banner-Hardy, father to Fenella and widower of Lady Penelope, who had overdosed on prescription sleeping pills when little Fenella was still in primary school. The coroner's inquest produced a verdict of suicide. Being abroad at the time of Penelope's death, no suspicion fell upon the apparently distraught husband and father.

Knighted for his services to British industry, Sir Brandon headed Banner-Hardy Construction Ltd, a company with a string of building developments in its extended portfolio. Currently, BHCL owned forty-three high-rise apartments, five city blocks similar to Hardwicke Row, three multi-storey car parks, and shopping malls in London and throughout southeast England.

BB, as Sir Brandon's close friends called him, married into Penelope's money, and narrowly avoided bankruptcy during the recession of the early '90s. In 1998, he bounced back into profit, with the spectacular refurbishment of a significant section of London Docklands—an area backing onto London City Airport. The identity of the consortium responsible for stumping up the seed money for the Docklands development had never been released but, at the time, unsubstantiated rumours relating to Russian oligarchs abounded.

Between 1998 and 2011, Sir Brandon and BHCL were

cleared of financial misconduct in no less than four separate National Crime Agency and Serious Fraud Office investigations. If that information alone wasn't enough to send Kaine's internal warning systems into overdrive, BHCL's recent business expansion most definitely was.

In 2014, the company diversified into the hospitality business when it bought the ailing King's Langdon Golf Course & Restaurant. Similar acquisitions continued, and BHCL's current portfolio included a string of hotels and Michelin-starred restaurants in London and the Home Counties.

"So," Kaine said when Lara paused in her briefing, "Sir Brandon owns a number of high-profile restaurants and is pressuring the owners of a small bistro in an up-and-coming area of London. Am I reading this right? Is this whole thing just about Sir Brandon securing prime real estate for his next venture in the restaurant business?"

Lara smiled and, once again, shook her head.

"Oh no," she said, "it's not as simple as that. Not by a long shot," and then continued, adding more detail to complete the back story.

"That's really interesting," Kaine admitted after allowing time for the information to sink in, "and it makes perfect sense. I don't suppose you've found anything specific to help us take the bugger down?"

Lara's wicked smile gave him his answer.

"Do you know what, Vincent? I rather think I might have."

"Go on."

Her eyes shone, and her enthusiasm bubbled down the phone connection. "I found a rather important function on Sir Brandon's social calendar. It's part of the celebrations for his sixtieth birthday and coincides with the launch of a new development. It's a formal, black-tie affair his company's been organising for months. It's one he simply can't afford to postpone."

"Sounds intriguing," said Kaine, his interest levels growing. "Do tell."

The moment she'd finished outlining the reason for the party and the nature of the invitees, Kaine couldn't do anything but agree with her. The "formal, black-tie affair" *was* too good an opportunity to miss.

"That's fantastic, Doc. You are brilliant," Kaine said, rubbing his hands together.

Lara beamed. "What? You have a cunning plan, Baldrick?"

Kaine took his turn to smile. "I rather think I might, Lady Blackadder, and I need you and Uncle Cuddles to help me make it work."

"Hang on a minute, boss," Rollo barked. "Who are you calling Uncle—"

"Fire away," Lara said, cutting across Rollo's complaint.

She angled her mobile for Kaine to see both her and a scowling Rollo at the same time. Rollo had levered his huge frame away from the back of the recliner and was sitting up, paying close attention to the conversation.

"Tell me," Kaine said, "how long will it take you to find the contact details of every current and former resident of Hardwicke Row? The former residents who've been 'encouraged' to sell up recently, I mean."

"Let me see," Lara said, tilting her head and raising a finger to her lips. "About ten seconds. I already have them on file."

"You do?"

"We've not just been lying around soaking up the sun,

you know. We've been working hard, too. What do you plan to do with the information?"

"I'd like you to write a compelling letter, inviting all the residents to a meeting of the Hardwicke Row Residents Association."

Rollo spoke. "Is there such an association?"

"Not yet," Kaine answered, still smiling. "After sending the letters, you need to contract a firm of keen and willing solicitors. The more thrusting and ambitious, the better. And I need a firm that isn't averse to working long hours and stretching the rules of law just a tad."

Rollo laughed. "Doubt we'll find a law firm that isn't."

Lara shot Rollo an impatient look before turning back to the camera. "What on earth do you have in mind?"

"I'll also need a notary of a similar disposition."

"Ry—Vincent!"

"You wanted a cunning plan, Doc. Pin back your ears."

By the time he'd finished explaining, Danny had risen from his dark pit and descended the stairs in nothing more than his boxers and a T-shirt. As he stood in the doorway listening to the outline plan, a wicked grin as wide as Lara's formed on his unshaven face.

"Nice one, boss. Love it."

Kaine returned the grin.

"I somehow thought you might."

Chapter Twenty-Four

Monday 26th October – Justina Constantine

St Catherine's on the Green, Lambeth, London, England

Justina took a steadying breath. She glanced from Arana to the wonderful Mr Abernathy—her family's Guardian Angel —before squatting in front of her babies and checking each in turn. They needed to look their very best for Ore.

"Kora, Rena, please listen carefully," she whispered to encourage them to follow her example, especially Kora. "Daddy is very much looking forward to seeing you, but you must be on your very best behaviour. Daddy has a terrible headache, and we all need to be very quiet, yes?"

Rena nodded, unable to speak. Her head tilted up to look at the tall men standing behind Justina on either side of the door to Ore's new room. One had a soft Irish accent, and both looked splendid in their smart uniforms. Mr Abernathy had just explained they were private security guards funded by a charity called The 83 Trust. A marvellous charity that would protect them and make their lives better. Justina could hardly take it all in.

Kora's eyes filled with tears, and her lower lip trembled. She had not been inside a hospital since her birth, and it clearly frightened her.

"Don't like this place, Mama. Smells icky."

"That smell is the disinfectant, *moraki mou*. It fights germs and is helping Daddy get better."

After wiping her eyes with her fists, Kora pulled in her lower lip, and said, "If it makes Daddy all better, then I *do* like it."

"Good girl. You can only stay for a short while. Children are not really allowed into this room, but the nice nurse with the long, red hair is giving us special permission. Remember"—she put her finger to her lips—"we must keep very quiet. Just give Daddy gentle hugs and kisses and tell him how much you love him. It will make him feel even better."

Justina stood, took each girl by the hand, and looked at her sister through happy tears. "I will bring them back out in a moment, Arana. When Orestes learns of the letter and the money, it will bring him such happiness."

Arana returned her smile and kissed Justina on each cheek. "Go, tell Ore the good news. He's been worried sick for weeks. It'll help his recovery."

Before leaving, Justina turned to her family's saviour and said, "We will not keep you long, Mr Abernathy."

"Take as long as you need, Justina," he said, speaking softly, "and please, call me Vincent."

Oh no. She could never do that. To Justina, he would always be Mr Abernathy.

———

"THANKS, love. Seeing the girls was … brill," Ore said, tears filling his dark brown eyes.

He lay propped up in his bed by pillows and looked so much better since they moved him out of intensive care and into the recovery room—the private recovery room, paid for by The 83 Trust. His colour had improved, and his eyes were less shot through with blood.

"The doctors would not let them in before," she said. "They have been desperate to see you. Rena wrote a poem … a prayer, really. And Kora has been colouring lots of pictures for you. I will bring them in tomorrow, to brighten the room."

"Thanks, love. That'll be … great."

"How are you, *polyagapiménos*?"

He gave her a brave smile. "A slight headache, but … a lot better than I was. Better still now I've seen the girls."

A curl of his hair had worked its way out from beneath his bandage. Gently, she brushed it away from his forehead.

"You do look stronger today," she said. "Much stronger. Oh Ore. You gave us such a fright."

He took her hand and kissed her palm. "I'm sorry, darling. Sorry for everything."

"You were not to blame. It was Lovejoy and the people he works for. His boss."

Without releasing his hand, Justina dragged the visitor's chair closer to the bed and sat.

"Who are those men?" Ore asked, breaking the short silence.

"What men?"

"The ones in the uniforms. They've been hanging around in the hall outside ever since they moved me into this room. I keep seeing them when the nurses open the door. And now you've brought someone else. The bearded one in the suit." Ore frowned. "Strange though. He looks familiar somehow. What the hell's going on, love?"

Justina kissed Ore's cheek and wiped away her lipstick with a snick of her thumb. He needed to shave but at that moment she didn't care how much his whiskers prickled her lips. Her Ore was awake and getting better, and Justina was thankful to the Lord her God for it. Gently, she pulled Ore forwards and fluffed up his pillows.

"The doctor said your concussion was very serious and they had to, what did he say? Induce a coma? They put you to sleep to help stop your brain from swelling. We were all sick with worry. But after the surgery, they woke you, and you are improving so quickly, yes?"

Ore rolled his shoulders, but kept his head still while doing so. "Stiff neck, thumping migraine, hideous cut to my scalp, but yes, it's a definite improvement on being comatose." He smiled his warm and beautiful smile.

Justina leaned in close and kissed him again, this time full on the lips. Then she leaned away and slowly shook her head.

"Orestes Constantine, I love you dearly, but you are an idiot."

Ore frowned. "Huh? What was that?"

"I said, I love you, Orestes Constantine."

"Yes, I love you, too, darling. But the other thing? I'm an idiot? Why?"

Justina allowed a chuckle to bubble up and escape her

lips. "I do not know *why* you are an idiot. It must be a trait of all Greek men."

"A joke? You're making fun of me? What makes you so happy? I'm in hospital with a broken head, we're about to lose our home and business, but you're giggling like a schoolgirl. You're getting hysterical. And you still haven't explained the men outside the door. Will you please tell me what's happening."

Justina stopped smiling, sighed, and leaned back to take a full view of her handsome, if battered and bruised, husband.

"How much do you remember about the day of the accident?"

Discomfort flickered over Ore's face as he struggled to sit up straighter only to collapse back against the pillows. He closed his eyes and sweat appeared on his forehead below the bandage.

"Oh my God," he gasped, looking towards the closed door. "The gun. Those men are cops, come to arrest me for trying to buy a gun!"

"Shush, Ore," Justina soothed, resting a hand on his shoulder and lowering her voice. "It has nothing to do with the gun. Those men are here to protect us, nothing more. I will explain everything if you answer me one question."

Ore stopped struggling and, breathing heavily, stared deep into her eyes. "You want me to pass a test?"

"One question only."

"And then you'll answer *my* questions?"

"I promise." Still smiling, she nodded.

He exhaled loudly. "Ask away, you … you bully."

Again, Justina giggled.

"On the day you were injured, I signed for a registered

letter addressed to you. Since the attack, I have searched, but I cannot find it. What did you do with that letter, Ore?"

His frown deepened, either because he couldn't remember, or he was embarrassed about what he had done with it. She would soon find out.

"Letter? I-I can't ... Wait a minute, I remember it now. I ran the bloody thing through the shredder, unopened. Lovejoy and his pressure tactics totally pissed me off."

"Aha, I knew it," Justina said, wagging her finger at him. "As I say, you are a *vlákas*. You should always open your mail and read it before you shred it. Let this be a lesson for the future."

He gave her his "little boy lost" look. "Have a heart, love. What are you banging on about?"

"Ore, that letter contained a bank cheque for ten thousand pounds, and you put it into the shredding machine. If that is not the act of a *vlákas*, I cannot say what is."

Ore's open mouth looked ready to catch flies. "Ten grand? Who the hell would send us ten grand?"

"A very nice man called Mr Abernathy."

Ore lifted a hand to cover his open mouth and he rejected the idea of catching flies.

"Abernathy?" he said. "Abernathy? Hang on, I know that name. Wasn't he the man who gave me first aid?"

"Yes, Ore," she said. "That is he."

Ore closed his eyes. "Oh God. Ten grand. I destroyed ten thousand quid?" He almost choked on the words.

"It would appear so," Justina agreed, unable to prevent herself laughing as the recently won colour drained from her darling husband's stunned face.

———

"SO, I really did shred a cheque for ten grand?" Ore croaked, still having difficulty in believing what the envelope had contained.

Mr Abernathy nodded and added a gentle smile.

"I'm afraid so. Well, nine thousand, nine hundred, and fifty pounds, to be exact."

"Bloody hell," Ore said, looking at Justina, who smiled at his discomfort. "Bloody hell."

"But don't worry," Mr Abernathy said. "There things we can do to recover it."

"Really? I thought that bank drafts were … I don't know … like cash. Destroy them and they're gone."

"There are ways around it. So long as the bank can verify the draft hasn't been cashed, it can cancel it and issue a replacement. Don't worry. The Trust will handle it."

"So, you can replace the money?"

Again, Mr Abernathy nodded. "And more. As I said, the whole point of the Trust is to help out where we can."

"So, the night of the attack, you weren't just passing by?"

"No," Mr Abernathy answered, looking uncomfortable. "Not exactly."

Ore blinked and shook his head.

"What *were* you doing?"

"Conducting a follow-up visit. Or trying to."

"A follow-up?" Orestes asked, glancing at Justina who had had more time to absorb the information and the shock.

Justina had also been given more time to become accustomed to the idea that they had been saved from financial ruin. She sat back on the uncomfortable visitor's chair, and she relaxed, and she smiled, and she watched her husband struggle to take in the news. Justina could not remember the last time she had felt so happy and so content. It was as though the grip that had restricted her heart had been removed and it could run free.

"That's right, Orestes," Mr Abernathy said, adding another gentle smile. It relaxed his face and made him look years younger. "You'd be surprised how many of our clients think the banker's drafts are some sort of scam. It's a sign of the times, I'm afraid. You're actually not the first recipient to have destroyed the draft instead of taking it to their bank for authentication. That's why, whenever possible, we make a follow-up visit in person."

Again, Ore looked at Justina.

"See," he said, grinning, "I'm not the only idiot."

"No, Ore," she answered, shaking her head, "you are not the only one. But it is not something of which you should be proud."

"And when I saw what had happened to you ... the attack," Mr Abernathy continued, "I made a few inquiries. Wasn't pleased with what I discovered, either. Hence the security detail outside the room. And don't worry, The Trust is covering all the expenses. We're also protecting the girls, as a matter of course. Which is why, right now, we have a team following them back to Golders Green."

Ore nodded, relaxed into his pillows, and turned to face their guardian angel.

"We can't thank you enough for your help, Mr Abernathy," he said. Ore paused for a moment before continuing. "The money will help. Of course it will, but ..." He winced and closed his eyes.

"But?" Mr Abernathy prompted.

Ore opened his eyes again, and stared through the window at the rain battering the glass. He sighed.

"I hate to sound ungrateful, but ten thousand pounds will barely cover our moving expenses."

"Ore!" Justina gasped.

Her husband raised his hand in apology.

"I'm sorry, love, but it's true. Without the Bistro, we'll be … destitute. Homeless. Arana can't house us forever and we'll never be able to afford a new—"

"Orestes," Mr Abernathy jumped in, "excuse me for interrupting, but when you destroyed the bank draft, you also destroyed the covering letter we sent with it. The letter explaining who we are and the help we can provide."

"The letter?"

"Yes, Ore," Justina said, leaning forwards in her chair. "The letter."

"What letter? What did it say?"

Mr Abernathy's smile lit up his green eyes. He had a way about him. A way that encouraged, no, forced Justina to trust him. She had no other choice but to do so.

"Amongst other things," he said, "it explained that the bank draft was only the first payment due to your family. We like to think of it as a demonstration of our goodwill. If necessary, we can provide much more. For example, in certain extreme circumstances we can …"

Justina listened to Mr Abernathy repeat what he had already explained to her a little earlier. It did not take long, and towards the end, when Ore finally understood the consequences of what The 83 Trust had to offer, tears of joy and relief burst from his brown eyes and rolled down his stubbled cheeks. Justina leaped from the chair, and while they hugged each other tightly, giving each other comfort, Mr Abernathy continued talking, and for a long time.

"…the upshot is this, Orestes. You have no need to worry about the future. You are financially secure. If you like, you can sign the BHCL contract and leave the Bistro behind. Buy a home in the sun and retire. Or you can invest in another restaurant. Alternatively …" He opened his hands and allowed the remainder of the sentence to drift in the air.

Still hugging Justina tight, Ore spoke through his tears.

"But we love the Bistro, Mr Abernathy," he said. "It's our home. I've lived there all my life, and so have the girls. They love their school, too. We don't want to move, but … the bastards are forcing us out. And they've done the same thing to others in the block."

Mr Abernathy pursed his lips and nodded.

"That's what our investigations have shown."

"We're too young to retire," Ore said, "and we'd prefer to stay where we are, but …"

"The building is tainted," Justina said, speaking for them both. "Those men have threatened us. They have—"

"I fully understand," Mr Abernathy said. "If it's a question of your safety and you'd rather stay put, there might be another way. A way to stop all this and give you your home back."

"Will your way make us safe?" Justina asked.

"Yes," Mr Abernathy said. "It will. I promise."

The certainty in his words, their conviction, filled Justina with hope, with confidence. Mr Abernathy was a man they could trust. She absorbed his certainty, and so too, did Ore. She could feel it through the strength of his grip.

"What d'you think, love?" Ore asked, looking deep into Justina's eyes. "Do you want to stay?"

Justina answered without hesitation.

"Of course," she said. "Of course we should stay! As you said, the Bistro is our home. The girls do not want to leave, and neither do I!" She looked to Mr Abernathy. "As my husband says, we are too young to retire."

Their saviour smiled again.

"In that case," he said, "leave it with us."

"Can we help?" Justina asked.

"Possibly," he answered. "If so, I'll be in touch. Can I have your phone number, please?"

"Of course."

Justina took her mobile phone from her handbag, and they exchanged contact details. Strangely, Mr Abernathy had a small mobile that looked incapable of accessing the internet. Perhaps he was older than he looked and did not feel the need to use a smartphone.

As Mr Abernathy turned to leave, Justina leaped from the bed and embraced him.

"Thank you," she said. "Thank you so much."

"No need to thank us," he said. "We're here to help."

A flicker of sadness or regret crossed his face, and then he turned and left the room.

Chapter Twenty-Five

Wednesday 28th October – Brandon Banner-Hardy

The Corpulent Canard, Hounslow, London, England

BB hid a bored yawn behind a monogrammed handkerchief. A small man—wearing a white jacket and trousers, blue-and-white-striped apron, and a gingham skullcap—stood over BB's table, bowing and scraping. The bloody creep couldn't have been any more obsequious if he tried, and BB loved every second of it. Jordan Christie, the head chef of the Corpulent Canard, a ridiculous figure with black, horn-rimmed glasses and a gap between his front teeth, rattled on. In effect, he told them about how he'd prepared, seasoned, skinned, and "sphericised" his home-grown garden peas to make them look and taste like, well, garden bloody peas.

BB tried to make it look as though he was listening intently. After paying through the nose for the little twerp's reputation, he needed to keep the guy sweet. Sweeter than his reconstituted peas, at any rate. There were plenty of restaurateurs around who were prepared to poach the man from under BB's nose if he gave them half a chance, and that wasn't happening any time soon.

How the diminutive prick could talk such twaddle to anyone and still keep a straight face was a complete mystery, but he did, and the normal clientele—bless their silk shirts and designer dresses—totally lapped it up. The same patrons also called months in advance for a reservation and didn't baulk at paying a small fortune for the cuisine served up by the TV celeb with his three Michelin stars. Three stars and counting.

Not tonight, though, oh no. Tonight was too important to allow anyone but friends, colleagues, stakeholders, and other sycophants into the restaurant. BB had filled the place with his acolytes and with people he owned to make sure that everything went perfectly. Nothing could go wrong in front of his latest marks, the ones he'd flown in from all over the world on leased private jets.

"...and you see the result," Christie finished, finally ending his delivery.

BB looked down at the little, green balls and the other miniature vegetables apparently dropped randomly into his bowl from a great height. They swam in a puddle of clear liquid that could have been tap water, but was billed as fresh tomato consommé—from home-grown tomatoes, no less. Christie didn't mention whose home had grown the bloody things. Probably a kilometre-long polytunnel in the middle of Spain.

"A work of art," BB said, earning another bow from the internationally renowned chef, aka, the "twit in the funny gingham hat".

BB managed not to snort.

"*Bon appetite*," Christie said in his nasal, Midland's accent and backed away, hands clasped to his flat belly, the scrawny, little git.

How could anyone ever trust a skinny chef?

BB expanded his chest, threw open his arms to the moneymen, his potential investors, and said, "Dig in, my friends. You are going to *love* this. I promise you."

And if you don't, who the fuck cares? At least you'll have something to tell all your rich friends.

Three Japanese, two Saudis, and a Russian, picked up their silverware and started eating. All chose the correct spoon—even the Russian. BB half-expected the ignorant peasant to pick up the bowl and lap at the contents with his tongue. Still, good table manners meant fuck-all when your family owned most of the coal mines in Kemerovo. Manners mattered even less to BB when the same low-brow family was falling over itself to invest in the London property market.

Lord above, if Ivan belched aloud and picked his nose between courses, some of the planted guests would probably do the same to make the man feel right at home. BB owned the place, he owned the crowd, and they could damn well enjoy the colourful floorshow.

He took his time over his bowl which, strangely enough, tasted okay. Acceptable, but hardly worth twenty quid a teaspoonful.

He looked around at all the diners in their fancy clothes,

wolfing down the meals he'd bought for them, each reacting as though enraptured, and found it difficult not to burst out laughing. But oh no, that wouldn't do. That wouldn't do at all. He'd hold off laughing until the funds hit BHCL's bank account.

The Corpulent Canard and the six other restaurants in the chain were not only making millions in profits, they also served as great places to schmooze the existing stake-holders and the potential investors. An acceptable face for his widespread empire, and tax deductible, too. His disso-lute father, who'd shot BB's inheritance into his arm and forced his son to marry Penelope the chinless heiress, would have been so proud, during his occasional lucid moments. He never lived to see it though, the dozy, doped-up moron.

At the end of the first course, Ivan didn't belch or pick his nose, but wiped his mouth delicately with the Egyptian cotton napkin provided.

Who'd have thought?

"Good?" BB asked, catching the eye of each special guest in turn.

They all nodded enthusiastically, adding praise in garbled English, apart from the Arabs, whose perfect diction matched his own and demonstrated the benefits of a classical education bequeathed by the former British Empire. One of the Saudis had actually attended the same prep school as the next-in-line to the UK throne—God bless his future Majesty.

BB clicked his fingers and the uniformed waitresses—selected for their looks as well as their skills at delivering silver service—swooped in to clear the bowls and the bread baskets. A second team arrived to set the table for the fish course. Christie had promised some sort of reconstructed, or deconstructed, or renovated, or reimagined sushi or sashimi, or some such. Anything to keep the Nips on side.

The upcoming arrival of the fish course allowed him time to think.

In spite of the tension he'd felt boiling in his guts since learning of the carnage in Halcyon Tower, the food was so far slipping down rather well. In the few days since he'd sent Fenella to dry out in the clinic, BB had doubled his personal, close-protection team. He'd also revamped his security protocols, and had maintained a close watch on Hardwicke Row, but nothing had happened to cause concern. No threats, no anonymous mail or phone calls. No attempted attacks on his person or personnel. Nothing.

As a failsafe, Brutus had geared the team up for a possible visit by Carstairs, the man Fenella had called an "old guy with a weird sense of humour". But the same man who'd escorted her to the taxi and saved her blushes had failed to make any contact with BB or his organisation. It confirmed BB's initial interpretation of events. Carstairs was an enforcer for Lovejoy's supplier. End of story. Fenella had survived by the skin of her teeth. Silly, little girl. Since her mother's "accidental" overdose, the idiot had turned from an average but compliant child into an empty-headed socialite.

Carstairs had killed Tugboat, Lovejoy's pet gorilla, and left Lovejoy a broken, paralysed lump. No bloody good to BB now, not from a hospital bed. The cripple claimed not to know why he'd been attacked. A burglary gone wrong, he'd claimed. Stupid moron. Fair enough, his description of Carstairs matched the one Fenella had provided. Average height, slim build, thirty-five to fifty-five years old, dark, wavy hair, and a greying beard. But it could have been any one of a million men in London.

So far, the combined resources of the police, BB's security team, and a raft of private investigators had failed to find any trace of the man, but BB could live with it. The "enforcer" had done part of BB's job for him when he'd wiped the building's surveillance recordings clean. Furthermore, after BB had greased a load of sticky palms, the "fix" was in. The police were treating the whole incident as a drug-related lover's tiff, and Tugboat's death as self-defence. The upcoming coroner's inquest would produce a verdict of death by misadventure and, given Lovejoy's medical condition, the Crown Prosecution Service was unlikely to bring the case to court. Best of all, his airhead daughter's presence at the scene would forever remain a secret.

A nice, quiet end to the event.

While the waitresses delivered the fish course—starting at the top table—Jordan Christie spouted some bollocks related to "sustainable fish stocks" and "translucent infusions" of something or other, which BB completely blanked out. When the twit in the gingham hat stopped talking, everyone finally started tucking in.

BB forked a morsel of fish into his mouth. It tasted like salt-cured cod. Nice enough, but hardly the reinvention of the century that the menu promised. So much bullshit.

As for Lovejoy, Brutus would ensure he kept his mouth shut in return for the round-the-clock medical care he needed—at least until the fuss died down. After that, the cripple would more than likely meet with an unfortunate accident. Easy enough to arrange. At some stage in the not-too-distant future, the useless fuck would roll his wheelchair down a flight of stairs and break his neck. Poor, unfortunate fellow.

It wasn't as though Lovejoy's loss mattered a damn. Irrespective of his unspoken aspirations, the piece of low-life slime would never have amounted to much inside the company. Simply by snapping his fingers, BB could find a dozen men to fill Lovejoy's place. On top of everything else, Fenella was better off without the prick leading her astray.

BB smiled to himself. Lovejoy actually thought his liaisons with Fenella had gone unnoticed. It simply went to show how deluded the man actually was. Lovejoy's departure was no great loss to the firm. No loss in the slightest.

All in all, it had turned into the perfect outcome for BHCL and BB's other business interests.

As for the elusive Carstairs, the longer he stayed away, the more convinced BB became. Lovejoy had pissed all over some other lowlife's flowerbed. He'd probably involved himself in some sort of turf war. Like as not, Lovejoy had tried to branch out on his own little side business and burned his fingers—or had his back broken—in the process.

Moron. Good fucking riddance.

Although employing people from the lower echelons had some merit—they worked for peanuts and weren't averse to getting their hands grubby—they were hardly the most reliable creatures in the firmament.

BB mopped his plate with the handmade bread provided and surveyed the room, mentally washing his hands of the bothersome and unpleasant penthouse incident.

He soaked in the atmosphere and smiled at his vacuous, but well-heeled, guests. Inwardly, he smirked. One way or another, he owned every last one of them. Altogether, he counted three senior police officers, a junior government minister, half a dozen MPs, and dozens of local authority councillors and planning officers, and their "significant others". All in his hip pocket, either bought and paid for or coerced into submission. In general, things looked good, but BB was nothing if not cautious.

The useless prick, Inspector Blackstone, should have been sitting with his nose in the trough alongside his more senior colleagues, but BB had ordered the fucker not to show. Unable to find a sniff of Carstairs, the bugger had proved himself useless. BB would be damned if he'd pay a small fortune to feed the useless waste of space.

In the wake of Lovejoy's incapacity, and to lower any potential media exposure, he'd placed a moratorium on pressuring the Constantines, but their time was growing short. While work on the upper floors of Hardwicke Row was progressing nicely, he'd been forced to put the street-level refurb and the Bistro extension on hold, which was causing a nasty, little bottleneck. The contractors were charging by the day and the excess fees had started eating into his expansive bottom line.

It was getting time to push ahead with the programme, which meant sending in the bully boys to clear the Constantine-shaped logjam. But first, he needed to raise the capital for his next great project, the Thames Estuary Development. After all, the best businessmen never risked their own money.

The twit in the gingham hat surpassed himself with the main course. It arrived on silver platters to rapturous and spontaneous applause from the whole room. For each table, he'd created a representation of the London skyline in food, with some sort of grey-brown, gelatinous slime representing the Thames. Christ knew what the London Eye was made of, but the flashes of yellow light shining through the windows in the Houses of Parliament had to be pure, edible gold.

The meal was costing BB an arm, a leg, and one testicle,

but the investment would be worth it if it helped to lock in the venture funding and, judging by the favourable expressions on his investors' faces, the contracts were all but signed.

He allowed a self-congratulatory smile to form, but before BB could instruct the waitresses to start serving, the heavy, velvet curtains in the far corner of the room billowed and a man he didn't recognise entered the dining area. The man stood near the curtain, smiling, and rubbernecking the place like a Goddamned tourist. With his grey beard, long, grey hair tied back in a loose ponytail, and horn-rimmed glasses, he looked like a street poet or an academic. The man's blue jeans and his sports jacket with leather patches at its elbows confirmed him in BB's mind as an academic. A college professor.

Clearly a hick on a once-in-a-lifetime visit to see how the other half ate, the professor must have arrived on the ridiculous off-chance of finding a cancellation.

Pathetic creature.

How the hell had the bugger found his way past security?

BB tipped a nod to Brutus, but, as usual, the big Georgian was way ahead of him. He spoke into his wrist mic like a real-life Secret Service agent, and two dark-suited men materialised in the reception area. They spoke quietly, checked the newcomer's identity, and waved a sleek metal detector over him.

The professor smiled at the attention and probably assumed it *de rigueur* for anyone visiting such a high-value establishment. If the bodyguard insisted on it, the ignorant rube would probably have allowed a public cavity search, so long as it earned him the chance to dine in one of the world's most exclusive eateries.

BB snorted at the ridiculous image running through his head.

After the electronic search, the professor said something to Brutus' men and pointed to the main door. Whatever he said must have satisfied their curiosity. The guards exchanged looks, and one spoke into his wrist mic.

"Brutus, what's happening?" BB asked, speaking quietly and hiding his mouth behind his napkin.

BB's head of security pressed the earpiece harder into his ear and listened before answering. "This is surprise presentation. Lady Fenella arrange it before her ... sabbatical."

Brutus nodded, and the men next to the professor disappeared behind the curtains.

"Did she clear it with you first?" BB asked.

Brutus scowled and shook his clean-shaven head. "No, Sir Brandon. You know what she is like."

BB sighed. "I do indeed. The girl never could follow instructions. Just make sure your men are awake."

"Yes, Sir Brandon. They are."

"I don't see anyone. Where are they all?" he asked, still keeping his voice down.

Brutus, eyes locked on the professor, raised his wrist, and pressed the earpiece again. "Alpha teams, report."

He listened for a few moments.

"Beta teams, report."

Another pause.

"They in position and aware of new arrival. We are secure, Sir Brandon."

"But where are they, man?"

"Out of sight. I did not want display of strength to upset guests, sir. Alpha teams are inside building. Beta teams are outside, front and back. There is one man in kitchen,

275

two on each exit point, and two at reception. I also have two men on street in front, and two in rear car park. Restaurant is safe and we are good. You can enjoy meal and floorshow."

BB nodded his acceptance.

Brutus had been on his staff for the better part of nine years and received a healthy salary in return. If the big, Georgian muscleman couldn't be trusted to do his job properly, no one could.

The pretty, dark-haired waitress at his side said something BB didn't catch.

"Yes, my dear?"

"Do you have any preference, Sir Brandon?" she asked, a cheeky smile playing on her plumped lips. "Chef Christie suggested you'd particularly enjoy sinking your teeth into the House of Lords."

BB laughed and wondered how much the sweet thing would charge to let him sink his teeth into her inner thighs. In an avaricious world, everyone had their price.

"Go ahead, I'll have a corner of the Palace, a mouthful of St Paul's, a piece of the Shard, and a spoonful of the Thames."

She did the honours and dipped low enough while loading the plate to give him a fair glimpse of her more-than-adequate assets. Well, if she didn't want him looking, she shouldn't take such pride in displaying the goods.

Brutus stepped back to his normal position against the wall, but kept his eyes on the professor, who continued an animated conversation with the Maître D'. Slowly, the Maître D's haughty expression turned to one of compliance and his complexion took on the shade and texture of Thames Embankment mud at low tide.

BB clicked his fingers. "Brutus, what the fuck's happening over there?"

The bodyguard started raising his wrist to his mouth again, but BB chopped his hand through the air.

"Don't just stand there, man. Go find out for yourself."

Brutus shook his head and leaned closer, keeping his voice to a deep-throated murmur. "No, Sir Brandon. My job is to protect you. I remain here. Send Charlie."

With a smile pasted in place to fend off the questioning glances of Ivan and the others, BB replied in a whisper, "Fair enough, just hurry him up, the marks are starting to wonder what's going on."

Brutus retreated a pace to make the call. One of the restroom doors opened and the besuited Charlie arrived. He straightened his jacket and weaved between the tables to the reception area. He stood at least five inches taller than the professor who had to crane his neck to hear what Charlie said. They exchanged a few words before the professor pointed at something out of sight. Charlie stiffened, nodded, and hurried towards it.

The Maître D' ducked behind his desk and reappeared a second later. He passed a microphone to the professor, who tapped it, causing the metallic thumps to boom through the PA speakers. Cutlery stopped scraping expensive, monogrammed crockery, and the background noise fell to a low murmur.

About fucking time something happened.

Reluctantly, BB took a break from eating his delicious serving of London, crossed his fork over his knife, and left them in the centre of the plate.

"Ladies and gentlemen," the professor said, "I'm sorry to interrupt your evening, but, as you know, this is a very special occasion. You've all met him before, but I'd like to introduce you to the *real* Sir Brandon Banner-Hardy on the eve of his sixtieth birthday."

Professor pointed at BB and indicated that he should stand.

Really?

"Please, everyone, a round of applause for your benefactor, the birthday boy, and the owner of this wonderful establishment. Sir Brandon, please stand to take your well-deserved plaudits."

The specially invited guests took their cue from Professor Sycophant and started clapping. One man shouted, "Bravo," and another put his fingers to his mouth and whistled.

To remain seated in the face of such adulation would have been impolite and impolitic. Smiling, BB stood and bowed slightly, still uncertain of what to expect. He glanced at each of the men at his table in turn. None seemed offended by the disruption to their dining pleasure. In fact, Ivan actually appeared impressed.

Maybe BB needed to reassess his opinion of Fenella. Perhaps she wasn't such an empty-headed, hopped-up bimbo after all. Nothing at all like her shit-for-brains mother. Perhaps he should move her into the organisation— after she'd completed her rehab, of course. He'd start her at a junior level to begin with. She'd need to prove herself. Work her way up from the sub-basement.

The smiling Professor Sycophant stopped clapping and waited for the applause to die. Without his orchestration, it didn't take long.

"I expect," Professor Sycophant continued, "you've noticed Sir Brandon is looking a little surprised. Well, that's because he's a modest man and had no idea we'd arranged this little presentation for him. One moment please, while my glamorous assistant sets up the audio-visual equipment."

Charlie reappeared, wheeling in a trolley on which stood a TV the size of a small cinema screen. Still murmuring, the crowd settled down for a showing.

BB found himself keen to learn what Fenella had laid on for him. He started to sit, but Professor Sycophant shook his head. "No, no, Sir Brandon. Please keep standing so everyone in the room can see your reaction to our version of *This is Your Life*. I can assure you, it won't take long. The first scene takes place a short distance away from this very building. I think everyone will find it fairly self-explanatory." He took a remote control from his pocket and pointed it at the screen.

When BB saw the first few seconds of film—a man on a motorbike outside Bistro Mykonos—he lost control of his legs and collapsed into his chair.

Chapter Twenty-Six

Wednesday 28th October – Brandon Banner-Hardy

The Corpulent Canard, Hounslow, London, England

A frantic BB summoned Brutus and hissed into the big man's free ear. "Shut that fucker down. Do it now!"

"You are sure? It will create scene and might require force."

"I don't fucking care if you have to rip his shitting head off," BB hissed. "Get rid of him!"

"Yes, Sir Brandon."

On the TV screen, the leather-clad biker threw a large brick and the restaurant window exploded. The diners gasped. The film paused on a close-up image of two little girls, mouths open, clearly screaming as their father vanished beneath a shower of shattered glass.

While Brutus barked orders into his wrist mic, Professor ... Professor *Bastard* began his narration, shouting above the growing hubbub.

"Ladies and gentlemen, I'm sorry if the film ruined your appetite, but what you see on the screen is more than a simple act of random violence, much more. The man on the motorcycle was paid to force the owners of Bistro Mykonos into selling their business and the lease to their part of the building. If we pan out on this shot"—he worked the remote again—"you'll see the block in which this restaurant is located, Hardwicke Row. Do you notice all those other businesses on the street, the pub on the corner, the betting shop, the butchers? During the past eighteen months, every one of them has changed ownership or announced closure except for Bistro Mykonos." Professor Bastard paused and let his gaze roll over his audience.

"And now, ladies and gentlemen," he continued, "take a look at the scaffolding on the upper floors and the weatherboard on the windows. It looks as though a major refurbishment is underway, doesn't it? Right in the heart of London, too. When I first saw the block, I wondered who the developer might be, as there aren't any of the usual signs you'd expect to see on the scaffolding. Just the standard health and safety notices."

He stopped, probably to drive home his point and to confirm he had the attention of BB's marks and the rest of the punters in the audience.

Standing beside Professor Bastard, Charlie looked on in confusion while Brutus gathered his men and led them towards the reception area, but too bloody slowly. What the hell was wrong with the morons? They only faced one man, and he was short, no taller than BB himself. Slim, too, a weakling.

A weakling?

Fuck no. He couldn't be Carstairs. Could he?

No. Not possible.

BB listened with growing dread as Professor Bastard started up again. "It didn't take me long to find out who was responsible for the refurbishment works, though. It's amazing what a little online research and a trip to the local planning office will turn up, eh? And what do you know? Apart from Bistro Mykonos, that whole block is now owned by—"

BB shot to his feet. "What on earth is the meaning of this interruption? Who the devil are you?"

The soon-to-be-dead professor smiled through his ridiculous, grey beard.

"My name isn't important, but you could say I was sent by the man your daughter, Lady Fenella, told you about. His name is Alan Carstairs." He smiled and added a little half-bow. "Ah yes, I see from your reaction that Lady Fenella did tell you about dear, old Alan."

Not Carstairs.

Of course not. He couldn't be.

Professor Bastard raised his hand to halt the approaching security detail.

"Ah, there you are, big fellow. The fiercely loyal—to anyone prepared to pay your exorbitant salary—Brutus Novikov," he said, the smile fading. "Yes, that's right, I know your full name, Brutus. I also know that you've murdered at least five men on the orders of your boss, over there."

BB stared hard at Brutus. As usual, the big bruiser didn't react. Didn't waste time trying to deny the accusation, either. Professor Bastard had just signed his own death warrant, but he didn't seem to realise the fact. BB had met plenty of academics who didn't appear to live in the real world and, clearly, this halfwit was no exception.

"I've done my homework," Professor Bastard continued. "Stop right there, Brutus. I'm almost finished, and we don't want to create any more of a scene. Not with all these people working their cameras." He held up his arms and waved them towards the diners.

BB looked around him. At least half of his guests—some of them his so-called friends—had mobile phones raised and active. Some of the phones flashed for stills. Hot bile rose from his stomach, threatening to bring his expensive, gold-laced meal up with it.

"So, where was I?" Professor Bastard asked as though delivering a lecture. "Ah yes, I remember now. The company with the freehold to Hardwicke Row, the block you see on the screen, is owned by none other than Banner-Hardy Construction Ltd, BHCL which, in turn, is owned by our illustrious host, Sir Brandon Banner-Hardy. Ta-dah! So, you get the *picture*?" He paused for a beat before adding, "Please excuse the pun, but I simply couldn't help myself."

"So what?" BB asked, swallowing the bile and finding his voice. "I own a number of properties throughout London. On occasion, some of them might be the target of wanton vandalism. I know what you're doing. You're trying to suggest I had something to do with this terrible and shocking incident. You actually think I would attack an innocent family? That's preposterous. In fact, it's slanderous."

BB avoided looking at the screen, hoping the camera lenses would remain pointed at him. He'd faced down many a hostile crowd in his time, from shareholders who'd learned that their dividends were being cut, to trade unionists who'd been informed about mass redundancies. Professor Bastard was no worse than any of them. He certainly wasn't Carstairs. He didn't kill Tugboat and maim Lovejoy. No way could a man so ... slight and inconsequential have beaten those two, not with his bare hands. Carstairs had to have been bigger, or mob handed. Professor Bastard was a lightweight, who looked as though he hadn't exercised for decades.

No, this was a huge bluff. The academic had nothing but innuendo and rumour.

Professor Bastard straightened an arm and pointed at BB. "No, I'm not suggesting anything, I'm levelling a direct accusation. One of your employees, an individual named Alfred Lovejoy, paid the biker, Barnard Mortensen, to terrorise the owners of Bistro Mykonos. And you, Sir Brandon, ordered the attack."

"That's an outrageous accusation!" BB shouted over another gasp from the audience. "Spurious! You have no proof, and anyway, why would I do such a thing?"

"I'm coming to the reason, but as for proof."

He hit a button on the remote once again and the picture rolled forwards to reveal the inside of the Halcyon Tower penthouse, the timestamp coincided with the date and time of the attack on Lovejoy and the gorilla. Fortunately, it only showed the desk and the kitchen, not the bloody mess on the floor that BB had viewed in crime scene photos.

"You see, the laptop in the picture contains all the evidence I need to prove he ordered the attack that risked the lives of those two little girls you saw earlier and hospitalised their father. The laptop contains other damning evidence of his wrongdoing, collected by Alfred Lovejoy, but this is not the time or the forum to discuss those particular crimes."

Oh fuck. Oh Jesus fuck. No!

BB breathed in through his nose, mouth clamped tightly closed, trying to force the panic, and rising bile, back down.

"For those of you unable to see him clearly in this subdued lighting," Professor Bastard said, mocking, "Sir Brandon has just turned a rather fetching shade of vomit green."

He clicked, and the image on the screen changed to a looped sequence of the rock smashing the Bistro window and the little girls' silent screaming.

"By the way, before you release your attack dogs, Sir Brandon, I sent the information from that very laptop to the local police station this evening. I'm expecting them to arrive at any minute."

The local police station?

BB suddenly saw a way out and almost laughed. The local police? Fuck them. BB *owned* the local police.

"This is a disgraceful pack of lies," BB yelled. "I've had more than enough of this. Brutus, kindly escort that deranged man from the premises. Take him through the kitchen and use the service exit. I'm worried about his mental state. Please take all the usual precautions."

Yes. Kill the bastard and make it painful, but find any remaining evidence first.

Finally making a decision, Charlie lunged. Professor Bastard snapped out his arm and Charlie fell backwards as though having been shot in the head. A woman in the crowd, close to the action, screamed. Professor Bastard's arm had moved so fast BB couldn't tell exactly what he'd done.

Brutus and his men stopped for a moment, giving

Professor Bastard the time he needed to recover his position behind the trolley.

"One moment please, Brutus," he said. "If you let me finish, I'll come quiet—"

Brutus and his men swarmed forwards but, rather than resisting further, Professor Bastard held up his hands in surrender.

"Okay, okay, I'm done. You can take me away if you wish," he said, as though still in control, and meekly allowed them to escort him, unrestrained, through the dining area and towards the kitchen.

The audience hum increased to an excited chatter and then to a roar. The camera phones turned towards BB once again.

BB stood tall and held up his hands. "My dear friends, please excuse the rantings of a fantasist who has clearly read too many conspiracy theories. I can assure you—"

Beside BB, Ivan stood. He summoned his underlings from the adjacent table and prepared to leave.

"Mr Andropov," BB said, "there's no reason to go. This means nothing—"

"Sir Brandon, thank you for such an interesting and … entertaining evening," Ivan said, his thick, Russian accent melting into a perfect, if slightly arcane, received pronunciation, "but I am unable to do business with a person of such low moral turpitude. My family simply would not allow it. Perhaps you need to look for your investment elsewhere? May I suggest you approach the owners of your Premier League football clubs?" He smiled and gave a slight nod.

While Ivan talked, the Saudis and the Japanese left without saying a word. BB sank into his chair once more and watched his specially selected guests and his former friends, desert him in droves and without a sideways glance.

Well, fuck the lot of the ungrateful bastards. He didn't need them. He'd pay them all back for their disloyalty. Each and every one of the ignorant, lily-livered bastards.

As for the current situation, Brutus had Professor Bastard and would beat the evidence out of him before dumping his body in the Thames.

BB took a deep, cleansing breath, picked up his cutlery, and re-focussed his attention on his plate of cold London.

After finishing the main course, he planned to search out the delicious waitress and demand the dessert he'd paid over the odds to enjoy.

Chapter Twenty-Seven

Wednesday 28th October – Evening

The Corpulent Canard, Hounslow, London, England

Fully aware of Brutus behind him and the two thugs at his flanks, Kaine scoped out the kitchen, confirming that little had changed since the previous day's scouting trip.

White-smocked sous chefs and other members of the cooking brigade, ten in all, stepped aside as Brutus' men led him into the kitchen. Brutus walked two paces behind to ensure that Kaine couldn't spring any surprises.

The security team's discipline and Kaine's prior research, told him they were reasonably well-trained professionals. They were armed and likely to be no pushovers. Before allowing them to lead him from the dining room, he'd gambled on them being unlikely to use their weapons in the kitchen in front of witnesses. The odds weren't in his favour until they took him outside.

Outside, he was prepared.

Outside, he had Danny with a rifle, and Danny rarely missed what he aimed at.

But inside, Kaine was vulnerable. Once in the kitchen, he'd planned to make a rush for the back door, but the best laid plans sometimes failed.

When preparing for battle, advanced reconnaissance often paid dividends. Unfortunately, during his earlier visit, the big thug in the tight suit standing guard at the rear door hadn't been there. The unexpected addition of a guard inside the back door as well as the one outside, was bad enough, but the cleaver held in his hand—the shiny cleaver that didn't look as though it had seen a side of beef since it left the cutler—made the situation much, much worse.

Kaine risked a glance over his shoulder.

Brutus threw a bolt on the kitchen door and snapped the barrel lock. He smiled and drew a Glock 17 from his shoulder holster. One of the chefs, a young woman in spotless whites and a paper hat, gasped. Brutus raised a finger to his lips, said, "Shut up, bitch," and held the pistol across his chest, muzzle pointing at the ceiling.

Kaine relaxed a little. At least it wasn't pointing at him, not for the moment.

Brutus leaned against the closed doors. "You are going nowhere, asshole," he said to Kaine before addressing the kitchen staff. "You lot fuck off outside for twenty minutes while we show asshole how to make fish fingers—with his own fingers."

Smiler, the man at Brutus' side, who hadn't stopped

grinning since they'd marched Kaine from the dining room, barked out a cruel laugh.

"Nice one, Brutus," he said, his voice more high-pitched than Kaine expected.

None of the staff moved. The same blonde woman started crying. The slim, young man at her side threw a protective arm around her shoulder, but trembled and looked close to tears himself.

"Well?" Brutus bellowed. "What you wait for? Fuck off. Mauro will not stand in way."

The head chef, Jordan Christie, gathered his courage and stood as tall as a man of his stature could manage. "What's the meaning of this? Leave my kitchen immediately!"

Christie's stance would have been magnificent if his voice hadn't cracked half-way through the second sentence.

Kaine nodded at him.

"Don't worry, chef," he said, keeping his volume low to avoid sparking early action from Brutus and his death squad. "You and your staff won't be out in the cold for long. I think it's even stopped raining. I'll try not to make too much of a mess in here."

His bluster sounded good even if it raised another sarcastic laugh from Smiler.

The TV chef threw Kaine a sad look that suggested he thought Kaine's comment was nothing more than the bravado of a condemned man. He gathered his brigade and ushered them past Mauro and out into the rear courtyard beyond. An icy blast of damp air ruffled Mauro's dark, wavy hair as he slammed the door on the last of them.

"Okay, men," Brutus said, his grin as wide and as cruel as Smiler's. "Now we have fun. Sir Brandon will not mind paying for damage we cause to kitchen."

In his position by the rear door, Mauro slapped the side of the cleaver against the heel of his free hand. It rang like an out-of-tune bell.

Still laughing, Smiler took a pace forwards, as did his mate. Kaine stepped to the side and took a defensive position with his back to the walk-in freezer. He spoke directly to Brutus, the alpha dog.

"Before you start, let me tell you, Banner-Hardy's going down," Kaine said, "and when he does, there'll be no money to pay your salaries or bonuses. You know that, right?"

Smiler and the other man exchanged glances. Smiler turned to Brutus, who frowned.

"This man playing for time. He thinks cops will ride to rescue, but they not coming. The boss is protected, understand?"

Kaine took his chance. "If you mean the one sitting out there, Superintendent Coverdale of the Bow Road police station, I wouldn't bank on it, Brutus, old chap."

The name struck home. Brutus' eyes narrowed, and he absently tapped the Glock against his shoulder. Kaine recognised the action of a man not as well-trained in the safe use of firearms as his dossier suggested. He was lucky the Glock didn't discharge by accident. Kaine filed the information away for future use.

He continued. "I saw the good superintendent hiding in the corner out there and, judging by the sick expression on his overstuffed face, he knew his secondary income stream was about to dry up—along with his police salary. In fact, it wouldn't surprise me to find Coverdale is in the process of calling Inspector Blackstone and they're both running through their exit strategies as we speak. What do you reckon, guys?" he said to the others.

Smiler stopped smiling. "Fucking hell, Brutus. Are you hearing this? If we ain't getting paid for topping this mouthy fucker, it ain't worth the risk."

Brutus shook his head, but the deepened creases on his forehead and narrowing of his eyes showed doubt, hesitation.

Kaine added to the pressure. "I was sort of fibbing before, too. This afternoon, I sent the information from the laptop and my report to the Independent Police Complaints Commission, the IPCC, not to the local plods. I have to say, it must have made good reading for them. As a backup, I also sent a copy to the National Crime Agency. They absolutely love investigating police corruption."

"Sod this," Smiler said, as quick at decision-making as he had been to laugh. "I'm off. You coming, Baz? What about you, Mauro?"

"Too fucking right," Baz said.

Mauro dropped the pristine cleaver on the nearest chopping surface and backed out of the door, ignoring Kaine, but never tearing his eyes away from Brutus and the primed Glock. Smiler and Baz raced after him. They moved quickly. Almost as fast as the late Tugboat had done.

Kaine slowed his breathing and loosened his shoulders and neck. How would Brutus react?

"So," Brutus said, taking two steps closer, but keeping out of reach, "just you and me now, cowboy." He grinned.

Kaine nodded. "Yep. Just you and me."

"But I have gun."

Kaine couldn't argue with that.

"Out there," Brutus said, using his empty hand to point to the dining room, "you accuse me of killing people for Sir Brandon, but you wrong, little man. Dead wrong. I kill people because I fucking enjoy it. So what is stopping me from shooting you in face for pure pleasure of seeing you die? Tell me that."

Slowly, Kaine looked up and pointed at the light fitting in the middle of the ceiling. "Smile, you're on Candid Camera."

Brutus looked up. He couldn't help it.

Kaine drove forwards from the freezer, shot out an open-handed, left uppercut, and struck the base of Brutus' nose with the heel of his hand. The big thug yelped as his nasal bone exploded. Kaine followed up with a snap-kick to Brutus' left knee and a simultaneous clubbing, backhanded right to his temple, landing the full-powered blow with the side of his fist. Both kneecap and skull crunched.

Brutus' eyes rolled up into his head and he teetered for the briefest of moments before toppling backwards to the floor. His head made a sickening thud when it bounced off the shiny, ceramic tiles. Blood and gore splattered across the floor.

Kaine took the Glock from the killer's dead hand, turned, and raced after Smiler and his cronies. No point checking for life signs. No human could have survived the trauma or the impact with the floor.

He burst through the outer door. The chill wind blasted away the sweat that had formed from the kitchen heat and the short bout of exercise.

He needn't have worried.

Smiler, Baz, Mauro, and a fourth man were sitting, cross-legged in a puddle in the middle of the car park— hands on heads, fingers interlaced. A relaxed Danny covered them with his Colt C8 carbine.

The young man from earlier, still with his arm around the pretty sous chef, looked as though he'd died and gone to heaven. She leaned against him and didn't seem to mind his close attention.

A harried chef, Jordan Christie, rushed towards Kaine. "Are you okay, mate? What happened to that Russian arsehole?"

Kaine nodded, said, "I'm good, Brutus isn't," and added a wry smile. "But he's Georgian, not Russian."

"Oh, right. Who knew?"

I did.

Behind the trademark, horn-rimmed glasses, Christie's eyebrows lifted a fraction. "Would it be okay to take my people back into the kitchen? It's freezing out here."

Kaine scrunched up his face. "Wouldn't recommend it. Dead bodies aren't pretty, and you wouldn't want to disturb a crime scene. Best go around the front to the reception area. Call out who you are first. I have a couple of men rounding up the other guards."

"We called the police as soon as we got outside. I'm surprised they aren't here already. The cop shop's only around the corner."

"Don't worry about that, but, can I ask a favour?"

"Anything," Christie said, worry clouding his face.

"Please wait fifteen minutes before you call again. Only this time, dial 9-9-9 and ask for someone more senior, someone in charge of serious fraud, or anti-corruption, or murder. Definitely not the locals."

"Fifteen minutes?" the chef asked, frowning. "You need the time to bugger off?"

"Something like that."

"But the other diners will have called the police, won't they?"

Kaine glanced over his shoulder and shook his head. "I doubt that very much. Most of those people will want to distance themselves from the whole event. Wouldn't surprise me to learn that half of them are on their way to Heathrow right now, desperate to find a country without an extradition treaty with the UK."

Christie laughed. "In that case, no problem. You'll have your fifteen minutes, my friend."

Kaine shook the chef's offered hand. "By the way, I'm sorry to have ruined your service."

Christie flashed his teeth. "Kidding aren't you? I'll be making a meal out of this for years—if you pardon the pun. This whole incident is going to form the basis of my next book. Just you wait. I'll be creating a whole new menu called *Killers in the Kitchen*, or *Death in the Dining Room*. I'm considering a beetroot-based starter." He stretched his neck and squinted towards his domain. "Plenty of blood in there, I'm guessing?"

"A little, but I didn't hang around long enough to make a study."

"Doesn't matter," he said, eyes shining as bright as his smile. "I'll use my imagination."

Judging from what Kaine had seen of the chef's creations, the man certainly didn't lack for anything in the imagination department. As for his taste and his culinary skills, they remained open to debate. Kaine hadn't had a chance to sample any of the man's creations.

"After tonight, you might consider looking for a new backer."

Christie scoffed. "That won't be a problem, mate. There's an honesty clause in my contract with BHCL and, for some reason, people keep falling over themselves to throw money at me." He looked over his shoulder to make sure his brigade couldn't hear and whispered, "Between you and me, I have no idea why anybody would fall for my bullshit when all they need is a bit of good pub grub. Still, I'm making a pretty decent living, so who's complaining?"

"Not you, clearly," Kaine said, warming to the diminutive chef.

Christie turned sideways to bring the others into the conversation. "We were watching your film show through the monitor in the kitchen. Mind if I ask who you are and why you risked your life tonight?"

Kaine raised a finger to his lips before answering. "Best you don't know."

"You mean if you tell me you'll have to kill me?"

Christie's laugh caught in his throat as he flashed a glance towards his kitchen and tried to imagine what might have happened to Brutus. He quickly shook his head. "Sorry, bad taste. I'll go before I piss you off."

"Good idea," Kaine said, adding a dead stare before winking.

The celebrity chef hurried away, shepherding his troops around the side of the building and out of sight.

Kaine closed on Danny, who hadn't moved since Kaine emerged from the kitchen.

"You okay, boss? I saw you wringing your hand."

Kaine looked at the outside edge of his right hand. A small split in the skin over the knuckle showed where he'd crushed Brutus' skull. "Brutus had a strong nose, but a glass temple."

"I would have let these fuckers go and come to help you out but ... well, one-on-one, I didn't think it would take you long to deal with the big bugger."

Kaine stared Danny down and showed him the Glock. "You know he had this?"

"Ooops," Danny sniggered, "my bad. Still, it didn't

seem to cause you too much of a problem, did it? What we going to do with these clowns?"

"There's a walk-in freezer in the kitchen. It has a lock."

"Cool." Danny laughed. "Sorry. The air's full of bad puns tonight, eh? I'll go put them on ice for the good cops."

Kaine groaned. "What about the rest of Sir Brandon's security team?"

"Just got the news," Danny said, tapping his earpiece. "Fat Larry and Slim rounded them all up and have them secure. What do you want done with them?"

"They're only the hired help. Let them go."

"What if any kick up a fuss?"

"They won't."

"But if they do?"

"Larry and Slim will know how to handle them."

Danny grinned. "Yes, boss. I guess they will."

Kaine checked his watch and lowered his voice. "We'd best hurry. There's a crowd waiting and a load of paper-work to complete before we can catch our cross-channel ferry. France awaits."

"In a hurry to get back to a rather attractive horse doctor, boss?"

"Get on with your work, Corporal," Kaine snapped.

"Yes, boss. Certainly, boss. Right away, boss."

Danny twitched the muzzle of the C8. The four captives jerked. "Okay, boys, up you get. Time to chill out."

"Corporal!"

"Sorry, boss. Can't help it."

"Force yourself."

"I'll try, boss," Danny said, still grinning as though he was having the greatest time. "Oh, now this is nearly over, you wanted me to remind you to give your friend in Porton

Down a bell. He can send Mortensen to the police now, right?"

Kaine thought about it for a second before answering. "There's no hurry. Mortensen's going to spend the next few years in jail. He might as well get used to rectal probes."

Danny winced and prodded a reluctant Smiler between the shoulder blades with the muzzle of his C8.

"Oh dear, and you say *my* jokes are bad?"

"Who's joking? With a haircut and a shower, Mortensen's going to scrub up nicely. He's likely to prove very popular with the old lags on C Wing."

Danny marched the prisoners towards the kitchen, entertaining them with a half-decent rendition of Jailhouse Rock.

Chapter Twenty-Eight

Wednesday 28th October – Evening

The Corpulent Canard, Hounslow, London, England

Kaine helped Danny feed the compliant prisoners into the freezer and lock the door on them.

"Want to make certain he's dead?" Danny asked, pointing his rifle at Brutus.

Kaine shook out his hand and flexed his fingers. "You can if you like, but I'll lay good odds he's breathed his last."

Danny shuffled closer to the body and took in the depressed fracture in the large Georgian's temple. "Bloody hell, boss. Didn't pull your punch, did you?"

"I thought it best not to waste any time."

"You aren't wearing gloves. Want me to splash his face

with bleach? There's bound to be a bottle around some-where and you wouldn't want the cops to find your DNA."

Kaine nodded. "Good idea. I knew there had to be a reason to keep you around."

"You can be really hurtful, you know," he said, smiling and looking anything but upset. "While I clean this piece of detritus, are you going to do the business with Sir Brandon?"

"Well now, Danny." Kaine broke down the Glock, examined its barrel for pitting, checked the load—Remington UMCs—and reassembled it within seconds. The gun would serve its purpose. At a pinch. "That's exactly what I'm going to do, and I'd best get a move on. The police won't be long."

"Sounds like a plan. Mind if I have a nibble on some of the posh nosh lying around? It'll only go to waste if I don't."

"Feel free. I doubt Chef Christie's going to object and it's already been paid for."

Kaine left Danny to his housework and his scavenging, grabbed a dishcloth from a hanger, and used it to unbolt the inner kitchen door. Quietly, he entered the dining room. On the way past, he picked up the TV's remote—the only item he'd touched in the dining room—and dropped it into his pocket. Sir Brandon, alone at his table, sat with his back to Kaine, speaking quietly into a mobile phone. Kaine couldn't hear what was being said, but the urgency was obvious in the man's arm-waving actions.

Kaine cleared his throat. "Hello there, BB. Bet you didn't expect to see me again."

Sir Brandon twisted in his chair. His eyes bugged wide, and his jaw dropped. The mobile slipped from his hand and clattered onto his dirty plate. The businessman jumped to his feet, pushing the chair away with the backs of his legs.

At the same time, his right hand slid under his jacket, reaching towards his armpit.

Kaine raised Brutus' Glock, aimed, and, in a flowing movement, squeezed the trigger twice. Two loud cracks reverberated through the room, and two small tufts of white lining burst from the right shoulder of Sir Brandon's otherwise-immaculate, black dinner jacket. Corresponding holes drilled into the wall behind him.

Sir Brandon squeaked and fell back into his chair, hands shooting towards the candelabra that dangled from the ceiling.

Kaine allowed himself a mirthless smile.

"Brutus had no idea how to maintain a weapon," he said. "If this Glock didn't shoot high, you'd have a ruined shoulder right now."

Kaine lied about the Glock. Its accuracy wasn't that far out, but, in his experience, very few things focused the mind better than being shot at, and he didn't want Sir Brandon's writing hand incapacitated. He extended his arm, pointed the Glock at the older man's sweaty forehead, and stepped further into the room. Sir Brandon's eyes narrowed, and his gaze never left the muzzle of the gun. He seemed transfixed by the weapon's power over life and death.

Once Kaine reached the table, he slid into the seat directly opposite the multi-millionaire construction magnate and thoroughly nasty individual. His aim never wavered.

The curtains at the entrance fluttered. Larry's gaunt face poked into the room followed by his stick-like frame. Like Danny, he carried a Colt C8 carbine. Anyone who didn't know better would have seen him as emaciated, a man barely capable of carrying his own weight. They would have been mistaken. Once, after a particularly harrowing and extended search-and-rescue mission, Kaine and his unit had returned to base, bedraggled and threadbare, but intact. A team of medics had tried to rush Larry into hospital. They wanted to treat him for dehydration and malnutrition when he needed nothing more than a shower, a change of clothes, and a good meal. "Fat" Larry Kovaks had the body fat percentage of an elite marathon runner and the strength of a bear. As with all of Kaine's chosen men, Larry could manage a twenty-five-kilometre route march over mountainous terrain carrying an assault rifle and a thirty-kilogram Bergen, and barely break into a sweat. Somehow, Larry consumed as much as two normal men and still looked like he hadn't eaten in days.

"Everything okay in here, boss?" he asked, his deep, booming voice at odds with his wiry frame.

Kaine nodded, said, "No problems here," and turned and twitched the Glock at Sir Brandon. "What about you, Sir Brandon. Anything to say?"

Sir Brandon showed enough sense to keep his mouth shut.

"We'll be out in a minute," Kaine told Larry. "I just need to impress on our well-dressed friend here the precarious nature of his current situation."

"Not that well dressed, is he. He's gone and messed up his fancy jacket."

Kaine smiled. "Shame that, isn't it."

"Sure is. We'll be ready for the off as soon as you are, boss," Larry said and melted back behind the curtain.

Sir Brandon swallowed hard. He started to lower his hands but shot them up again when Kaine shook his head and twitched the Glock once more.

"W-What do you want with me?"

"First things first. Take out your gun, and please, please give me an excuse to shoot you in the face."

Driblets of sweat ran from Sir Brandon's receding hairline and tracked down his gaunt cheeks. They joined underneath his chin and dripped onto his shirtfront.

"I-I ... don't know what—"

"Best you move very slowly and use your left hand."

He tried to comply, but with his left hand, he struggled to remove a small-but-deadly Ruger 380 Auto from the suede holster tucked under his left armpit. Eventually, he managed to tug it free.

"Place it on the table, barrel pointing towards you, and push it across to me."

Sir Brandon followed the instructions carefully. Kaine lowered the Glock and aimed it at the red cummerbund encircling the man's belly.

Kaine took the Ruger, unloaded it, and dropped it into his jacket pocket. Not the most accurate or reliable weapon ever made, but deadly enough at close quarters.

Sir Brandon raised his hands again, slowly. "H-How did you do it?"

"How did I get the better of Brutus and his men?"

He nodded.

"Doesn't really matter, does it? What you really need to know right now is what I want and how you're going to get out of this alive. Am I right?"

The Knight of the Realm nodded again, and another drop of sweat fell from his chin.

"That's really simple," Kaine said, checking his watch— two minutes before Chef Christie would phone the police and a few more before they would arrive. "You and I are going on a little drive."

Sir Brandon stiffened. His mouth opened. A strangled sound emerged, but no words.

"Don't fret, old chap," Kaine said. "You still have a chance to survive the night."

"W-Where are you taking me?"

"Not far. It'll be a nice surprise."

"Oh God. You're going to kill me?"

"Isn't that what you ordered Brutus to do to me?"

"I have money. I-I can pay you. P-Please don't ..."

"Death is nothing less than you deserve, but money might help persuade me to let you live a little longer. We'll see."

Behind the fear and the tears, the light of hope shone in the man's pale eyes.

"Anything," he whimpered. "I-I'll pay anything."

Yes, you will.

The image of two little girls screaming and their father lying face down in his own blood returned to stoke the fire of Kaine's anger. He barely retained control. For two pennies, Kaine would have pistol-whipped the pitiful creature with his own little gun. But Kaine was better than that. His personal code wouldn't allow him to beat a helpless, old man into a pulp. Besides, his plan required Sir Brandon to remain unmarked, coherent, and in full possession of all his teeth and all his faculties.

"You can lower your arms now, but keep the hands in view, there's a good chap." He reinforced his command by twitching the Glock yet again.

Sir Brandon dropped his hands to the table and rattled out an audible sigh.

"Don't relax too much, old sport. Your writing hand's going to be doing a load of work over the next few hours."

"What?"

"I'll explain when we reach our destination. Now, up you get, you miserable piece of excrement. Move smoothly and quietly to the exit where your carriage awaits."

BOW ROAD WAS as quiet as Kaine had seen it. A few private cars and taxis rolled along each carriageway, headlights dipped, and even the traffic lights cooperated by changing to green when needed.

Behind the wheel, Slim Simms—built like a Dutch barn and the owner of a right cross powerful enough to fell a small oak—stopped the Range Rover alongside Bistro Mykonos' boarded up window. It was an ironic gesture not lost on Kaine or the prisoner at his side.

"Oh God," Sir Brandon said the moment he recognised the area.

The window's destruction marked the start of Sir Brandon Banner-Hardy's fall from grace, and it was about to mark the end of BHCL as a going concern. That the story would conclude at the Bistro within the following day or so also seemed entirely fitting.

"Do the words 'chickens' and 'roost' come to mind?"

Cleverly, Sir Brandon chose not to respond to Kaine's question.

Kaine's old Astra was already parked on the street, courtesy of a fast-driving Danny, and the Bistro's soft lights through the undamaged windows bathed the pavement in a cheery, yellow glow.

Slim killed the engine and yanked on the handbrake. He turned to face Kaine, as did Larry in the front passenger seat. Both grinned like hard-working men on the cusp of receiving their healthy, year-end bonuses—which happened to be the case.

"Ready to meet your audience?" Kaine asked.

Sir Brandon turned to Kaine, chin trembling. "What do you want from me?"

Kaine smiled ever so politely. "Just your signature on some contracts. Nothing onerous, I can assure you. Now, let's go and have ourselves an Inaugural Meeting."

Sir Brandon edged away, shrinking back into his seat.

"Oh no you don't."

Kaine pocketed his Glock, grabbed hold of a torn shoulder pad, and dragged the reluctant, soon-to-be-former-millionaire businessman from the car. With Slim and Larry acting as a defensive rear guard, he pushed their reluctant prisoner through Bistro Mykonos' front door.

Chapter Twenty-Nine

Wednesday 28th October – Evening

Bistro Mykonos, Tower Hamlets, London, England

The Bistro was packed. Angry-looking men and women occupied each chair, and at the back of the room, more people had been forced to stand. Kaine pushed a resisting Sir Brandon further into the dining room and held him still, a trophy on display. Every face turned to the front and the loud babble subsided.

Roger Finchley, a heavy-set man at the table nearest the broken window, stood, making his presence felt immediately. He had unruly, white hair, an argumentative beard, a huge beer belly, and his nose held the colour of sundried tomatoes. Kaine had identified the one-time owner of the pub on the corner as a natural leader of the former residents, owners, and leaseholders of Hardwicke Row. Kaine had also spent most of the morning detailing his proposals in advance. After asking a number of searching questions, some of which Kaine was reluctant or unable to answer, Finchley announced himself as a fully-fledged supporter of the project.

"Mr Finchley," Kaine said to the publican and turned to the others, "ladies and gentlemen, thank you for coming at such short notice."

The publican began his performance with a sneer, and he pointed at Sir Brandon. "This him, is it? The man responsible for everything?"

For the second time that night, Kaine found himself introducing Sir Brandon Banner-Hardy to an audience, only this one comprised innocent victims, not villainous and greedy pond scum.

A man at the back called into question Sir Brandon's heritage. Others joined in. A woman at a table next to the kitchen offered to remove his privates with a pair of rusty scissors. Kaine allowed them to vent for a few minutes before raising a hand for silence, but it took several moments for the crowd to quieten. Without careful handling, they could easily have degenerated into a mob.

Sir Brandon backed towards the door but, with a nod from Kaine, Larry and Slim stepped forwards in unison and stood on either flank, giving him no room to do anything but stand and squirm.

Kaine moved to one side to give the crowd a clearer view of the figure of hate. He allowed himself a few moments to take in the gathering. A few former residents were no-shows, but most had turned up keen and ahead of time. Lara's letter and its promise of healthy compensation had proved a really good draw.

The Smithson family—wife, son, and two teenage daughters—filled a table in the middle. They'd owned the grocery store until Alfie Lovejoy and Tugboat paid a visit one weekend and put Mr Smithson in hospital with a compound fracture of the right leg. At another table, the Howdens—an elderly couple in failing health—threw furious glares at Sir Brandon. They'd been forced out of their home on the top floor of the row after an arson attack left them terrified. Kaine's gaze wandered over faces that told a dozen stories, each of them minor in the great scheme of things, but life-changing to the individuals concerned.

Another family missing from the room was the one Kaine had come to help, the Constantines. But they were safe and under protective guard. Their lives and livelihood would be restored, even in their absence. Kaine would make certain of that.

He broke the simmering, festering near-silence. "I imagine you'd all like to see this individual"—he jerked a thumb at a cowering Sir Brandon—"strung up by his man parts and dangling from the nearest bridge?"

Some in the crowd cheered, others nodded. One woman shouted, "Too bloody easy on him!"

"I agree entirely," Kaine said, "and while you would gain some momentary satisfaction, it wouldn't return you to your homes or earn you the compensation you deserve."

"Your letter said we'd learn summat to our advantage," Finchley shouted above the growing noise of dissention. "That's why we're all here, but I'm happy to string that bastard up right now. I'll even provide the rope."

The crowd cheered.

Kaine held up his hand again and shouted, "I fully

understand, but if you give me a few more minutes of your time, I have a much better alternative."

Finchley took a moment before taking over Kaine's role of crowd control. "Okay, settle down you lot. Let's hear what the man came to tell us."

He turned and gave Kaine a surreptitious wink before passing the baton over to him once again.

Kaine signalled to Danny, who'd been in the kitchen, standing guard by the rear door. "Let them in now, please."

Danny opened the door and stood aside to allow three men and two women to enter. Each wore a dark suit and carried a fat briefcase. They were business-like, serious-looking, and stopped in the kitchen before entering the dining area.

As a body, the audience turned to study the newcomers.

Kaine spoke up. "Let me introduce you to the four senior partners of Prescott, Blaire, Smith, and Brown, legal representatives to the recently formed Hardwicke Row Residents' Association. The man at the back is Mr Owen Jenkinson." A bookish, fifty-something man in a dark suit offered a shy smile to no one in particular.

Kaine took his notes from his pocket and read aloud. "Mr Jenkinson is a Notary Public. Which means, he is a legally appointed officer of the court whose role is to certify any documents signed tonight. Once he has testified to the validity of said documentation, officials in any country will accept them in good faith."

A muted rumble from the group suggested they were impressed, but still confused.

Kaine returned his notes to his pocket and continued. "Inside those briefcases are contracts made out to each resident of the row. While I encourage you to read the paperwork, the gist is pretty simple. Each of you will get your homes and businesses back—if that's what you want. You'll also receive five times the highest offer made by BHCL to compensate you for the inconvenience you have suffered, and they have caused. Furthermore, the building renovations will continue until the work is completed to a high standard, and this work will be supervised by a firm of contractors of your choice. As for those people not here at the moment due to illness or injury—our hosts, the Constantines, for example—we have obtained their powers of attorney. I promise you, no one is going to lose out."

He paused to let the information sink in before hitting them with the knockout blow.

"Finally," he said, "by the end of next week, Banner-Hardy Construction Limited is going to deposit twenty-five million pounds into the association's bank account—"

A rippling gasp cut into Kaine's announcement. Sir Brandon groaned, and Larry and Slim had to hold him up to stop him sinking to his knees.

"Yes, ladies and gentlemen, I'm completely serious," Kaine said, unable to stop himself from smiling. "The association will take over the running of the row, but you'll own it as a group. There's a whole lot more in the contracts about freehold and leasehold and annual maintenance fees and Council taxes, and so on, but the solicitors are here to take you through all that. They'll remain here for as long as is necessary, and their time during this process will be paid for, in its entirety, by BHCL."

Kaine paused and allowed silence to bleed into the room. Eventually, the quiet was broken only by London's evening traffic and Sir Brandon's laboured breathing.

"Oh, and before I forget," he said, "even if it takes all night and all of tomorrow, Sir Brandon will be here to countersign each and every contract. So, take your time and help yourselves to the refreshments we've laid on. I don't want anyone to rush into anything. To be legal and above board, this has to be done by the consent of all parties. Now, before we continue, are there any questions?"

"Where do I sign?" a wag shouted, laughing, seemingly in disbelief.

Another man cheered and the room filled with applause, whistles, and table thumping.

Kaine turned and took two paces towards the doorway. He locked eyes with a snivelling Sir Brandon. "Do you have a problem with signing any of those contracts?" he asked, making sure even the people in the back could hear. "I want it made perfectly clear that you are signing these contracts of your own free will and without duress."

The beaten man swallowed.

"I-I …"

"Last chance, Sir Brandon," Kaine said, leaning closer and dropping into a whisper. He patted the pocket containing the Glock. "You wouldn't want me to choose my preferred option, which involves dragging you away from here and introducing you to the present Brutus gave me before I crushed his skull."

"You crushed his …? God. No, no. I'll … sign anything you want. Just don't hurt me, please."

"Louder, please."

Sir Brandon coughed and shouted, "I'll sign," in a dry, creaky voice.

"Of your own free will?"

"Y-Yes … of my own free will."

"And without duress?"

"A-And without duress!"

Kaine smiled, patted the man's sweat-dampened cheek, and leaned closer, whispering again. "And don't think you'll be able to renege on the deal later. I've had my team of solicitors working on those contracts for days. They are completely watertight. And, to keep you totally 'honest', the information I found on Lovejoy's computer is enough to put you away for the rest of your life. The charges will include fraud, tax evasion, bribery of officials in a public office … Oh and of course, multiple counts of murder. Try to wriggle out of any one of those agreements, and I'll send the files to the National Crime Agency."

Sir Brandon straightened. He blinked and stared into Kaine's eyes. "You mean … you mean the police aren't involved yet?"

"No, not yet," Kaine answered, meeting the man's eye. "The police and I don't really get along. So, just to make sure you understand, I'll keep hold of the files to make sure you keep to your part of the bargain."

The man who'd aged ten years in a single evening raised a shaky hand to wipe his forehead. "Thank God. May I sit down, please?"

"In a minute. Before you relax, there's one thing you can do for me personally," Kaine said, gently.

Sir Brandon started shaking again. "What? Oh God, what now?"

"Nothing onerous. It's just that my men and I incurred some expenses cleaning up your mess. I'll need you to transfer some funds into our offshore account."

The man frowned and shook his head as though he needed to clear out his ears. "Y-You're blackmailing me? For money?"

Kaine scratched the top of his head. "Not at all. I prefer to call it my organisation's consultancy fee. But don't worry, I'm not greedy. Five million pounds ought to cover our costs, assuming you transfer it before midnight. One second later and the fee doubles." He checked his watch. "You have forty minutes."

"You're mad," Sir Brandon spluttered. "I don't have that amount of cash available … and I can't access anything at this time of night."

"Really?" Kaine said, dropping a heavy hand on the liar's shoulder. "What about your instant-access account in the Federal Bank of Liege? As of three o'clock this afternoon, your available funds were a smidge over eight and a half million Euros."

Sir Brandon's jaw dropped.

"Y-You know about that account?"

Kaine drove his thumb into a pressure point on the man's shoulder hard enough to make him squeal. "I know everything I need to about you, old chap. I could demand it all—every last penny—but, unlike you, I'm not a greedy man. And you'll need some money for legal costs, I imagine."

Sir Brandon nodded. "Okay, okay. Please … please stop."

Kaine relaxed his grip. "Excellent, I knew you'd see sense in the end. See that tall, blond chap in the kitchen?" He pointed to Danny. "He has a tablet set up with the bank account details. All it needs are your authorisation codes and your thumbprint. To be honest, we don't really need the codes, and I could hack off your thumb if you prefer."

"No, please. I'll do it. But, what's to stop you coming back for more?"

"Nothing, old chap. But, here's my promise. This is a one-time only deal." He patted the older man's hollow cheek once more, and added, "You can trust me. I happen to be a man of my word."

Kaine nodded to Larry, said, "Take him to the kitchen.

He's finally seen the light," and stood back. He'd had more than enough close contact with the slippery bastard for one night.

Larry and Slim pushed Sir Brandon forwards, but he struggled against them and turned to face Kaine.

"Who are you?"

Kaine smiled through his annoyance. "My name isn't important."

"But why are you doing this to me?" he asked, sounding every bit the plaintive and whiny child.

Kaine finally lost his cool. He grabbed the pig by the lapel and spun him to face the weatherboard panel.

"That's why, you mealy-mouthed piece of filth," Kaine hissed. "Anyone prepared to do that to an innocent family deserves punishment and gets my undivided attention. Just be happy there's no broken glass left in the pane, or I'd mash your face into it. Now get him out of my sight."

He threw the badly shaken man back to his guards, who hurried the quivering wretch towards Danny. The members of the recently inaugurated Hardwicke Row Residents' Association burst into another round of spontaneous applause. Roger Finchley clapped Kaine firmly on the back and raised Kaine's arm, forcing him to acknowledge their plaudits.

Kaine lowered his head. If they knew his true identity, they'd likely start baying for his blood along with Sir Brandon's.

Chapter Thirty

Thursday 29th October – Evening

The English Channel

According to the notice on the Brittany Ferries' information desk, the overnight crossing from Portsmouth to St Malo was one of the roughest on record. Had the conditions been any worse, the sailing would have been cancelled. During the trip, even the highly experienced crew struggled to keep upright while performing the most routine of tasks.

Most of the passengers spent the journey with faces buried in reinforced paper bags, leaving the full-service restaurant empty apart from the two ravenous, former-SBS operatives. They took their time over a late dinner, neither saying much and savouring both the food and the relaxed atmosphere after a job well done.

Kaine pushed away his empty plate and swirled the rather decent Fitou, enjoying the way the full-bodied red wine clung to the inside of the glass. His palate wasn't sophisticated enough to make out the "ripe plum and peppery spice" promised on the label, but the wine was a first-rate accompaniment to the roast lamb, Duchess potatoes, and green beans he'd recently enjoyed.

Across the table, Danny vacuumed up his steak and frites, washed down with a second bottle of Danish lager.

"Grub's good here, Captain," he said. "The chef must be a proper sailor. Remember that weak-kneed clown in the galley on *HMS Fabricant*? Useless beggar couldn't boil an egg unless the sea was flat calm."

"I remember," Kaine said, draining his wine and emptying the remains of the half-bottle into the glass. He didn't often allow himself the luxury of a third glass, but after such a successful—and rewarding—outcome, he considered it fitting and relaxed his own rules. The fact that he was heading back to France and a certain medic didn't do anything to dampen his celebrations, either.

Danny leaned back, beer in hand, and laughed. "The look on BB's face when you made him face that broken window. Wish I'd had my phone camera handy."

Kaine squirmed in embarrassment. "Afraid I lost my cool a little there. The slimy git got under my skin with his hard-done-by attitude. Miserable piece of excrement."

Danny took a deep swig before speaking again. "Don't pull your punches, Captain. Tell me what you really think." He grinned and drank a little more.

"Sorry, Danny, but when I think what could have happened to those girls and what did happen to their father … my blood boils."

He allowed the thought to fade and rode another

rolling, twisting dip in the ship's forwards momentum. A huge wave boomed against the port bow. Somewhere outside the restaurant, a woman screamed.

Not a good sailor, that one.

"What do you reckon, boss?" Danny asked, holding his plate to stop it sliding off the table. "Force 8? 9?"

Kaine shrugged, then nodded. "Something like that, but the wind's coming from the southeast. It'll ease right back when we reach the lee of the continent. Be flat calm in a couple of hours, I'd bet."

Danny read the time from his watch. "When do we dock?"

"Oh-seven-thirty. Give or take. Might be a bit of a delay with the weather."

"And then what? A ten-hour drive to your villa?"

"If we hurry."

Danny's face broke into one of his cheeky smiles. "And you are going to hurry, right, boss?"

"Easy, Danny."

Kaine tried to snap, but Danny was correct. The lad could read Kaine's mood no matter how hard he tried to mask it.

"If you're in that much of a rush, why didn't we fly?"

"Oh dear, Corporal. You seem to have forgotten the basic principles of covert travel."

Danny paused for a moment's thought before answering, "You mean the one that says never travel back the same way you went out?"

"Spot on. Give the man a bonus."

"You've already done that, boss. And a nice, healthy one it was, too. Who knew Sir Brandon would be so generous?"

Danny waited for the ferry to climb out of another deep

trough before speaking again. "Good working with some of the old troop, eh?"

"Agreed. Civilian life hasn't dulled their edge one bit. I've a feeling I'll need to call on them from time to time."

"They'll all be willing, boss. And they'd do it even without the healthy wage packet."

They fell silent for a few moments, and Kaine allowed his thoughts to roam. It didn't take long for them to fetch up on a sun-drenched beach in Gironde. He looked forward to the tranquillity—amongst many other things.

"Changing the subject, boss. Are you sure you don't mind me crashing at your place for a couple of nights?" Danny asked after taking another swig from his fast-emptying bottle.

"On the way to your friends in Spain?"

"That's right. They won't reach Madrid until Sunday, and I don't have the key to their gaff. Besides, it will be good to see Uncle Cuddles again."

They laughed.

"Don't let Rollo hear you call him that."

The brightness of Danny's smile dipped a watt or two, before lifting again. "Of course not. Be nice to see the doc again, too."

The cheeky young git double-hitched his eyebrows.

Kaine sighed. Time to stamp out the minor insubordination before it spread through the ranks.

"Corporal Pinkerton, there's nothing going on between the doc and me. My only goal is to keep her safe until I'm certain no one wants to use her to get to me. And that's all. Do I make myself clear?"

Danny straightened his face and sat more upright. "Yes, boss. Absolutely, boss." He paused a moment before adding,

"In that case, you wouldn't mind if I asked her out for a meal while I'm visiting? On a date, I mean." His eyes glistened with mischief.

"Forget it, Danny," Kaine snapped. "She's way out of your league!"

And mine.

Danny slapped his hand on the table hard enough to make the crockery jump. "Ha! I knew it. You do like her, don't you? Can't blame you, mind, she's a wee bit special. And you're dead right. She's way too good for the likes of me."

"Good. And now we're going to drop the subject," Kaine said, delivering it as an order, not a request.

Danny nodded and became serious for a moment. "Sorry, boss. Just wanted to let you know Rollo and I couldn't be happier for you." He coughed and shifted in his chair. "And to change the subject again, that information you found on Alfie Lovejoy's laptop ..."

"What about it?"

"Are you really planning to hold onto it?"

Kaine leaned back and toyed with the wine glass. "Only until BHCL has deposited the money into every account. Should take no more than a week to release all the funds. After a short delay to ensure there aren't any shenanigans, I'll send the files to DCI Jones, and he can distribute them as he sees fit. Sir Brandon Banner-Hardy is going to prison and what's left of his fortune won't save him."

Danny threw his free hand to his chest and gave Kaine a look of mock horror. "You mean, you lied to Sir Brandon? Shame on you."

Kaine laughed. "I'll say three Hail Mary's next time I'm in church."

"Bloody hell, you still go to church?"

"Not recently."

As if any church would have the likes of me.

The trill of Kaine's mobile interrupted his reply. He dug the phone out of his pocket, hoping to see *Uncle C* or *Doc* as the caller ID, but the display showed an anonymous text.

Pick up the next call. A friend.

He turned the screen towards Danny, who set his bottle on the table, but kept a tight hold to its base. The mobile trilled again, this time with a call.

"Going to answer it, sir?"

"Don't see why not, do you?"

Danny shook his head, and Kaine hit the speaker button.

"Hello?"

A man spoke. "Hullo there, Mr K. How you diddling?"

He sounded young and cheery, the accent a sort of Cockney mashed with the hint of an Aussie twang. Almost as though it was forced.

Kaine sat up straighter, eyes searching the restaurant for signs of danger, but they still had the place to themselves. Even the waiter had disappeared into the galley. Danny leaned closer, straining to catch the caller's words above the crashing of the sea against the hull and the shuddering throb of the powerful, twin marine diesels.

"Hello yourself, Mr …?"

"You can use the name Corky, Mr K. Before this goes any further, congrats are due. You did a real good job at the Corpulent Canard last night. Nice one. That Brutus were a real big dude. Evil, you know? But you took him apart just like that."

The snap of clicking fingers jumped out of the mobile phone's speaker.

"You saw that?"

"Yep. Corky were spying through the gaff's surveillance cameras. Caught a good view of the kitchen. The way you took the Georgian apart. Spectacular. Corky better remember never to upset you, Mr K."

Kaine lifted his gaze from the phone and looked at Danny, who opened his eyes wide in appreciation. The man with the cocksure voice, Corky, had watched the take-down without putting up any interference. It sounded promising.

"How did you get this number?" Kaine asked, trying to calm his churning thoughts.

"Don't worry about that for the moment, Mr K. You're safe. Corky ain't told no one where you are or where you're going, and he never will. You gotta remember this. Corky is your friend."

Kaine found it difficult to trust someone who referred to themselves by their first name. Again, he glanced at Danny, who shrugged and shook his head.

"How can I be sure of that?" Kaine asked.

Corky barked out a laugh.

"You're still free and clear, and on that big boat to … well, let's keep your destination off the airways. Best to be on the safe side until we get to know each other a little better. 'Kay?"

"Okay. What do you want?"

The strange man on the other end of the call released a deep sigh.

"Corky don't want nothing but to help you, Mr K. He didn't introduce himself properly last time—"

"Last time?"

"Ain't you twigged it yet?" he said. "Corky's the one who

texted you about the Constantines. He's the one who gave you the heads-up about them needing your help."

Kaine and Danny shared another glance. He had twigged. Of course he'd twigged.

"You're the texter?"

"Yep," he said, chuckling.

"Why didn't you introduce yourself properly?"

"That's because Corky wasn't sure you were serious about helping the families, the ones you call The 83. He was worried your trip to Scotland last month might have been a one-off."

"Are you satisfied now?"

"'Course. Corky wouldn't be making this here call otherwise, now would he?"

Despite his high state of alert, Kaine smiled. The man was gently irritating, but hard to dislike. The fact that Danny dropped his shoulders and raised the bottle to his lips showed that he felt the same way.

"Okay," Kaine said. "Explain yourself. What do you want and why?"

"Like Corky said before. He only wants to help you protect The 83. Ain't it obvious? You see, at the moment, you're talking to a bloke what is probably the best information acquisition specialist on the planet."

"'Information acquisition specialist'?" Kaine said. "You mean you're a hacker?"

"Mr K, you don't have no cause to go insulting Corky like that. Hacking is a game carried out by spotty kids in basements who don't have the first clue what they're doing. They just get lucky now and again. As for Corky? Well ... Corky's what you might call an artist. A Rembrandt of the keyboard if you like. Trouble is, if he's being totally honest with himself, Corky's a little bored. He don't have no real challenges left in life. It's like this, Mr K. Once you've made a fortune from robbing a few dozen dodgy companies it gets a little stale, y'know?"

"Really," Kaine said and relaxed enough to take another sip of wine.

"By the way, Mr K. How's the Fitou?"

"What the hell?"

Kaine shot to his feet, but the restaurant remained empty, and he'd confirmed the absence of surveillance cameras in the area before making his choice of tables. Danny reached for the knife in his boot, on high alert.

Corky laughed. "That got you, didn't it? No, Corky don't have no eyes on you, but he does have access to the electronic point-of-sale tills on that ferry. How was your steak? Or did your mate what don't like being called Pinkie, have the beef while you had the lamb?"

Another chuckle burst through the speaker. Kaine and Danny exchanged another glance. Danny puffed out his cheeks and pulled his hand away from the dagger.

"That was nothing but a little demonstration of Corky's skills. Of course, he wouldn't have had a clue what you'd bought specifically, but as you're the only ones in the restaurant, it weren't difficult to guess. They don't have cameras in the posh dining room, but Corky did see you head into the place a little while back. Corky saw you checking out the duty-free shop, too."

"Okay," Kaine said, retaking his seat. "You've made your point. What do you want, money?"

"No!" Corky snapped. "Corky told you, he don't need money. He's got plenty of cash. Corky don't want nothing but to help you. Didn't he prove that already with the Greeks?"

"Okay, in that case, tell me how you knew they were in trouble."

"That's the easy part. Corky's been watching The 83 ever since he learned you wanted to protect them, and—"

"How?" Kaine interrupted Corky's flow.

"You what?"

"How did you learn I wanted to protect The 83?"

Corky tutted. "Corky was coming to that, but let him finish one story first, then he'll tell you another. ... So, Corky set up a load of stealth programs to flag up any major changes in The 83's circumstances. You know, anything that might show them as being in difficulty. Told you Corky was clever." He chuckled.

"Yes, you did."

Not exactly bashful, are you.

"Anyhow, a few months ago, before you shot ... let's just call it 'the incident', and before Corky started snooping on them, the Greek restaurateurs had that sudden drop off in till receipts. Last Thursday, Corky found out that someone were putting the pressure on them and had done the same thing to most of their neighbours, and *that's* why Corky sent you the text."

Kaine nodded to himself. Corky had answered one question, but plenty remained.

"Okay, Corky. You've given us the demo, and I have to say I am impressed. What happens next?"

"Dunno, Mr K. That depends on what Corky's algorithms say and what you want him to do for you. If you like, he can be your ears on the world."

"Not sure I need another pair of ears."

"If you mean that stunning bird what lives in Paris? She ain't nowhere near as good as Corky," he snapped, showing signs of mild annoyance for the first time. "She never told you 'bout the Constantines, did she?"

"The woman in question is busy. She has to work for a living."

"Yeah, that's what Corky means. If you let him, Corky can help you full time. Corky's loaded, see. Rolling in moolah. He don't need to do no more paid work if he don't want to. You and Corky can decide who to help together." He paused for a moment before asking, "Well, what do you reckon?"

"I call the shots, Corky. No one else. Tell me how you found me, and I'll give you my answer."

Corky sniffed. "Promise to keep it to yourselves?"

"I can't make that sort of promise on insufficient information. But if you play straight with me, I'll do the same with you. Will that do?"

"Yeah. Suppose it'll have to."

Kaine looked questioningly at Danny, whose expression remained noncommittal.

"So, how did you find me, and why are you so interested in me and my problems?"

"Okay," Corky said, "Corky's gonna hold you and Corporal P to your promise. Don't think he won't find out if you jabber but … well, Corky's been sort of taking an interest in what a senior cop who works in Birmingham has been up to."

DCI Jones?

"You've been doing what!"

"Yeah, yeah, Corky knows. Please don't tell the old geezer. Corky's sort of taken a shine to him, you know? He's become a bit of a father figure to old Corky. Been teaching him about computers, social media, and the internet and stuff. Baby steps. Trying to help drag him into the modern world has been a bit of a struggle, mind. Don't worry, though. He's learning. Bloody sharp geezer when he puts his mind to it. Trouble is, he'd go ape-shit if he knew Corky were checking up on him."

Kaine scoffed. "You think?"

"Yeah, okay, but it's for his own good, too. He's starting to tread on important people's toes, and Corky wants to look out for him."

"In what way?"

"Er, in what way's Corky looking out for him?"

"No, Corky," Kaine said, exasperation edging into his voice. "In what way is 'the old geezer' upsetting the important people?"

"Oh right, Corky's got ya," the hacker answered. "Well, you know he's trying to get you a full exoneration, right? Trouble is, it don't suit the UK government's official position on a certain arms company. In short, the beggars are happy to hang you out to dry. Mr J's kicking up a fuss, but they're freezing him out. Corky's a bit worried he'll do something stupid like go to the press or resign or something."

"Hold on one second," Kaine said, hitting the mute button as the waiter appeared with Danny's pudding. He pressed it again when the man, looking a tad the worse for the wild motion of the ferry, staggered back to the galley with their empty dinner plates. "Sorry about that, Corky. What can I do to help?"

"You might want to think about releasing your evidence to the press. Corky knows you kept copies. It would take the pressure right off Mr J."

"Thanks for the advice, Corky. I'll talk to Mr J and see what he has to say on the matter."

"You do that, Mr K, but don't tell him you and Corky have been chatting."

"I won't."

"Good. Anyhow, that's it for the first part. If you're happy to receive Corky's help, he'll keep in touch. Now, Corky bets you're keen to know why he called you tonight rather than leaving it for later, yeah?"

Kaine sighed. "Okay, I'll bite. Tell me."

"Ever been to Haarlem?"

Kaine shot a look at Danny, who'd started tucking into his apple pie and *crème anglaise*, a thin and insipid version of English custard that Kaine found excessively bland. Clearly the youngster had lost interest in the conversation and had resumed his primary goal of cramming as much food into his face as possible. In his current guise, he'd have given Larry Kovaks a run for his money.

"Harlem, New York?" Kaine asked.

"Nah, Haarlem, the city just outside Amsterdam."

Danny stopped in the middle of loading his spoon and nodded.

"My colleague has, but I've never had the pleasure. Why, what's in Haarlem?"

"Ah, now here's an interesting thing. One of The 83 just landed himself in a spot of bother."

Danny lowered his spoon to the plate, wiped his mouth with the cotton napkin provided, and leaned closer, concentration written all over his face.

"What sort of bother?" Kaine asked.

"The 'killing a young woman and getting banged up for murder' kind of bother. You interested?"

Danny nodded. Kaine agreed.

"We're all ears."

"Okay, it ain't much, but Corky'll tell you everything he knows. There's this kid with special educational needs …"

Corky talked for ten minutes before ending the call abruptly with, "That's all Corky's got for now, but he's gonna keep digging. Be in touch with more, soon as he's found anything worth telling you."

Kaine lowered the phone to the table and drained his glass. "What do you think?" he asked Danny.

"I reckon we're heading to Holland, don't you?"

"Yes," Kaine said. "I rather think we are. How long will it take to reach Haarlem from St Malo?"

"A good few hours," Danny said, digging out his mobile and hitting the power button. "I'll find out, assuming the internet's still operating on this tub in this weather."

"Thanks."

Kaine picked up his phone and started dialling.

"You calling the villa?" Danny asked without raising his eyes from the screen of his smartphone.

"Yes. Rollo needs to know where we're going, and I need to know he can still look after the doc."

"Yeah," Danny said, smiling. "Sure you do."

"Danny!"

"Sorry, boss. Can't help myself."

"Try harder."

Kaine hit the call button but after ten rings the villa's voicemail kicked in. He left a coded message and called Lara direct, but it transferred straight to voicemail, too. The same thing happened when he dialled Rollo's number. He left a third coded message and waited for the call back.

And waited.

Thirty minutes later, with Kaine's emotions in turmoil and dozens of scenarios running through his head—each more worrying than the last—his mobile finally vibrated.

"Hello?" he almost shouted into the phone.

"Ryan, it's me. Is everything okay?"

Lara's educated and carefree voice calmed his shattered nerves. The relief flooding through his system stopped him reprimanding her for breaking telephone protocol by using his real name.

"What took you so long to call back, *Doc*?"

After a slight hesitation, she said, "My … friend and I were … swimming. We've only just picked up your messages. What's wrong? Is the weather really bad?"

Before the ferry sailed he'd reported to Rollo and given him their weather-affected docking time. Standard operational procedure wherever possible.

"No, nothing's wrong, but there's been a development. We've had to change our plans."

Kaine winced in preparation for her angry response, but her calm, almost casual, "What's happened?" came as a surprise. It seemed as though she didn't care. His joy and relief at hearing her voice turned into an unreasonable disappointment. He took a breath before launching into his explanation.

"Texter called. Turns out he really is a friend, and he wants to help. As it happens, he knows our mutual friend from Birmingham."

Kaine paused, hoping for a response, but none came.

"Are you still there?"

"Yes," she said, her tone flat, almost emotionless. "We're still here. You're on speaker, by the way."

"Good, okay. Someone in the Netherlands needs our help."

"Really?" Rollo asked before adding, "Good evening, boss. How's the trip? Has the young whipper-snapper started throwing up yet? The poor chap never was much of a sailor."

Danny rolled his eyes towards the ceiling, but kept quiet.

"Good evening, Alphonse," Kaine said.

He interpreted the amusement in Rollo's tone as the sergeant's way of keeping Lara in check—his recently redis-covered "Uncle Cuddles" persona rearing its benign head.

"I understand you're changing your itinerary?" Rollo asked.

"Exactly," Kaine said and started talking.

Chapter Thirty-One

Friday 30th October – Morning

Ferry Terminal, St Malo, Brittany, France

The on-board announcer called the foot passengers to the mustering point—in French, English, and Spanish—and Kaine shunted his Bergen into a more comfortable position on his shoulder. He'd had a fitful night's sleep, kept awake in part by worrying about how to deal with the Lara situation and by the idiot in the next cabin whose roaring snores drove straight through the wafer-thin partition wall.

At 03:00, Kaine considered storming the information desk and demanding to change cabins for one with at least a hint of sound insulation. Then the snores stopped. Danny must have turned over in his bunk. The next thing Kaine remembered was being woken by the melodic, Breton harp music flooding the PA system in Brittany Ferries' quaint version of an alarm call.

He and Danny had eaten a full breakfast in a near-empty café, and now stood side-by-side, waiting to disembark. They'd pre-booked a hire car and were bound for the bustling mayhem of Haarlem instead of the more restful delights of Gironde.

"Weather's cleared," Danny said, looking through one of the salt-stained windows to a view of the Napoleonic port. "Should get some decent sun today, according to the forecast."

Kaine yawned but didn't respond. Unlike the energetic Danny, he would never consider himself a morning person and could cheerfully have lasted another three hours without talking. A uniformed officer drew open the bulkhead door, thanked them for sailing with Brittany Ferries, and wished them a safe onward journey.

Kaine stepped into the covered gangway and inhaled the cool, clean air of Northern Brittany. With passport in hand and Danny at his back, he shuffled forwards with the rest of the passengers. In the customs zone, the Bergen just about squeezed into the tray and passed through the x-ray machine without sounding the alarm. Danny's less well-filled pack caused less of a problem, and they made it through into the port terminal within a few minutes.

Dozens of people filled the baggage claim area, but Kaine focused his attention on the signage, searching for the car hire bureaux. A slim, dark-haired woman crossed his line of vision. The way she moved seemed familiar. His heart flipped.

Lara?

Couldn't be. She'd been playing on his mind, screwing

with his imagination. The woman passed behind a big man in a heavy, roll-neck sweater.

Rollo.

No doubt. It could hardly be anyone else.

"Well, bugger me," Danny said, dropping his backpack to the floor. "What the hell are they doing here?"

Lara stepped out from behind Rollo, a huge smile lighting her face. Kaine stopped midstride and his Bergen crashed to the floor alongside Danny's. He couldn't decide whether to be angry or delighted.

He chose both.

Rollo marched forwards, picked up Kaine's Bergen in one hand, and led a spluttering Danny away without offering an explanation.

The crowds around Kaine and Lara melted away to nothing. Silence descended.

"Surprised to see me?" she asked, smiling, eyes shining.

"Stunned more like. Furious, too. What the hell are you doing here? And how did you get here so quickly? Damn it, woman. Why can't you just listen to me for once?"

Kaine stopped talking when her smile faded. He let go of the anger, gave into the delight, and took a step closer. She did the same in a hesitant dance. He lost control and tugged her into his arms.

Before he knew what was happening, they kissed.

Their first real kiss and he was lost. Completely defeated.

It seemed to last for hours and for moments. Her hand caressed his neck, easing away his tension. He broke the connection first, didn't want to, but needed to come up for air.

Her body felt good in his. Firm and soft and round. Christ he enjoyed the feel of her. The touch of her.

"That's better," she said, pulling away and searching his eyes. "Much better."

He licked his lips. "You taste sweet."

She laughed. "I've just finished my second hot chocolate while waiting for the boat to dock."

Kaine blinked.

"Er ... it's a ship, not a boat," he said, searching for a way to smooth any awkwardness. "A ... boat can fit on a ship, but a ship can't fit on a boat. And I didn't taste any chocolate."

"Ryan Liam Kaine," she whispered, after first checking to make sure no one was close enough to overhear, "you could at least try to come up with something more original."

"Give me time. I thought about saying the earth moved, but after the storm we just sailed through, I was worried you might question my sea legs. Not the thing to do to a Royal Marine. You shouldn't be here, Lara. It could be dangerous, and I don't want you hurt."

"My word, you are such an old romantic."

Kaine sighed. She'd ripped apart his determination to stay aloof and professional. Luckily there were two top-flight marines guarding their backs. Unluckily, both currently wore goofy smiles and looked as though they were about to start cheering.

Not so good in terms of security, but first rate in terms of improving his morale.

"So," he said, edging her closer to the safety of the goofy ones, the older of whom showed a comforting bulge under his left armpit, "mind answering my questions, Doc?"

Lara frowned in concentration and hugged his arm in both hers as though to stop him running off. "Okay, in order of delivery. Rollo and I are here to help. A close friend of mine lives in Amsterdam, and she's married to a lawyer. Last night, Sabrina's system alerted us to the young man's arrest, and we were already on our way here to meet you when you called.

"We took turns driving and kept checking the villa's message system. The phone signal kept dropping out, which is why it took us a little while to return your call. We had to find a quiet lay-by so you wouldn't hear the traffic. Rollo didn't want you to know what we were doing in case you ordered him to turn back to the villa. An order he didn't want to break."

Kaine fired a glance at his once-trusted friend. "The minute I have a chance, Sergeant Rollason and I are going to have some serious words."

"Please don't be angry with him, Ryan. He loves and respects you. You know that, right?"

"Hmm. He's a military man to the core. Wouldn't thank you for using the 'L' word. By the way, you've left out one question."

"The one about my not listening to you?"

Kaine threw her a scowl, not that he meant it. "Yes, that's the one."

"Oh Ryan, I'll always listen to you. Doesn't mean I'll obey, mind. I'm not one of your awestruck squaddies."

"In the marines, they're called booties, not squaddies."

"I stand corrected," she said, beaming.

He hugged her again, enjoying her warmth. "God, woman. You're impossible."

"I know." She laughed. "We make a good team."

"Not if you keep putting yourself in danger."

She pecked his cheek.

"So, what are we going to do next?"

Kaine looked from her to the awestruck booties. "I guess we're all heading to Haarlem."

"Good answer."

She rested her head on his shoulder.

While the other passengers hurried about their business, Kaine found himself in an island of tranquillity, if only for a few moments.

The END.

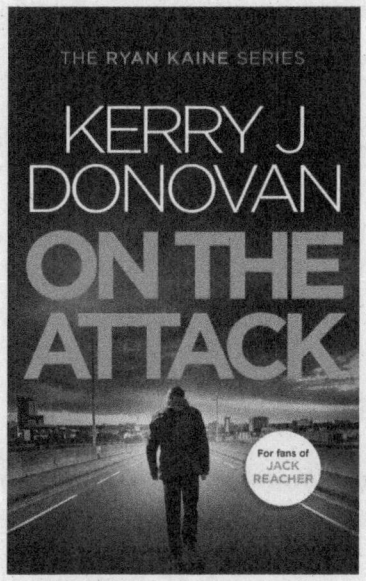

On The Attack: Chapter One

Monday 23rd November – Jerome Tedesco

Ocean Village, Southampton, Hampshire, England

Jerome "Teddy" Tedesco glared at the empty whisky glass in his hand. He'd have thrown the fucking thing at the wall, or at the Kraut, but his therapist kept telling him to meditate, to find his inner peace, not to vent his anger on others so readily. To do so wouldn't help relieve his underlying stress, or lower his blood pressure, or sort out his anger management issues, or whatever.

Well, screw her. Screw the overqualified, overcharging bitch into the wall.

She knew nothing.

So far, he'd paid the woman a small fortune to leave her Harley Street clinic and make weekly house calls and, after

340

twenty-three sessions, the best coping strategy she could come up with was meditation?

Total bloody shit.

"Think things through before you act, Mr Tedesco," she'd said, before clocking up another fucking invoice. "You'll find it works."

Yeah, and what else had he been doing all his Goddamned life?

Fuck.

It was little better than the things Mother used to tell him as a boy.

"Count up to ten, Jerome. Count up to ten. If you do that, the anger will fade, and the world will seem a much happier place."

If he'd listened to Mother, he'd have saved tens of thousands of pounds worth of therapy over the years, but ... sod it. If he'd listened to Mother, he'd still be working for the Shylock in the back street betting shop, and he wouldn't be the owner of all he surveyed—half of Southampton's seafront. He wouldn't own any of his businesses, the casinos along the south coast, the fishing boats, the pleasure cruisers, the stud farm on the South Downs, or the racecourse. Where would he be if he'd counted to ten and toed the fucking line?

Nowhere. That's where.

He let the Kraut on the other side of the desk, Schechter, sit and squirm a little longer before delivering judgement.

The moron would be doing plenty more squirming in a minute, but Teddy kept him dangling. He liked to see the minnows suffer. It suited his management style, and it made the ending all the sweeter. The two slabs of meat standing either side of the door already knew what he was going to say—he'd told them before they let Schechter into his office, his inner sanctum. They'd be ready for any reaction from the stupid Kraut.

German efficiency be fucked.

Teddy had to admit, Schechter looked the part. Tall, blond, square-jawed, broad-shouldered, intelligent, blue eyes. He was the archetypical Aryan—one of Hitler's super-men. But everyone knew what happened to Hitler and his bully boys. They bottled out and ended up losing a war they should have won. Schechter had come highly recommended by a man Teddy once trusted, but that hadn't worked out too well. Not so far. Not for the Kraut, and not for Grady, the Kraut's sponsor.

Fuck's sake, who did he have to screw over to get things done properly these days?

Teddy held up his empty glass and the nearer of the two guards, Ginger, rushed to refill it for him.

A good monkey. Well trained.

Teddy warmed the glass in his cupped hand and inhaled the rich vapours. Smoky, oaky, warm. The aroma of peat bogs, oak casks, and heather. Precisely the aroma a Macallan Speyside single malt should give off. Reassuringly expensive. He raised the lead crystal glass and touched the liquid to his lips, allowing his skin to absorb the moisture. He licked away the residue.

Very pleasant. Very rewarding. Well worth the price.

"Tell me, Schechter, how difficult should it be to dispose of a corpse?"

The Kraut stared back, said nothing. His open-mouthed expression, dumb and stupid. Not a good look for someone about to plead for his life. Plead and fail.

Teddy lowered the glass to the coaster in case he lost

control, which was on the cards. Wasting any of the glorious nectar wouldn't do. Wouldn't do at all.

Meditate. Count to ten.

To make certain, he rolled his chair further away from the desk, distancing himself from the glass and the Kraut. It gave him more perspective. More room to operate. More room to think.

"It isn't a rhetorical question, man. Answer me!"

Schechter stiffened. For the first time since he'd joined the organisation, the German showed real fear. Damn right, too. On the other hand, it was the first time he'd fucked up in all that time. Simple thing, but it had caused Teddy a monumental fucking headache.

"I apologise, Mr Tedesco," he said in his fucking annoying, stiff and precise accent. "It was the result of unforeseen circumstances. We thought—"

"You thought! Fuck off. You didn't *think* at all. When Grady recommended you, he said you were bright. A university graduate, no less. It's not like Grady to be so fucking wrong. A shame really. He used to be my go-to guy for new personnel, but not anymore. Timothy and Ginger have acquainted him with a hospital bed. The fucker's going to be drinking his meals through a straw for the next few weeks. He's not 'going-to' go anywhere for quite a while."

Ginger sniggered.

Teddy grabbed a book off the shelf behind him and hurled it at the redheaded fucker, who caught it mid-flight, in front of his nose. Good reactions. It reminded Teddy why he'd kept the bugger around for two years. Not as efficient or bright as Timothy, but acceptable. Although Teddy still needed to keep him on his toes. Didn't pay to let the hired help grow too comfortable or to have ideas above their station.

"What the fuck you laughing at, shit-for-brains? Your job is to stand there, look mean, and do as I say. Did I tell you to laugh? You're not laughing, are you, Timothy?"

The enormous, black South African at Ginger's side stared at a point above Teddy's head, giving it the thousand-yard stare.

"No, Mr Tedesco. Not at all, sir."

Good boy, Timothy.

"That's right. See that, Schechter? Timothy knows when to answer and when to keep his mouth shut. Pity Ginger doesn't learn from him. He doesn't know when to keep his ears open and his mouth shut. He will though, given time."

Ginger shut the book quietly and hugged it to his chest. A thick, leather-bound volume it was, something about the decline of the Roman Empire. Teddy's interior designer—the limp-wristed queer—had bought a truckload of the dusty books to build what he called the room's "ambience". In the end, Teddy approved of the look and had even started to read a couple of the monstrous tomes. After all, they'd cost enough. Might as well get some use out of them other than as fuck-off, expensive wallpaper.

"You can put it back where it belongs, Ginger. We all know you never learned to read. Yeah, you can laugh at that one. It's meant to be a joke and people can laugh at my jokes."

Timothy smirked as Ginger marched across the room, replaced the book with its mates, and returned to his post without so much as a snicker or a twitch in his expression.

Teddy sat still, giving Schechter the evil eye the whole time. What the fuck was he going to do? Things were beginning to slip sideways. If he didn't get business back on track, the London hyenas would rumble south and start circling the *veldt*, and he couldn't let that happen. Teddy valued his position in society—and his neck—too much to allow it. No way. Best to cauterise the dead tissue before the infection spread, and what better way than to make an example of a young, German smartarse.

Top of his head, Teddy could list a dozen ways to dump a corpse, and all of them would have been better than the one Grady and Schechter had chosen, stupid mutts. Most of the methods, he'd already utilised himself on his way to the top.

Dig a hole in the woods somewhere and plant the body as fertiliser. Chop it up into pieces with a woodchipper and feed it to the pigs. That was a good one, possibly the best. Pigs loved human meat. Ate everything—bones, teeth, hair, the lot, and then they crapped it out over the fields as manure. Wonderful. The circle of life.

Back in the day, you could drop a body into the foundations of a bridge or a new building and cover the bloody thing with a thousand tonnes of ready-mix. Couldn't do that easily these days, though. Not since builders became so bloody security conscious, fenced everything in, and rigged up surveillance cameras. Teddy blamed the Health and Safety Executive and all the other Nanny State, do-good bastards. Fuck them and fuck all the so-called terrorists who gave good, honest thieves a bad name. Ignorant, towel-headed cretins who blew themselves up for a pack of virgins. What use is a virgin to a fucker who's blown himself into tiny pieces? The lack of logic was hysterical. Comedians would write sketches about it if they weren't so shit-scared of the fallout.

Count to ten, Teddy. Savour the moment. Watch the Kraut squirm.

"Okay, Schechter. Let's have it. I gave you and Grady the simple task of losing Tubby Malahide's blubber-filled carcase and the whole thing ended up like a dog's breakfast. Tell me what happened in your own words, and tell me what you're doing to rectify the situation."

The Kraut clasped his hands together. Bubbles of sweat formed on his upper lip.

Yeah, that's right, Schechter. You should be sweating.

Teddy leaned forwards, retrieved his drink, and took a real sip, soaking up the golden liquid. He waited for a story that might just save the German's life—but he doubted it.

Schechter swallowed and took a breath.

"Come on, Schechter. I don't have all fucking day."

"I apologise, Mr Tedesco. I was trying to gather my thoughts. I need to make this as clear and concise as possible." The Kraut covered his mouth with a hand and coughed. "On Saturday, Grady called and told me we had a task to perform on your behalf."

"Yes, yes. I know all that bollocks. Don't think you can shift all the blame onto poor, old Grady just because he's not here to defend himself. I already have his explanation and want your side of things before making my final decision. See how generous and fair I can be? That's why they call me the nicest boss on the south coast. Isn't that right, Timothy?"

The South African dipped his head.

"That's right, Mr Tedesco," he said, in a deep, rumbling voice that could shatter bricks—and kneecaps. "Absolutely right."

"Good. Now get on with it, Schechter. I'm not a patient man."

The German shuffled in his chair. "Grady called me to his flat and told me to bring a tarpaulin and a car with a big enough boot to take the, ah, package—"

"Fuck's sake, man. We're all grownups here. Call a shovel a fucking shovel."

"*Entschuldigen sie?* Excuse me?"

"Tubby wasn't a brown-paper parcel headed for the post office. He was a corpse, a cadaver, a body, a stiff. He might have been dipping his hand in my till, but he'd already paid for it with his life. Show him some fucking respect!"

"*Jawohl!* Yes, sir." Schechter swallowed before continuing. "I drove Grady and the ... *body* to the quarry, under his directions. It was not a place I had visited before. He said it would be deserted at that time in the evening, but when we removed the body from the car, a dog barked."

"The mutt you shot?"

"Yes, sir. That's correct. A woman of middle-age, maybe forty-five, was exercising her animal around the lake that had formed from the quarry workings. The animal was brown and white, and stood about so high." He raised his hand about two and a half feet above the carpet.

"I don't give a shit how big the mutt was. This isn't Crufts, you fuckwit. Get on with the story!"

Teddy jerked his hand and some of the expensive whisky splashed onto his fingers. He licked them clean. Strike one for the Kraut. Any more errors and he was out. This wasn't baseball. No second or third strikes in Teddy's organisation.

"Grady yelled at me to get her. He can't run because of his bad knees and one of us had to stay with the ... corpse. I gave chase."

"How far away was this old biddy?"

"Across the lake on the other bank. No more than thirty, thirty-five metres straight across."

"So, this little, old lady was only a few yards away, but she was too fast for you, and you let her escape?"

Teddy squeezed the glass so hard, he worried it might shatter under the pressure.

"It was not like that, Mr Tedesco. Thirty metres in a straight line, but the shore was curved, and she ran directly into the woods. I could not run straight across, because the *wasser* was too deep. I had to run around the shoreline. The woman was faster than I expected, but I gained quickly upon her."

"And you had a gun, right?"

"Yes, sir. I was close enough to shoot her without missing when the dog attacked. Vicious. Look!" He rolled up his shirtsleeve and showed the bandage covering his forearm. "I shot the animal two times in the chest, but it landed on me. Took me down to the ground. By the time I threw it off, the woman had disappeared. It was dark and pouring rain, and I had no *taschenlampe*, ah, flashlight. And then I heard a car roar away."

He took a breath before continuing.

"All this time, Grady was yelling at me to come back, so I picked up the dog and carried it back to the car."

"You took the dog?"

"Yes, sir. I thought it best not to leave any evidence. You know, the bullets inside the animal?"

Teddy took another sip. Collecting the mutt showed initiative. The Kraut had just earned back his first strike. He might be on his way to earning a full reprieve, too. Although it was too early to tell.

"Also," Schechter said, growing more confident, his voice firmer, "the rain was pouring down. It was heavy enough to obscure our tracks, I thought. And there was one other thing, Mr Tedesco."

"Which was?"

"The dog was in good condition. Despite the rain, I

could tell it had been professionally groomed. Well looked after. Expensive collar, you know?"

"So what?"

For the first time since his arrival, Schechter's shoulders relaxed a little. A ghost smile stretched his thin lips. He reached into his pocket. Timothy and Ginger stiffened and started moving forwards, but Teddy raised his glass and shook his head to send them back to their posts. In his left hand, the one not holding the tumbler, he gripped a SIG Sauer P226—the weapon of choice for the US military. Good enough for the Americans, meant good enough for him. Teddy would never be without it and, with Schechter on the other side of the desk at a distance of less than two metres, he wasn't likely to miss.

Despite the state-of-the-art gizmos protecting his office —the body scanners, the x-ray and infrared cameras, the metal detectors, and the other electronic countermeasures —Teddy was not going to drop his guard. Too many high-ranking "businessmen" had grown lazy thinking they were Teflon-coated and died as a result. Well, not Teddy Tedesco. Nobody was going to catch him on the crapper with his trousers around his ankles.

The Kraut's hand came out of the pocket holding a white, plastic disk, no bigger than the lid of a jam jar.

"If that's a bomb ..."

Teddy set the tumbler on the coaster, racked the SIG, and pointed it at Schechter's face. The Kraut's eyes bulged, and his jaw slackened.

"No, sir. I-It is a microchip reader. Given the dog's well-kept condition, I-I thought it a possibility that it had been microchipped. I bought the device at a pet shop this morning."

With his thumb, Teddy pressed the gun's de-cocker to

lower the hammer and make the weapon safe, but he kept it in plain view and Schechter's eyes stayed locked on the muzzle. Hardly a surprise. Teddy'd been on the wrong end of a gun a few times in his life. There were few things in the world more terrifying than seeing the black hole open up in front of you, especially when it was being held by a nut job with evil in his heart.

"And was it?"

"Chipped? Yes, sir," Schechter said, drawing his gaze from the muzzle back to Teddy. "It was, and I now have the name and address of the owner."

He turned the scanner to let Teddy read the screen.

Mrs Angela Shafer,
#3 Railway Cuttings,
Old Mill Lane, Hampshire.

Teddy nodded and allowed himself a congratulatory smile. The kid had done well. Saved his own life even if it did upset Timothy and Ginger, who looked as though someone had opened their last Christmas presents by mistake. Not to worry, he'd be able to feed someone else to his murder monkeys soon enough. There were always plenty of people around who tried to put one over on Teddy Tedesco. So far, none had succeeded. At least, not for long—as Tubby's ghost would confirm.

"Nice one, Schechter. What's your first name? Grady told me you were smart, but never gave me your full name."

"Hardy, sir," Schechter said, swallowing after Teddy slid the SIG back into his top drawer. "My mother named me after the actor, Hardy Kruger. She had a girlhood crush—"

"That's enough of the back story, son. Don't get too comfortable. You're still a fuck-up. All you've done with that"—he pointed at the scanner—"is bought yourself a little grace period."

The grin fell from Schechter's face.

"Yes, sir. Sorry, sir."

"I assume the old dear went screaming to the filth?"

Schechter worked a finger between his shirt collar and his neck, and pulled. Fucker must have found it difficult to breathe in such a tight collar and with the tie done up so high. Well, sod him. He needed to show some respect and all Teddy's employees knew the correct dress code. Professional attire at all times. The Kraut should have bought a shirt with a better fit.

"Yes, sir. I have been following the investigation on the police scanners," Schechter managed to say. "As I expected, they found nothing at the quarry. It would appear they have closed the investigation, more or less."

"Any press coverage?"

"Minor reports on the local radio and in the local newspaper, but nothing national."

The information tallied with his own research. Teddy paused for a minute before retrieving the glass.

"Okay, that's acceptable. What did you do with Tubby's carcase in the end?"

"Grady knew the location of a different quarry with a lake. Apparently, there are many such abandoned workings in the region. We weighted it down with rocks, sliced the body open from here"—he pointed to a spot below his navel and ran his finger up to his sternum—"to here, to vent the accumulating gasses, and threw it off the cliff into the water. It sank like a boulder. No one will ever see Tubby Malahide's mortal remains again, sir. I promise you."

Teddy took another sip. It tasted good again.

"They'd better not, Schechter. You won't survive for long if they do."

Again, the Kraut shot him a nervous smile.

"You want me to pay a visit to Mrs Shafer? Make sure she does not speak to the police again?"

Teddy was about to agree but had second thoughts and shook his head. "No, that won't be necessary. I have a better idea. Pony's been bored recently. I'll set him on the woman. He can have his fun."

Ginger shuffled his feet and shot a sideways look at Timothy.

Timothy didn't move. He knew better.

Colour drained from the Kraut's already-pasty face.

"Pony?" Schechter asked, his voice thin and scratchy.

Inwardly, Teddy smirked. The Kraut had definitely heard the whispers. Who inside the organisation hadn't?

"You've met my little brother?" Teddy asked, already knowing the answer.

"No, sir. But I know him … by reputation."

Teddy laughed and drained his glass. His eyes watered as the rich heat scoured the back of his throat.

"So, you've heard the stories?"

Schechter dipped his head. "I have, sir. Yes."

"All true. Every single one of them. But the stories everyone knows about aren't the half of it. I could tell you some that would turn your hair white, if you weren't already an albino."

Schechter raised his right hand and smoothed his hair into place in a reflex action he probably didn't realise he was doing.

"But if you really want to know, I'll get Pony to tell you himself. Would you like that?"

Schechter shook his head emphatically. "No, thank you, sir. That will not be necessary."

"That's a shame. He loves an audience. A special case, my baby brother. Very special. Now bugger off, but keep your mobile powered up. I might need you later today. One of my tenants is a few days late on her rent."

Schechter jumped to his feet, clearly unable to leave the room quickly enough. While the Kraut's back was still turned, Timothy looked at Teddy, a question formed in an arched eyebrow.

Teddy shook his head, confirming that the trick with the microchip scanner had saved Schechter's life. Timothy nodded but couldn't hide his disappointment. Spending the first fifteen years of his life under the apartheid regime, the big South African had every reason to hate blond, white men, but he'd have to pull in his horns, for the moment.

Timothy opened the office door and Ginger escorted Schechter from the room, probably about to tell the German how close he'd been to ending up lying alongside Tubby Malahide.

Teddy grinned. No value hiding the truth from the men. They needed to be kept in line.

"Don't worry, Timothy," Teddy said, reaching for his phone. "There's a little action on the cards in Lymington. A couple of trawlermen have developed sticky fingers. You'll have plenty of opportunities to flex those big muscles of yours."

"Thank you, Mr Tedesco. Looking forward to it. Want me to leave the room while you talk to your brother?"

"What do you think?"

The big *kaffir* tapped a finger to his forehead in the nearest action he would ever make to a salute.

"Be right outside when you need me, Mr Tedesco. Don't

forget your dinner with Mrs Tedesco. Roast chicken's on the menu tonight, sir. You asked me to remind you."

Fuck. He had forgotten. So many things to think about.

"Thanks, Timothy," he said, punching buttons on the phone number pad. "I did remember. And Mother can damn well wait."

Sorry, Mother. Didn't mean it. Just for show.

Timothy closed the door quietly behind him and the call connected.

"That you, Teddy?" Pony asked with his standard, girly voice.

"And who else would be calling you on this private line, baby brother?"

"You got something interesting for me at last?"

"Fancy taking a little trip into the country with that arsehole boyfriend of yours?"

"Which one?" Pony asked, his high-pitched giggle squealed down the phone line. "I have so many."

"I was thinking of the one with the beard and the muscles, Pavlovich. You still seeing him?"

In other words, "Is he still alive?"

"No. I have a new special friend. Johnno Ashby. The sweet boy needs an education though. What's the job?"

Teddy gave him the outline.

"Any constraints? Want me to make it look like an accident?"

Teddy snorted.

"Don't care what you do so long as the bitch doesn't talk to the filth again. You can make it quick if you like but, knowing you, it'll be slow and ..."

He allowed the sentence to trail off, waiting for Pony to jump in. It didn't take long.

"You know me so well, big brother. I enjoy toying with them. How old is she?"

"No idea, bro. All I have is her name and address. Want me to put one of my investigators on her?"

"Nah. Don't bother, Teddy," Pony said, using his serious "down to business" voice. "Doing the deep background stuff makes it all the more fun. Adds to the enjoyment, you know? The excitement of the hunt tastes every bit as sweet as the kill itself. By the time I'm finished, I'll know everything about her from her favourite hairdresser to her daughter's bra size. Assuming she has a daughter."

Again, he broke off to giggle—a sound that prickled the fine hairs on Teddy's neck.

"Give me a few days and I'll have her begging for release." He let out the breathless laugh that must have made his victims wet themselves. "And I don't mean the sweet release of a good, long screw, if you know what I mean, bro."

Teddy wrinkled his nose in disgust.

"Spare me the details, Pony. Just get the job done and make sure no one finds the body. Disposing of a stiff is what gave us this problem in the first place."

"Ah, Teddy. You were always the squeamish one. But I don't think of this as a problem. Oh no. This situation is what I like to call an *opportunity*!"

The line clicked dead on Pony's intimidating laugh. Teddy dropped the phone in its cradle. For a brief moment, he almost felt sorry for the Shafer woman. He shuddered again.

Poor cow.

Still, business was business. Move on or move out. Time to dress for dinner. Mother did so love to see him in a smart suit.

On The Attack: Chapter Two

Friday 27th November — Angela Shafer

Spire Road, Andover, Hampshire, England

In the dark behind Angela, a door slammed. The hollow noise boomed through the near-deserted car park. Footsteps clacked, hurrying towards her. Was it *him*?

Oh God. Why can't he leave me alone?

The breath caught in her throat. She increased her pace, up on her toes, avoiding heel-strike, trying to quieten her footfalls.

Where did she park the car? There. Up ahead. The other side of Brian's Volvo.

She tried to calm her rapid gasping. Could he hear her breathing? Could he see her in the poor light? God, was he there, hiding in the darkness?

The chasing footsteps faltered, shuffled, continued. He hadn't seen her, didn't know where she was. She ducked, keeping below the roof level of the few remaining cars. She should have left with the others, but there was always one more thing to do. Brian needed the Brick Street property details for the morning's viewing, and she'd volunteered to stay late.

Stupid, stupid woman.

Still on the move, panting, heart thumping, shivering, she fished in her handbag for the car keys, gripping them tight. She reached the Volvo and ducked between it and her battered Fiat. The button on her key fob hadn't worked for years. Couldn't use it anyway. The flashing indicators would give away her position.

She pushed the key into the lock, turned, tried the handle. Nothing. Still locked.

God! The other way. Turn the key the other way! Idiot!

The footsteps drew closer, louder, echoing through the car park. *He* was there! Nearly upon her.

Angela tried again and turned the key anti-clockwise. The alarm disengaged, and the door buttons popped. More noise. Inside on her plastic seats, she slammed the door closed and pressed the security door lock. The buttons popped again.

Safe. Oh God, safe.

Angela sat, stiff but shivering, gripping the steering wheel with both hands, trying to quell the shakes. The keys dug into her palm, hurting, but she couldn't relax her grip until the panic attack faded.

Knuckles rapped on her driver's window.

Angela jumped. A short screech burst from her mouth.

She spun to face the noise. The hand tapped again. Its

owner bent at the waist. A familiar face appeared. Smiling. Friendly.

Brian! Thank God.

"Angela, are you okay?"

She breathed again.

"Brian, you … startled me. I was miles away. Just a sec."

She jabbed the key into the ignition and turned it enough to feed power to the windows. She hit the button and waited for the glass to shudder down its channels in the doorframe.

Brian grinned at her through the opening.

"Sorry to scare you. Should have called out. Forgive me."

"No, no. It's my fault. I've had so much on my mind since … well, you know. And with Bobbie away at university, I've been left on my own, stewing."

If only that were all. She tried returning his smile, but it felt unnatural—forced.

Brian stepped back from the car and stood up straight. Typical of the man, so thoughtful. He didn't want to crowd her.

"Yes, I know. Things have been tough on you recently, and I … we … I mean everyone at the office wants you to know we're here for you. If there's anything you need. You didn't take any time off after the … after the plane crash. We all care about you, you know?"

Angela's face heated. Embarrassed by his gentle and supportive words.

"I do know. Thank you. Everyone's been so very kind. You and Alan in particular." She straightened her shoulders. "Was there something you wanted?"

Brian frowned in the way he did when trying to remember something lost and on the tip of his tongue.

"Ah yes, right," he said, fidgeting in his jacket pocket, still frowning, but less so. The ridges on his forehead softened. "You left this on your desk." His hand came out holding her mobile phone. "I thought you might need it tonight."

She sighed and took it from his hand, trying to show gratitude and hide the fear haunting her life. "Thank you, Brian. You didn't have to go out of your way."

He smiled his disarming, warm smile again. Her heart rate slowed a little, and the shakes diminished with it. If she confided in him, would he help? Could he? No, she couldn't do it to him. Brian had a family—Beatrice and the girls—and telling him would put them in danger, too.

Why was this happening to her? What had she ever done to deserve it?

"You might need it," Brian said, casting his eyes over her ancient, little Fiat, which was one more MOT failure away from the scrapyard. "You have a long drive home. And Old Mill Lane is awfully quiet this time of night. I'd hate for you to be caught without a mobile if this old wreck packs up on you."

A stab of fear returned to halt her heart, as the thought of the long drive home to her quiet, empty, exposed, little house suddenly terrified her.

How had *he* found her? How did *he* know where she lived?

Brian leaned back, still taking in the old car with its rust and its dings, shaking his head sadly. "Do we really pay you that poorly?"

"Excuse me?"

"Well, I might be stepping out of bounds here, but your car is a wreck. I hate the idea of you breaking down in the middle of nowhere. And it's not as though you can resort to public transport, not in that rural backwater of yours."

He laughed at his own joke—Hampshire hardly justified the tag "rural backwater".

"I mean, there aren't any buses out where you live. Why don't you upgrade? If finances are a problem, Alan and I would be happy to countersign a loan application. We might even consider some sort of leasing arrangement on the business." He paused and shook his head. "Oh, sorry, I'm being pushy again, aren't I?"

"No, no. Not at all."

Shocked anyone would care, Angela fought back the threatened tears. She so wanted to confide in him, but no. No. She couldn't take the risk.

"Well," she managed to say through her nerves and the sense of gratitude, "as it happens, money isn't an issue. In fact, I've been considering changing cars recently, but … it's just … I've been too busy."

Maybe she should leave the area. Up sticks and run. She had enough money now, but the man on the phone had found her once and she couldn't guarantee that he wouldn't find her again.

Dear Lord, what could she do?

"Is anything wrong, Angela?"

"N-Nothing. Why do you ask?"

He opened his hands in a shrug. "It's just that for the past few days you've been so distracted. Most unlike you. I know your sister passed away recently, but … Alan and I have been worried it's more than that. Is it something either of us have done or said? Or not done and not said?"

"You've been talking about me?" she snapped.

She didn't want to snap but couldn't help it. Her nerves had been shredded ever since Breaker's Folly.

"No, Angela. It's nothing like that. We're worried for you. Actually, we're being selfish. The office would grind to a dismal halt without you holding it together for us."

"Oh, I'm … really grateful, but there's nothing you can do. It's just that … I'm missing Jackie."

That's right, you coward. Blame everything on your dead sister when she has nothing at all to do with it.

"Sometimes," she continued, losing herself in the moment, "I see a figure in the street, and I call out, thinking it's her. Then I'll be sitting in front of the TV and remember watching the same show with Jackie and find tears rolling down my cheeks. No reason, no stopping it either. It kills me every time I see a news report of the crash."

Brian pushed a hand through the open window, breaking the barrier between them. He rested it on her shoulder. The first time they'd touched since hugging at Jackie's memorial. A funeral with no body. Jackie's remains still lay at the bottom of the North Sea. Divers had recovered the black box flight recorders and most of the aircraft, but not all the bodies. The risk and expense wasn't deemed worth the reward and she and Bobbie had ended up burying an empty casket.

Brian pulled his hand away. "It's only been a couple of months," he said. "Your emotions are bound to be raw, but they'll ease. I promise."

He meant well, but his words didn't help. She took a tissue from a packet stuffed in the pocket of her car door and wiped the tears. Turning her head away, she blew her nose and crushed the tissue into a tight, little ball.

"Listen, Angela, do you have any plans for tonight? We could have dinner if you like. Talk things over."

Angela looked at him in shock.

"What about Beatrice and the girls? Won't they be waiting for you?"

Brian's mouth dropped open and his eyes bugged. "My word, no. I didn't mean it that way. I meant for you to come home for dinner with the family. I'd call ahead. Beatrice and the girls would be delighted to see you again."

Angela threw her hand up to cover her mouth. How embarrassing. What was wrong with her?

"I-I'm sorry. Didn't mean it like that. I was just worried they'd wonder where you were. Thanks again for bringing my phone, and thanks for the offer of dinner, but I already have plans for tonight. I'll see you in the morning. Bright and early."

She turned the key in the ignition. The Fiat coughed into life and belched out a cloud of dirty, blue exhaust fumes. Brian stepped away, his nose wrinkled.

As usual, the transmission crunched as she engaged first gear and pulled the car slowly out of her space. She left the car park with the image of a bemused and waving Brian D'Costa burned into her memory.

He'd been completely correct about Old Mill Lane. Eight miles of winding, two-lane road, deserted and unlit after sunset, it would be one of the worst places in the region to break down. She'd never even tried dialling from her car—and why would she? Although a mere twenty miles from Southampton, for all she knew, the place was a communications black spot.

After a slow but uneventful drive, she crunched into a lower gear to negotiate the tight turn into Railway Cuttings and slowed right down to make the sharp corner into her driveway. A terrace of three Victorian cottages faced her. The one on the end bought by Mum and Dad in 1986. He'd been so proud of the place. His first and, as it turned out, only house purchase. He'd renovated it and lavished great care on it until Mum died. After that, he curled into a metaphoric ball and allowed the place to disintegrate slowly around them all.

No lights on in any of the windows.

Oh God.

She'd be alone in the Cuttings again.

The other two houses in the row were second homes, owned by London couples who only visited on weekends and during the holidays. Before *he* started calling, her cottage had seemed peaceful and safe, but now ... it stood out silent, ominous, and scary.

She drove the wheezing Fiat onto her gravel drive and turned the ignition key. The engine spluttered on for a few more turns before coughing and dying. What did that mean? Why didn't it just stop?

Angela rolled down the window and strained her ears, listening for anything unexpected. The wind whistled in the conifers behind the cottages, a cat mewled, a motorbike roared along the nearby road, but nothing stood out as unusual. No strange cars filled the other drives. No unusual sounds. No smells.

She took a steadying breath.

Since Breaker's Folly, her life had been one long, waking nightmare. The police had found nothing and basically accused her of fabricating the whole story. During their final meeting before he closed the case, the silver-haired detective sergeant actually asked whether she was taking any medication. The fool indirectly suggested she'd imagined the whole affair.

"If I've been hallucinating, where's Lady?" she'd asked, slapping her hand on the desk between them in the cold, grey interview room.

"Perhaps your dog simply ran off. Did she like to chase rabbits?"

"She's a Border Collie. They are bred to herd sheep and cows. She doesn't chase rabbits. She was shot, I tell you. Shot dead!"

The policeman frowned impatiently at her before checking his watch.

"Mrs Shafer," he said in the condescending way officials often used when bothersome members of the public interrupted their tea break. "As I told you earlier, we searched Breaker's Folly thoroughly and found nothing. I'm sure your dog will find her way home. Have you considered posting a reward?"

He stood, pointed her to the door, and that was that. The policeman dismissed her as though she meant nothing. On her way home, she fumed, contemplating ways to punish the man for his laziness. She'd call the local paper, the radio. She even considered talking to her solicitor, the one handling Jackie's estate, but she didn't get that far. The man with the quiet, posh voice and the scary laugh started calling.

The first call interrupted her typing the email to her solicitor. At first, she thought it was a cold call, a man selling life insurance. He knew her name and address, and was very polite. Then he told her not to talk to the police again, threatening all sorts of harm to her and Bobbie if she did so.

He knew about Bobbie!

Morning and night, he called. Said he'd be watching her and would pounce when she least expected. Whenever she lowered her guard.

Dear Lord, what am I going to do?

Sitting in the car with her hands still gripping the wheel

tight, warm tears ran down her cheeks. She'd never felt so scared. Not just for herself, but for Bobbie, too.

Again, she listened to the night. Again, she heard nothing unexpected. Could she leave the car and brave the darkness? Her house stood no more than ten metres away, waiting for her, bathed in the Fiat's headlights. It offered sanctuary, but something stopped her moving.

Maybe the man had been bluffing. Maybe she had nothing to worry about. Bobbie was safe in Norwich, and she could move on with her life. After all, what had Angela really seen? What could she really do if the police wouldn't listen?

With teeth gritted, she unpeeled her hands from the steering wheel and turned off the headlights. She rolled up the window, removed the key from the ignition, and grabbed her handbag, clutching it to her chest as though it would protect her.

She reached for the door handle and pulled. The lock clicked, the door screeched open, and the courtesy light flashed a dim yellow. She sniffed the air, but the lingering stench of unburned exhaust fumes told her nothing other than her car needed a completely new exhaust system. Well, no, thank you. She'd waste no more money fixing a car that was so old and so tired. She was going to buy a brand-new car. A BMW or a Mercedes. A white one with leather seats.

Lord, how her mind wandered.

Concentrate, Angela.

She sniffed again, but no strange smells—no aftershave warning her of *him*—could have punched through the odour of partially burned premium unleaded.

Unsatisfied by her precautions, but unable to see an alternative, Angela unclipped the seatbelt and climbed out of the car. Ten more paces and she'd be home, safe again for another night.

The courtesy light in the car stayed on long enough for her to identify the Chubb key to the front door. The movement-activated security light over the front door would help, but she wanted the key ready to avoid delay.

A hand fisted in her hair. Before she could scream, a second hand clamped over her mouth. A hard body slammed into her back, forcing her against the side of the car.

Oh God!

"Told you I would come, Angela. Didn't think I was kidding, did you?"

He cackled.

A firm bulge, where a man's groin would be, pressed against her backside. Her knees buckled, legs unable to take her weight, but he held her mashed against the side of the car. Crushed and helpless.

Oh God. Please. No.

She tried to struggle but he was too strong. Too solid. Immovable.

She should have gone home with Brian and his family.

Family ... her family. Bobbie.

How was she going to save Bobbie?

Oh God. Please make it quick. Please make it be over.

On The Attack: Chapter Three

Friday 27th November – Angela Shafer

Old Mill Lane, Andover, Hampshire, England

Hot, nicotine-fouled breath scorched Angela's ear.

"Did you think I was lying, bitch?"

Tightening his grip on her hair, the man forced her face against the roof of the car. The freezing metal burned her skin. She whimpered as he ground his hips harder into her buttocks. The bulge felt bigger, more solid.

Her crying out aroused him?

Quiet, Angela. Be quiet. Don't encourage him.

If she stayed calm, maybe she'd find a way out. Her phone. Could she reach it? No, too dangerous.

Stupid woman, he'll kill you.

She had to stay alive. Stay alive for Bobbie.

"We're going to have some fun, you and me."

He chuckled, the same mirthless laugh he'd used on the phone. Angela closed her eyes and clamped her knees together, trying not to pee.

"Well," he continued, "not sure how much fun it'll be for you darling, but me? I'll be having a ball."

Car headlights snapped on, flooding her front garden in their harsh, white glow.

Saved! She was saved!

She struggled, fought, twisted around to face the car.

"Help! Please help!"

She bucked her head. Screamed again. Flailed her arms. Reached up and behind, trying to find the man's eyes with her long fingernails.

He jerked his head away, out of reach. His arms were too long, too powerful. She couldn't get close and turned her fingers to scratch the exposed skin at his wrists.

The animal, the pig, snarled. He cracked her head into the car's side pillar. Blinding lights flashed behind her eyes.

The pig's cruel laugh echoed through the night.

"Stupid bitch," he said. "No one's here to help you, and I don't need any assistance, thank you very much. I can do whatever I want to you all by myself. I'm going to take this slow and steady, and I'm going to enjoy every single second. Those headlights aren't from a knight in shining armour, darling. There is no Good Samaritan. Oh dear me, no. They're from my car, and that's Johnno driving it. He's my ride home. He likes to watch, too. Might even join in when I'm finished with you. If there's anything left of you for him to play with, that is."

He stopped talking long enough to lick her neck. She nearly retched.

"Now, let's go in the house. It's cold out here, and I do like my central heating."

Without warning, he dragged her by her hair, forcing her along the path with him. She caught sight of his face for the first time.

He wasn't one of the men she'd seen at the Folly. More than two people involved. A gang? God, how many of them were there? One of these people shot Lady. Why hadn't she kept her stupid mouth shut?

Pig's evil smile showed clean, perfectly aligned teeth. Dark eyes but pale skin, almost translucent in the harsh light of the car's full beams. A clear view. No mask. She could see his face, and he didn't care.

She was going to die. He was going to kill her!

Headlights bathed the scene bright as day. Yet her attacker didn't waver. His smile widened, and he nodded towards the other car.

Warm pee dribbled down her legs. Angela couldn't stop her lower lip trembling and her chin jumping. Tears rippled her vision, ran down her nose. She sniffled, and the man's eyes sparkled.

Showing fear *did* excite him.

Be brave, Angela. Show him nothing.

She had to stay strong. Stay alive for Bobbie. Keep him talking. Maybe it would help. Give her time to find a way out.

"W-Why are you doing this?"

Pig's evil smile broadened. "Haven't you got it yet, sweetheart? I'm doing it because I enjoy inflicting pain. Because I enjoy fucking people who don't want to be fucked. Men or women. Boys or girls. I don't care. Do you get it now, darling? I'm going to make you plead for mercy, and then I'm going to kill you."

"P-Please don't hurt me. I'll be good. You can do whatever you want, but I'll—"

He yanked her hair again. Pulled her closer.

"You'll be good? You'll be *good*? Yeah, darling, you'll be excellent. This is going to be the best sex I've had for weeks. By the time I've finished with you, there won't be a hole I haven't rammed, or a piece of your flesh I haven't tasted. We've got all weekend, baby. You are going to be *so* good."

It wasn't happening. It couldn't be happening. She'd wake in a minute, sweating and screaming. She'd had panic attacks before, nightmares. But her scalp hurt where he'd torn it, and her cut cheek bled inside her mouth.

No, not a nightmare. Reality.

"Johnno! Get over here!"

The headlights snapped off. A car door opened and slammed shut. Footsteps crunched on gravel.

"W-What do you want me to do?" Johnno asked, meek as a kitten.

Pig wrenched her hair and rammed her head against his hip to hold her in place. She scrambled sideways. Bent at the waist, she had to grab the back of his jacket to avoid falling and losing more hair.

"Either kick the front door open, or find her keys, you fuckwit!"

They were going inside. The hall. What could she use? Something. Anything. The telephone table. She could swing it. Smash Pig's head in. But what about the other one? What about Johnno?

An open-handed blow clapped her cheek, rattling her teeth and slamming her head against the bony part of his hip. Once again, lights flashed behind her closed eyes.

"Where are your keys, bitch?"

Angela could barely hear him through the ringing in her

ears. It hurt so much. Maybe if he hit her again, she'd lose consciousness and miss the worst of what was to come.

He pulled her hair again. She squealed, scrunched her shoulders to protect her ears, grabbed his jacket. So much hurt. So much pain.

Don't cry. Don't let him hear you cry.

"Answer me or I'll smash the window open with your face. Don't try my patience, woman."

Although his words were vicious and callous, the only time he'd raised his voice was to call Johnno from the car. Somehow, the quiet, controlled speech was scarier than when he yelled. She answered. Couldn't help herself.

"By my ... my handbag," she said. It was all she could manage.

He pulled her head up until it was level with his once more. She had to stand on tiptoes and put her hands on his chest for balance. His pecs tightened, and his sneer turned to a smirk.

Petrified, she froze. She couldn't pull her hands away. She couldn't move.

"Where is it?"

"I-I dropped it."

"Stupid bitch."

Johnno moved in the darkness. Gravel scattered. Clouds rolled away.

"Here they are," he said quickly, sounding eager to please. "I have them."

The keys rattled on the ring.

More footsteps. The gate opened, hinges screeched. Somewhere in the back of her mind, she remembered the can of lubricating oil on the top shelf of the garage.

Why was she worrying about that now, of all times?

Johnno scurried along the path to the front door,

searching through the keys. The security light snapped on, blinding her.

"Come with me, you," Pig said.

He lowered his hand and started walking, forcing her to crab along beside him. She had no choice. His fingers tangled tighter in her hair, pulling, wrenching. Hurting.

Her hair would be such a mess. Would Geraldine be able to rescue it?

Hair? You're worried about your bloody hair?

Johnno reached the front door, pushed it open, and found the light switch. Her hallway. Her home. It should have been a sanctuary, but … the phone stand!

She reached out for it, but Pig moved too quickly, pulling her through the hallway, following his acolyte towards the front room. Johnno turned on more lights. The curtains would be open. Someone passing might see, might help.

But, no. At night, the lane would be quiet. Lonely. No one would drive past. No one would save her.

Pig dragged her into the front room, threw her on the single chair in the corner, and stepped closer. She kicked out. Landed a glancing blow to his shin.

"Fucking bitch!"

Angela barely saw his hand move before his fist smashed into her face.

———

SOFTNESS BENEATH HER. Nothing above.

Warm air. Quiet.

"Wake up, darling. Wouldn't want you to miss any of the fun."

Angela squeezed her eyes tight shut, but a slap stung her cheek and spun her head. She had to look.

"Awake now?"

Her front room. Still alive. Why?

Sore. Everything hurt.

Pig stood above her, a cruel smile twisting his lips. Lights on, curtains still open. He knew they wouldn't be disturbed. She was alone, helpless with a madman. No, two madmen.

Johnno stood in the open doorway. Watching, silent, face pale.

She was alone with two men. Totally vulnerable. She stared at Johnno. Dressed the same as the pig, but half the size and about ten years younger. He looked at her with what, pity? Could she use that information somehow? Would he help her?

"Yes, that's better," Pig said, rubbing his hands together. "Now we can get started."

He reached for her blouse, undid her buttons one at a time, slowly. What had happened to her jacket, her overcoat?

The blouse parted, exposing her bra, her skin. Her belly trembled. She moved her arms to cover herself, but he grabbed her wrists and twisted them outwards. It hurt, but she gritted her teeth, trying not to cry out. It was what he wanted.

Still smiling, Pig kept twisting. Pain.

He was breaking her arms.

"Stop, please," she whimpered.

He released her wrists and grabbed her hair again, forcing her head towards him, tearing more out from the roots. He stopped when her face was centimetres from his groin. The outline of his penis stood out clear through his tight trousers.

Oh God, no.

Pig's white shirt—starched and perfectly pressed—clung to his flat stomach. His free hand moved lower, its thumb hooked into his leather belt.

"Like what you see, darling? Want some of this meat inside you? Think you can take it all, do you?"

If she just allowed him to get it over with, gave him what he wanted, maybe he'd let her go.

Anything, Angela. Do anything. Stay alive. Survive.

"Don't hurt me. Please don't hurt me anymore."

Pig's grip on her hair tightened, his other hand reached for the zip, then pulled away.

"'Please don't hurt me anymore'," he mocked. "Darling, I haven't even started yet. I told you, we have all weekend."

Her cheek throbbed from where he'd hit her. She'd bitten her tongue and her cheek, and tasted blood. More than one tooth in her head was loose, but if he put his thing anywhere near her mouth, she'd bite down and bite down hard. Her stomach lurched at the thought of what he'd do afterwards, but she'd bite down anyway.

She turned to stare at Johnno, trying to lock eyes with him, but the creature looked away.

Coward. You filthy coward.

Pig slapped her again. Not as hard as before, but hard enough to rattle her teeth.

"Look at me, not Johnno. I'm the one in control!"

She lifted her eyes and stared into his.

Dark, they were. Empty of all, even hate.

"After I've fucked and killed you, I'm going to leave your body to rot. Got it?"

She tried to nod, but his fist in her hair was too tight.

"Yes, yes, I—"

"Then I'm going to pay a visit to Norwich."

Bobbie? He knows where Bobbie is? How?

Fear changed to terror. Terror became anger, rage.

"W-What did you say?"

"Yeah, that's right. Finally getting the message?"

Pig turned to his minion.

"Hear that, Johnno?" he said. "The bitch is finally getting the message."

He pulled her forwards on the chair and pushed his head towards her face.

"Oh yes, we know all about your daughter. Pretty, like you, only young and fresh. Nice, big tits, too. Bigger than yours and firmer. None of that middle-aged, wrinkly, drooping bollocks. And none of that flabby belly shit, either."

He punched her in the stomach, knocking the wind out of her. She gasped and pulled her knees up to her chest, struggling for breath. Darkness encroached at the edges of her vision.

Bobbie! Oh God, Bobbie. What have I done?

Pig continued. "When I'm finished with you, dearie, Johnno and I are going to pay darling Bobbie a little visit. We'll be able to compare notes. You or your brat. Which one's a better fuck."

"Bastard!" Angela gasped. "Don't you touch my daughter. I'll kill you!"

She struggled. Kicked out, aiming for his shins again, but she missed, and it only made him laugh louder.

"That's it, bitch. I love it when they fight back. Much more enjoyable. Johnno!" he yelled. "Time to have some fun. Come here."

Johnno didn't move.

Pig pinned her head to the back of the chair by her hair. He grabbed her breast and mashed it against her ribcage.

Angela tried to push his hand away. He punched her in the face and grabbed both her wrists, holding them together in one hand. He wrenched her arms over her head. Hot tears flooded her cheeks.

"Bastard!" she screamed. "Animal! Pig!"

She kicked out again, aiming for his groin this time, but he twisted, and her shoe glanced the side of his hip.

"Fucking bitch."

He hit her again and again, and the strength ebbed away. Vomit rose, burned her throat. She swallowed it back.

The pig took hold of her skirt and pulled up. The gash he had for a mouth spread into another grin.

"Now, open wide, honey … this is going to hurt."

———

ANGELA STARED at the ceiling the whole time Pig was on top of her, grunting, tearing, thrusting, pummelling. Breathing on her. Hot, wet, foul air. Used air. Staring at her without blinking, his eyes empty, dead. He was waiting for her to react.

She didn't.

She was numb and sore and humiliated and angry and terrified. But she gave him nothing. The whole time he was on her, in her, Angela chewed her cheek, tasting blood. It reminded her she was still alive. She had to keep going—for Bobbie.

Fighting Pig had only brought pain and a few moments of blackness. He was too big, too strong. Nothing seemed to hurt him.

Angela crawled inside herself. She withdrew from the room. She visited Bobbie in Norwich. A beautiful city. Lots of flowers that smelled so nice in the warm, summer sun.

Clean and light and bright and happy. The cathedral with its spire pointing to heaven, reaching up to God.

Where was God now?

Why had he deserted her?

THE PIG GRUNTED AGAIN. Pulled out of her and punched her in the mouth, laughing.

"Not bad," he said. "I've had worse. Your turn, Johnno. I've warmed her up for you."

Oh God. No!

Her body responded and she screamed. Tried to sit up, but the pig held her down, slapped her again.

Johnno, still by the door, watched but did nothing. A strange expression clouded his face. Was he enjoying it? Getting aroused? He was going to be next. Take his turn. But did he want to? Why did she care?

God, stop this, please. Let it be over.

"No, I-I can't," Johnno said, shaking his head, waving his hands in front of his chest. "Don't make me."

Pig pushed himself to his feet and pulled up his underwear and trousers. "Get over here, fuckwit. I'm taking a breather. Your turn. Make her suffer."

Angela curled into a tight ball and covered her face with her hands. She cried through closed eyes, trembling. She wanted to throw up, but nothing happened when her stomach rippled.

No more. Please, no more.

Outside, a door crashed open.

An explosion and a flash of blinding, white light.

Johnno flew through the air, screaming. The coffee table splintered under his crashing weight.

Someone—a man—yelled, "Down on the floor!"

Another shouted, "Get down! Do it now!"

A man dressed head-to-toe in black raced through the open doorway. A second followed close behind.

Pig spun. His hand reached into his pocket.

Angela's eyes stung, and her ears rang.

A blue-white light flashed.

Rapid clicks followed, partially drowned out by Pig's agonised screams. His eyes rolled up into his head and he collapsed in a heap on the floor in front of her, twitching and convulsing. Blood dribbled from his mouth and his hands clenched into fists. Feet thrashing and legs flailing wildly.

Bastard!

Angela kicked out. The pointed toe of her shoe connected with Pig's jaw. He fell backwards, and his head cracked against Johnno's knee. He stopped moving. She jumped up, screamed, kicked him again, and stamped her foot into his groin. Something soft and squidgy moved beneath her heel.

"Bastard!' she wailed and stamped again. "Bastard, bastard!"

She raised her knee again but lost balance and teetered sideways. The first man in black rushed forwards, one hand outstretched.

Angela screamed and threw out her arms to fend him off. She fell, hit the carpet hard, and scrambled on her backside, hands and feet scurrying, pushing her into the corner of the room.

"No more. Oh God. Please, no more!"

Grab your copy...
vinci-books.com/ontheattack

About Kerry J Donovan

#1 International Best-seller with *Ryan Kaine: On the Run*, Kerry was born in Dublin. He currently lives with Margaret in a bungalow in Nottinghamshire. He has three children and four grandchildren.

Kerry earned a first-class honours degree in Human Biology and has a PhD in Sport and Exercise Sciences. A former scientific advisor to The Office of the Deputy Prime Minister, he helped UK emergency first-responders prepare for chemical attacks in the wake of 9/11. He is also a former furniture designer/maker.

kerryjdonovan.com